THE
LOST
SISTER
OF
FIFTH
AVENUE

BOOKS BY ELLA CAREY

DAUGHTERS OF NEW YORK
A New York Secret
The Lost Girl of Berlin
The Girl from Paris

SECRETS OF PARIS
Paris Time Capsule
The House by the Lake
From a Paris Balcony

Beyond the Horizon
Secret Shores
The Things We Don't Say

ELLA CAREY

THE
LOST
SISTER
OF
FIFTH
AVENUE

bookouture

Published by Bookouture in 2022

An imprint of Storyfire Ltd.
Carmelite House
50 Victoria Embankment
London EC4Y 0DZ

www.bookouture.com

ISBN: 978-1-80314-544-0
eBook ISBN: 978-1-80314-543-3

This book is a work of fiction. Whilst some characters and circumstances portrayed by the author are based on real people and historical fact, references to real people, events, establishments, organizations or locales are intended only to provide a sense of authenticity and are used fictitiously. All other characters and all incidents and dialogue are drawn from the author's imagination and are not to be construed as real.

Maisie Lawrence—this one is for you. x

It is not enough to win a war; it is more important to organize the peace.

Aristotle

Imagination is the only weapon in the war against reality.

Lewis Carroll

PROLOGUE
SUMMER 1943

Martha hurried through the Conservatory Garden. Her fingers flew to the tiny silver cross around her neck and clutched it as if they might tear it from its delicate chain and send it crashing onto the smooth raked gravel beneath her feet. She clipped along and every person she laid eyes on, every family she passed in her wake, and especially each breathing, smiling young woman only served to make her shoulders quake.

Night and Fog, *Nacht und Nebel*, the treacherous words thudded in time with Martha's footsteps and beat along with her heart. How could brave, invincible Charlotte possibly have been arrested and swept away under Hitler's latest decree? How could the world that Martha had known and trusted all her life have become so torn apart?

Martha slumped down onto an empty seat. She pressed her hands into the flaking surface of the bench. Splinters pierced the tender skin on her palms, and yet she did not flinch. How were she and Papa supposed to cope with not knowing if Charlotte was alive or dead? Did the Nazis not realize that every person they spirited away was loved? That the agony of not knowing the whereabouts of loved ones punctured families' hearts?

Banks of seasonal flowers spread before Martha as if smiling in the face of her despair. Box hedges were trimmed into a sea of swirling curlicues, just like they were in France. Martha squeezed her eyes shut. It had been a mistake coming to the French gardens in Central Park. As much as she adored this place and knew it as well as she knew the traceries of her own heart, it was, like France, redolent with memories, imbued with everything that had happened before the last four years had unfolded like some grisly tale. Its beauty only served to remind her of what the world was like before kindness was replaced by hate.

If she opened her eyes, everything in front of her would look like the gardens she loved in Paris. Everything would remind her of France. Her mother had lived and died in Paris, and now her sister had gone missing in the same country.

The letter burned in Martha's handbag; its stark words were branded onto her like a tattoo. Ever since receiving it, she'd become glued to the newspapers, whose stories spun an insidious web of horrible truths around the disappearances in France. There had been increased Resistance activity since the German invasion of the Soviet Union. German counterintelligence had redoubled their effort to capture French Resistance members and saboteurs. Those caught under the Nazis' Night and Fog decree were taken to Germany upon capture.

Charlotte had disappeared in the night.

No one had heard officially that she'd been taken, because the Night and Fog decree forbade prisoners to have any contact with loved ones. The whole point was that relatives at home would not know a prisoner's fate.

Martha had read and re-read the letter in her pocket at least ten million times, or so it seemed. Charlotte had gone up to Paris for the day, but she had simply never returned. Her co-workers in the South of France now suspected she had been involved in the Resistance, under what guise, they knew not; of whom she worked with, they knew nothing; of what she was doing in Paris, or whom she met, they had no idea.

Martha leaned forward and covered her face with her hands. A death in the family was one thing, but when a person went missing it was as if you lost your compass, your world, and your soul. She and Papa were helpless, not knowing whether they should grieve. The dim flickers of hope that fired Martha up in the darkest hours came crashing down every time she considered the realities.

The Nazis knew what they were doing. People said they were mad, but Martha knew they were not. The cruel wrench of this agony was not wrought by crazed killers, it was fashioned in cold, knowing blood. The intimidation for family members was akin to a living death. The mortality rate amongst Night and Fog prisoners was incomprehensibly high, according to the newspaper reports that were filtering out from Europe.

Martha sat. Two little girls in cherry-red summer dresses, their hair flying along behind them like streaming kites, skipped along the well-tended paths in Central Park.

In Paris, children cowered under Nazi rule.

Two questions burned in Martha's mind. She had no idea whether her own adored sister, Charlotte, had been working for the French Resistance or not. And she had no idea whether Charlotte would have the privilege of growing old.

1

FIVE YEARS EARLIER, SPRING 1938

Martha would never forget the day the telegram arrived from Paris. She was sitting in the window seat at home. The treetops in Central Park were sprinkled with creamy blossoms, all spread out below. Martha allowed herself a wistful moment to gaze down at the secret glimpses of lawn where she and Charlotte used to play as children. Charlotte had always taken on the audacious roles, while Martha was content to follow in her twin sister's tempestuous wake, accepting without complaint that she would always be the gentle assistant, while Charlotte held absolute sway.

Martha reached for the novel that lay idle in her lap. Sighing, she allowed herself a small smile. She'd always found her bliss embarking on adventures within the sanctuary of a book. She tugged at her unwieldy dark brown curls, pulling them free from the tortoiseshell clasp she wore to work at the New York Public Library. Today she'd been working on the reference desk in the Children's Room, never growing tired of the way the kids raced across the tiled floors and installed themselves in the window seats with books in hand. Martha always felt a pang of delight when a child signed the registration book and received their first library card. She'd ask them to hold a hand up while they pledged to take good care of the books. For Martha, every story was a treasure that would take a child away to far-flung lands.

When there was a knock at the front door, Martha forced herself away from the prospect of an idyllic hour reading before she and Papa met for a glass of sherry in his study. He was tucked away in there now and she would never think to interrupt him at the sound of the door knocker. She trotted down the hallway, her stockinged feet muted on the polished parquet floor. When she opened the front door, her rosebud lips widened in an automatic smile, only to compress again at the sight of a young delivery boy holding a telegram.

Charlotte.

Martha narrowed her honey-colored eyes and clutched at the skirt of her printed floral dress.

"Good evening," Martha said.

"A telegram for Mr. Laurence Belmont and Miss Martha Belmont."

Martha reached out, her hand moving involuntarily. "Thank you."

The telegram boy swung around and moved back to the elevator.

Martha pulled the front door closed behind her and stood stock-still in the hallway, her heart thumping in her mouth in time with Papa's grandfather clock. No matter how she tried to rationalize things, the fact was, she'd grown up with her late grandparents' tales of the terror they'd felt when telegrams had arrived in this very apartment during the Great War. Martha and Charlotte's papa, Laurence, had been in France, and every time Martha's grandparents had heard a knock at the door, they'd talked of how they braced themselves for nightmarish news from the Adjutant General that their only son had been officially reported as killed in action on the Western Front.

Now Charlotte was in France, and every night, Martha was witness to the anxious look that clouded Papa's features. Worry for his daughter was etching lines between his eyes.

Martha moved back to the living room. The telegram was pinched between her fingers. She hardly dared to open it. She hardly dared to take it to Papa.

The Great War might be done, but the newspapers that she tidied away in the library were filled with headlines shouting of how Adolf Hitler was determined to dominate continental Europe. Just last month, in March, Hitler had sent his armed forces into Austria and proclaimed its union with Germany. No matter how Martha wished she could avert her eyes and ears, there was no avoiding the fact that new waves of tension were sweeping across the entire European continent. There was no doubt that Hitler was casting covetous eyes toward further conquests. His terrifying persecution of minorities, already imposed on the people of Germany, was now being put into effect in Austria.

Despite Papa's insistence that Charlotte must come home to the United States if things heated up too fast, Martha knew only too well that Charlotte would do no such thing. She would throw herself into the thick of trouble, while here at home, Martha and Papa must sit and listen to the radio each evening like a pair of worried birds, while Washington debated the monumental question as to whether the United States would or would not turn its back on the "European problem."

Papa would not cope with any worrying news when it came to Charlotte. Martha opened the telegram herself, her fingers fumbling and slick with sweat.

MR. LAURENCE BELMONT AND MISS MARTHA BELMONT

PARIS, FRANCE

25, RUE LAFFITTE

DEEPLY REGRET TO INFORM YOU OF OUR
DARLING ANITA'S DEATH. ALL THE LOVE OF MY
HEART AND SYMPATHY TO YOU BOTH. LETTER
FOLLOWING.

CHARLOTTE

An ache lodged at the back of Martha's throat. She read and re-read the distressing, unthinkable words until her head spun, and she placed her head in her hands, letting the piece of paper spiral like a fallen leaf to the floor.

Anita had been the closest person to a mother that she and her twin sister Charlotte had ever known after their mother, Chloé, had died fifteen years earlier in 1923 when her little girls were nearly four years old. Anita had been one of Chloé's closest friends, and she'd embraced Chloé's two little motherless American twins as if they were her own, coming all the way to New York from Paris to stay while Papa was away on his sabbaticals, researching the important academic history books he wrote when he was not translating European works of fiction into English.

Sometimes, when Papa went away, Anita insisted Martha and Charlotte stay with her in her apartment on Rue Laffitte in Paris, overflowing with art because the gallery she owned downstairs was similarly spilling over with the paintings she loved.

Martha swallowed, a lump forming in her throat at the memories she treasured of Anita, of how she used to display the works of her artists by pegging their paintings like laundry on clotheslines; how she'd host wonderful dinner parties after every exhibition, inviting her artists, their families and friends to celebrate the launch of their careers; how she'd carefully nurtured so many young Parisian artists, taking them by the hand and guiding them through the minefield that was the European art world.

Martha took a deep breath to still the tears that fought to stream down her cheeks. Anita had that certain something, a swish of her smooth chestnut hair, a twinkle in her dancing eyes, and a *je ne sais quoi* that made everyone who met her fall in love with her on sight. It was the reason she'd remained so successful in the cut-throat world of selling art, because her passion was infectious.

It was inconceivable to imagine Paris without Anita. It was impossible to imagine that Anita was gone.

Slowly, Martha rose from her vigil, and walked step by weighty step down the hallway to Papa's study.

He'd never recovered from the loss of Martha and Charlotte's mother. Anita was the closest link they all had to her. Martha must break Papa's heart in two all over again.

A little later, Papa sat in his wood-paneled study, brooding in his favorite wing-backed chair. His pipe was poised in one hand. He stared, disconsolate, at the fireplace, and struck a match, holding the flame to the surface of the tobacco, and moving it around the bowl. He puffed through the pipe until it was all lit.

Martha sat opposite him, her hands clasped tight in her lap and a frown gathering on her forehead. She felt a pang of nostalgia at the way Papa's feet stuck out in front of him at odd angles when he sat, and how the cardigan he wore was ruffled around his middle, while his gray hair was disheveled around his still handsome face. He lifted his gaze toward her, and his red-rimmed blue eyes held volumes of unspoken grief.

"Shall I light the fire?" Martha asked. Despite the promises of warm weather that came with the spring, it was chilly in here. And she had to do something. Anything to lift the disquieting veil of silence with which Papa surrounded himself.

Absently, Papa nodded. He averted his gaze, his jaw clenched, his lips pressed closed.

Martha winced at his tightly controlled distress. She busied herself, collecting logs from the basket by the fireplace, ensuring they were as thick as her fist, and placing them at the bottom of the grate, then adding a layer of small logs, and one or two more of kindling, spacing the wood out so that the fire would have enough air to breathe. Finally, she added some sheets of old newspaper, filled with printed stories about Hitler's covetous greed for the Sudetenland in Czechoslovakia. What country would he thirst for next?

The answer hung, unthinkable, between her and Papa, every day, every night. Everyone knew that the idea of taking France tingled Hitler's insatiable tastebuds.

Martha struck a match, staring at the tiny new flames that licked in the grate. She swept a hand across her forehead, her heart breaking for the loss of Anita, and laced with an unsettling fear for Charlotte, because Anita had been Jewish, and now, Charlotte would be a young woman, alone in Paris, working in a business owned by a Jew.

Papa dug for a handkerchief in his pocket. "We must escalate our efforts to remove Charlotte from all danger." His voice broke, and he stared down helplessly at his hands. "This is unthinkable. Anita's loss is..."

Martha took in a breath. "Darling Papa. Charlotte says Anita was talking for some time of an evacuation plan to protect the French National Museums' public collections of art in case Hitler invaded. I am certain she would have prepared to keep not only her collection, but Charlotte safe." Martha turned back to face the fire, unable to finish her sentence, trying to quell her obvious distress.

Papa remained silent, his head buried in his hands.

From the beginning of this year, the Nazis' crackdowns on Jewish people had become more ferocious, increasing the expropriation of their property, and stealing their possessions, impeding their efforts to emigrate, while plans for German expansion escalated, and domestic preparations for war accelerated. It was all part of the process that was known as "Aryanization." Martha closed her eyes, images of the deep green front door that led into Anita's narrow building on Rue Laffitte in the old streets of Montmartre crowding into her mind, her and Charlotte reaching up to knock, while Papa stood behind them under the blue Parisian skies, the sun shining on the windows of the buildings in the charming Parisian thoroughfare. Papa, holding their luggage, would tilt his bowler hat in acknowledgment at passersby. When it was especially hot in August, and Paris was empty as people flocked to the seaside, Anita would whisk Martha and Charlotte down to the Loire Valley, to her family's magical Chateau d'Anez with its endless cool green lawns and a lake lined with willow trees for swimming. Especially wonderful for Martha, there were marvelous hidden places where she could tuck herself away for hours and read a book. She opened her eyes again, only to come face to face with Papa. His eyes were clouded with grief.

Martha held his gaze. Seeing Papa in such deep distress was too much. There was only one thing to do. "I shall book a passage to Paris, Papa. I will persuade her to come home."

Papa reached for an old silver-framed photograph of Anita and his beloved Chloé. Anita beamed out at the camera, her dark chestnut curls blowing in a soft Mediterranean breeze, while Chloé, her fair hair whipping around her face, smiled radiantly.

Martha's earliest memories of her childhood during the early years of *Les Années Folles*, the Roaring Twenties, in Paris were vague. It was Anita who had filled in the details with her talk of dancing late in the jazz clubs and music halls where Josephine Baker and Maurice Chevalier launched their careers, of driving around the Loire Valley in open-topped cars and waving cloche hats in the air, of visiting the picture houses where the world's first silent movies were shown. It seemed so long ago now, another world. Martha had moved to New York with Papa and Charlotte in 1925 and had not been back to Paris since 1933 when things had changed so dramatically in Europe after Hitler came to power.

Papa looked up, as if forcing himself to divert his eyes away from the photograph.

His brows drew together. "I cannot allow you to do that. I'm her father, I should be the one to go."

Martha searched his face. Paris held too many tragic memories for Papa. She couldn't sit by while he went to Paris. Every time they went there, Papa would spend the least time he could in the city where Chloé had died. It was as if this was an unspoken agreement in the family, as unspoken as their acceptance that Papa was never going to get over his loss.

"There is something else."

Martha stilled.

Papa spoke in low, resolute tones. "I fear dreadfully for Anita's parents, Élise and Olivier. An elderly Jewish couple, their only daughter dead."

Martha stood up. Outside, twilight had fallen over Central Park, and the blossoms were muted, the park awash with soft sepia tones.

Papa went on, the words grating out from his lips: "If I were to lose anyone else that I loved in France, I don't know that I could—"

"That is why I must go." Martha swung around. "Charlotte needs to understand that the thought of losing her is impossible. Impossible for you. I shall convince her that she must come home to New York. I am resolute, Papa. There is no alternative."

Papa clutched the photo of Chloé and Anita, pressing it close.

"I shall bring them all back. Charlotte, Élise and Olivier." Martha went over to him, kneeling at his feet, taking his hands in hers. "You will not lose her too. I promise you, hand to my heart."

A frown line seared between his eyes. He shook his head. "Martha—"

"I'll take one of the regular French Line Cabin Services. Seven days at sea is nothing to me. I'm a good sailor and—"

"I end up curled up on my cot in the cabin confoundingly ill." Papa's grip on her hands tightened. "Please, bring her home. Bring them all to safety. I hate the idea of another war." He ground out the words, his face falling into shadow.

Martha swallowed. She had to do this for her father, for Charlotte. It wasn't just that Papa was a feeble sailor, but if anyone was to persuade Charlotte to come home, it was Martha. Despite their differences, they were sisters, and Martha hoped that would be enough now. There was a selection of ships going every few days, SS *Champlain*, SS *Lafayette*, *Rochambeau*. There was her inheritance from Maman to pay for a return ticket and she could use her savings from the New York Library.

Martha squeezed her eyes closed. "In two months, we shall all be here. Safely. Please, Papa, don't fret anymore." But Martha's insides curled at her falsely confident words, and one question seared at her heart. *How far would Charlotte go to protect all that she loved in Paris, and was there honestly any hope to convince her to leave?*

Papa turned away, the expression on his face unreadable, and Martha focused on the gold-red flames in the fireplace that scorched the soft, beautiful wood, before transforming into a brilliant, blazing blue.

Martha

"You must have a traveling wardrobe. It is the least I can do."
Vianne Conti adjusted the hang of a fashionable *robe de style*
here, smoothed the bodice of an organdy blouse there, all
displayed beautifully on mannequins dotted around the atelier
she had built into one of the most fashionable in New York.
Vianne turned to Martha, her blue eyes wide. "I can't imagine
what you are going through. I'm so sorry. This is my small way
of sending you off feeling a little stronger."

Martha's eyes wandered up the staircase to the *galerie,*
where Vianne kept the haute couture pieces she designed for
her most discerning clients. Vianne's attendants assisted the
clientele, their voices muted and discreet.

"In times of crisis, it is even more important to dress well."
Vianne bowed her head, and tucked her hands into the white-
faced pockets on her contemporary black costume, with its
stand-up white collar and flaring skirt that skimmed her hips.

Vianne's ability to create things of beauty when times were
difficult was legendary. It was how she'd survived the last war.

But could she, Martha, hope to summon the same strength of purpose as the women of her mother's generation if large-scale war came to Europe—or, dare she think it, to the United States again? Charlotte could, that was certain. But what about her, Martha?

She wrapped her hands around her waist and turned away. The fact was, Anita had never once complained about the horrific injuries that she must have seen nursing during the Great War with Martha's mother, Chloé. Vianne never talked of the last war, not once. Martha had always seen strength in the older women's silence, but she dared not think of what they had endured. There was a sort of complicit loyalty between them to that time, that place and the memories of war that would always bind them close.

The reality was, Charlotte showed the same singular strength of purpose that Anita had in spades. There was almost no fighting chance that Charlotte would turn around meekly, climb aboard a boat, and leave the fires of Europe to burn. Martha gazed down at the swirling patterns on the carpet beneath her feet.

The beautiful designer, whose sister-in-law, Sandrine, had been the third member of Chloé and Anita's friendship trio back in France, took a step closer to Martha, her hand reaching out to stroke her arm. "While your father has considered me a good friend to you and Charlotte, I know that Anita was the substitute French mother whom you both adored."

Martha folded her hands in a knot. The last few days had been a whirlwind, and she'd deliberately kept herself busy to stop herself from falling apart, booking her passage to France on the SS *Champlain*, informing the New York Library that she would be gone for several weeks.

"When do you sail?"

Martha sighed. "In ten days' time. I don't want to put you to any trouble. I already have such a lovely spring wardrobe." It was true. When Papa had arrived in New York with Charlotte and Martha after Chloé's death, Vianne had swept into their lives, and Martha and Charlotte had been two of the best-dressed little girls in Manhattan. They both adored Vianne.

"Oh, my darling girl." Vianne shook her head. "The moment your father told me of the dreadful news, I got out my little design book and began to sketch. My seamstresses know the nuances of your body to a T," Vianne went on. "Once I've given them my ideas, they will begin cutting out the patterns and will be able to fashion you a wardrobe in no time." She lowered her voice. "You know, Martha, with your tumbling chestnut curls and extraordinary golden eyes, you will be the belle of the cruise."

Martha took in a sharp breath. The belle of the cruise? Again, that role was for Charlotte, not her. Martha knew where she belonged. Why try to change anything now?

Vianne was watching, her expression astute.

Martha winced. "A couple of skirts and blouses is all I'll need."

Vianne's big blue eyes widened. "You are going in ten days' time?"

Martha nodded.

"Well then." A look of contemplation crossed Vianne's exquisite features. "That means you will be sailing on the same passage as dearest Clyde."

Martha's stomach quivered. "Clyde?"

"Clyde Fraser, dear. He's been in Virginia but is returning to Scotland."

"Vianne—"

"Clyde is a friend of my sister, Anaïs, and her husband, in Scotland." Vianne took in a breath and eyed Martha. "He's a doctor, and a member of the Gordon Highlanders, such a brave battalion."

Martha frowned. Clyde Fraser would undoubtedly do what

every other young man who met Martha did. He would ignore her, and in this case, find some fashionable set aboard the boat with whom he'd amuse himself until they berthed in Plymouth, and he went off to Scotland, after which she'd never lay eyes upon him for as long as she lived. Martha knew how it would be.

But there was little point in arguing with Vianne. Martha would simply climb aboard the boat with a trunk full of books and read her way across the Atlantic Ocean just as she always did.

Several days later, Martha returned to Vianne's atelier to collect her wardrobe. Her mind was aswirl with plans for the crossing, and not least, her worries at leaving Papa. At present, he was translating a modernist novel from Italian into English. He'd been pacing around the house muttering that he wished he could meet the author. He'd grumbled at breakfast this morning over the fact that he couldn't go to Rome because of "that infernal Mussolini."

Martha had sighed in despair. Mussolini had supported Hitler in the decision to invade Austria and had written an article aligning Italy with the idea of an Aryan race. The prospect of traveling to Italy right now was as worrisome as going to Germany. Everyone was wondering when, or if, it would ever be safe to move around the world freely again.

Martha took a deep breath and took the stairs up to Vianne's hallowed *galerie*.

When Vianne appeared outside the door to her office, with its picture window looking down on Park Avenue, she clasped Martha's hand and led her to a private fitting room. Vianne pushed open the walnut door to this exquisite space, with its soft carpets and modern curved sofas. Dotted about the room, all displayed on mannequins, were some of the most beautiful outfits Martha had ever seen.

"Vianne, these are extraordinary," Martha whispered. Surely, they were for a new collection or for some fashionable girl raised in the Upper East Side? But when Martha's eyes landed on a nautical-inspired travel outfit, with a tight-fitting sweater and a pair of soft-flowing matching navy trousers, she drew her hand to cover her mouth.

There were two evening gowns, one simply draped to the waist, before flowing to the floor with an asymmetric shoulder design in burnt orange, and another in silk jersey designed in Ancient Greek style with the drapery held together by hidden drawstrings. Then, there were shirt dresses with front button fastenings, a high-waisted skirt of black satin, and a blouse of pale pink lamé, along with a smart dove-gray suit that could be worn with fur lapels and with a cape, with a fitted blouse untucked under the jacket.

Martha drew in a sharp breath. A cream diaphanous dress was embroidered with delicate pale pink flowers made of ruched fabric seeming to encircle the wearer's body as it flowed to the ground.

"For dinner, and for dancing aboard the ship," Vianne murmured. "I wanted you to have something special."

Martha turned to Vianne. "It is too much," she said, simply. It was impossible to find any other words.

Vianne held a soft finger to Martha's lips. "Anita would not have wanted you to mope about in black, *chérie*. She would have wanted you to live your life to the full." Vianne's expression clouded. "And this is more important than ever now. Because everyone knows that the time just before night falls is the most enchanted. And I am afraid that the skies are about to darken over my beloved Europe again."

Martha's fingers shook as her hands glided over the soft fabric.

"Will you try it on, so I am content that it truly fits?"

Martha's sigh was deep and weighted. "I don't know what to say," she whispered, honestly.

"Just say *oui*," Vianne replied. She unfastened the dress from the mannequin and led Martha into a secluded little dressing room.

Ten minutes later, Martha stepped out, her curls tumbling down her back. She knew her cheeks were pink and glowing, and she couldn't help taking a little twirl for Vianne.

"Why, it's gorgeous," Martha said. The branches of the pretty pink blossom that trailed down the floor-length diaphanous skirt were counteracted by black for the branches, and there was a black velvet ribbon fastened around the waist.

"Come out to the mezzanine gallery," Vianne said, "I shall check everything in a clearer light." Vianne's expression softened, and her blue eyes were filled with warmth. "Martha, you are an extraordinarily gorgeous girl. Promise me, you will wear this special gown to a ball aboard the ship. Promise me you will dance the night away. You must not hide away anymore. You know?"

Martha blushed, and the breath she took in shook a little.

As she stepped out of the private salon, Martha came to a sudden stop. For coming up the stairs, his long legs striding in a pair of trousers with a perfect crease down the center, and wearing a smart double-breasted suit with peaked lapels, was a heavenly good-looking man with smooth blond hair and green eyes who stopped in his tracks, his gaze landing on Martha and staying right there.

Martha drew a hand to her mouth. She pulled her tumbling hair back from her face.

But the man's voice seared into her back. "You look sensational," he said. "Don't change a thing."

Martha froze. Slowly, feeling ridiculous now, she said, "I should go."

But Vianne laid a hand on her shoulder. "Clyde," the older woman said, moving forward and embracing him.

Martha's eyes widened. Clyde Fraser.

"Sorry I'm late for our morning coffee, Vianne," Clyde said, his words lilting in a soft Scottish way, his eyes twinkling back at Martha.

Martha folded her arms across her body.

"I'm afraid I got waylaid at the station talking to some chap who wanted to visit the Highlands for the trout fishing. I gave him my card and it seems, Hitler or no Hitler, he's coming to stay at the local inn."

Martha glanced about for an escape route. If only she could fall through the floor and not come up for air until he was gone. How naughty of Vianne to engineer this.

"How charming and typically kind of you." Vianne turned to Martha, her hand moving from Martha's shoulder until she tucked her hand into Martha's arm. "This gorgeous girl whom you have been rightly admiring is my dear friend Martha Belmont. And she will be traveling on the same boat as you across the Atlantic, so I imagine you will get to see Martha and this gown all over again."

"I have a mission aboard the ship. I won't be troubling anyone for entertainment." She sent the Scotsman a look. It was true. She was on a mission to convince her sister to come home. Martha bit her lip at the easy way the story rolled from her tongue.

Clyde's eyes danced. "A mission. How intriguing."

"I won't be needing entertainment," Martha went on, wincing, too late, at the fact that she was repeating herself. She was not good in these situations. Her arms fell to her sides.

"I didn't realize I was an entertainer," he said, his green eyes dancing now.

"If you will excuse me, I must get back to Papa." Martha shook her head, gathered her skirt and rushed back to the privacy of the salon, where she slipped inside, closed the door behind her and collapsed against it, her fingers curling around the soft folds of the stunning gown.

"I think the prospect of your Atlantic crossing has become more enchanting for you, Clyde, dear. Hmm?" Vianne's soft voice purred through the closed dressing-room door.

Martha closed her eyes.

"Although she is a poor dear. Traveling for such a sad reason. You simply must look after Martha. Make sure she does not spend the entire trip to Paris on her own".

Clyde spoke in low tones. "Given the circumstances which we're going to find in Europe, I'm happy to do anything I can do to cheer up a fellow passenger, if it helps."

Vianne lowered her voice. "The spirit of helping one another is going to be more important than ever in the coming months."

"I'll make sure she's in the swing of things," Clyde said. "The last thing anyone wants to do right now is brood."

Martha sighed, and she tried to beat down the sinking sensation that, from hereon, everything was going to change.

3

Charlotte

Charlotte stretched her legs underneath the breakfast table in the shade of the glorious linden tree in the *parc* at Chateau d'Anez. The feel of the cool, freshly mowed grass between her toes was delicious. She leaned her head back, her glossy black curls tumbling down her shoulders and her dark eyes half closed. But her ears pricked as the other members of the house party walked across the lush green lawn that spread out like a verdant blanket around the magnificent chateau. The morning sun gleamed on the grand Napoleon III building, catching on the floor-to-ceiling French windows and the mansard roof, the golden light lending even more beauty to the magical chateau's richly decorated facade.

If it were any other summer, Charlotte would be looking forward to a breakfast spent chatting, eating, sipping coffee, and reading the papers well into the day. There would be a wonderful discussion about food and the markets, for Anita's mother, Élise, now in her seventies, had always taken great pleasure in cooking, and much to her late mother-in-law's disgust, insisted on commandeering the vast chateau basement kitchens herself when she was younger, resulting in complete delight on the part of her guests. Now, Élise took on the role of supervisor in the kitchens and still enjoyed her daily trips to the local markets, where she was a well-loved customer.

This morning, Charlotte had risen early, taking her usual walk up the long driveway flanked by old, grand trees to the chateau's huge wrought-iron gates, before weaving her way back through the *parc* and returning to her private *salle de bain* for a deliciously long bath. Now, her stomach grumbling, she eyed the gorgeous spread before her with satisfaction: fresh fruit, *pâtisseries* from the local *boulangerie*, *croissants*, *pain au chocolat*, homemade jams and brioche. But this summer, the guests at Chateau d'Anez were not assembled for pleasure, nor were they here to simply enjoy Élise's wonderful menus. This year, the guests were here to discuss the impending war, and how Hitler continued to simply ignore the Treaty of Versailles, amassing thousands of warplanes and building an army of 300,000 men, before marching into the Rhineland in blatant defiance of the terms struck at the end of the Great War.

"We can assume the Nazis would enter France from the east should they attack France." Monsieur Lavigne's voice carried across the *parc* as the house party came closer. "The Loire Valley is one of the safest areas for the collection of the Louvre. It is close to Paris, and yet far enough from the German border. And should further evacuation be necessary, it is reasonably close to England."

Charlotte sat up taller in her seat, leaning closer to catch the words of the senior curator from the Louvre. She'd sat, spellbound, half in shock, and half in awe while the esteemed fine arts administrator, sent to the chateau by none other than Jacques Jaujard, the deputy director of the entire French

museum system, les Musées Nationaux, had addressed Élise
and Olivier last night at dinner. Monsieur Lavigne had arrived
with a startling proposal. He had offered Olivier and Élise a
small subsidy for the use of Chateau d'Anez to store some of the
treasures of the Louvre if France was invaded. It seemed he was
reiterating his plans today.

Charlotte's heart went out to Anita's mother, who had
tended and loved Chateau d'Anez for decades. Élise's brow
furrowed with concern, her usually perfectly styled gray hair
pulled back into a hasty knot at the nape of her neck, her
fingers, glittering with the jeweled rings that Olivier had given
her during their long and happy marriage, clasped in front of
her soft green skirt.

Beside her, his hand loosely holding his wife's, Olivier's
head was lowered as he walked, the expression in his emotive
dark eyes unreadable. But Anita strode with her head high, and
when her coppery gaze met with Charlotte's, she did not flinch.
Anita came to sit at the table, a flurry of Guerlain's Sous le Vent
swirling around her smart red shirt-waisted dress.

"We are asking several local owners to be inspired by patrio-
tism, or, by your love of art, to help France." Monsieur Lavigne
settled himself down in a seat opposite Charlotte. He sipped
from his tall glass of water and sat back in his chair, folding his
arms in his pressed linen suit.

Charlotte did not miss the way Élise's hands shook when
she placed her white linen napkin on her lap.

Even before Monsieur Lavigne's arrival and his proposal,
vexation for Élise, Olivier, and Anita had kept Charlotte awake
at night, along with frustration at the prospect of losing the
French way of life that she'd come to know and love. This was a
way of life that was gradually inching her closer to putting
together a picture of the mother she'd lost.

From the very first time she'd been able to fully compre-
hend the tragedy of Chloé's death at the hands of a rogue

vehicle in Paris, Charlotte had lifted her chin and realized that she had to live enough of life for *two* people. But, sometimes, she worried that she was living for three, because her sister, Martha, had retreated into herself when Papa had finally explained what had happened to their mother that dreadful day. Charlotte had taken on the role of protector of her quiet, watchful sister, and yet, she was also drawn so very strongly to France, and this had led her to moving here just a few months ago, leaving her sister behind.

Charlotte cast her eyes about the sun-kissed, deep green lawns of Chateau d'Anez. This enchanted place was Charlotte's connection to a living, breathing family.

Until talk of Nazi invasions had threatened to blow their world apart.

Charlotte listened intently while Monsieur Lavigne talked of plans to evacuate France's precious art out of Paris.

"It was decided three years ago that Chambord would be the primary depot for the collection of the Louvre," he said. "We will use the great chateau as a way station, where the masterpieces will be checked as they are evacuated from Paris, and then sent onto their final destinations. The fine arts administration is presently finalizing what those destinations will be, and that means we are looking for specific chateaux."

"I understand why Chambord has been chosen," Olivier said. "With miles of forest surrounding the building, it is isolated enough, and it should not be bombed in error, because it is so easily recognizable from the air."

Charlotte swallowed. "But what about the sculptures? *The Winged Victory of Samothrace?* Surely that will be too heavy to move away from the Louvre."

Monsieur Lavigne sighed. "We are in the process of working this out."

Charlotte reached for a croissant. Across the table, she caught Anita's eye, and smiled at the way her mother's friend nodded encouragingly. Charlotte was asking questions and taking part in this important conversation about the protection of France's heritage like the professional gallerist she wanted to become.

Charlotte had learned everything she knew about art from Anita, as well as everything she knew about running a successful business. While Charlotte recognized she had a long way to go, she reveled in the fact that she could wake up every morning, throw her shutters open wide onto Rue Laffitte, and work with people who were engaged with life, who adored living as much as she did: artists and collectors and dealers who did not wish to waste one precious day.

Monsieur Lavigne cleared his throat. "There is something else." He turned to Olivier. "What plans have you, to keep your family safe? Your daughter, your wife…"

There was a silence.

Charlotte sat up, looking to Olivier.

"I'm sure I don't have to inform you of what may happen should Hitler's… forces march into France," Monsieur Lavigne continued, barely hiding his grimace. "In January, they began to Aryanize the very economy in Germany. Your home, your art collections, not to mention your welfare, are all under grave threat."

Even Charlotte lowered her gaze. How dare this man raise such a thing while enjoying the hospitality of a Jewish family? Had he no sensitivity?

But Monsieur Lavigne went on. "You must know that Jewish owners are being forced, in Germany, to sell their businesses. They are prohibited from working in any office. Your daughter's fine gallery—"

Anita pushed back her chair and stood up. She reached for her father's silver cigarette case. "Do you mind, Papa?" she asked.

"Oh, do go ahead, *chérie*," Olivier muttered. He crossed his arms but remained silent, allowing the curator from the Louvre to continue.

Charlotte sighed at Olivier's pragmatism. He was not one to blow off steam.

There was a soft rustle in the leaves above their heads, and Monsieur Lavigne looked around sharply, as if there could be Nazis listening in the linden trees. "This month, the Germans have launched the *Entartete Kunst*—the exhibition of 'degenerate' artwork in Munich."

Anita raised a brow and blew out a perfect smoke ring. "Imbeciles," she muttered. "Hitler would have everyone paint in the old-fashioned ways of a hundred years ago to satisfy his hopelessly dated tastes."

"Artwork of the modern kind that your daughter, with due respect, has championed in France throughout her entire career is exactly what Hitler blacklists," Monsieur Lavigne continued, oblivious to Anita's dagger gaze. "We can only assume he'll do the same thing in France."

Anita scoffed. "Never."

Charlotte's head went from Anita to Monsieur Lavigne and back.

He lowered his voice. "The Nazis will not only target artworks. If they arrive in Paris, they will most certainly turn on those who work with them. Being a Jew and a proponent of modern art places you at great risk, Anita."

There was an awkward silence. Élise brought her hand to her mouth and Olivier cleared his throat.

Monsieur Lavigne went on. "The situation is stark. It is not anticipated to improve. Monsieur Goldstein, Madame, if things worsen, and if Germany does, indeed, become gripped by anti-Semitism, would you consider removing your family from Europe? Have you thought about relocating to the New World?"

Élise placed her coffee cup down with a clatter. Milky brown liquid pooled over her perfect white linen cloth.

Later that morning, Charlotte waited in the *entrée* to Chateau d'Anez, holding the wicker basket that Élise always took to the local markets in Amboise. The thought of wandering through the colorful stalls where the vendors set up along the tree-lined avenues seemed like the perfect idea after Monsieur Lavigne's dire warnings at breakfast. Élise had stood firm that she would visit the markets, just as she had done twice a week for the last thirty years. She'd also insisted that Anita not change her plans to meet with a collector who was interested in buying some paintings from a young Italian artist whom she had taken under her wing.

The stiffness in Charlotte's shoulders lifted at the sound of Élise's familiar footsteps on the parquet floors. But while she waited, Charlotte could not avert her eyes from the beautiful portrait of Élise as a child that hung on the wall. The artist had highlighted the young Élise's silky brown hair with streaks of gold, the expression in her deep brown eyes was pensive below her delicately curved brows, and the way her little arms were folded around her body was suggestive of an inclination not to sit perfectly still for Monsieur Pissarro at all. Throughout the airy rooms of the vast chateau, there were dotted several beautiful pieces of such importance to the hearts and minds of Olivier and Élise that they were almost like glue, binding their family to each other, and to the artistic family legacy that they shared.

Charlotte tore her eyes away from the painting, and her thoughts away from Hitler, as Élise made her way through the four huge reception rooms that flowed across the ground floor, one opening to the next through floor-to-ceiling solid double doors. The sun shone through the majestic French windows that overlooked the *parc*, and when Élise came to a stop next to Charlotte, pausing to arrange her green felt hat in the ornate mirror in the *entrée*, it was easy to pretend that the traditions and way of life at Chateau d'Anez would never change. It still seemed fantastical to contemplate Hitler's soldiers invading France.

Élise collected the keys to her Renault Nervastella. She tucked her arm into Charlotte's, and Charlotte handed Élise her basket, searching Élise's face for any traces of her brief panic when she spilled her coffee at breakfast time.

"Oh, thank you, *ma chérie*," Élise said. She patted Charlotte's arm. "I'm determined to make things as normal as possible in spite of the worrying news." She lowered her voice and eyed Charlotte, her dark eyebrows raised. "I'm glad that Monsieur Lavigne has left us. I admire plans to save the treasures of the Louvre, but..." She turned her gaze toward Charlotte, anxiety piercing her eyes. "You don't think the Nazis will come into France, Charlotte dear?"

Charlotte frowned. "Of course not," she said, attempting to sound as convincing as possible. But yesterday, Olivier had walked out of the salon, throwing a newspaper in the trash that told stories of physical assaults against Jews in Poland and how Hitler was holding grand parades of his troops in Nuremberg. The insidious nature of Hitler's anti-Semitic undertones added a deeper layer of darkness than Germany's imperial ambitions had twenty-five years ago in the Great War. "You must not worry, Élise." She squeezed the elderly woman's arm, her own heart dancing a nervous tune.

Élise stilled. She opened her mouth as if to speak, only to close it, instead, clipping purposefully out the front door toward the stone steps that led to the elevated entrance of the chateau.

That's the way. Hold your head up and be fearless. Charlotte followed Élise out to her waiting car.

But when they climbed into the Renault with its formidable

grille in front of the hood, Charlotte started at the sight of the single tear tracing down Élise's cheek.

Charlotte rubbed Élise's shaking back, her worry escalating at the feel of Élise's perspiring hand. "It is nonsense," she assured Élise. "The entire situation makes no sense."

"I ask myself, what does Hitler have against us?" Élise said. "What right does he have to take out his hatred on peaceful Jews?"

Charlotte took in a deep breath. "I simply don't know," she said.

Élise looked up; her eyes streaked with traceries of red. She gripped Charlotte's hand, her knuckles whitening. "What if it turns out that we must leave Chateau d'Anez at short notice? What if Monsieur Lavigne is right, and the newspapers that Olivier is throwing in the trash, thinking I shall not pick them up after him, are indeed correct…"

Charlotte closed her eyes, her grip tightening around Élise's fingers.

Élise balled her gnarled fist. When she spoke, her voice was soft, but gripped with something new and stirring. "The thought of my portraits hanging on some Nazi's wall. The thought of Olivier's sculptures being thrown into some truck and driven away. This is what Monsieur Lavigne is worried about. I overheard him talking to Olivier last night. Monsieur Lavigne thinks the Nazis will target Jewish collectors if they invade France. There seems little doubt they will exclude us from basic freedoms, as they are doing in Germany. They have no respect for us as human beings, and Monsieur Lavigne says the Nazis may avail themselves of our beloved possessions without a second thought. These things mean so much to me. Charlotte, I want to stay in France, but I fear we must leave our home, and then what…" She shook her head. "I don't know how I could say goodbye to my whole life. Do you understand?"

Charlotte's heart thumped against her chest. How anyone

could contemplate packing up and abandoning their entire life in the face of impending war and persecution was beyond comprehension, but, incomprehensibly, it was something that Anita and her parents may have to face. While Charlotte was determined to alleviate Élise's worry, she had also come to a resolution of her own.

"I shall stay and ensure everything is taken care of properly, until you return." Charlotte grasped Élise's hand. "I swear it. The Nazis will not touch your precious home." *And they will not touch you, Anita or Olivier*, Charlotte swore to herself.

There was a silence, and slowly, Élise's dark eyes locked with Charlotte's. "I cannot risk your safety."

Charlotte took in a ragged breath. In her own way, she'd thought this through as well. She'd thought it through because she knew so well that Papa would place her safety above anything else. His letters were coming frequently, and Charlotte knew he was panicking. Panicking because he'd lost Chloé to France, and panicking because there was a real worry that he was not strong enough to go on if he lost Charlotte too.

Charlotte spoke evenly. "As a neutral American, I am perfectly placed to stay. The Nazis will not—they *cannot* —target me."

Élise shook her head, her ringed hands pressing into her temples.

"I swear it," Charlotte said. And she meant what she said. The Nazi party had made their interest in art clear from early on. They'd already "purified" German art galleries, removing thousands of pieces of modern art from collections all over Germany, from the Impressionists to the modernists, and that meant works just like Pissarro's portrait of Élise as a young girl. They'd waste no time in purifying France, but Charlotte would not sit back and let that happen if she could avoid it. She reached out and stroked Élise's shoulder with her free hand.

"Your collection is part of your family. It is a legacy that is the beloved fruits falling from famous artists' hands."

Élise drew in a ragged, shaking breath.

Charlotte gazed out the car window over the still green gardens, spread out on this perfect summer's morning. The fact was, if Chateau d'Anez were to be a repository for treasures from the Louvre, it would be well guarded. France would safeguard the priceless works from the country's collections at any cost. What Monsieur Lavigne was proposing, acquiring the chateau as a repository for artworks, could be the best way to keep Élise and Olivier's beloved heirlooms safe. And if Élise and Olivier had to flee, so be it. Charlotte *would* be above suspicion and of no interest to the Nazis. She would be the perfect person to stay in France to protect the family heirlooms and the home that Élise and Olivier cherished.

Charlotte closed her eyes. Papa would have to understand. How could she abandon everything that this family loved when Anita had welcomed her into their world? It would be unthinkable. It was simply not something she'd ever do. Going to sit quietly in the United States while her beloved France was at war? She may as well run herself a bath and lay in it while Europe burned. No, the idea of leaving France was impossible. She was too bound up in it, as it was in her.

She might be American, but she was also half French, and something told Charlotte that her own mother would have never run away from such problems. She would not have hidden. She would have fought, just as she had donned a nurse's uniform and gone to northern France to tend to the horrific wounds of the Allied soldiers in the last war. That image was enough to galvanize her.

"You can rely on me. I want to be here," Charlotte said.

Élise wiped her hand across her forehead and eased herself to a more upright position in her seat.

"We shall go to the markets." Charlotte fired up the engine

on the Renault and sent Élise a determined glance. "And we shall live every day with a great appreciation for our way of life."

Charlotte drove down the long driveway, overhung with trees, at a cracking pace. Beside her, she sensed Élise stiffening as they approached the wrought-iron gates. How much longer would the family be able to stay here, and get to drive through these beautiful gates?

4

PARIS, SUMMER 1937

Charlotte

Charlotte hauled her groceries up Rue Laffitte, the honey-colored buildings that lined the narrow street seeming to close in on the sidewalk in the oppressive summer heat. She stopped a moment, taking in the one sight that never failed to remind her why she loved Paris more than any other city in the world.

Rising in the shimmering haze at the end of the street, the majestic white cathedral of Sacré-Cœur soared like a white-painted castle above the Notre-Dame-de-Lorette church. Below this, the old village of Montmartre spread like an enticing canvas, its streets resonating with the lives of painters such as Picasso, Miro, Toulouse-Lautrec, Renoir, and Van Gogh. This was the world that Charlotte's parents had inhabited back in the 1920s. This was the world that Charlotte wanted to contribute to, a contribution that was worthy of her mother's memory.

The plaque, welcoming young ingenues and collectors alike to Galerie A. Goldstein, gleamed in the golden sunlight. Charlotte let herself in, pushing the heavy green door closed behind her with her back, and allowing herself a moment to catch her breath in the cool interior of Anita's beloved space.

Her trained eye swept around the ground floor, where preparations for the opening of Anita's latest protégé's exhibition tonight were almost complete. The walls were lined with Sandro Luciana's striking, joyous paintings of people in calm, everyday scenes.

Charlotte remembered the day the young artist first came to Anita's gallery, talking quietly of his passion and hard work and pulling from his portfolio a selection of his expressive modern works filled with color, pattern, and fluid lines.

Now, the way the young artist had captured the daily life of the Parisians seemed even more poignant, given the conversations that had taken place out at Chateau d'Anez, and Charlotte swallowed hard as she gazed at the images in the paintings: the cobbled streets of Montmartre, Parisians sitting at wicker chairs in pavement cafés, sipping coffee and whiling away the mornings, strolling in the formal Tuileries Gardens, peering through golden lit windows in the enchanting streets of the Left Bank, rain blurring the sidewalks, walking, arms entwined, over the romantic bridges that looped across the River Seine. How long would this world last?

Only yesterday, Anita had stood up and left her favorite café, La Rose Blanche, abandoning her coffee when the couple next to them had talked of Hitler's malignant programs and the destruction of the Great Synagogue in Nuremberg. The Nazis already seemed to be infiltrating their way of life.

Charlotte's eyes were drawn to the picture that was closest to her heart here in the gallery, a painting of a model lounging in a Parisian apartment, wearing a red coat and exotic trouser suit with a book at her feet and a bunch of roses in a vase. The painting was filled with beautiful, patterned details, and the model, who looked at the viewer in the most confident and striking way, was none other than Anita.

Sandro had asked her permission to paint her, and Anita had vowed she would always keep this portrait as a special reminder of the talented young artist she was about to launch into the world on this day. Charlotte determined to protect this and the family's other treasured artworks.

When Anita appeared through the door to the back rooms of her gallery, Charlotte came forward and embraced her dear friend. "I think it's going to be a real occasion tonight, Anita. I can feel it in my bones." Charlotte crossed her arms. "I know I have a long way to go when it comes to helping you discover artists, but Sandro Luciano, to me, seems like the real thing."

Anita clasped her heavily ringed fingers to her heart. "Well, you know, I am the most excited I have been in all of my career."

Charlotte took a step back. "You are serious?"

Anita nodded, gazing around the room, and barely hiding her delight. "Now that we have all Sandro's paintings on the wall, I see a young Matisse."

Charlotte shook her head. "You truly think that Sandro has that sort of potential?"

Anita took a practiced glance around the gallery. "I am certain. And I am determined to sell Sandro's works for a price that is worthy of his potential. Even though he is unrecognized at present. Someday," Anita said, "his name will be familiar in every household of France. And I intend to support him and ensure his work is valued accordingly. From day one." Anita arched a brow.

Charlotte nodded, only too aware of what *not* to mention right now, the fact that Anita had once been swindled by her arch-nemesis, Monsieur Gerard DuPre—a well-known gallerist who had stolen one of Anita's earliest and most promising artists away from her by telling him that Anita, a woman, would not fetch high enough prices for his work.

This travesty had happened once when Anita was young, but never again. She'd confronted Monsieur DuPre and demanded he steer clear of her clients. And she always explained to her artists that she would do her utmost to achieve the best commercial outcomes for them. As a result, she had not lost one artist since, and she'd not only built up a loyal clientele, but she was one of the most coveted gallerists in Rue Laffitte. Every day, at least one young artist would walk in the door holding a portfolio of their work, and Anita, often with Charlotte looking over her shoulder, would sit down with each one of them and take a serious look at their potential.

"So," Anita said, leaning down to pick up Charlotte's grocery bags, "I shall settle into the kitchen and cook for our celebratory dinner after the show. Darling, please, take a rest for an hour or so. You've been slaving away since dawn."

Charlotte stretched. A bath would be heavenly. Today, she'd not stopped: contacting the press one last time to get Sandro as many mentions in the papers and magazines as possible, checking and rechecking the final layout of his paintings in the gallery, subtly shifting the lighting to maximize its effect, before collecting the printed pamphlets for the guests. Next, she'd rushed off to the markets to buy flowers for the show, running back with armfuls of summer roses, which she'd arranged on Anita's desk in the gallery and in the apartment upstairs for the dinner tonight. All this while dealing with her day-to-day administrative tasks, fielding queries from artists, negotiating with collectors. She'd been on the telephone to every single first-time guest to the gallery, giving them clear directions to Galerie A. Goldstein, mainly because she did not want their precious guests being lured into the garishly signposted Monsieur DuPre's gallery across the street. Then, she'd run back to the markets this afternoon to collect the second round of fresh, afternoon baked baguettes and produce for the celebratory dinner. Anita treated her artists like a family and here in Rue Laffitte, Charlotte felt as if she were part of a family with the very biggest of hearts.

. . .

That evening, Anita's dining room was alive with chatter and brimming with the delicious scents of Anita's summer menu— leeks in vinaigrette and roast Provençal chicken—that permeated from her country-style kitchen next door. The French doors of the dining room were flung open to the tiny balcony that looked out over Rue Laffitte, allowing the warm summer evening air to filter into the apartment, filled with the work of Anita's beloved prodigies. Paintings lined the walls in every room, and in the long hallway, the floors were stacked with canvases that could not fit on the walls. Charlotte joked that Anita needed a grand apartment on the Champs-Élysées to store her collection, but Anita always smiled and said that she'd never leave the fringes of Montmartre. Here, she said, was where you found real life.

The sounds of Benny Goodman's clarinet filled the room, the needle scratching on the record only lending an even more romantic air. Next to Charlotte, the young artist Sandro Luciana sat with a twinkle in his sensitive eyes, and a flush in his cheeks, for downstairs every one of his marvelous works had sold, apart from the portrait of Anita that would never leave Anita's home, and she, in turn, was hailed as having discovered a major new talent.

Charlotte clapped her hands, along with every other guest in the room, when Anita served her signature *Hazelnut Dacquoise*; the layers of nutty meringue and whipped coffee filling covered in a chocolate glaze soothing and enlivening her taste buds all at once.

"You are like a midwife," Sandro's father, Giuseppe Luciana, who had traveled from Rome to Paris to view his son's first solo exhibition, said. The slight, middle-aged Italian turned back to the table, from where he'd been examining the stunning modern works that hung on the dining-room walls. He sat down, peering at Anita over the bowl of red roses that lent drama to the striking paintings that edged the room. "Giving rise to all these wonderful young artists? It as if you are giving birth to a new generation of talent."

Anita's beautiful face lit up in a genuine smile. "I do what I love. I find life is simpler that way," she said.

"Well, we are all the more grateful for your philosophy." Giuseppe leaned forward and picked up his half-full glass of champagne. "A toast, to Anita Goldstein, may she continue her wonderful work!"

The guests echoed Giuseppe's sentiments, and Charlotte raised her glass, catching Anita's eye, a tiny pang of doubt piercing the joy she felt. Today's front pages were emblazoned with photographs of Nazi storm troopers parading along Germany's ancient, cobbled streets, singing out National Socialism's challenge to the nations beyond the frontiers of the Third Reich. All throughout Germany, political speeches proclaimed a need for more land. Hitler was insisting that today Germany belonged to him, but tomorrow, he'd own the world.

Sandro Luciana turned to Charlotte, drawing her away from her troubled thoughts. "I cannot thank you enough, Mademoiselle Belmont. You have worked tirelessly for me. I will be forever grateful."

Charlotte smiled at the young man. "Now, you promise me, you won't be lured away by that rogue Gerard DuPre. He won't look after you half as well as Anita."

Sandro's dancing eyes met hers. "Oh, but I have promised this to Anita." He tilted his head to one side. "You know, Anita runs her business like a man, and cares for her artists like a mother. I believe this is a winning combination, no?"

Charlotte sighed. "I hope that one day, there will be many more women like Anita running art galleries in Montmartre." Her hope was that she'd be one of them.

Sandro raised his glass.

Out of the corner of her eye, Charlotte saw Sandro's father looking over at them, a little anxiety crossing his features. Charlotte frowned. He'd spoken to her earlier of his worries that Mussolini was following so closely with Hitler. *Il Duce* had signed a military alliance with Hitler and Giuseppe had said he was worried for Sandro should he come home and be forced to make an allegiance to an ideology he would detest. Sandro was an artist, his concerned father had explained, not a soldier.

Charlotte sent a sympathetic smile toward the older gentleman, and he nodded at her and took a sip of his champagne. But as she sat amongst the happy, cheerful guests around Anita's welcoming table, she worried what all their fates would be when the Nazis struck, because everyone was now saying it was no longer a matter of if, but when.

The following evening, Charlotte stood with Anita outside the Basilica Sacré-Cœur. They'd taken a summer stroll through the winding streets of Montmartre. Later, they'd return to Rue Laffitte to enjoy the spinach quiche and salad of grated carrot with Dijon vinaigrette that Anita had prepared for their evening meal.

Charlotte looked out at the landscape, all of Paris sprawling below. If she closed her eyes, she could imagine how this hill and its surrounding countryside were once dotted with windmills, and she felt the familiar tug at her heartstrings at the sight of the Eiffel Tower pointing up toward the heavens, while behind the monument, the sky was washed in a luminescent golden glow and the sun sank, a stunning tangerine orb beneath the horizon. Beside her, Anita was quiet, her brown eyes narrowed in contemplation.

Anita balled her hands tight. "Look at this. Paris. The city of light and dreams for so many." She turned to face Charlotte, her dark eyes narrowing. "I'd rather throw myself into the Seine than lose everything I love. As for living under the Nazis' rule?" She shook her head. "I'd rather stab myself with a dagger and end it all."

Charlotte froze and a deep coldness pierced her chest. "You must not talk that way."

Anita punched out her words. "Living under a government whose very legal framework allows for the persecution of Jews would be impossible. No, I'd be better off at the bottom of my beloved Seine."

Charlotte whispered her words. "I shall never let you be hurt, as long as I draw breath." She swallowed hard, her throat sticking. She'd been too young to do anything to save her mother, but she'd rather die on the tip of a sword than sit by and do nothing to protect the woman who had been there for her entire life. "I shall protect you and everything you've worked for with every fiber of my heart. When it is all over, we will dance, and we will celebrate in the streets with all of Paris, just as people did after the Great War. And then, you and I will come up here, and together, we will watch the sun set over Paris from Sacré-Cœur."

Anita turned, slowly, to face Charlotte, and she sent a quick, frightened glance up to the white basilica above their heads.

5

SS CHAMPLAIN, SPRING 1938

Martha

Martha moved to the farthest corner on SS *Champlain's* upper deck, well away from the passengers who were playing badminton in the fresh sea air. The click of rackets tapping shuttlecocks and the chink of glassware filtered around the deck, while the sounds of conversation were lost in the warm spring breeze. Martha sank down into the lone deckchair that appeared to have been placed exactly for her, the soft navy-blue trouser suit that Vianne had designed melting around her body. It was effortlessly comfortable, as if she were wearing a pair of elegant pajamas. What bliss.

She raised her face to the sun for a moment. Virginia Woolf's *The Years* sat enticingly in her lap, and the great ocean liner cruised through the aquamarine water as if she were cutting through a piece of shimmering silk. Above Martha's head, the sky soared in a lustrous arc of blue.

Martha gazed out at the sea until her eyes locked on the distant horizon. What was beyond it? What was over there? The books she adored were set in Europe and the British Isles, where the turrets of magical castles peeked through soft rings of clouds atop distant blue hills, rising as if out of fairy tales, where green parks dotted with gracious old trees spread for miles and women in white dresses sat with parasols sipping tea, and where villages built of honey-colored stone held local markets filled to the brim with bright, delicious produce and artisan makers sold their wares.

All of this, the old world, was a world that she and Charlotte had glimpsed when their mother was alive, only to be thrust onto a ship just like this one after Chloé had died, and taken to New York with Papa. The New York Library was the only place where Martha could bury herself and try to catch glimpses of the places she might have seen more of in Europe, had her mother not died so young.

On board the ship, Martha had adopted her usual routine: do what was necessary in the real world, and spend the rest of her time escaping from it. If she ate early, she could return to her cabin to read before the other passengers had slipped on their dancing shoes and strolled through the moonlight to one of the dining rooms. The ship's crew had already realized that she was alone, ushering her to the quietest table or the farthest seat in the library, to the most secluded booth in the salon.

Martha sighed. Of course, she really had no interest in the cabaret shows that were paraded out night after night in the grand salons aboard the ship, and the idea of standing about in the ballroom waiting for someone to ask her to dance caused her stomach to churn. Life aboard ships could be heinously over-planned—deck games, mad antics in the swimming pool, sack races, exercise classes, lectures on everything under the sun and daily guided walks around the ship.

Last night, she'd taken a quiet stroll up here on the deck while the dining rooms were at their busiest. She'd leaned on the railings of the ship, staring out at the moonlit water, stars spangling the night sky, laced with milky clouds.

"Miss Belmont."

Martha stilled. The voice was coming from behind her. Instinctively, she sank down deeper into her chair, closing her eyes, her fingers pressing into the hard cover of her book. She should have stayed in her cabin if she'd not wished to be disturbed. But her visitor strolled around her deckchair and hovered, insistently.

"Hello there."

Martha opened one eye. She brought her hand up to shield her gaze from the sun, which had suddenly turned brilliant and golden, glimmering around the figure looking down at her, rendering him almost in shadow.

She sank even further into her seat. "Mr. Fraser," she said.

"You look like you've found a good wee spot." Clyde Fraser extended the last word, his Scottish accent coming to the fore. One of his dark blond eyebrows rose toward the sky, and he leaned on his badminton racket, crossing his ankles. "I saw you walk past. I waved, you know."

Martha nodded, trying not to savor the smooth scent of Pour Un Homme de Caron that lingered around Vianne's impeccably dressed Scottish friend.

Clyde Fraser ran a hand through his blond hair, his green eyes crinkling above the dark V of the white tennis sweater that he wore over a white open-neck polo shirt and a pair of crisp white trousers. "You're avoiding the organized sport, Miss Belmont," he said.

"As you see," Martha said. "Call me Martha." Her brow wrinkled.

"Martha. It's a lovely name you have."

Martha folded her hands in her lap. If only Charlotte was here to flash her dark eyes, link her arm through Clyde's and march him off to the badminton court, where she'd proceed to annihilate him at the game, and then, she'd smile at him and tell him she had so much to do today, so many things to take care of... he'd disappear from Martha's radar.

By contrast, men would talk to Martha for a few moments, perhaps attracted by her chestnut curls and her eyes with their golden flecks. But then, they would find her odd, too dull, and unenticing, and they'd soon make their excuses and melt away. She knew the pattern. There was really no point in drawing this conversation out.

"You will want to return to the games," she said. "Don't let me spoil your enjoyment of them." She edged her copy of *The Years* a little closer to her nose.

But Clyde Fraser squatted down in front of her.

Martha's pulse quickened.

"Virginia Woolf? How interesting."

"Yes. Well, then." Martha flipped the hard cover of the book open, her heart drumming away.

There was an awkward silence. "Have dinner with me tonight. You can tell me all about it."

Martha forced herself to read the words in front of her on the page, but for once, that was all they were. *Words.* Words floating and blurring in front of her eyes.

Have dinner with him? Was he mad?

Martha sagged down in her chair. Vianne's instructions to him whirred in her mind. *Poor, dear. Traveling for such a sad reason. You simply must look after Martha. Make sure she does not spend the entire trip to Paris on her own.*

Martha chose her words carefully. "It's very kind of you, but I've got an enormous amount of work to do." She chewed on her lip.

He tilted his head to one side. "I forgot about your wee mission. Is it top secret? You're not going to assassinate someone?"

Martha glared at the book, but she pressed her lips together to hold in the chuckle that rose in her throat. "Not today, I'm reading."

Clyde reached out, and gently pulled the top of *The Years* down so that it was not entirely obscuring Martha's face. She could see the faint traceries of lines fanning out from his eyes, the way his cheeks were tanned from the spring sun. His hands lingered on the book.

"I'd rather swim the Atlantic than spend the rest of the week playing organized sport, you know." He spoke softly, whispering, almost, but his eyes burned with intensity.

She tore her gaze away.

"I'm only dressed for the part." He tugged at his jumper and sent her a sheepish grin. "But I really don't fit in."

Martha glanced across the deck at the groups of young women her age leaping around the badminton court. The fashionable girls were famously embracing Mary Bagot Stack's Women's League of Health and Beauty, with its motto, "Movement is Life."

"Well," Martha said, knowing she sounded a little wry, "the ship is full of people who will try to convince you to. Fit in, you know."

Clyde folded his arms. "I'm intrigued by the way you are managing to keep well out of it. I want you to promise to tell me how it's done."

Martha leaned forward, folding her forearms around her knees. She gazed at him, her eyes meeting his, direct. She smiled and shook her head. "If I did that, I'd be letting us both down."

He grinned, spinning his racket in his hand. "You, by giving up your solitary state, and me, by proving it is more easily broken than I thought."

Martha jumped at the sound of a girl shouting that she'd won a point. She glanced at her watch, and turned her gaze out to sea.

Clyde went on, in his impossibly soft, lilting Scottish brogue. "Vianne tells me you work in the New York Public Library. Do you know, it's my favorite place in New York?"

She shook her head. "I see." She tried to focus on the rolling waves, the way they swept in and out, taking deep breaths to calm her nerves. How long would it take him before he'd had enough? Three more questions? Four?

"I have a great affection for the old maps they keep," he continued.

Martha sighed. She loved the old maps too, filled with places afar that she hardly dreamed of visiting. She'd whiled away many of her own lunchtime breaks poring over maps of the Far East, the kingdom of Siam, the sacred Ganges, the fragrant island of Java, and Ceylon.

"I love nothing more than to sit at one of the long tables in the quiet, hushed reading room and look at maps. I like to dream up places to visit one day. The Far East fascinates me. What do you think?"

Martha turned back to him, and he smiled at her, his eyes lighting up in genuine interest. She frowned.

"Forgive me," he said, "but I think you are a real traveler too. Content in your new surrounds, not needing to be constantly entertained and distracted or reminded of what you are missing from home."

"Perhaps," she murmured. She fingered the pages of her book. Surely he was going to give up soon.

"I have a theory that we are either born travelers, or we are not."

"Rather discriminatory of you."

"Some of us have a wonder for new things, new places and the stories that go with them."

Martha frowned. "Honestly, you don't have to—"

"And some of us do not," he went on. "Complaining about the foreignness of French cuisine, or asking if there are hamburgers on the menu." He lowered his voice, shooting a glance toward the badminton players. "I admit, I can tell who's who."

Despite herself, Martha felt a smile playing around her lips. Being insular, a closed book lost in the detours of her imagination, was so entwined with who she was, and yet, somewhere deep inside, a small voice screamed that he'd picked up how she really felt. Inquisitive. Wanting to learn new things, yearning, deep down, to *experience* life, not hide away in the shadows.

But, that voice inside herself also reminded her, this was a dangerous world. Look at what had happened to her mother when she threw herself into life, fell in love. No, it was far safer to hold back than let go and completely live. And that, Martha reminded herself, was what she was traveling to France to do, to bring Charlotte back to safety. To convince her to look after herself. She worried day and night that Charlotte did not realize that she couldn't play with fire and not get burnt.

Clyde leaned a hand on the armrest of her chair. "I'd love to chat with you more," he said. "Could I meet you for a drink?"

She held up a hand. "Really, there is no need, Clyde. As you point out so well, I'm not in need of entertaining. I'm very happy taking care of myself. But thank you for the offer," she added, a little wistfulness seeping into her tone.

"No one can say no to a quick drink, Martha." He rolled his r's deliciously.

Martha looked down at her lap.

"If you find me a bore, then you can leave after ten minutes," he went on, sounding jovial. "You don't even have to finish your French 75," he said, mentioning Martha's favorite cocktail. "Although, how anyone could ever go wrong with champagne is beyond me."

Martha toyed with her curls. She sighed and sent him a little shrug.

His face broke into a genuine grin. "Is it a deal then?" he

asked, his voice soft. "Can I meet you at seven thirty outside the *salon*?"

"But I'm not traveling first class."

"Well, I am," he said. "So why not give it a try?"

She opened and closed her mouth.

"I'll be there. I'm looking forward to it more than anything in a long time." He sent her a wide grin, and wandered away, waving goodbye with his badminton racket in the air.

Martha slumped down in her deckchair and opened her book, her eyes scanning the pages furiously for several moments, her breathing accelerating and her heart palpitating away in her chest. She turned the book up the right way again and took in a lovely, calming deep breath.

When the sun had gone down, Martha stood inside her cabin in her dressing gown, staring at her reflection in the mirror. The red-headed girl named Marian from South Carolina who was sharing her cabin lay on her bed enjoying a selection of Hershey's chocolate and reading *The American Magazine*.

Martha leaned against one of the pair of enamel washbasins that sat opposite the two single beds with their peach-colored counterpanes, the wooden side rails sitting firm on the beds, just in case the ship took a lurch.

"Fancy meeting a Scotsman for a drink in first class instead of me?" Martha said, eyeing the back of Marian's magazine.

Marian placed the glossy magazine down on her lap and laughed. "Darlin', you're not fooling no one with that red lippy and those shining eyes. Get out of here. Go and have a good time."

Martha frowned at her reflection in the small mirror. Her brows were fashionably pencil thin, and she'd applied a little of the latest light creamy eyeshadow to highlight the flecks in her eyes, along with mascara from its cake, with its tiny brush. Deep red Max Factor lipstick traced over her lips.

Marian leaned up on one elbow. "If the Lord's willing and the creek don't rise, I'll see you back here with more flush in your cheeks than you can poke a stick at."

Martha caught the other girl's eye in the mirror in disbelief.

"Sometimes," Marian said, "it takes a stranger to tell you the truth that's right under your nose. Put on one of your lovely dresses and go, sweetheart."

The Greek-style cream silk dress that Vianne had designed sat untouched in the open wardrobe, its carefully gathered shoulders, complete with intricate embroidery detail, waiting achingly to be worn.

"Hadn't you better get dressed already?" Marian said, leaning up on one elbow.

"Thought you said you were meeting this swell at half-past seven. Because you've only got minutes until then." She popped a chocolate in her mouth. "Too late to cancel now, sweetheart."

Martha folded her arms.

Marian went on in her languid tone. "The only person who has shown any interest in me was some guy in his eighties, who asked me to form the numbers for his game of bridge. See what I'm saying?"

Martha closed her eyes. "Goodness help me and tell me this is not the silliest thing I've ever done," she murmured.

She counted to three and reached for the stunning cream silk Greek dress.

Clyde Fraser was standing by the staircase leading to the first-class salon, wearing a London cut suit with wide shoulders, the double-breasted jacket and lapels faced with gleaming satin. His blond hair was smooth, and his stiff-fronted white dress shirt was pristine.

Martha clutched onto her silk evening purse and asked herself for the millionth time why she'd agreed to something that she knew would end in embarrassment. She only hoped that Anita's resting soul would forgive her for doing something so frivolous when she was mourning her loss.

"You look stunning," Clyde whispered. "Thank you for joining me." He paused, the expression on his face unfathomable. "I'm honored you did."

Martha shifted a little in her shoes.

"Shall we go up to the top deck?" he asked, tucking her free hand under his elbow.

Martha regathered the skirt of the dress, holding the tiny train along with her purse, and walked with him up the glamorous staircase to the first-class salon. If anyone had asked, she would have said she felt as if she were an extremely awkward heroine in a film.

Her brows drew close together at the sight of the beautifully dressed first-class passengers who were seated at deep mahogany tables and lounging about on plush velvet chairs. They were the very people who'd been playing badminton today, and here was Martha right in their midst. She followed Clyde tentatively into the room, struggling with those old feelings that told her she didn't belong.

A jazz band sat atop a podium and there was a ceiling made of opaque glass, softly lit around the edges with modern, subtle lights. There was a hush in the room, an ambience that was muted by the soft carpets underfoot. On the far wall, a vast tapestry soared from the floor to the ceiling, and the room was surrounded with French doors that were decorated with flowing curtains of golden silk.

A waiter appeared and led them to a table by the French doors. Martha slid into the soft chair he pulled out for her, gazing for a moment over the brilliantly lit upper deck, strung with a myriad of tiny glowing lights. Beyond this, the sea moved, mysterious and murky, as if holding secrets untold in the dark. She sighed, wishing for one moment, that she could be out there on the deck, staring at the ocean.

When the waiter had brought them each a cocktail, Martha's French 75, and Clyde's Sidecar, along with a selection of *caviar frais*, *toast Melba*, *olives vertes* and *olives noire*, Clyde lifted his glass in a toast.

"Here's to a wonderful journey, and a fruitful and successful *fait accompli* for your mission." He took a sip, his eyes twinkling.

Martha turned to look out the window. She covered her hand with her mouth.

"I'm sorry," Clyde said, leaning forward. He was quiet a moment. "Martha..."

She sighed, staring down at the soft folds of the beautiful dress in her lap. "I shouldn't be here," she murmured, shaking her head. "It was a mistake." *Too soon*, she wanted to add. Too soon to be out enjoying herself after Anita had gone. Martha had hardly had time to process the loss when she'd been catapulted into sailing to Paris.

Clyde leaned forward, folding his hands on the table. "I'm sorry. I've chosen the wrong venue." He attempted a grin. "There aren't so many options to choose from aboard the ship. I wish I could have taken you for a walk in Central Park, or perhaps to the beach for the day. But," he said, softening his voice, "at least you can look at the sea here. There is that."

She took a sip of the gorgeous champagne cocktail. This was awful. But it wasn't Clyde's fault, and his mention of the park and the beach was thoughtful. "No, I'm sorry. You see, recently we lost a—"

Clyde reached out, placing his hand on the white table-cloth. "Vianne told me. Your friend in Paris. I'm sorry."

The band struck up "Thanks for the Memory."

Martha nodded, and there was a silence. "I guess I'm not much fun to take out for a drink," she said.

"But there's no one else I'd rather be sitting with right now, you see."

Martha shifted in her seat. He couldn't mean it. He must only be being polite. "You are traveling home to your family in Edinburgh?"

He nodded. "I'm afraid they're all very normal. You have grown up surrounded by such interesting people. Vianne, a fashion designer, and your dear late friend, who owned an art gallery?"

"Normal can be wonderful."

Clyde sighed. Something passed across his features, and Martha waited, watching him, her interest piqued.

"I have two younger sisters, Kirsty and Bonnie, and my parents live in Edinburgh, in a big old terrace house, with a huge basement kitchen, where we spend most of our time."

She nodded.

His features softened as he spoke of his family. "There are Labradors, and living rooms with old, faded sofas and worn Turkish rugs that, despite their age, my parents refuse to replace. My mother always fills the house with fresh flowers, and she spends a lot of time in her garden, which is her passion, you see. I'm afraid it's not at all exotic or unusual."

Martha smiled into her glass. "It sounds perfect. It sounds just fine."

Clyde sipped his champagne, looking thoughtful. "Yes, but, you see, if there is a war, then I worry that I have everything to lose." He raised his face, his green eyes grazing against hers. "Being happy comes with a risk."

Martha chewed on her lip. Was it a risk she wasn't willing to take? Was that her problem? Fearing being happy?

His eyes were intent on her and she cast about to change the topic. "Vianne says you know her sister in Scotland."

Clyde nodded, offering Martha the plate of olives. "Vianne's sister, Anaïs, married a cousin on my mother's side, Archie MacCullum. Anaïs had a terrible time of it in the last war."

"She was very brave, according to Papa." Martha shook her head. Everything that came out of her mouth seemed to be loaded, and she had no idea why. Bravery? That belonged to Charlotte. Happiness? It was the thing she associated with her mother and the past. She took in a shaky breath. Was this why she avoided social situations like the plague because they seemed to throw up all her inadequacies at once and send her into overdrive?

Clyde switched tack. "Archie owns an estate in the Highlands, and every summer, we go up there as we have a house there too. The Highlands are very much a part of my heritage."

Martha glanced up. She'd read that the Highlands of Scotland were wild, beautiful, remote. There were no crowds, she could be quite alone with nature... "I've long wanted to go there," she said, meaning it, reddening.

"One day, you must come..." Clyde faltered. He adjusted his cufflinks and cleared his throat.

Martha looked down at her lap.

"What I mean is, I think you'd love the Highlands if you visit. I hope that one day, you get to see them, and if you ever want to look us up..."

He waited, and she cast about for conversation. "I understand you are a doctor?"

He leaned forward, cupping his hands together. "I've been studying to become a surgeon at the University of Virginia in Charlottesville, until I decided to return home... Let's not dwell on Herr Hitler tonight, but I've also done military training. As part of the family tradition, I'm a proud Gordon Highlander."

Martha's brow wrinkled. Vianne had mentioned his military connections. "Did you have to cut your studies short to go back to Scotland?"

"No," he said, softly. "I've finished. So, good timing on that front, if you can possibly use that term in these times."

She looked at the table. Every one of the *hors d'oeuvres* plates was empty.

"Martha?" Clyde said. "Are you... That is, I'd love you to stay on and join me for dinner if you'd like to."

Martha folded her hands in her lap. He couldn't be serious. She was all ready for him to make the same excuses to leave that every young man always made when they had the misfortune to find themselves alone with her.

And then, she couldn't help it. She laughed. "Not that woman over there?" she said, indicating with her head at a girl laughing animatedly at another table in a pink dress. "Or that girl?" she asked, her eyes tilting toward a young woman who was dressed in a stunning black Chanel evening gown entering on the arm of an elderly man. "Because I'd quite understand. I'm not one for social graces. You honestly don't have to put on a show for me."

He leaned forward, folding his hands on the table, his eyes dancing. "Sweetheart, I'm a Scotsman. Gruff, monosyllabic. The occasional outburst if I feel strongly about something. And I feel strongly that I'd like to have dinner with you."

Martha shook her head, grinning at the tablecloth. Darn it. She liked this man. "Well then, I'm happy to stick around in that case."

His face lit up in a smile. And he pushed his chair out, holding out his hand. She took it and was certain she felt the lightest squeeze.

Several days later, Martha stood amongst the crowded passengers on the deck of SS *Champlain* as she glided toward the docks in Plymouth. Clyde leaned against the ship's railings, his suitcases sitting neatly by his side. Masses of people lined the docks to greet the great liner in overcoats and hats, some waving them in the air, others gaping at the mighty ship that had crossed the Atlantic Ocean to bring their loved ones home again. Overhead, the sky was gray and misty and drops of soft rain drizzled down onto the shores of the British Isles.

Martha felt a pang of sadness as the great liner edged closer to the docks. The last few days on board with Clyde had been easy and companionable, and yet, there was a tension brewing inside her, causing her to toss and turn at night, to steal covert glances at him, sending her imagination into what the future might hold for them, ridiculously, and most of all, setting her to wonder if he felt the same impossible pull toward her.

She and Clyde, as if by unspoken agreement, had gotten themselves into a routine these last few days. Martha had come to love the delicious anticipation she felt each morning, knowing Clyde would be waiting for her at the bottom of the polished staircase, where he'd escort her up to the first-class breakfast dining room, insisting she choose from the sumptuous menu, complete with fresh fruits, strawberry, apricot and Reines-Claudes jams, fresh juices, eggs scrambled with asparagus tips, broiled hams, bacon, buttered toasts, brioche and croissants.

After they'd lingered too long talking over coffee, they'd freshen up in their rooms, before going to the very spot on the deck where they'd first met. They'd read, Clyde showing a deal of interest in the small suitcase full of books that Martha had brought on board the ship. After a day or two, a pair of chairs sat at the far end of the deck, and the crew had tactfully left the companionable arrangement in place for them.

They'd read and chat all morning, before donning their swimming costumes and exercising in the pool, or taking a long walk around the decks, never running out of conversation about

Edinburgh, Charlottesville, New York, the library and Clyde's dream to work in one of the leading surgical hospitals in his home city of Edinburgh. He'd opened up to Martha, sharing his hope that new anesthetics would make surgery less painful, and safer as well. He'd been inspired by the surgeons in America who were treating patients who could not afford surgery for free, with nearly forty percent of some states' populations on government relief because of the crippling Depression.

And then, in the evenings, they'd meet for dinner. Once, they'd danced in the ballroom, and yet, Martha had not worn her diaphanous dress. Somehow, she felt that if she put it on, it would signify something, her growing feelings, perhaps, which she was fearful of showing, and because she'd been wearing it the first time they'd met and wearing it may spark off something that she couldn't bear to end. Because she knew that if something did start, a romance, then Scotland was a long way from New York.

No matter how much she enjoyed Clyde's company, and no matter how devastatingly handsome and intelligent he was, she could not contemplate leaving Papa for a beau across the Atlantic Ocean.

Here, on board the ship, she'd felt safe enough to let go, but the cruise ship was not the real world, it was a bubble in which she'd been able to pretend that the things beyond its confines and the feelings of inadequacy that haunted her didn't matter anymore.

What was more, Clyde had not once mentioned keeping in touch after they parted ways in Plymouth before Martha sailed on alone to Le Havre, catching the train to her destination, Anita's beloved gallery in Rue Laffitte.

Martha stared out at the folks lining the docks, her own hands pressing deep into the wooden railings of the ship. They drew in closer to shore, finally berthing, the engines that had guided them safely from America winding down and the sounds of people cheering from the shore filtering up through the hazy gray air. The passengers on board the ship joined in, sending up a heartening roar, and Martha turned to look up at Clyde, her eyes searching his face, her heart thumping a tune she'd never felt before. She did not want this to be the last time they said goodbye. She couldn't bear never to see him again.

He looked down at her, his expression unfathomable underneath his stylish Homburg hat. And then, as the ship's horn rang out one deep, last note as a final parting to those who were leaving her, Clyde's eyes ran across her face. His brow furrowed, and he leaned a little closer to her. Her breath quickened, and in that one, still, silent moment, even as the passengers started moving in a great swell around them, she stared up at him and he shook his head.

"Martha?" he asked, murmuring her name in a way he had not done before, and she felt the shift in him, the tension, the conflict that, perhaps, he was feeling in the same way as her. Or had it just been a diversion for him? Did he view her as a friend for this journey, whom he'd never lay eyes on again? "I'll cherish this past week." His eyes began their frantic search of her face again, moving fast as if to take in any final details.

"I will too," she whispered, and despite the pushing and moving that was going on around them, they stayed put, stuck, neither of them seeming willing to move forward, as if in their own private space, while the SS *Champlain* too sat in wait, perfectly still. Despite the talking, and the chatting around them, the clarion call of gulls screeching to each other high in the sea air, and the soft lap of water against hard docks, Martha only wanted to drink in the last sight of Clyde.

He shot a glance beyond her, where, she knew, the crew must have set up the gangplank and the passengers would be lining up to disembark. She'd made this journey enough times to know the pattern, to know how it all would end.

"Martha, can I write to you?" Clyde said suddenly.

Martha almost slumped with relief. Her laughter was shaky and was lost in the misty air. "You must promise," she whispered, and she stumbled back a step, almost falling into another man's back.

Clyde reached out to steady her, his arm circling her waist so that she was even closer than before. "It's been wonderful," he murmured. "I want to see you again."

She nodded, and her hand in its white glove came up to rest on his cheek. Without hardly realizing it, her knees were wobbling, and he took her hand, and turned it over, carefully slipping off her glove and placing a kiss on her upturned palm.

And all the tension in her shoulders, the not knowing, the wondering, the nights spent lying awake, melted away, for one lovely moment.

Until the ship's horn rang out again, and Clyde tipped his hat and smiled at her, that green-eyed Scottish smile that she knew she'd never forget. Without saying goodbye, he turned and was lost amongst the crowds leaving for the shore.

6

Chloé

Paris was sparkling. Germaine Bongard's apartment was filled with gorgeous guests and the scent of wonderful perfumes floated in the air, Floris' Special No. 127, Caron's Narcisse Noir, and the famous Parisian fashion designer Paul Poiret's Nuit de Chine. Chloé took a covert look around Paul Poiret's sister's salon, her gaze falling upon Germaine Bongard's wonderful exotica no matter where her eyes landed. From the gilded mirror above the white marble fireplace to the oriental lampshades and golden statues from the Far East were reflected the one hundred guests, here to celebrate Paris's first proper winter season now the war was finally over.

It was Christmas Eve, and everything was magical. The apartment was a showcase for Poiret's designs. It was all too delicious, from the jewel-colored turbans to the harem trousers Poiret had made sensational in society before the war. Women wandered around in his famous lampshade dresses, their wide tunics held out with wire as if in challenge to the unthinkable desolation of the last four years.

Such a display seemed almost unimaginable after four long years of war. Chloé fought hard to reconcile this splendor with the memories that still burned of nursing in rudimentary first-aid stations behind the front lines for three years, until these were developed into proper field hospitals and she'd assisted teams of American surgeons under tragic circumstances.

Chloé swallowed as she thought of those wounded young men who were no different from the gentlemen in evening dress who graced this room. It seemed like yesterday that she was confronted with the sight of boys all laid out on stretchers, things moving too quickly to process, as she informed patient after patient wheeled in from the ambulances outside that even minor wounds could result in amputated limbs.

Chloé closed her eyes in relief when Laurence moved toward her, wrapping his arms around her waist. Thank goodness, her new husband had not been one of those patients to whom she'd had to impart distressing news. She'd cared for him as he recovered from a nasty shrapnel wound to the leg, and to this day, he swore that it was her cheerful ministrations and the laughter they'd shared in desperate times that had restored him to full health.

Chloé leaned into him as he dropped a secret kiss on her neck. "You know you look sensational," he said, in that American accent that had captured her from the start. "Just wait until I take you to New York."

Chloé screwed up her nose. The thought of the golden, quiet vineyards that surrounded her parent's old *mas*, their farmhouse in the South of France, had sent her into spirals of homesickness during the war. She was feeling somewhat lost in Paris while Laurence was working here, translating books into English and getting in with the burgeoning literary crowd, writing away in cafés on the Left Bank, his shirtsleeves rolled up, his glasses perched on his nose, and his braces showing off his handsome figure. How would she possibly manage if they were to relocate to New York?

Here in Paris, Chloé was more than aware that she had everything a woman could want, but she was struggling with a type of discontent that she could not put her finger on, and it was unsettling her.

She shook her head at Laurence. "Oh, you are ridiculous, *mon amour*," she said. "What would I do in in New York?"

Laurence's eyes twinkled. "Why, you'd do exactly what you do in Paris. Charm everyone you meet."

Chloé swiped him playfully. It was said that Parisian men were charming, but her American husband, Laurence Belmont, was something else. He was full of contradictions, one minute laughing with her, the next becoming so moved by something that tears would fill his golden-flecked eyes. No, Laurence was a person who lived by extremes, somewhat like Chloé's nursing companion, Anita. Their other friend, Sandrine, was of a far more even temperament, bless her.

Chloé had gotten him through the dark days of his injury by reading to him from the few books they had in the field hospital —he'd loved the *Hundred Best Poems*, and she'd been touched by his genuine displays of emotion when she read aloud to him.

When he'd translated some of his favorite poems into Italian, Spanish, and French from their original English, and he'd written them out for her, decorating the verses with exquisite little drawings, Chloé had been enchanted. Soon, he'd taken to leaving her little notes on his bedside chest in different languages, which she'd had to beg him to translate for her, laughing the entire time. She'd adored reading to her patients during the war, and she'd found solace in the small book collection in the hospital, losing herself in a different time, a different place even for five minutes. And books had brought her closer to Laurence.

But now, she found herself wandering aimlessly around

Montmartre when Laurence was out working for the day, because she'd lost that sense of having a vital role in the world, and there seemed little hope of her finding the fulfillment that she craved. Women were not being employed after the war. They were being turned away in droves after manning the factories, driving the trolley cars, ticketing the Metro, doing all the vast array of things that men used to do before the war came along and changed everything.

And was being married to someone who was going out into the world, who was engaging it, enough?

Chloé forced herself to abandon her own troubling thoughts, instead turning to her husband, his chestnut hair combed neatly and his eyes intent on her, his tall figure prominent even in this room with its parade of beautifully dressed guests.

He nudged her and indicated that she look across the crowded room.

"Oh, *vraiment*? Truly?" Chloé murmured, squeezing his arm as his eyes twinkled with amusement.

The room was filled with the young diplomats who were arriving in Paris each day, filling the city to the brim prior to the peace conference. Tonight, they were all dressed in boiled, stiff dress shirts, hair neatly combed, their conversation all about the possible terms of the conference that was scheduled for January 18 in the New Year.

But Chloé's gaze fixed on the spot Laurence had pointed out for her. Typically, Anita had found the only man who did not fit into the room of diplomats. Even from across the room, Chloé could see how Anita's head was thrown back in appreciation, how her dark eyes sparkled, and how she clapped her hands with delight. Chloé brought her hand up to cover her mouth at Anita's companion's appearance, his hair cut in the shape of an upturned bowl, his tiny round spectacles, and his shirt all patterned with diamonds and flowers.

"Tsugurharu Foujita, you know. Typical of Anita to find him, and I have to say, it's very intelligent of her." Anita's mother, Élise Goldstein, appeared next to Chloé and laid a hand on her shoulder.

Chloé turned to take in Anita's beautiful mother. If she were honest, she was in awe of the chatelaine of the fabled Chateau d'Anez, the woman who had procured invitations to tonight's select party.

Élise Goldstein stood, dressed in a stunning purple kimono jacket decorated with flowers and with a fashionably narrow hem, the dark velvet band at the neck highlighting her exquisite almond-shaped eyes. "Foufou, to those who know him well. You should go and say hello, Chloé, dear. My daughter will delight in showing him off to you."

"I have not seen him before." Chloé had heard of him. Of course, she had. Anita was working hard to open her own art gallery, and she talked non-stop about her passion for supporting the lost youth of Paris, the painters who could not afford the rent on studios and who were converging on the city with a dream in their hearts and, most of all, a desire to put all that the war stood for behind them, to capture the new, modern world on canvas, and perhaps more than that, to be a part of the growing community of creative young things in Paris. Many of them were sharing beds in flea-infested studios on the Left Bank, drawn by the hope that they may be one of the chosen ones who could make a living out of doing what they loved.

Anita's companion, Foujita, was the success story many of the young artists whom Anita dreamed of helping aspired to. Anita joked that she'd be the luckiest girl in the world if she were to discover an artist as talented as Foufou, who had famously become the envy of everyone, because he could afford a bathtub with hot running water in his studio at 5 Rue Delambre.

Chloé sighed. She envied Anita her focus. If only she, too, could find something to become excited about.

"A most interesting young man. He is friends with all the greats—Picasso, Modigliani, Matisse." Élise tapped Chloé on the shoulder. "He flies from model to model, from muse to muse. Legend has it, he woos them to his studio to sit for him with the promise of a hot bath! Anita does well to talk with him if she really wishes to open her own gallery." Élise's fine brow crinkled. "I despair of my daughter getting married and settling down. Independence is a wonderful concept, but loneliness is a reality my daughter professes to ignore."

"Anita will never be lonely," Chloé said, turning to Élise. "When she opens her own gallery, she shall be surrounded by kindred spirits. Don't you see?"

Élise shook her head. "I don't know why she resists the idea of falling in love so insistently. Ah well," she laughed. "This is no subject for a party, especially not this one. Go, meet Foufou, and see what you make of him."

Chloé kissed Élise Goldstein on her cheek, grabbed Laurence's hand and pulled him across the room.

And then it happened. Just as she came to a stop at the edge of the large group that was slowly gathering around the eccentric Foufou, who was passing a tiny, fluffy white kitten around the delighted guests, another man appeared, and Chloé came to a standstill, because she saw Anita pale.

Her usually unimpressible friend, who would shrug when a young man was captivated by her sparkling eyes, her deep, sultry voice, the way she moved, and how she wore her clothes with a true Parisian sense of *je ne sais quoi*, looked as if she might swoon.

"Why, Sumner! What a treat!" Foufou said, forcing Chloé to pull her gaze away from her mesmerized friend.

Instead, she turned to see the subject of Anita's gaze, and came face to face with one of the most strikingly handsome men she had ever laid eyes on. Chloé struggled to take her own eyes off him, and she sensed that Anita was simply struck dumb. The newcomer, who was slapping Foufou on the back as if he were a very old friend, was immaculately dressed in a white dinner suit, which he wore with all the aplomb of a handsome young swell out rowing a girl in a boat down a river lined with willow trees. And he spoke with the very same languid American accent as Laurence when he shook Foufou's hand.

"Sumner Green," Laurence murmured in her ear. "It seems that what everyone says is true. All of America is coming to Paris."

Chloé turned to her husband; the question that was burning on her lips lost as Foufou let out a delighted squeal.

"Anita Goldstein," Foufou said, placing an almost proprietary arm around the staring Anita, "you simply must meet Sumner Green. And Sumner, this charming young thing is Anita. I suspect you'll both be illuminating Paris like sunrise bringing in a new dawn, and I can't wait to watch."

"Hello again, Sumner," Anita said, her voice lower and huskier than Chloé had ever heard it before.

There was a silence. Foufou's bowl-shaped head swung from Anita to Sumner and back.

And then something flickered in Sumner Green's eyes.

That evening, Chloé sat with a thump on the sofa at Anita's apartment, while outside, in the streets of Montmartre, a new kind of music filtered through the air. Even inside, the syncopated strains of the audacious new sound with its insistent, strange, and strong rhythms permeated through the closed windowpanes.

Chloé watched her friend, who was standing by the fireplace, an unreadable expression in her eyes.

"You were awfully rough on poor Laurence," Anita said.

"Sending him off with Foufou to go drinking. Foufou will corrupt him, you know. I think dear Laurence was quite stunned and I'm not sure he really wanted to go, but he'll do anything for you, darling. You know he'll come home full of absinthe and ridiculous stories—that's if he makes it home at all. He'll probably end up sleeping on one of Foufou's sofas in that famous studio of his, surrounded by models who'll try to fall in love with him."

But Chloé didn't want to talk about herself, nor Laurence, nor Foufou, for that matter. Like a pair of boxers eyeing each other in a ring, Anita and Sumner Green had circled each other throughout the rest of the party, neither of them approaching the other.

"Who is he?" Chloé kicked off her T-bar shoes and lay back on the chaise longue, staring out the tall French doors at the velvety sky, sparkling with a smattering of glittering stars. "I simply must know."

Anita had kept up a steady stream of nonsensical chatter when they'd ridden the Metro home from the party, filled with passengers delighted to be out on the first normal Christmas Eve they'd had in years, avoiding the question that burned on Chloé's lips. All through the war, Anita had remained impervious to the many wounded soldiers who begged her to write to them when they returned to the front, and while both Chloé and Sandrine had come home to Paris engaged, Anita had refused, steadfastly, to entertain the idea of falling in love, of marrying or having children one day.

Anita went to stand by the French doors that led out to the tiny Juliette balcony with its elegant balustrade. "I met Sumner at Chateau d'Anez in the summer of '13."

Chloé's eyes sparkled. "A history. I thought so."

Anita swung around, moving across her moonlit salon to one of her mother's tiny antique tables, spiraled with gold leaf. She picked up a cigarette, placed it in her long holder, and lit it, the embers sending a tiny glow into the otherwise dim room.

Chloé waited.

"Sumner was one of Maman and Papa's artistic summer guests." Anita's expression clouded, and she blew a smoke ring into the room. "They collect them, you see."

"So, you got to know him well," Chloé murmured.

"Oh, Maman and Papa were enchanted by him, because he showed a prodigious talent when they met him at some soirée in Paris. Added to that, Maman took him under her wing because he was having trouble with his parents back in America."

Anita paused.

"They were insisting he study commercial art as a compromise for his wanting to paint full time. He hated illustrating for the *New Yorker* and wanted to create his own works. Maman invited him to Chateau d'Anez for the summer, so that he could paint uninterrupted. She offered him a room, food, good company. What young aspiring artist could resist?" Anita shrugged, and waved her cigarette holder in the air, but she folded her other arm tightly around her waist.

Chloé rolled over onto her stomach, leaning on her elbows, resting her chin in her cupped palms. *And what young woman could resist such a handsome house guest in turn?*

Anita moved back across the room. "Maman and Papa were entertaining many other established, important guests of the artistic world in the chateau that summer; Paul Poiret was staying, along with his sister. I think they all knew the war was about to erupt, and so it was special, there was a heightened intensity, as if they were trying to hang onto the way of life they all knew was going to go."

Chloé nodded. Her own parents had sat at their simple farmhouse table when the war was announced, their hands folded on their laps, her father's gray brow creasing, her mother pale with worry for France.

"I was starting to tire of the endless rounds of established artists and designers that Maman and Papa would bring home." Anita chuckled, deep and low. "They all seemed the same, Chloé. Settled. Knew what they were doing. Commercially successful. Sumner was different. Through him, I saw the struggle that so many young artists endure. These are the artists whom my parents don't necessarily support."

Chloé sighed. She was entranced with the idea of Chateau d'Anez and could only imagine what it must have been like, growing up there with an endless round of house parties, filled with exotic artistic guests and fun during the Belle Époque. Indulgence had been everything during those golden years, and Anita's exotic parents were a product of that generation.

Chloé rolled onto her back, staring at the ceiling. How fortunate Anita's parents had been.

"Sumner would hardly remember the girl who used to sit with him by the lake while he painted under the linden trees, handing him his brushes like a fool." Anita shook her head, her dark hair catching in the soft lamplight.

"But I'm certain he did," Chloé whispered. "Remember you." She'd seen it. The faint flicker in his eyes, the hint of recognition, before he'd been swept away by Paul Poiret.

Anita gathered her shawl around her shoulders. "I was eighteen. He was twenty-three. I'm afraid I was terribly naïve." A faint shimmer of something drifted into her voice, as if it were going to crack.

Now, Anita was trying to reconnect with those days by supporting other young artists, just like Sumner had been. How intriguing. Chloé sighed.

"Sumner inspired me to open my own gallery," Anita said, suddenly.

"Of course, he did," Chloé murmured. She heard Anita pacing around the room.

"No. You see, he gave me the confidence to finally broach

the topic with Maman and Papa. He sat with me while I told them of my dreams, and I think it was only because he was there that they entertained the idea with any seriousness." Anita sighed.

"I understand that all too well." If Chloé were to approach her parents and tell them she was feeling bored, a married woman with little to do, they'd look at her blankly. She pulled a pillow onto her stomach and frowned. If Anita had a man sitting with her, lending support, it would probably help her situation. She felt for her friend.

"Back in Paris," Anita said, "Sumner introduced me to Berthe Weill, one of the first women gallerists in Montmartre. And that was when I thought it might be possible. That was when I thought my dreams were not just a whimsy."

Anita had said how much she admired the formidable Berthe Weill, the Jewish art gallery owner in Montmartre who was famous for spotting and representing some of the finest new artists in France. Recently, Berthe had been helping Anita with her plans to open her gallery right below this apartment.

Chloé drew in a breath. "And what happened after his visit to France?" She winced at the inevitability of her own question. *The war.*

"Maman mentioned that he sold six of his watercolors to the Brooklyn Museum after he returned from naval service." Anita lowered her eyes, her dark eyelashes forming a soft curve over her wide cheekbones. "I think he's on the cusp of making it."

"And now, he's back, and the old flame is still alive within you," Chloé whispered.

Slowly, Anita raised her eyes. "You know I don't want to get involved with a man. I want to have a career, Chloé."

"So, what are you going to do?" Chloé stared at her friend. "Have a husband and a career?"

Anita stood stock-still. "You make it sound so simple."

Chloé stood up, and in the light of the moon over Paris, she placed one arm across her friend's shoulders. "That's because it is."

Anita let out a short laugh. She leaned her head on Chloé's shoulder. "Oh, Chloé, I do adore you so."

Chloé straightened her shoulders. "And I you."

Paris felt different after Anita left to ring in 1919 with her family at Chateau d'Anez. While the streets of the Right Bank were crowded with diplomats who were cramming the hotels to capacity, sleeping on bathroom floors and on sofas, according to the newspapers, Chloé found herself alone, staring out the windows of the small apartment she shared with Laurence while he was working, as snowflakes fluttered down over Paris, and the sky remained steel gray.

Rugged up in her warmest woolen coat, gloves and a felt hat several days into the new year, she made her way out of the Vavin Metro stop and walked through the Quartier de Montparnasse, with its tiny, cobbled streets filled with old bookshops and warm brasseries. As Chloé strolled along the Boulevard de Montparnasse, she allowed herself a small smile at the sounds of a couple chatting, their American accents vibrant in the cold winter's air. The rents in Montparnasse were cheaper than in Montmartre, and that was why there was a shift from the old center of the Belle Époque to the Left Bank.

Chloé came to a standstill outside the café where Laurence had asked her to meet him for lunch. Under the large sign that read *Le Dome*, the sidewalk teemed with tiny wooden tables set with oval-backed wicker chairs. Chloé had to crane her neck to try to find Laurence in the crowded café.

He'd been working here regularly, finding the busy atmosphere of the Left Bank cafés a wonderful foil to the solitary nature of his translating work. Laurence was coming home each evening delighted with the growing crowds of expatriates who frequented the cafés, and adored rubbing shoulders with the writers and publishers for whom he worked.

Chloé paused a moment as she spotted her husband. Next to Laurence was a woman with her hair pulled back into a tight bun. She was holding a cigarette in one hand, and in front of her, sat a cup of coffee, but what was most striking was her unusual mode of dress. Laurence's companion was wearing a deep green velvet buttoned-up vest over a white shirt with a large black bow at her neck, and Chloé could also discern that this was tucked into a long, old-fashioned gray flared skirt.

When Laurence caught Chloé's eye, he raised a hand to wave her over, standing up and rushing off to get her a chair from one of the crowded tables.

Chloé threaded her way through the diners and stood, rather awkward, staring at the woman, who gazed right back up at her in turn, as if appraising her. Chloé reddened. Perhaps this was one of Laurence's esteemed authors. She was becoming used to feeling out of place amongst the literary people with whom Laurence worked, and the feeling that she had nothing to recommend herself other than her status as Laurence's wife right now was not appealing. She was neither university-educated, intellectual, nor artistic, but, fighting to push aside that unsettling thought, Chloé slipped down into the chair that Laurence had procured for her.

"Chloé, darling." Laurence leaned down and placed a kiss on Chloé's cheek, squeezing her hand. "I'd like you to meet Adrienne Monnier. Adrienne, this is my wife, Chloé."

"*Enchantée*," the woman said, her voice deep and resonating.

"Good afternoon. Charming to meet you," Chloé said in English, for Laurence's sake, only to flush at the amused expression on Adrienne Monnier's face, because Laurence was a translator and spoke more languages most likely than either she or Madame Monnier put together.

Chloé fussed about pouring herself a glass of water from the glass bottle on the table, suddenly wanting her hands to be doing something, not sitting here still, like a gaping fish. Oh, it seemed impossible to get things right. Why did she always feel so awkward? So out of place? She'd felt more a part of things during the war because she'd had something to do.

When Laurence was waved over to a table by a man Chloé recognized as one of the authors he translated, Chloé placed her glass down on the tablecloth. Now she would have to have a conversation about which she knew precisely nothing.

"Your husband has been telling me about your passion for books," Adrienne Monnier said.

Chloé heaved out a breath. "I am simply a reader, not a writer, or an artist," she said. It seemed wise to get this over with, rather than draw things out.

Adrienne narrowed her intelligent-looking brown eyes. "But Laurence tells me you read him back to life after his injury during the war. He tells me that you read him poetry so beautifully that you quite restored his spirits. So, I would say you fit in perfectly on the Left Bank of Paris."

Chloé lifted her eyes, searching the other woman's face for signs of condescension or patronization, but she could see neither.

Adrienne Monnier lowered her voice. "It is a matter of not being intimidated, of cultivating an inner confidence, you see. Look around here. This is as new to everyone else as it is to you."

Chloé bit on her lip. Was it so obvious she felt out of place?

"Those who speak loudest and have the strongest opinions may not be the most intelligent beings in the café," Adrienne continued. She leaned back in her chair, folding her hands in the lap of her voluminous skirt.

Despite not knowing at all how she might fit in, Chloé

chuckled. "I do always find that the more intelligent a person is, the less opinionated they are."

"Forgive me," Adrienne said, suddenly.

Chloé lifted her face to meet her companion's gaze.

"I see that you have a husband who is very occupied, Chloé. And I'm wondering whether a woman like you, a trained nurse who chose the very books that would especially appeal to injured soldiers, might consider a proposal I have?"

Chloé waited, curious.

Adrienne smiled. "I run a bookshop on Rue de L'Odéon."

Chloé stilled. "How wonderful," she said, meaning it.

"Well, it is a bookshop, and a library of sorts. I love to be surrounded by books, whether I am selling them, reading them, or talking about them with my friends. Every week, we have readings by authors, and my store is something of a gathering place for poets. André Breton used to come in often during the war."

Where was this intriguing woman going with this?

Adrienne was quiet a moment. "My business is thriving, and I need another assistant in my store."

Chloé took in a sharp breath. "You do?"

"It is called *La Maison des Amis des Livres*—The House of Friends and Books—and when I mentioned that I was looking for a new assistant, your husband stepped right up and told me you'd sold him on several modern poems he would not have considered worthy of reading before you introduced them to him. He says you could sell milk to a cow." Adrienne's eyes twinkled.

Chloé sat back in her seat. The sounds of intelligent conversation, conversation of the university students and the young intellectuals that spent time around here, conversation that usually intimidated her, all seemed to merge into one continuous flow, and she simply stared at the woman sitting opposite her. "You must have so many other people to choose from, Madame."

Adrienne shook her head. "But I have practical motives, Chloé. You speak English perfectly, and are married to an American, so I confess there is merit in my asking you to come and work with me, because Montparnasse is starting to be filled with expatriate Americans, and who better to understand their reading tastes than a Frenchwoman who is married to one of their countrymen?"

Chloé felt a slow smile spreading across her face. A bookshop on the Left Bank of Paris? She wound her hands tightly in her lap.

"I publish an independent literary journal," Adrienne continued, "for which I write essays, so, you see, I am finding myself extremely busy and in need of more help in the store."

Chloé shot a glance toward the table where Laurence was sitting, sleeves rolled up to the elbow, a glass of wine in front of him, immersed in conversation with his companions. She turned back to Adrienne, quite resolved. The House of Friends and Books? It sounded like just the place for her. If she could fathom all the conversations!

Chloé lifted her chin. "Well, I could try. I can't promise you that I could keep up with all the chatter, but I can tell you that I do love to recommend books. And I like to help people." She lowered her gaze. Perhaps, this was a new way of contributing, a far more hopeful way than she'd had to endure by nursing the wounded during the war. She'd be taking care of those who came to her in a different manner, nurturing their hearts and minds, and what better way to celebrate peace?

Adrienne's face broke into a wide smile. "I'm delighted to hear it," she said. "Would you like to walk to Rue de L'Odéon with me after lunch today, so I can show you the store and you can meet everyone?"

Chloé nodded. "Absolutely, I would." She could hardly believe her luck.

Adrienne smiled. "I cook roast dinners for my staff regularly, where we sit down and discuss what we have been reading." Adrienne regarded her. "I will need you to read several books a week so that you will know what to recommend to my customers."

Chloé bit on her lip so as not to let out a cry of joy. If she'd known Adrienne better, she would have reached out and enfolded her in a hug.

Adrienne leaned forward. "Laurence tells me we have another thing in common."

Chloé waited.

"We are both country women at heart. That is why," Adrienne said, "my other love is cooking. In fact, why don't you stay for dinner with us all tonight? Let me cook for you after work, and after a dinner at the long wooden table above my shop with the other staff, I can send you home with a lovely pile of books to read. How does that sound?"

"Heavenly," Chloé breathed, speaking the truth. She'd work for Adrienne for free if she could be surrounded by books all day. But she wasn't going to tell the angel sitting opposite her that.

When Laurence came over to their table, full of apologies, Chloé stood up, threw her arms around her husband, and placed a kiss on his cheek. She'd not known a time of peace since she'd become a woman, and if this was what it meant, then Chloé hoped fervently that there'd *never* be another war.

Charlotte

Charlotte stood in Anita's empty dining room in the apartment on Rue Laffitte, the scarf that she'd tied to secure her hair while she dusted Anita's adored home leaving a faint line of perspiration on her shiny forehead in the searing summer heat. In front of her, Sandro Luciana's stunning portrait of Anita hung above the silent dinner table. The French doors were thrown open to the balcony, and the room was brimming with memories of Anita. If Charlotte closed her eyes, she could almost hear the laughter of all the dinner parties they'd enjoyed here, the wine, the lovingly prepared menus, the flowers, and the joy. Now, the dining-room table that Charlotte had polished with beeswax sat forlorn, the chairs all pushed neatly in as if to say goodbye.

Charlotte tore herself away from Sandro's striking likeness of Anita, her dark eyes sweeping confidently over the room. She made her way down the staircase to the gallery, the scent of dozens of bunches of flowers assailing her, as they had every day these past, lonely weeks. Each day, yet another artist whom

Anita had discovered and nurtured would arrive, head bent, beret in hand, offering a tribute to the woman who had kick-started their career.

Charlotte picked up one of several new miniatures of Anita, posthumous gifts painted by her adored protégés, surrounded by glorious blooms, roses, daisies, peonies, lilies. All of summer brought into the apartment. No matter how Charlotte tried to escape the beautiful gloom in here, it seemed impossible to hide from the cruel fact that Anita was gone whilst Paris was alive with summer. When she took some quiet time in the gardens of the Palais Royal, Charlotte was assailed with an explosion of floral color, petals pirouetting on the warm summer breezes, floating off into the air, only to be lost in a few seconds. Here so briefly, only to be swept away with the wind.

Charlotte wrapped her arms around her waist. For the first two weeks since Anita's death, she'd been poleaxed, unable to move, think or work, accepting the stream of visitors who came to the door with all the alacrity of a wooden doll. Élise and Olivier had made their slow way to Paris from the Loire Valley, ashen-faced, red-eyed, quiet, tossing and turning in the guest bedroom that Anita had always kept for them, and wandering around her beautiful apartment like a pair of birds who had lost the very reason they'd built their nest. Chateau d'Anez and art were their passion, but their daughter Anita had been their world.

Now and then, Charlotte would find Élise stroking Anita's possessions or gazing up at one of the paintings, all the works she'd so carefully curated and kept, because she loved them. And yet, while Élise and Olivier grieved for Anita, not once had they talked of the worry that was at the forefront of everyone's minds. The worry that was about to come to a head this after-noon, because Martha was due to arrive.

No matter how much Charlotte wanted to see her sister, she

knew that Martha would come with a proposal. It was going to take every ounce of Charlotte's strength to tell her that her hopes were in vain. With Anita gone, Charlotte could never abandon her friend's life's work. She was the only person who knew how to operate Galerie A. Goldstein. And yet, how could she tell her sister that this was more important to her than being home with Martha and Papa? Because, no matter how she dressed things up, this was what it came down to.

Charlotte settled at Anita's small wooden desk, her heart full of the memory of Anita right in this spot, lowering her tortoiseshell glasses onto her straight nose, and examining contracts with all the aplomb of the experienced business-woman she was. In the more recent, lonesome evenings, Char-lotte had worked her way through Anita's leather book of business, becoming familiar with her considerable contacts in the world of art, familiarizing herself with Anita's list of valued clients, with every transaction they'd undertaken in the past twenty years. Charlotte had learned which paintings they'd bought or sold, had read all the notes on their potential future interests, who had referred each client, whether she had anything in stock that might interest them at present.

Like the luminous modern portrait of Anita by Sandro Luciana, and Pissarro's painting of the young Élise that was safely at Chateau d'Anez, Charlotte knew that Anita's leather-bound book of business was priceless. It represented the past, present and future income of the gallery and was locked away in a safe built into a panel in the gallery every time she left the premises without fail.

In the last week, Charlotte had been proud to add some new names to the hundreds of collectors and artists who graced the well-turned pages of the great leather-bound book. But despite Charlotte's determination, another dark sense of fore-boding festered in Anita's home and in the streets of Paris,

where people's faces were pale with worry, the older generation's foreheads creased because the tension between Germany
and Czechoslovakia was increasing to an almost catastrophic
state.

Hitler had launched a war of nerves against Czechoslovakia, the Führer claiming that the Germans living in the
Sudeten region of Czechoslovakia were being mistreated by the
"tyrannical" Czechs. He was demanding they be incorporated
into the greater German Reich, but if the Czechs gave in to this,
it would deprive them of their fortified frontier facing Germany
that they had acquired in 1919. Czechoslovakia was resisting
Hitler's demands, because they had faith in their alliances with
not just the Soviet Union, but also with France. And what that
meant for France was the topic that scourged everyone's hearts
and minds.

In the last few weeks, Élise and Olivier, knowing that
another war seemed more possible than ever, had begun practical arrangements with the Louvre for the collections from
France's premier art museums to be stored at Chateau d'Anez.

And this month, the National Museums of Art had started
to actively mobilize. Charlotte knew they had sought trucks for
evacuation. Every day, huge packing cases and trunks were
being delivered to the Louvre.

Charlotte closed the great leather book and gazed around
the paintings that sat peacefully on Anita's gallery walls. If
Hitler announced he would take the Sudetenland by force,
Europe would be on the brink of war. She stood up and paced
around Anita's gallery, her eyes lingering on some of the pieces
that Anita had acquired in the weeks before her death, in the
weeks before she'd left the suicide note one dreadful, beautiful
summer morning on the pillow of her perfectly made-up bed.
Anita's anger, the tension that had boiled inside her toward
Adolf Hitler and his despicable treatment of Jews in Germany
and Austria, had tipped to boiling point, but Charlotte had also

noticed a deeper melancholy creeping beneath the surface of Anita's wrath.

When Anita had taken to her bed for several days, only sleeping fitfully and refusing to see anyone other than Charlotte, she had called the doctor—of course she had. But the elderly practitioner had shaken his head and informed Charlotte that the only treatment available for Anita's condition may well be surgery to destroy her prefrontal lobe, which would have, he told her, a calming effect.

Charlotte, horrified, had spoken with Élise and Olivier, who had refused to countenance something which could alter their darling Anita's personality to such an extent that she may not be able to make any decisions at all.

So, they had watched and waited, hoping for the return of their passionate, fiery Anita.

But all Charlotte was left with were the tragic words of the final, handwritten note she'd found atop Anita's pillow. In the darkness of the night, she'd taken a train somewhere to the coast, and waded into the sea, ending it all. She'd not said where she was going, and she'd insisted that no one know. Anita had not stipulated whether she'd chosen the stormy Atlantic Ocean, or the balmy Mediterranean for her swansong.

Charlotte was only drawn out of her dark reverie by the sound of a creak in the gallery's green front door. She froze for one split second at the sight of the person standing framed by the sunlight in the doorway, before she bolted across the gallery, uttering a cry.

"Martha," she said, coming to a sudden and momentous stop, her eyes widening for one long moment as her gaze landed on her darling, bookish sister, who stood there in a terribly chic soft navy trouser suit with her luggage in her hand. Vianne. Vianne would have designed it for her. Oh, for one second, how Charlotte missed everything about New York!

Martha pulled the small navy hat she wore from her typically tangled curls, and opened her arms out wide.

Charlotte threw herself into her sister's embrace. "I cannot believe it," she managed. "Thank goodness you are here."

Charlotte wept into her sister's shoulder.

Martha held her at arm's length. "Charlotte," she said, tears pooling in her own eyes. "I've been so dreadfully worried about you."

Charlotte took in a shuddering breath. "Coffee," she said, firmly. She eyed the two neat suitcases that sat by Martha's feet. "And then we will unpack your things." She tucked her arm into her sister's, and led Martha upstairs to Anita's empty, silent home.

That evening, Charlotte allowed her eyes to roam around the beautiful and tranquil gardens of the Palais Royal. Next to her on one of the benches that lined the formal garden, sat Olivier, Élise and Martha under the lime and chestnut trees. All around them, the seventeenth-century architecture looked down upon their grieving party, as if reassuring them that France had been through great troubles before, and Paris's beauty would never die.

The only possible plan had been to get out of the apartment tonight. With Martha here, Anita's absence left an even greater gaping hole than before, and they'd all sat in the salon, staring at one another, Martha seeming unable to process the fact that Anita no longer breathed life into the apartment on Rue Laffitte.

Once they had settled in the Palais Royal gardens, Martha had spoken in her typically soft and gentle manner, relaying to them all how Papa was begging for Charlotte to come home. He was horribly concerned about the situation in Europe and was offering sanctuary to Élise and Olivier in his apartment too, with his assistance to obtain the necessary papers they'd need to migrate to America. They belonged, Martha said, together. Anita's family had been Chloé's family, and Papa couldn't bear to have them at terrible risk, given the news from Germany that was blistering from the radio each day.

For a moment, no one spoke. Charlotte broke a piece of crusty baguette from the checked tablecloth that Élise had spread with a picnic between them on the bench. No matter how bad things were, Élise always had time to prepare lovely food. Charlotte spread her crusty bread with soft *chevre*, her eyes roaming over the crackers, fruits, cornichons, butter, sandwich meats, and a cold salad sprinkled with a little vinaigrette.

Élise folded her ringed hands in her lap, and Olivier leaned forward in his seat, entwining his gnarled old hands, his perfectly pressed cream linen trousers immaculate, even though the world he'd known and loved was falling apart.

Charlotte swallowed, a lump forming in her throat at his dear persistence in the face of tragedy.

Papa was right. The elderly couple had to leave Europe. Especially now that Anita was gone.

"I have had a letter from my dear friend Georg in Vienna," Olivier said. He sighed. "In the last four months since Hitler marched into Austria, he has created chaos amongst the Jews. Georg writes that public harassment of individual Jews is common on the streets now the Nazis have occupied that beautiful city." He shook his head, his voice shaking and brittle, as if his own words were almost incomprehensible, even as he spoke them. "All Jewish students of high-school age attended their last school day at the end of the semester in June and are now banned from any formal education."

Charlotte stilled.

"Teenagers like Georg's son have no idea what to do, so they either stay home or try to congregate in the parks, until the local Hitler Youth groups or other German citizens demand their departure." Olivier lifted his hand and took Élise's, holding it close to his heart. "Rumors, Georg writes, abound amongst the people as to what might happen if Jews must remain in Germany and Austria, and in other territories if Hitler carries out his plan."

Charlotte stared at Élise's lovely picnic, her stomach curdling and her appetite falling away.

"I have been glued to the radio, and at the recent hastily put-together conference in Evian, right here in France," Olivier went on, "no government showed any willingness to open their borders to Jewish refugees from the Nazi rule. Georg says this month, thousands of Jews are queueing up in Vienna to petition the occupying German authorities for the documents to permit emigration. Apparently, they can expect days waiting in line. Georg and his wife have sent their son to stay with cousins in Berlin, because they anticipate that they will not be home in the coming weeks. They will be waiting for safe harbor. They are talking of going to America."

There was a silence. The sounds of Paris whirring on around them, taxicabs and trolley cars, the crunch of people's feet on the neatly raked gravel that lined the park, seemed surreal in the face of this stark, awful reality.

"I think the takeover of remaining European countries by Hitler by whatever means is only a matter of time," Olivier said, his voice deadly quiet. "The only place that makes sense for us is America. Martha, Élise and I will accept Laurence's offer that we leave France for New York." He lowered his head, his face ashen. "I only hope that one day, we shall be able to return to Chateau d'Anez under circumstances that are far better than we are facing now."

Élise turned her dark eyes toward Charlotte. "Dearest Charlotte, I'm afraid that I think Georg is right."

Charlotte frowned. Without her realizing, she'd curled her fists into two tight balls.

"We cannot ask you to stay in France, Charlotte, no matter how scared I was last summer," Élise went on, her voice carrying with the whisper of the leaves in the breeze. "Come to New York with us. We should all sail together, *chérie*."

Charlotte turned in alarm to face Anita's mother.

"I worry that dear Georg knows more than even he is letting on to us all." Élise's dark eyes were serious. "I saw the expression on your face when you were reading Georg's letter from Germany, Olivier."

Charlotte's eyes locked with her sister's. Martha's expression was pleading. But Charlotte sat tall. She cleared her throat and chose her words with great care. "There are other Jewish gallerists in Paris talking of packing up and leaving their businesses in non-Jewish manager's hands. I am perfectly placed to help. As an American, I shall not incur suspicion on the part of the Nazis. Don't you see? I can keep things running for you. I promise that I will keep your home and Anita's business safe."

There was a silence, and Charlotte squeezed her eyes shut, taking in a deep breath, and willing the spirit of Anita to strengthen her resolve.

"I am determined that Anita's life's work will not be destroyed, and I am determined to do all I can to ensure that Chateau d'Anez remains exactly as you will leave it. This is my commitment to you all. You can trust me; I promise you that."

Charlotte's heart was beating wildly. Surely, Martha would argue with her, tell her she was quite mad. But then, she felt the warmth of her sister's hand pressing against hers. And they sat there, a strange little family, about to be separated in the face of a thundercloud, swollen with a portent that none of them could hope to understand.

Charlotte gazed out the kitchen window into Rue Laffitte in the early hours of a beautiful warm morning. With just days left until Martha, Élise and Olivier sailed for New York, she was going to have to get used to being alone in Anita's apartment. Despite her resolve to stay here in Paris, the enormity of her decision was only just starting to hit home. She'd lost Anita for good. Élise and Olivier were going to New York. Having Martha here had made things much closer to bearable. But Martha would be gone very soon too.

Charlotte looked up at the sky. It was luminous, its warm glow bathing the buildings opposite in pearly summer pinks. She'd always been told she was determined, she thought nothing of fighting for those she loved, and her decision to stay and protect the Goldsteins' livelihood was as natural to her as swimming in a lake, but one fact remained: she was going to be alone. She was going to have to dig into her deepest reserves to forge ahead without the comforting presence of those she knew and loved.

Tearing herself away from her reverie, Charlotte threw open the window, brewing coffee and placing the fresh baguettes that she'd bought for breakfast along with summer raspberries, strawberries and preserves on a tray. Somehow, keeping the simple rituals going seemed vital.

From Élise and Olivier's bedroom came the sounds of Élise's chatter about her visit to the Opera Garnier this evening, as special guests at the performance of *Salammbô* in honor of the royal visit by the King and Queen of Great Britain.

Charlotte turned to see Martha moving into the kitchen, her chestnut curls tumbling about her face, her peach silk dressing gown gathered loosely around her slim waist.

"I am indulging," Martha said, accepting a cup of steaming black coffee from Charlotte and cradling it in her hands. "The wireless is crowded with talks about English literature, British Art, and broadcasts of Shakespeare. The royal visit is accompanied with a cascade of all things English. It is a wonderful distraction."

"And distractions are so very you," Charlotte smiled, pulling a stray curl away from her sister's cheek. Paris had been in a fever of anticipation for the royal visit, and the newspapers were full of the inseparability of Britain and France. "But," she went on, "literature aside, everyone knows the royal visit is just a buttressing of the entente cordiale between France and Great Britain. It's clearly a warning for Hitler, Mussolini, and Co."

Martha pinched a strawberry from the tray and popped it into her mouth. "I for one am not going to complain about staying home tonight and listening to Shakespeare while you are at the opera with Olivier and Élise fighting to catch a glimpse of Queen Elizabeth and her fashionable gowns," Martha said.

Charlotte grinned. "But Queen Elizabeth is providing such a diverting interlude." She'd gone with Élise to stand amongst the well-wishers on the Champs-Élysées as the King and Queen of Great Britain had driven by in their cavalcade to the Quai d'Orsay Palace, which for three days was hosting the royal couple and returning to the splendors of Louis XV.

"The fact that Parisians, who consider themselves leaders in world fashion, are praising Queen Elizabeth's gowns is rather lovely," Martha said.

Charlotte stepped closer to her sister. She'd been waiting for a moment alone with her to broach the topic that each day, seemed more and more obvious to her. Martha's cheeks had been unusually flushed when she'd first arrived, and, while this could be put down to the abundance of fresh sea air aboard the ship, Charlotte had noticed her sister daydreaming and gazing out the kitchen window one too many times. "Honey," Charlotte said, "who is he?"

Martha looked up from her cup of coffee.

Charlotte glanced at the kitchen door, but there was no sight of Élise or Olivier yet.

Martha laid her coffee cup down on the bench and raked a

hand through her curls. "It is nothing. I'm far more concerned about you."

But Charlotte shook her head. "I'm not talking about me."

Martha grimaced. She sighed and rested her head in her hands.

Charlotte folded her arms, and, at the same moment, she burst into laughter just when Martha did the same, her shoulders shaking.

"Dramatics don't suit you," Charlotte laughed. "You don't fool me."

Martha lifted her head. "He's a Scotsman. He lives in Edinburgh."

Charlotte's dark eyes held strong. She waited.

And then, Martha took in a ragged breath. "I think I've fallen in love."

Charlotte pulled out a chair and sat down at the table. Slowly, she raised her eyes to meet with her sister's. Words hung, unspoken, but acknowledged between them.

"But how do you feel about him being such a long way from New York?" Charlotte said. She sighed, lowering her voice. "He must be very special, but I know how much you love home. I know I made the choice to move to France a few months ago, but at times, even I feel homesick for New York." Charlotte squeezed Martha's hand.

Martha held her gaze. "How could I ever leave Papa?" she whispered, her voice cracking. "He needs me to be there."

Charlotte tented her hands on the table.

"I can't bear to leave Papa."

"Oh, Martha," Charlotte murmured. "I'm sorry," she whispered.

Martha was an angel. Charlotte had left New York and had chosen to come and work in Paris as soon as she could without a second glance. It had been exciting, modern, her right. But Martha was made of far more sensitive material. She'd struggle to do something solely for herself. And, deep down, Charlotte knew that Martha would also struggle to take a risk that might lead to heartbreak, but that might also lead to her finally finding the happiness she'd hidden away from since the death of their maman.

Charlotte reached a hand across the kitchen table, resting it atop her sister's. "Why not see where things take you?" she said, knowing that Martha would not lead her own charge, as she, Charlotte, was so wont to do.

Martha shook her head. "It's impossible."

"No," Charlotte insisted. "It's only impossible if you say it is."

But Martha looked away to the side, her jaw tight.

That evening, Charlotte stood in the foyer of the Opera Garnier, the magnificent gilt porticos that lined the vast room glittering in the light of the hundreds of electric candles on the golden chandeliers. She gazed around the magnificent space, Martha's revelation still ringing through her heart. She'd never thought for one moment that Martha would fall in love with a man who lived on the other side of the Atlantic from Papa. She'd never thought she'd feel guilty that her reasons for being away from home outstripped Martha's, and Martha would accept this, just as she always did.

Charlotte accepted a glass of champagne and took a long sip.

Élise and Olivier were at the center of a crowd of artistic friends underneath one of the classical paintings that adorned the walls. Exquisite sculptures lined the room and the sounds of champagne glasses and muted conversation filtered through the air. Out of the corner of her eye, Charlotte caught a glimpse of the lovely Queen Elizabeth of England, chatting graciously with an elderly gentleman. Her long white dress, typical of the entirely white wardrobe she'd worn for this tour, glistened with a multitude of tiny beads and flowed to the floor. Her expression was beneficent and mild, and the idea of Hitler seemed about as far removed as the moon from where she was standing.

Charlotte tore herself away from gazing at the gracious Queen Elizabeth at the feel of a gloved hand pressing her arm. She turned, coming face to face with a woman of around fifty years of age, whose soft gray eyes held Charlotte's.

"Sandrine," Charlotte said, leaning forward and kissing her mother's old friend, Sandrine Mercier, sister-in-law to the fabulous Vianne Conti, and the third member of the trio of nurses that had Charlotte's mother Chloé and darling Anita. Now, Charlotte held her mother's friend at arm's length, her presence, the fact that she was the last one of them alive, lending an extra poignancy to the evening.

"You look perfectly lovely, Charlotte," Sandrine said. "Enchanting." Her gray eyes roamed up and down the cream halter-neck gown Charlotte wore, with its softly draped flared skirt and striking embroidery of gold tendrils around the neck, the pattern repeated several times in a circular fashion down the dress. "One of Vianne's gowns?"

Charlotte tucked her arm through Sandrine's elbow. "Oh yes. This was designed by your wonderful sister-in-law," she said.

Sandrine's brow furrowed. "I don't know when I'm going to be able to see her again."

Charlotte squeezed Sandrine's arm. She knew how much Sandrine admired the fabulous New York career of her talented sister-in-law, but despite her modesty, Sandrine had become a successful businesswoman in her own right.

Since her husband, Jacques, had returned from the Great War in a state of ill health, Sandrine had single-handedly run his father's business—an antique store named Celine in Paris's Marais district—turning it from the brink of disaster to its former healthy, profitable state, and yet Sandrine always insisted that Vianne was the formidable member of the family.

After her husband's untimely death, Sandrine had continued to keep the antique store, becoming well respected in cultural circles for her ability to adapt to trends in furniture, design, and *objets d'art*, always seeming to stock Celine with items that would appeal to her late father-in-law's clientele, while steadily building up a strong list of her own customers over the years.

Charlotte led Vianne's sister-in-law to a quieter corner in the crowded room.

"I hear that you will stay in France, that you will take over and continue Anita's work?" Sandrine said, her expression serious.

"Coming from an experienced businesswoman to one who is a fledgling in the nest, it is a real compliment that you've asked."

"Like me, you have rapidly inherited an established business. One you never dreamed would be yours. I know something of that."

Charlotte heaved out a sigh. "What can go wrong?" She lifted her champagne glass in the air.

Sandrine spoke with care. "Having lived through one war, I have no doubt that should what seems inevitable indeed eventuate, then we shall all need friends whom we can trust. You know I am here for you, Charlotte."

Charlotte squeezed the delicate-looking middle-aged woman's hand. Sandrine was as finely built as a frail leaf in the fall, but her soft expression belied a determination that Anita always said Sandrine had not been born with but had grown within her.

"I shall be here," Sandrine said. "You can count on me."

Charlotte closed her eyes. In promising to keep Anita's business going, she was letting Papa and Martha down, but she'd forgotten about the quiet presence of her mother's friend, Sandrine, and the fact that she'd continued a family business in the face of tragedy and early death was something. So, perhaps, she was not such a bad person after all.

Sandrine smiled, her delicate features lighting up. "You must know that Anita and Chloé live on in you. I yearn for them every day, but you embody them both."

Charlotte held her champagne poised at her lips. "I'll drink to that," she whispered.

Just then, Élise turned to her from a distance, catching her eye and seeing her talking with Sandrine Mercier. And Anita's mother raised her fingers to her lips, and kissed them, mouthing something that Charlotte was certain, were the words, *God Bless You Both.*

Several days later, Charlotte stood on the platform at Gare Saint-Lazare, the train that would take Martha, Élise and Olivier to the port of Le Havre sitting ready to leave on the tracks. Charlotte swallowed. Beside her, Élise and Olivier were busying themselves triple-checking they had their tickets, their wallets, passports, and tickets.

Charlotte stood face to face with Martha, who was dutifully returning to be with Papa. Charlotte shook herself. It was not duty that bound Martha to their father. The tie that bound Martha to Papa was love.

Charlotte reached out and stroked a tendril of hair underneath Martha's hat. She was dressed in a smart dove-gray suit, her small feet planted firmly on the platform, her face pale.

"If you decide to change your mind," Martha said, "go back, get your passport, jump on this afternoon's train and I'll meet you on the docks." Martha went on, her words clear, even amongst the crowds gathered on the platform, "Please, Charlotte. Hitler has no mercy," she whispered. "I don't think any of us have any idea what will eventuate."

Charlotte pulled her sister into a rough hug, closing her eyes against the familiar feel, hating the way she could almost hear Martha's heart beating hard in her chest. "I love you and I love Papa," she said, murmuring into her sister's ear. "But Paris is part of me, and I it, and should I leave—"

Martha pulled back, holding Charlotte at arm's length. "You would feel the same way I would, should I abandon Papa," she said, her voice cracking, tears running freely down her cheeks.

Charlotte held Martha's gaze for a long moment, savoring the sight of those tawny eyes she'd grown up watching for sadness, protecting her sister when she was teased at school for holding back.

"Paris is my New York, Martha," she murmured.

Martha grimaced, swiping a hand across her cheeks, nodding, her mouth working. "Don't take risks," she managed.

The train's whistle pierced the air, and next, Martha had torn herself away, and was rushing off, her shoulders shaking.

Charlotte, staring helplessly at her sister, asked herself for the millionth time why she simply could not play the safe game, why she could not flee to safety like everyone else. But soon, she was enveloped in Élise's embrace, the older woman crying into her shoulder, Olivier's arms around them both.

And then, the guard blew his whistle, and Élise pulled back, her hand pressed to Charlotte's cheek, her dark eyes filled with tears. Charlotte, for one wild moment, yearned, ridiculously, to just get on the train with them. To run away.

But she never ran. She fought.

And now Europe was facing the fight of its life.

So, she stood there, a lone young woman on a platform filled with strangers, and she watched in silence while those she loved most in the world left.

Charlotte stared at the hard concrete below her. They might be leaving now, but she swore that it wouldn't be for good. Charlotte promised herself that, one day, the people she loved would be able to safely step onto French soil once again without any fear of persecution and without any fear that their home would not be safe, and she would be here to meet them.

8

PARIS, WINTER 1919

Chloé

Chloé's maman always said that people who were happy wished for others to be happy too. Joy spread joy. It was as simple as that. La Maison des Amis des Livres was all prepared for tonight's soirée, and Chloé's nerves tingled with excitement about the person she'd secretly invited to attend. She'd been working here for a year now, and had loved every minute of it, but hopefully tonight would top it all. Chloé moved toward the bookshop's closed front door and unlocked it to allow this evening's guests to flow into the warm store from the cold.

He'd popped into the bookstore this morning, and Chloé had not been the only person to pause and take a second glance at the tall, handsome American as he perused the selection of art books in French. There'd been whispers behind the backs of hands, and one of Chloé's fellow workers had sauntered over the room to nudge her.

But Chloé wasn't staring because she was about to become enamored with anyone other than her dearest Laurence. Chloé couldn't take her eyes off Sumner Green because she wanted to get him into the same room as Anita and he'd just given her the perfect opportunity.

She'd wandered over to the well-dressed artist, helped him find the book he was seeking—on Matisse's time spent painting in the beautiful light in Nice—and invited him to tonight's soirée. It had been simple, of course, to pick up the telephone after this and insist that Anita come to hear the luminous French poet, Paul Valéry, tonight. Chloé had told Anita there would surely be artists coming along who were looking for representation.

So, it was a *fait accompli.*

Chloé had whizzed around since the bookshop closed, tidying the bookshelves that lined the walls, and dusting the black-and-white portraits of famous writers that hung above Adrienne Monnier's beloved books. She'd set out wine and nibbles, even though the croutons had to consist mainly of carrot straws and savory wartime biscuits made without butter, because milk was still in short supply.

Now, she moved toward the bookshop's closed front door and unlocked it to allow this evening's guests to flow into the warm store from the cold. She hung the small sign that she'd made announcing the event on the door. Outside, in the cold, crisp street, people strolled before dinner, walking past the large windows that looked over Rue de L'Odéon wrapped up in scarves, coats, and hats. Chloé could see breath curling from people's lips and the warm pink glow on their cheeks.

When the first customers appeared, Chloé stood back and let them in, the small bell above the door tinkling and bringing in fresh flurries of cold Parisian air. She leapt into action, taking coats, pouring wine, and helping people to a seat on the rows of wooden chairs she'd set up this afternoon, all the while, her eyes darting about for a sighting of Anita, Sumner, or preferably, both of them.

Upstairs, Adrienne was having a quiet drink with Paul

Valéry before the event, and no doubt, they'd appear soon enough; Adrienne in her white blouse, velvet vest, and one of the customary long skirts that she favored.

As the bookshop filled with chatter, laughter and the shedding of coats and scarves, Chloé chatted and worried neither Anita nor Sumner would appear.

When Anita finally arrived, accompanied by Laurence, Chloé's stomach took a little lurch, for Anita's cheeks were pink with anticipation, and this was only about hearing Paul Valéry! Anita looked gorgeous in an elegant dress in deep red, loosely fitted with a high waist and a flaring skirt. The color highlighted the flash in Anita's dark eyes, and the shine of her dark brown hair.

Chloé resisted clapping her hands with glee. She ignored the stirrings inside her that said she shouldn't be meddling.

But it wasn't until the famous poet had settled down on a chair next to Adrienne, until the room fell to a hush and the guests stopped nibbling and were cradling their wine glasses in their laps, that the front door swung open, and Sumner Green swept into La Maison des Amis des Livres in a swirl of freezing air.

He was dressed in a swishing navy greatcoat, his cheeks flushed with cold, and he was rubbing his hands together and looking up from under his eyebrows. Chloé saw the way Anita's shoulders turned rigid. She raised a brow as Anita hastily patted her hair.

Sumner strode down the center aisle, scouting for a seat, and when his gaze landed on Anita and he stopped dead in the middle of the room, Chloé had to bite down on her lip to stop herself from letting out a delighted squeal.

Next to her, Laurence turned, his expression quizzical, but Chloé simply shrugged and indicated they watch the famous poet, who was beginning to read La Jeune Parque, which Adrienne considered to be his greatest work so far.

When the talk was done, people started turning in their seats, standing up and moving toward Adrienne. Chloé's eyes darted from Anita to Sumner and back again. He was heading toward her; she was looking up at him.

"Matchmaking, darling?" Laurence said, leaning close. "Didn't you say that Anita was a lost cause? Showed no interest in anyone during the war?"

"How could you be so cruel about my dear friend," Chloé murmured, flicking the idea away with a flutter of her fingers.

"I take it this is why we're going out afterward," he said, his voice low and incredibly deep. "And why you rang Anita to insist she must be here. I thought it was a little odd, but she, funnily enough, was touched by your thoughtful invitation."

"How brilliant you are, darling," Chloé whispered right back. "A regular sleuth."

When the store was almost empty aside from a couple of close friends of Adrienne's who were staying for one of her famous roast dinners, Chloé smiled at the sight of Anita and Sumner sitting on one of the sofas for two in a corner of the store.

"Anita?" Chloé said, wandering over and turning on one of her most ravishing smiles. "Laurence and I are of a great mind to go out dancing. You will come with us, won't you? And, oh! Mr. Green?" Chloé laughed. "How charming to see you here. You simply must join us. Laurence, my husband, insists!"

Anita spread out her hands and studied her painted nails.

"How could I resist?" Sumner Green said, his eyes twinkling. "And you," he said to Chloé, "must call me Sumner. Only people I don't like have to call me Mr. Green."

Chloé clapped her hands and introduced Laurence.

So. Sumner was fun too. Not a bore. Which was perfect. She and Anita had both been so disillusioned when the third member of their nursing trio, Sandrine, had taken up with the moody Jacques Mercier. He'd never come out with them.

"Simply perfect," Chloé said. The evening was going to be gorgeous, and so, Chloé knew, was Sumner Green.

Half an hour later, Chloé flitted around the crowded tables in Café de la Rotonde, Anita was ahead of her, stopping to chat with all the people she knew. Conversation buzzed around the café on the corner of Boulevard de Montparnasse and Boulevard Raspail, where painters, photographers, writers, and intellectuals shared their ideas at the crowded tables, and a Dixieland jazz band played "Tiger Rag" to set the mood. Chloé could almost have hugged herself. Paris was back.

Behind her, Laurence and Sumner had already been caught up at one of the crowded tables in Victor Libion's famous café, where, for the price of a cup of coffee, artists and writers could sit and work all day. Monsieur Libion was famous for his hospitality, and for turning a blind eye when a struggling artist stole the crusty tops from the baguettes that he displayed in baskets behind the bar. Rumor had it, he allowed his creative clientele to take chairs, napkins, and cutlery home. He didn't mind a jot.

Chloé wove her way past a table of young men loudly surmising that a new ideology for the world must be found after all the trauma and confusion of the war. If the catchphrase since the war was "out with the old and in with the new," then Café de la Rotonde was the center of it all.

Chloé stopped still at the sight of the infamous artists' model Kiki de Montparnasse, who, gossip had it, was being painted by Maurice Mendjisky. Kiki was, it was said, his muse. Chloé spotted an empty table, and moved toward it through the smoky, crowded room, sitting down and waving to Laurence, who blew her a kiss right back. He was sharing a joke with Sumner by the bar now and chatting with a man who kept pulling his pipe out and pointing with it, until they'd all roar with laughter and shrug their shoulders, their hands in the air.

Chloé smiled to herself. Laurence's gestures made him look perfectly French!

She looked around, taking in the café. The walls here were lined not with books but with napkin drawings from the artists that came to drink coffee. Picasso, Rivera, Federico Cantú... One of Anita's favorite paintings was set in this very café, and it was by Picasso and called *In the Café de la Rotonde*. Chloé had not glimpsed the famous Picasso yet, but Laurence had told her that his studio was right around the corner.

When Anita wove her way over to Chloé, ravishing in her red dress, her face lit up in a sensational smile. "We are celebrating tonight, *chérie*," she said.

"Oh, I know," Chloé replied, arching her brows and turning to look at Sumner.

But Anita clutched Chloé's arm, "Dearest Chloé, I have gained my very first client!"

Chloé's mouth dropped open, although she should not be surprised. Anita had been working like a demon to set up her art gallery in Montmartre. She'd told Chloé, proudly, how she'd put up a wooden sign saying *Galerie. A Goldstein.*

Anita indicated across the room. "That young man over there has agreed to allow me to represent him, and we'll be hosting his first exhibition as soon as I can organize it," Anita said. She sat down, cupping her chin in her hands. "He showed me some of his work just now. He had his portfolio right by the table over there. I looked at it, and I loved it, and I offered him to come see me tomorrow. After we talked for a few minutes, I simply knew we'd work well together. And he's being hunted by some of the other owners in Rue Laffitte." Anita looked more serious now. "I am utterly determined to make this work."

"And you will," Chloé said, meaning it. She cleared her throat. "*Ma chérie,* this is wonderful, and I'm more than excited for you, but, what about Sumner Green? The spark is still alive for you both?"

Anita chewed on her lip and sighed. "Chloé, it's not so simple."

But as if in a flash, Sumner and Laurence were standing at their table, Sumner resting his arm along the back of Anita's chair.

And right then, across the crowded room, Kiki de Montparnasse, the girl who everyone said was born as Alice Prin in Burgundy, stood up on her table and started singing a song. She danced to her own music and blew kisses to her many friends in the room.

"Look at her," Anita breathed, as if talking almost to herself. "We must all dance to the beat of our own drums. It is the only way to truly capture your fate in your own hands."

"I'll drink to that," Laurence said, sipping his wine.

Kiki kicked up her heels and everyone who understood what it meant to truly breathe life into Paris again clapped along.

When Chloé pushed open the door to Anita's gallery the following morning, Anita gathered her coat, flicked off the light switch, and came right across the empty floor, her expression dark. Chloé frowned. She'd come to chat about the wonderful evening they'd enjoyed last night. When she and Laurence had left Café de la Rotonde just before midnight, Anita and Sumner had been in deep conversation.

But now, Chloé followed Anita, whose face was pale, as she swept out of what was going to become her fledgling gallery. She closed and locked the green door behind her and marched ahead of Chloé along Rue Laffitte. Chloé felt a sickening sensation spreading through her body. She hoped that she hadn't caused Anita any pain by inviting Sumner along last night.

Chloé struggled to keep pace with her friend, whose feet were clicking on the cobblestones, her brow creased below her deep red velvet hat. She came to an abrupt stop alongside Anita at the top of the street, following her friend as she crossed Rue de Châteaudun, until they stood underneath the austere portico at the entrance to Notre-Dame-de-Lorette. The great church swelled up in front of them.

Anita let out a loud sigh, and, leaving Chloé no choice but to trail in her wake, marched right up the steps to the front door, pushing it open, and threading her way into the hushed interior of the Roman Catholic church with its magnificent gold-leaf decorations on the ceiling, and bright murals covering the walls.

Chloé crossed herself, kneeled at the altar and waited while Anita wove her way into an empty pew. There were only a few silent people in the church, and Chloé shook her head. Anita seemed to have hardly noticed that she was a Jewish woman seeking sanctuary in a Catholic church. But Anita had always maintained she had nothing against those whose religious views did not align with her own.

The fact that Anita had chosen the church where Chloé came to worship was touching.

Chloé slipped in next to Anita, sending her a sidelong glance. She could have boiled an egg on Anita's forehead; it was so lined with filmy sweat.

"Anita."

Anita closed her eyes. She threw her head back, her dark curls tumbling down her back, her hands clasped in two tight balls in her lap.

Chloé waited.

Anita whispered into the soft, muted shadows of the church. "I know now, why I have avoided relationships with men."

Chloé shook her head. She turned to Anita, wanting desperately for her friend to find the happiness she deserved. But sometimes, doubt and worry plagued Anita, and Chloé did not quite know why. She was a person whom, perhaps, Chloé would never fully know.

"My desire, my heart and my labor would all have to come secondary to Sumner, should I enter into a relationship with him," Anita continued.

Chloé held up her hands. "Surely, you do not believe that the world cannot move forward after all we have endured, and that things cannot be better for the women of our generation. Otherwise, what was it for?" Chloé sighed. There. Perhaps she did have more understanding of the intellectual conversations that were going on in the cafés than she gave herself credit for.

There was a silence, as they both, Chloé was certain, remembered the devastation, the loss, the havoc wreaked by war.

But Anita shook her head. "No matter what our theories are, the fact is that a woman is still expected to be loyal, docile and committed—but not to herself."

Chloé held her dear, complicated friend's hands. "Sumner would not expect—"

"All last night, Sumner talked of *his* aspirations, *his* dreams, *his* hopes to become a world-famous, internationally successful artist. Not once did he ask me about *my* gallery."

"But you would not be happy with someone who did not have hopes and plans," Chloé pointed out.

Anita swallowed hard. "You know how hard I have worked to set up my gallery."

"Of course." Chloé squeezed Anita's hand. "But that does not preclude you from love. Surely, you can talk to him. Tell him your hopes and dreams." She did not add that Anita and Sumner had only just met once again and that Anita's worries seemed premature. She knew Anita better than that. Her friend was always either all in or all out. She made decisions quickly, and nothing would change that.

"All my life," Anita continued, "I'd been waiting for a love that would bind me to it, and now that I've found it, all I can see is a loss of myself."

Chloé closed her eyes. She took in a breath, willing herself to find some way to help. "Anita, you are passionate," she said, finally, "you will never be happy unless you are with a passionate man, a man of equal feeling and intelligence to yourself."

She searched Anita's face, waiting for her to contradict what they both knew was true, but her friend remained silent, her eyes locked in some miserable pain that Chloé had never, ever experienced, but desperately wanted to alleviate.

"You are in love with him," Chloé said. "And that is confusing you. Throwing you. You would not settle for anything less."

Anita turned to Chloé, her eyes clouding, her expression unreadable.

Chloé drew her friend's head to her shoulder and looked up at the stunning altarpiece ahead. Peacetime was supposed to be simple. But love, it seemed, was just as complicated as war.

9

Charlotte

Charlotte looked up at the soft click of the gallery's front door. She placed the sketches that she'd been perusing aside, the portfolio from a young artist who'd dropped by this morning, eyes shining in anticipation because he was finally ready to share his work. The front door opened tentatively, and Sandrine Mercier stepped into the cool interior of the gallery from the hot August afternoon.

Charlotte rose to greet her mother's old friend, a feeling of warmth spreading through her at the sight of the well-dressed owner of the Mercier family's antique store, her blond hair neatly waved in the latest fashion, and the navy shoes that matched her smart costume clipping on the wooden floorboards. Sandrine was a businesswoman; Charlotte was becoming a businesswoman, and now, she was starting to meet Sandrine on increasingly equal terms.

"I have bad news," Sandrine said, a vertical line running between her brows. She sighed. "Dearest Charlotte, I'm afraid you are going to have to act."

Charlotte searched Sandrine's face. The older woman had been true to the promise she'd made at the Opera Garnier on the evening of the Royal British visit to Paris a year ago. Since Élise and Olivier had departed Europe for the safety of New York with Martha, Sandrine had been a consistent friend and adviser to Charlotte.

When Hitler had seized the remainder of Czechoslovakia in March this year, making it clear Poland was next, Sandrine had called Charlotte for coffee, ensuring she was informed and that she had a clear grasp of the political situation, because, Sandrine had warned Charlotte, what happened next might be crucial as to whether France went to war.

"I have just come from a meeting of volunteers at the Louvre." Sandrine averted her eyes toward the closed front door of the gallery.

Charlotte moved across the room, opening the heavy door, and placing her *back in ten minutes* sign on the handle, before firmly pulling it closed and securing the lock.

Sandrine shook her head. "The Louvre is preparing for war. They are packing the collections up today."

Charlotte sank down into Anita's chair, her eyes roaming sadly over the beautiful sketches of Paris that the young artist had dropped into her this morning. A question formed itself on her lips, but instead of voicing it, she sat in contemplation. The Louvre administrators had packed the collection up last September, going so far as to take every item deemed urgent out of the museum, in trucks to the Loire Valley, after Hitler had set his sights on the Sudetenland. But then the Munich Agreement had been signed, allowing Germany to annex the Sudetenland, and immediate war was avoided. So, the Louvre sent everything back to Paris. That was eleven months ago.

Charlotte picked up one of Anita's favorite pens and twirled it in her fingers.

"Tomorrow," Sandrine said, "the Louvre will begin evacuating the collection to Chambord before directing the pieces to their hiding places."

Charlotte took in a ragged breath. The thought of Chateau d'Anez, Élise and Olivier's beloved home that housed their own personal collection, filled with priceless objects from the Louvre was fitting, heroic, and yet, most of all, strange.

Sandrine slipped into the chair opposite Charlotte, the expression in her gray eyes filled with concern. "Charlotte, I have mixed news. News that I think you will not like, but news that is absolutely in the best interests of the Goldsteins."

Charlotte looked up, her eyes grazing with Sandrine's. She waited for the older woman to continue.

"Monsieur Jaujard, who, as the director of the Musées Nationaux, is leading the operation to remove all artworks in the public collections to safety, has announced that he will protect major Jewish collections along with the riches of the Louvre."

Charlotte stayed perfectly still. "You are saying then that the Goldsteins' collection at Chateau d'Anez comes under this umbrella? The state will protect it. That is good news." She sat back in her seat, a slow smile spreading across her face. "Why, that's marvelous." Her idea had been that the Goldsteins' collection that was already at the chateau could rest alongside those of the Louvre and that she would take care of it, but if the Musées Nationaux were officially going to look after Jewish collections, that left things in a much better light.

But Sandrine's gray eyes held traces of anxiety. She sighed and tented her hands together. "It is the urgency that worries me."

Charlotte waited.

Sandrine continued, her voice low, determined, and strong. "Charlotte, you *must* pack Anita's collection today, and prepare for its removal to Chambord."

Charlotte stilled, her body frozen, her eyes sweeping around the gallery that had been Anita's life work.

"From Chambord," Sandrine went on, "the Louvre will transport the pieces of Anita's that you wish to keep to Chateau d'Anez, where they will be guarded along with a collection of fourteenth- and fifteenth-century paintings from the Louvre. I know this is a shock, but the threat is very real."

Charlotte gazed around the gallery. The paintings for her next exhibition were all beautifully hung, ready for one of Anita's long-term artists to show to the collectors she'd invited for the opening show later this week. Upstairs, Anita's walls were lined with those works she'd loved, kept, treasured. Her paintings still sat, stacked against the hallway walls. Above Anita's bed, Charlotte had placed Sandro Luciano's striking portrait. Taking it away would mean abandoning Anita's dreams, her home, everything she'd fought so hard for during her career. How could Charlotte do such a thing?

She shook her head. "The Nazis cannot touch a gallery run by an American. I am neutral. They will respect that if they really do come..." Her words faded into the quiet room.

Sandrine's expression grew more serious. "They will view you as a collaborator. A collaborator with the Jews."

Charlotte stood up. She went across to the window overlooking Rue Laffitte. She'd promised Anita that after any war was done, they'd meet again at Sacré-Cœur. The Sacred Heart of Paris. How could anyone wish to destroy that?

She whipped back around to face her mother's friend.

But Sandrine leaned against Charlotte's desk, her pale fingers interlaced tightly, her expression pinched. "I was your age when we faced the threat of the last war. Very quickly, it became a reality."

Charlotte covered her mouth with her hands.

"Anita's paintings will have to be packed by midnight, at which time I shall arrive with a truck and a driver to load them

for removal, and then you must drive to the Loire Valley yourself. Take Olivier's car."

Charlotte stood there, poleaxed. She'd never feared danger.
And this felt like running away.

"And one more thing. Please. Remove the sign outside the
gallery. Remove all traces of identification belonging to Anita.
Pack as much as you can into the car. Destroy the rest. And,
darling, choose the pieces from her collection that you could not
bear to part with..."

Charlotte took in a ragged breath.

"Choose the pieces that you will want to see hanging here
once again, when you return to Paris, after this..." Sandrine
sighed. "After this atrocity is finished with."

Charlotte swallowed, bile sticking in her throat. She cast
her eyes about the dear, familiar gallery. Her heart was
thumping hard against her breast in the smart working dress she
wore, the reality that Sandrine had imparted rendering the
bodice impossibly tight. She was constricted, a young woman
who'd only known peace and opportunities in her lifetime,
thrust into the reality of war. Charlotte gasped. She stumbled
across the floor, only to slump back down at Anita's desk, her
head in her hands.

"If you are still harboring any doubts that this gallery will be
targeted," Sandrine continued, "just remember that Hitler
declared that the outbreak of war would mean the end of
European Jews."

Charlotte nodded. The reality was hitting her now. Tears,
dreadful, heated tears, slid down her cheeks. She'd let Anita
down. She'd not managed to save her business at all!

"The worst mistake we can make would be to underesti-
mate the Nazis. And I'm not willing to take that risk with any
daughter of my dearest friend."

Charlotte took in a shuddering breath. The Great War had

been her mother's war. Sandrine's war. Anita's war. This was going to be her war.

Yesterday, she'd walked past the Louvre and seen a watch-tower in place atop the roof of the Salon Carré, the room next to the Grand Galerie's eastern end. Atop it, two firemen were already keeping watch. She'd walked on by, still denying that things could possibly change. Still denying that Paris would ever be vulnerable. Even yesterday, she'd refused to contemplate the idea that the French government might not be able to cope with a German advance toward the capital.

But there'd been workers digging trenches in the Tuileries Gardens for the outdoor sculptures the last few days, while others piled sandbags in front of the windows of the Louvre. In the newspapers, it was said that every department in the Louvre had installed portable electric lamps, gas masks and pharmacy supplies in case of an enemy attack while they were preparing the collections for removal.

Charlotte exhaled. She sat at her desk and steeled herself. "Forgive me, Sandrine. I had to process the loss of Anita's home."

"There is no need to apologize," Sandrine murmured. "Darling..."

But Charlotte stood up and moved back toward the window. "I thought I would stand firm in Paris, but, reluctantly, I can see that doing so would place everything Anita loved at too great a risk."

"Yes."

Charlotte turned around to face her mother's friend. "But, Sandrine, I will *not* shy away from any danger that the Nazis might throw toward the Jewish family who have become my family." She pressed her hand against her heart. "I will do everything I can to protect their legacy, so that they have a home to return to in France. *When,* not if, this is all over."

Sandrine spoke quickly. "At the chateau, you must hide

everything. Pack the Goldsteins' entire collection away and store Élise and Olivier's beloved pieces amongst the items from the Louvre that will arrive as planned from Chambord. Especially, you must hide Anita's collection of modern art."

Charlotte nodded.

"Hitler hates modern art, but his officers will steal anything if it is Jewish. They will simply take all of this," Sandrine waved her hand in the air, "and they will deride it."

Charlotte folded her arms, which were shaking, but she held Sandrine's gaze.

"Hitler is looking to amass a private collection from the stores of Europe as he conquers each country. The cache from France will be one of his greatest prizes."

Charlotte grimaced.

"The curators of the Louvre are taking more than four thousand objects from the Louvre alone to Chambord. Then there are the other important public museums of France. The Louvre has hired professional packers as well as many volunteers to help."

Charlotte balled her fist against her mouth. She would pack Olivier's car in the cover of darkness, bring it around to the front of the building and load it up. "I shall place the pieces of Anita's collection that can go with the Louvre vehicles by the front door, and I shall be ready for you this evening."

Sandrine's eyes misted.

Charlotte gritted her teeth. "I swear it. None of the things the Goldsteins hold dear will end up in Germany."

Sandrine moved to the door. "I must return to the Louvre as I am required to help pack." She paused. "I am proud of you." Her lips curved in a sad smile. "I expected nothing less."

Charlotte winced at the sound of Sandrine softly clicking the green front door of Galerie A. Goldstein closed.

. . .

When there was a quiet knock at the door in the early hours of the morning, Charlotte slipped across the gallery to let her visitors in, the walls seeming to echo with reproach toward her in the gray gloom, crying out against the absence of the beautiful modern paintings that Charlotte had taken down, removing them as soon as darkness fell over Paris, so that she could legitimately close the shutters that looked out over Rue Laffitte.

Working carefully and quickly, her hands shaking throughout, Charlotte had packed up each work with the fire-resistant paper that Sandrine had delivered from the Louvre, then in leatherette to resist the humidity of France's hot summer, labeling the works A.G., for Anita Goldstein as she'd been instructed by Sandrine. She'd placed a number on each item, which she recorded in a corresponding logbook that she would keep on her person while she traveled out of Paris.

When the streets were finally quiet after midnight, Charlotte had undertaken one of the most devastating tasks of the evening. She'd slipped outside, a pot of paint in her hand, and she'd carefully painted over the sign that hung outside the window, her heart breaking as she concealed Anita's beloved words, Galerie A. Goldstein. She'd had to force herself to do this, reminding herself that she was protecting Anita's legacy as she'd promised. It was impossible not to remember it all, to hear Anita stepping through the front door, the sign shining in the sun, or draped in snow, heralding the warm, welcoming space inside, which had been a haven to so many artists, collectors and lovers of beautiful art. This gallery had been as much a part of the Goldstein family as Anita, Élise, and Olivier themselves.

Charlotte moved toward the door that led out to Rue Laffitte, opening it just wide enough to afford entry to Sandrine, still working after she'd been volunteering at the Louvre since she left Charlotte this morning, assisting the hundreds of professional packers, movers, and woodworkers as well as the dedicated volunteers who were carefully placing the great collections into thousands of numbered crates for removal to Chambord.

Instinctively, Charlotte leaned forward, kissing Sandrine on the cheek, as if that one Parisian gesture would lend some sense of normalcy to a situation that still seemed unthinkable and unreal.

Charlotte stood tall when Sandrine introduced her to the man standing next to her, a loyal Louvre volunteer, and eyed the open-backed truck. She moved across the room, indicating silently toward the stack of paintings, wrapped and labeled, leaning neatly against a wall. As if on cue, the man began collecting them.

"Godspeed," Charlotte whispered. She almost reached up to cross herself as the volunteer picked up the package that she knew held Sandro Luciana's portrait of Anita. The number on Sandro's work would have to remain engraved upon her heart until it passed safely through the way station at Chambord and was delivered to Chateau d'Anez along with the other items from the Louvre that were destined for the Goldsteins' country home. After that, Charlotte swore, she would not let it out of her sight.

"You have your book of business somewhere safe and accessible?" Sandrine whispered while the man loaded the cherished portrait into the truck.

Charlotte nodded. "But of course," she said.

Sandrine laid a hand on her arm.

Charlotte's eyes locked on the man through the open back of the truck as he lay the wrapped portrait of Anita carefully on its side. Sandrine had told her that the Louvre had trained each volunteer and packer meticulously, with a great emphasis on not ever placing a painting on the ground, lest someone should tread on it while all the packing was being carried out.

Charlotte's heart hammered. Olivier's car was ready to go,

next to the truck, filled with photographs, Anita's favorite books and the little ornaments from her dressing table.

Charlotte had stood, staring at Anita's wardrobe, her striking clothes still hanging there, before closing it silently. There were some things she could not take. But leaving Anita's clothes alone here felt like another nail in the coffin that was saying goodbye.

Charlotte stood with her heart in her mouth while the man placed a yellow sticker on the package that contained the portrait of Anita. That color, Charlotte knew, meant that, in accordance with the Louvre's system of priority, Anita's portrait was lowest down the scale. Sandrine had explained how there were three colors in use: yellow for valuable works, green for major works and red for world treasures. Sandrine had heard that the Mona Lisa, the Louvre's most valued treasure, was marked with three red stickers.

While to Charlotte and Anita, Luciano's portrait was worth a red sticker, Charlotte would think of all those other works of art, cherished by families and created by artists, which would not even be granted a yellow circle and would possibly be lost forever.

When the gentleman was done with the paintings that Charlotte had carefully packed for the Louvre, Sandrine turned to her. "If it makes you feel more confident, the system for transport has been in place for months, and in development for years. In the triage areas, the air is ringing with the sounds of typists furiously creating five copies of lists for the contents of each crate."

Charlotte nodded, unable to speak as the volunteer climbed into the front seat of the open-backed truck.

"Each crate only bears the initials, MN, for Musée Nationaux, and the number of each crate to discourage theft," Sandrine explained, her gaze moving to Charlotte's obscure labeling of Anita's largest works and nodding in approval. "And the shipping labels only say Chambord, to keep unauthorized people from knowing each item's ongoing destination. You followed my instructions to a T when it came to labeling and wrapping. Everything will be fine." But a shadow passed over Sandrine's features.

The reality of the situation hit as the driver turned over the engine on the truck. Charlotte covered her mouth, her breath shaking.

Silently, Sandrine hugged Charlotte one last time. "You will leave soon?" she asked, her eyes searching Charlotte's face.

Charlotte nodded, her heart threading itself into knots. Olivier's Hotchkiss Coupé sat right in front of her. How could she bear to climb inside and say goodbye?

Sandrine pressed a small notebook into Charlotte's hands.

Charlotte frowned, turning the book over in the dark.

"Charlotte," Sandrine said, almost mouthing her words, pressing her hand over Charlotte's fingers, "here you have a list of my business contacts for Celine, those customers who are interested in fine things in the Loire Valley. Word is, the art market will not fall flat." Sandrine turned toward the truck.

"*Sandrine?*" Charlotte called in a hoarse whisper.

Her mother's friend turned to face her, wiping a hand through a stray tendril of blond hair.

"If things become dangerous in Paris," Charlotte whispered, "You must come down to Chateau d'Anez. You will always have a bed there. A home." Charlotte swallowed. She knew she would be sharing the chateau with curators and guards, on the lookout to protect the famous works stored in the great house, but if there was one tradition of Élise's that she would continue, it would be hospitality. She would ensure that friends remained welcome at the chateau.

Sandrine nodded in the muted darkness. Then, in an almost imperceptible movement, she turned and climbed into the passenger seat of the truck. The sound of the engine rumbling to life rent the quiet street, and Charlotte turned back to Anita's depleted gallery, stepping inside, and gathering up her final belongings before resting her hand against the door. Then, holding back a sob that threatened to spill up through her chest, she pulled Anita's green door closed, and turned away for one last time.

10

NEW YORK, SPRING 1939

Martha

Martha stood next to librarian Anne Caroll Moore in the Children's Room. A small group of the New York Library's youngest members were mesmerized at the sound of Élise Goldstein reading aloud. Élise moved through the pages of Ludwig Bemelmans' splendid new book, *Madeline*, her French accent captivating her small audience, their little faces gazing up at her in rapture.

Martha turned to Anne, who had single-handedly advocated welcoming children into the library by giving them their own room with specially trained staff way back in 1906. Now, the elderly woman sat with a smile of satisfaction as Élise delighted her young audience.

"Mrs. Goldstein is wonderful," Anne said. "I loathe the circumstances under which she had to come to New York, but I am most grateful for her presence here."

Élise was carefully holding *Madeline* so that her audience could have the perfect view of the illustrations in the book.

Martha smiled. Given what Élise had been through in the

past months, Martha was more than relieved to see Anita's mother losing herself in the children's enraptured gaze. Élise had been understandably lost when she'd first come to Manhattan. Wandering around Papa's apartment, picking up objects wistfully, then turning them over and examining them like the true connoisseur that she was. The elderly woman would then place them down and sigh, her brow furrowed with worry about what was going on in France.

As an antidote to this, if there was one, Martha had encouraged Anita's parents to be tourists in New York. She'd accompanied them on her days off to Central Park, Brooklyn and the Metropolitan Museum of Art, but these expeditions had only reminded them of all they'd left behind, of the artistic life in France that they'd built up over decades together. They'd all returned home to Fifth Avenue, Élise and Olivier trying to be polite before making their excuses and retiring to their room as soon as dinner was done each evening. From there, Martha could hear their soft whisperings and the odd heightened argument about how they were to manage in New York.

But what was most moving was the way the Goldsteins sometimes sat down of an evening on one of the leather sofas in the apartment's library with its paneled walls full of Martha and Laurence's extensive collection of books. Olivier would be closed off in the pages of a book, but Élise's face would work through a range of emotions while she contemplated all that was happening in her beloved France. Martha had taken to sitting at Élise's feet, while Élise read out loud during the long, cold winter's nights, accompanied by a roaring fire. Martha had gently invited Élise in to read to the children in the library, and while it had taken her some persuading, she was delighted that Élise had come today.

"Martha," Anne went on, "why don't we employ Mrs. Goldstein?"

Martha started. "Employ her?"

"Mrs. Goldstein doesn't have to put up with being a volunteer and I suspect she has so much more to offer," Anne said. "I think she may bring many more children into the library, and, in the coming months, that will bring more joy to this place than any of us can hope to imagine." Anne lowered her gaze. She shook her head, reaching into her pocket for her handkerchief and wiping her eyes.

Martha grimaced. She wrapped her arms around her body. Hitler had invaded Poland two days ago. Great Britain and France were waiting for a favorable response to their demands to Hitler that he retreat. No one held out any hope for this. It was only a matter of time before Nazi troops advanced further. Martha had lain awake the previous nights, praying and yearning for peace. She and Papa had sent telegrams to Chateau d'Anez where Charlotte was based. They had not had a reply and had been wandering around at home like a pair of worried ghosts. The not knowing and the sense of anticipation for the announcement they all dreaded festered like a boil that needed to be lanced. Yet, if the not knowing was unbearable, Martha hated to think how an announcement might feel.

This morning, people on the trains and streets of Manhattan had been unusually hushed. Martha had noticed passengers of the older generations staring helplessly at young men in the carriages, talking behind their hands and shaking their heads.

Don't, Martha had wanted to shout. She'd looked down, burying her head in her book, furiously fighting to escape.

For the first time in her life, it hadn't worked.

For the first time in her life, Martha had not been able to find solace in the pages of a book.

Her gaze flickered at a movement by the door. There, Olivier stood, his hat in his hand, and his face ashen. Martha started, instinctively battling the urge to rush across the room to him, fear snaking in her belly and brewing until it was almost unbearable. She clutched her stomach. Her breaths caught and hitched. She stood up, pushing back her chair, mercifully clutching it before it clattered to the floor. Righting this, she swept across the room to Olivier.

It had happened. All she had to do was look at his face.

Olivier sank down into one of the comfortable chairs that were dotted about the room. He sat, bowed, with his head in his hands, his gnarled old fingers pressing into his temples, and his bowler hat resting on his knees.

"Olivier." Martha's heart went out to the old man, a man who was sitting here, on the other side of the ocean, while his extended family, friends, countrymen and his cherished home faced desecration through no fault of his own.

She closed her eyes, fighting the images that wanted to crowd there. It was the images of suitcases that affected her most, of children placing their hands in those of their parents, trusting them and walking by their sides, while overhead, bombers circled in the azure skies over Europe. Children, just like these in this very library, who had been unlucky enough to be born in the wrong place at the wrong time.

Young men, dying in trenches and falling out of the sky from airplanes, every day.

Air-raid sirens wailing over the old cities and towns of Europe.

Ships sinking.

The stench of death.

Slowly, Olivier raised his face. Martha grabbed his hand, and her heart broke at the way his eyes were bloodshot, his cheeks sunken and hollow. Martha shuddered violently. When he shook his head, Martha slumped down next to him, staring incredulously at the children whose little faces were turned to darling Élise, to a woman who had lost her own daughter but who was here, reading stories to the next generation.

Tears streamed down Olivier's cheeks freely now, while he

watched his wife reading to the children, when he'd lost his own, and then, the room rang with a chorus of laughter at *Madeline.*

Little voices, the sound of them soaring up to the very vaults of the library and echoing through the room. The next generation. What of them. Did the Nazis not have children too?

Martha clutched Olivier's cold fingers, until Élise completed the book and turned around toward her husband, as if, instinctively, she knew he was in the room.

As if, instinctively, she knew exactly why he was here.

Martha sat, unable to move, her body turned to stone and her stomach leaden while Élise made her way past the children who were looking at books with their parents, nodding at the people who wanted to thank her, moving straight toward Olivier, her husband, the man with whom she'd survived the last war.

Quietly, like a spaniel with a broken spirit, Olivier allowed his wife to lead him away from the crowded room. Martha, hearing the ripples of conversation and growing sounds of alarm at the news that the world was now at war, took the elderly couple to the small office she shared with several other librarians, and, closing the glass door, she helped Olivier, his face still pale as a sheet, into a chair and went to pour him a glass of water.

"M*on amour*," Élise whispered, her hand shaking as she stroked Olivier's own fingers. "We shall never forget this day."

Martha stood with her head bowed.

Élise touched her throat with her free hand. She squeezed her eyes shut. "Our darling Charlotte," she whispered. "My friends! No one else we knew could get out. Germany, oh Germany what are you going through? My home in France..." She grabbed onto the table and sank into a chair.

Martha leaned against the long table, her hands pressing into the impenetrable wood.

Olivier's dark eyes clouded. "So. Here we are again."

Ridiculously, Martha fought back a bark of laughter.

Olivier's lips were pale. He moved them as if to utter words, then shook his head, and placed his hands on the table, his fingers tightly curled into a fist against his palm. "We should never have come to America and left Charlotte alone in Paris."

"I asked her to stay." Élise's distressed eyes roamed the room. "I asked her to take care of our home."

"Élise," Martha said, her tone firm. "Charlotte is the bravest person I know." Martha went on, searching for and finding the only words that could possibly alleviate some of the pain in this room. "I tried," she said, "to convince Charlotte to come home. Whether you or someone else had asked her to stay in France, she would have remained. You must not, you cannot, blame yourselves." But Martha's hands shook. The only person she had to blame was herself.

Martha turned away. France would be one of Hitler's biggest prizes. Everyone knew that once he'd swept through Poland, he'd push straight on toward France. What would it take? A few months? Weeks? What would Chateau d'Anez look like, what would Paris look like, under Nazi rule?

The soft murmurings of Élise and Olivier trying to comfort each other faded into the background.

Martha pushed her chair back, assailed with worry for Papa. She needed to run home, to settle him. He would be beside himself. Shock would reverberate through them all at its own pace, in its own way. But nobody should have to deal with it alone.

Martha reached for her handbag, her jacket. Outside the window, on the opposite sidewalk, the queue at the newsvendor ran around the corner. People lined up, their heads bowed. The hope of a resolution with Hitler had been dealt a final blow.

Turning away from the window, Martha reached for the pocket of her skirt, her fingers curling around two envelopes that she kept like mantras on her person always. One, addressed to her in straight up-and-down masculine writing; the other, in Charlotte's loopy forward-sloping script was all about her love of working in Anita's gallery, about how proud she was that she'd gradually brought in new clientele. Martha's two beloved courageous souls.

Clyde's letter told how the Gordon Highlanders, men from Aberdeen in the northeast of Scotland, were toughened fighters who would not be daunted. He predicted that the Gordon Highlanders would be one of the first regiments to leave for France, should that country be drawn into war. He'd said the battalion's war cry was "You're nae a soldier if you're nae a Gordon."

Now, Clyde's bold words sank like lead to the bottom of Martha's heart.

Martha sat at the empty dining-room table that evening, her notepaper spread out in front of her in the fading light. She hadn't turned the lights on. It seemed wrong to bathe the room in warmth. Papa had refused dinner tonight. He and Olivier were shut away in Papa's study with the door closed. She scanned Clyde's last letter to her. Who knew what havoc war would play on the mail? From now on, Martha knew she'd only received sketchy details from him. He would not be allowed to write of how he truly felt, what he was seeing, experiencing, nor about the dangers he would face.

She picked up her pen. What to write now, on the eve of the announcement that had changed the course of his life? What to write to Clyde when his last letter to her had been so typically joyous? It was impossible to imagine him...

Martha forced herself to stop her train of worrisome thoughts. She reached for his latest letter to her instead.

Edinburgh, August 1939

Dearest Martha,

I am afraid I've battled to find a private space in this house where I can write to you! Kirsty has been following me about for the last half-hour, refusing to accept the fact that the letters that arrive from America are from Thomas A. Moore, as you address them, as much as I insist that is the truth.

I know we agreed we'd keep our letters private, between ourselves, so as not to upset your father. I do understand that and the last thing I want to do is cause him any distress at the thought of you writing to some fellow across the Atlantic, who admires you so very much and hopes to meet your papa one day. At the very least, I can convince him I'm a decent chap who wishes only wonderful things for his beloved daughter, but I hope he is not as insistent in knowing your business as my sisters are, or our secret, as we call it, shall be out before we know it, Thomas!

Kirsty and Bonnie, whom I hope you shall meet in the not-too-distant future, when all this infernal war talk is done and Hitler is back where he belongs, well out of politics and away from the German people, have both been successful in convincing our parents to allow them to train as nurses. They will be starting next week.

I am, I must admit, very proud of them both, but I think that Kirsty would possibly make a better spy than a nurse! I told her so, and she thought this was a great joke. I believe at this moment; she is discussing the option with our parents. Honestly, they are so vague, I expect they'll tell her to go and train in espionage!

I shall be finishing my work in the hospital soon. I will be going to the north of Scotland for further training, just as I thought. I'll continue to write to you, but I shall be limited by the rules of what I can include in my letters, alas, Martha. But please know, when we meet again, and when this is all over, I shall tell you as much as I want you to know, and as much as won't cause you any concern.

Martha laid the letter down. Dear man. *As much as wouldn't cause her any concern.*

In the meantime, our household is its mad, active, noisy self. I'm not sure how Mother and Father will manage without all the laughter and the uproar around them. The kitchen will be very quiet, and I think the dogs will get far more time to sleep!

Anyway, it will be good to get out in the fresh country air and to be doing something more concrete toward helping. All we have going on here in Edinburgh, apart from the obvious tomes about the German leader, are warnings about air-raid precautions, light-excluding fabrics for curtains, and sandbags.

We are trying to get our parents organized, but they hardly take any of this seriously, so I'm afraid I'm going to have to insist.

I hope things are far more sensible in America, and I also hope that you are managing to enjoy yourself. Please do. For both of us. I can't wait to see you to show you my home, my country, my heart, and I'm going to be optimistic and hope that it may be soon.

My dearest wishes and love,

Clyde

Later that evening, Martha tossed and turned. She lay awake until the early hours, worrying about the anguish Papa would feel if she were to tell him how she wanted to go to Edinburgh, that her relationship with a man on the other side of the ocean could be something real. But how could she leave her father, when he'd not coped with the loss of Chloé and was now worrying so much about Charlotte? How could Martha leave, knowing that she'd break his heart? What was more, she'd miss Papa and the peaceful life that she'd shared with him. But if she didn't follow her feelings through for Clyde, was she ruining her chances of happiness?

She either let down Papa, or herself.

The dining-room door opened, and hastily, Martha shuffled the letter away in the pages of a book.

Élise appeared, turning on the lights. She shook her head, a frown line appearing between her eyes. "Your father and my husband are both poring over maps of Europe and trying to make a logical argument for Hitler *not* reaching the Loire Valley. Martha, I feel useless." The older woman sighed. "I..." She shook her head, opening her mouth and then closing it, as if she were battling whether to raise something or not.

"Élise?" Martha reached for her wrap, throwing it over her shoulders.

Élise paced about the dining room, lifting silver objects, putting them back down again and gazing at a portrait of Martha and Charlotte's grandmother, her brows knitting. She heaved out a loud sigh.

"The news is distressing. Papa tells me not to read the papers continually, to turn off the wireless and walk in the park if it is too upsetting," Martha said. But she grimaced, knowing that to do this would be impossible. Charlotte's life was at stake.

Élise came to an abrupt stop, taking up a position by the window, where she peered out at Central Park. "I... Can we talk in the kitchen? Please, Martha," she said, almost stumbling for words.

Martha nodded. Carefully, she picked up the book that held

her letters, and tucked it under her arm. She frowned at the floor, following Élise out into the hallway, hating the fact she was writing to Clyde without Papa's knowledge. Goodness knew, they'd never held secrets from each other. She felt pierced with guilt that she was concealing her correspondence.

She followed Élise down the hallway, her heart melting at the sight in front of her eyes when they came to the kitchen. There was a checked tablecloth on the vast kitchen table, and a bunch of daisies sitting in a vase. Élise had set out two sparkling wine glasses and a bottle of chilled white wine. And on two white plates sat two perfect salads of crisp green lettuce, summer tomatoes and chicken that was cooked until it was golden and crisp, along with a basket of baguettes that Élise had procured from a French bakery in the Upper East Side.

"How lovely food can cheer up the gravest of days," Martha murmured, taking a seat.

She watched Élise, who bustled around to pull out a chair, sitting down and shaking her head, her hands folded firmly on the tablecloth. Martha bit on her lip. She hated to think of Élise suffering about something in silence. She'd been through so much already.

"Darling," Élise said, her voice low and sure, "you know, you *must* know that there are thousands of Jewish refugees, applicants in Europe, who are waiting for visas to get into America. You must be aware as to how hard it is to get into this country and how things have gotten worse this year." She lowered her head. "Olivier and I were only fortunate because, I fear, we are wealthy and have the means to support ourselves here. Were I to have applied on my own, it would have been a different matter entirely."

Martha was quiet. In June, she'd read, with her heart in her mouth, how the *St. Louis*, an ocean liner filled with Jewish refugees, had been turned away from the port of Miami, forcing its return to Europe. The newspapers had shouted that the argument for this was that *all* foreigners were suspect, and that Jews must not be considered immune.

Élise spoke softly. "I have a dear Viennese friend about whom I am increasingly worried." She wiped a hand across her cheek, turning away from her food, her chin wobbling.

Martha reached across the table. "You should have told us. Papa and me. Please, don't keep such things to yourself."

Élise's chest rose and fell. "You have done so much for us already. How could Olivier and I trespass anymore?" Her dark eyes were serious. "And as for what Charlotte is risking..." She stared down at her food. "Please, I am sorry."

Martha sighed. "You must talk to me. Please. I know the burden of holding things in." Her last words came out soft.

Élise's head whipped up, and for one moment, their eyes locked in understanding.

"Very well," Élise whispered.

Martha waited.

Élise spoke in low tones. "My dear friend Gisela lost her job and everything she'd worked for when she was stood down by the Nazis because she is Jewish, and then, knowing that staying in Vienna would be impossible, she fled to Paris."

Martha sighed.

Élise ran a hand through her hair. She went over to the kitchen dresser and pulled out a ream of papers, sitting back down and placing these on the checked tablecloth.

Martha stared at the papers that Élise spread out before her. Élise had a copy of the Immigration Act. Martha couldn't help it, she chuckled softly and leaned closer to the enterprising older woman sitting opposite her. "I am not even going to ask where you managed to get your hands on this."

Élise pulled out a pair of reading glasses from the pocket of her skirt. "Gisela Weber is the daughter of one of my oldest childhood friends, who sadly died when Gisela was young."

"Oh, I'm sorry."

Élise looked up. "Gisela is an incredibly intelligent woman. I have been—how do you say it?—a second mother to her since she was fourteen years old."

"Then she was incredibly fortunate," Martha said. "Her loss was supplanted by a very real gain." She closed her eyes. Two other little girls had benefited so very much from their association with the Goldstein family. She returned her attention to Élise.

"Gisela is now stranded in the South of France. She is there with friends. But now, I worry that she will not be safe there either. I know that the British are being told to evacuate France." Élise took in a breath, as if trying to struggle to control her own emotions. "She is fifty-three years old and has been, for many years, one of the most revered professors at the University of Vienna in their mathematical department."

Martha covered her mouth, nodding. Being blistered with photographs in the newspapers did not convey the reality that each person living in the shadow of war had a life, dreams, ambitions, careers, and families just like anyone else.

"Surely, I thought, one of the universities here would want Gisela," Élise went on, sadly. "One of the women's colleges. I asked myself, how could they turn such an inspirational person down? But to emigrate as a woman is difficult. And to come here as a Jewish woman?" Élise shook her head. "It is impossible."

Martha offered Élise the baguettes.

"Please, help yourself." Élise held up a hand. "Outside the small quota of people America are letting in each year, there is an allowance for academics, scientists, professionals."

"And Gisela has tried this?"

Élise eyed Martha. "Gisela would have to have employment lined up in the United States for the coming two years to even be considered." Her voice shook when she continued. "Offers for these places for emigration to America are for professional *men*, and their dependent wives and children. Look, it is in the Act!" Élise pushed the papers, covered with tiny print, across the table.

Martha scanned the relevant section. And there it was—the Act provided for a small quota of researchers and professors, along with their *wives*.

"I want to get her here," Élise said, her voice ringing through the quiet room. "I want to fight to give Gisela a chance. Because if we cannot help her..." Élise looked sideways, her mouth working. "I fear that it may be the difference between her being alive in the coming years, or dead."

Martha swallowed. "Surely it is not that bad," she whispered, wishing she were right. The Nazis were not killing Jews in Germany or the occupied territories.

Yet.

Martha glanced down at the pages in front of her. "Élise, the cut-off age for these special visas outside the quota is fifty-five years old. I—"

Élise placed her knife and fork down on her empty plate. And then, she tilted her head to one side, "Martha, there is room for more than one heroine in every family. You don't have to leave it all to Charlotte, you know."

Martha reddened. She stared at her hands.

Élise stood up. She moved across the kitchen, pulling a chocolate babka, the dough braided and filled with melted chocolate, out of the pantry.

"I think," Élise said, sitting down to the table, and offering the sumptuous cake to Martha, "I think it's time we found out what Martha can do." The elderly woman tilted her head to one side. "Adversity, I always told Anita, is only an opportunity to bring out your best."

Martha's brows drew closer. "The circumstances alone are so very against this..." She cast about hopelessly. "Maybe, if Charlotte were here—"

"Stop it," Élise said.

Martha jolted at the older woman's tone.

"Are you willing to help me fight to get a woman whom I love like family away from the Nazis?"

Martha stood up, pushing her chair back, moving to stare out the window at the still, silent treetops outside. She looked down at Fifth Avenue below. Cars whizzed, toylike, up and down the wide street. Tiny. Insignificant. Martha shook her head at the sight of New York rolling along while Europe was about to burn in flames. Slowly, she turned around to face Élise. The smile she sent the older woman was tight. "I have no idea how I could make any difference, or what I could do to bring her here. You have said yourself that it seems impossible."

Élise opened her mouth. But Martha felt a quiver in her stomach. She closed her eyes. And right then, she imagined Charlotte standing here, hands on her hips, dark eyes flashing.

She opened her eyes again. Élise was sitting there. Depending on her. Willing her to help. And the fact was, Charlotte was not here. She, Martha was.

Martha studied the floor. After what seemed an age, she raised her head, her eyes clashing with Élise's. "Élise, for the sake of your friend, I'll help in whatever small way I can."

Élise reached out, her eyes misting over. "Come and sit with me, darling," she whispered. "We shall plan. And between us, two women at a kitchen table, we shall see what we can do."

Martha wheeled over to the table, and her appetite swelling as it had not done in months, she eyed the delicious-looking cake. With a firm movement, she took in a deep breath, reached forward and helped herself to a generous slice.

11

CHATEAU D'ANEZ, SPRING 1940

Charlotte

Charlotte sat in Élise's small sitting room in the chateau. Outside, the garden sat serene in the warm evening, long shadows casting across the lawns from the linden trees as if nothing were wrong at all. If Charlotte closed her eyes, she could almost hear the lost sounds of guests chatting on the terrace, glass tinkling, men making witty jokes and girls in fabulous dresses laughing as the sun went down over the Loire Valley.

Now, the only talk that rang through the grand rooms downstairs was of Hitler. Everyone stationed at Élise and Olivier's home worried about Hitler's next move like dogs at a bone. All the time Charlotte had been here, she'd taken to sitting upstairs in Élise's small salon of an evening, preferring the sense of intimacy that it offered, with its pretty curtains sprigged with tiny blue flowers on a white background, matching wallpaper in the French style, and soft rugs underfoot to the vast, empty formal rooms with their furniture shrouded in white cloths and the paintings that had been taken out of the Louvre leaning against the walls. Some items were stored in the basements, and still others were in the old orangery that Élise had restored into a summer house.

Charlotte and her fellow occupants, the head guard and his family, several guards housed in the outbuildings, and the curators, a couple from the South of France who both worked at the Louvre, had settled into their new existence in the orderly manner that had been prescribed to them under the long-standing plans, the guards growing vegetables and raising chickens when they were not on watch, along with the addition of guard dogs in case attackers tried to enter the chateau from the surrounding woods.

Charlotte and the curators, Lucie and Armand, enjoyed a quiet existence watching over the fourteenth- and fifteenth-century paintings they'd been entrusted with. They'd cooked together in Élise's vast basement kitchen, almost lulling themselves into thinking that while France had declared war, nothing may eventuate.

Hitler had postponed his plans to immediately attack France months ago, back in September of the previous year. He'd delayed his offensive again and again, and throughout the last fall and winter, he'd undertaken very little when it came to military activity.

Charlotte sipped at the cup of coffee she'd brought to enjoy in privacy up here. She was becoming used to labels being thrown around the chateau. The U.S. and Great Britain were referring to this as the "phony war." The young French guards were scoffing at Hitler, and constantly alluding to the "drole de guerre." Charlotte went to turn on the wireless. She curled up on Élise's comfortable sofa as the sun sank down below the horizon, her shoes lying on the floor. And as the announcer's voice spelt out the news that they'd all begun to think was impossible, Charlotte paled, and for quite some time, she sat and stared at the glorious colors in the sky.

Armand often railed about the weakness of the Maginot Line, but when he did so, his wife, Lucie, would leave the room, shaking her head and refusing to acknowledge that France was not properly protected from a Nazi invasion. But then, Armand would turn his frown toward Charlotte, insisting that even with the concrete fortifications, tunnels and defenses along the French–German border, the Maginot Line had *not* been extended along the French–Belgian border, because Belgium was a neutral country. So, he said, how could it possibly protect France?

Charlotte's coffee turned cold, and her hands froze as the news continued, playing out the worst fears that had preyed on everyone's minds: Hitler's armies had made it into France. The Maginot Line, the announcer said in crisp, clear tones, had proven worthless. The Germans had swung around the Maginot Line into Belgium, before moving straight through the Ardennes Forest into France.

Charlotte turned slowly, as if unable to take her eyes away from the mild-looking wooden wireless that was changing their lives as she sat, when she sensed Lucie at the door.

"Charlotte?" Lucie ran a hand through her red-gold curls, a flush spreading down from her cheeks to her pale decolletage. Lucie paced across the room to the window, blocking Charlotte's view. "Armand says it is the beginning of the end for the defense of France," Lucie murmured. "The road to Paris is unprotected."

Charlotte sat up suddenly, only just remembering to place her cooling coffee cup down before she spilled the cooling brown liquid all over her lap.

Sandrine.

Charlotte spoke with her mother's oldest friend at least once a week. Sandrine's carefully curated, kindly given list of business contacts in the Loire Valley had been a real asset when it came to continuing to maintain Anita's gallery and sales.

Charlotte had managed to sell a good selection of the works done by the young artists she was still trying to advocate for in Paris. Refusing to let them down, she had simply packed up and run everything from Chateau d'Anez.

But now what? She glanced around at the contents of Élise's lovingly decorated room. What did the Louvre have planned next? Were they to remain here, with only a few guards? If the Nazis had come into France, what was the government going to do to protect its citizens from attack? Their homes, livelihoods?

How would Sandrine survive?

"The government are saying that they cannot guarantee our security, nor that of the French government itself," Lucie went on.

"It is unthinkable." Charlotte stood up. She took in a deep breath. She must stay calm. Prioritize. And when it came to the things that needed protecting, she would never, ever accept this lying down.

Charlotte paced around the room, the sound of Lucie's soft voice barely registering. First, there was Sandrine. Paris was in the firing line and Chateau d'Anez, for what it was worth, did have some protection, even if it was from loosely trained guards and dogs.

Charlotte must convince Sandrine to leave Paris. Sandrine must pack up Celine and move to the safety of the chateau. There was no question of this.

Charlotte stared out the window, not seeing, for once, the empty gardens, only seeing what threatened to eventuate in Paris.

She would drive Olivier's car to the capital and pick up her friend. Like she had done, Sandrine would have to choose what to bring, what to leave, and prepare to be able to flee with the minimum of burden to her person.

Charlotte turned to face Lucie and opened her mouth to

articulate her plans. But then, all at once, Armand appeared at the door to Élise's dear little room, his dark hair flicked back from his high forehead, his old-fashioned blousy artist's shirt hanging over his cream trousers, and his blue eyes ablaze.

"There is a bonfire in the courtyard of the Ministry of Foreign Affairs in Paris. The government of France are throwing their archives out the window and burning them in expectation that the Nazis will take Paris."

Lucie went to stand with her husband. She crossed herself.

Charlotte nodded, swallowing down the bile that wanted to rise in her throat. She curled her lip. Very well. She would go to Paris and bring Sandrine to safety now.

Armand's blue eyes grazed with hers, and in the front hallway of the chateau, Élise and Olivier's telephone rang.

Charlotte stood for one second, face to face with the two curators, and then, as if in choreographed motion, they all dashed toward the main staircase that led to the telephone.

And when they all came to a stop in the hallway, Lucie stood, breathless next to Armand, while he picked up the phone, speaking in rapid French for a few moments, barking out questions, and then, finally turning to Charlotte and Lucie, his brow creased.

"Chateau d'Anez has been deemed too risky to store the collections any longer. We must move everything out of here immediately. We must leave the chateau too."

Charlotte opened and closed her mouth, too torn to speak. Because she had to go to Paris. She was not leaving without Sandrine. But then, her head rang with questions. What did this mean for Anita, Élise and Olivier's private collection? Would it, too, be moved, along with the collections from the Louvre? Would Monsieur Jaujard still protect the Goldsteins' artworks, and would there be enough room in the transport convoys for wherever they were going next?

Charlotte cast about wildly. She'd packed Élise and Olivier's major pieces that they'd kept here in the Loire Valley months ago when they had first arrived before Hitler stalled his plans. The portrait of Élise by Pissarro sat against a wall in the dining room in a wooden crate, clearly labeled, and Olivier's beloved small Italian sculptures were packed nearby.

But Charlotte cast her eyes about the entrance to Élise and Olivier's beloved home. What of Chateau d'Anez? How could she simply walk away and leave? She would have failed them. She would fail in the promise she made to Élise during the summer of 1937.

Lucie came and rested a hand on her shoulder. "I know how much Chateau d'Anez means to the Goldsteins," she murmured, her eyes dashing toward her husband. "I know how difficult it will be for you to leave."

Charlotte shook her head. "It must be done." She closed her eyes, pressing her lips together, trying to stop the hot tears that wanted to course down her cheeks, trying to still the way her heart rose up to clog her throat, almost strangling her. She took in a shuddering breath, forcing herself to focus on Sandrine. "When are we to leave?" she asked Armand.

He frowned. "There is a small convoy of trucks arriving in the coming days. All I know is that we are going south and awaiting further instructions. I don't have any further details."

Charlotte wrung her hands.

"The museum administration does not know how bad the fight for Paris will be. Here in the Loire Valley, we are only minutes from Paris by air," Armand explained.

Charlotte nodded. "I understand, Armand." The priority had to be the treasures of France. No one was going to stay here and protect this, one of many beautiful chateaux. It would be looted. Charlotte's eyes peeled around the lovely hallway. The memories... this charming old home. She ached for the past.

"The Germans could inflict serious damage intentionally on the famous chateaux of the Loire, or," he lowered his voice, "the collateral damage from the battle for Paris could extend here. We are simply in the line of fire. We need to start preparing now."

Charlotte leaned against the hall table. In front of her was the dark patch on the wall where she'd carefully removed the portrait of Élise. She swallowed.

"All the Goldsteins' collection will come with us," Armand said, softening his voice a little.

Charlotte managed to nod. She turned away from the couple, who were talking in whispers, saying they must rouse the guards into action.

In the hushed hallway, Charlotte lifted her face. "I have to go to Paris," she whispered. "There is someone who must come with us too."

Charlotte saw the way the couple's gaze swiveled doubt-fully toward each other.

But Charlotte stood firm. "I shall be back at first light."

Armand's chest rose and fell, and his forehead was lined with a pale film of sweat. "We may need to use Olivier's car to transport the collections. You will have to ensure it is full of gas."

There were stores of fuel in Olivier's garage. She had hardly used the car these last months. Charlotte nodded. "I shall leave now."

Armand and Lucie were silent, a frown creasing Lucie's face.

"Sandrine Mercier?" Lucie asked.

"Yes, Sandrine."

Lucie had seen how helpful Sandrine had been to keeping Charlotte's business afloat these past months.

"The telephone," Charlotte breathed. "Now."

·   ·   ·

In the early hours of the morning, Paris sat silent as if under a dark cloak. The sound of a lone motorcycle was the only sound to rent the otherwise deadly quiet Marais district, where Sandrine's antique shop had thrived for decades until now. Charlotte cast her eyes around the store that was once the pride of one of the district's most beloved antique dealers, Gabriel Mercier, Papa to the wonderful fashion designer Vianne Mercier. Thanks to Charlotte and Sandrine's speedy packing up, the store was devoid of all its beautiful treasures. It was all empty now.

But still, the space remained lovely, from the shining wooden floorboards that were used to the clatter of Sandrine's efficient shoes, to the elegant display tables and cabinets that were cleared out, as if the life within them had been taken away. Charlotte had loaded as much of Sandrine's stock into Olivier's car as she could manage, while Sandrine had packed herself a suitcase in the Merciers' apartment around the corner. There had been no time for her to save anything else. Then, working swiftly, they had placed the remainder of Sandrine's stock into boxes, storing them out the back of the shop.

"I suspect the Nazis shall be too blind with greed for France's priceless treasures to bother themselves with these trinkets," Sandrine said.

Charlotte bowed her head.

This was the second time she'd had to pack beloved family things. Things that may not be of any value to governments, but that meant the world to those who lived with them, day by day. It was as if the life of France was being driven out and left to rot.

Sandrine picked up her suitcase. "I can't help but feel that I am failing." She turned to Charlotte; her gray eyes wide. "Vianne's father kept this store going through the last war. And the memories of my husband, here..." her voice choked up. "He was flawed, but I loved him."

Charlotte tucked her hand into Sandrine's arm. "This war, the speed of it, will be very different from the Great War. As unbelievable as it seems, it is happening again, but on a different scale, with new perpetrators, who are more deadly, even than last time," she whispered. "You must not feel that you are in *any* way letting the Mercier family down," she said, grimacing at the irony of her own words, given that failing the Goldsteins had made her wretched all the way from the Loire Valley to Paris. She hated leaving their home. Hated this situation. But, in the end, she'd realized that in the case of invasion, there was simply no choice but to tear yourself away from everything you loved, and only take what was truly irreplaceable. People, and great works of beloved art in their case.

"We must leave," Charlotte said, gathering herself. Armand had issued a stark warning when she left Chateau d'Anez. There was a severe shortage of trucks due to military requisitions and Olivier's car would definitely be required to transport the collection out of the chateau. Charlotte would have to load it and drive it herself because many of the guards did not know how to drive a car. They were used to zipping around Paris on motorbikes, and Charlotte was one of the few people who had her car license. Now, she moved forward, her expression grim, while tears slid freely down Sandrine's cheeks.

"How does one say goodbye to a whole life?" Sandrine cried.

Charlotte climbed into the car and turned to the pale Sandrine who slipped in beside her. "There are no words, dearest. The roads are going to be clogged. Please, try to get some sleep."

"Goodbye, Paris," Sandrine whispered.

Charlotte's mouth was turned down, grim. If this was the end of one chapter, she hated to think what the next one would bring. Nevertheless, Charlotte brought the engine of Olivier's car to life.

. . .

"Charlotte?" Sandrine stood in the doorway.

Charlotte turned from the small desk she'd requisitioned in Olivier's old office in Chateau d'Anez to carry out the business for Galerie A. Goldstein. She'd contacted the few local collectors who'd bought pieces from her lately, informing them that she must deliver their items in the coming days. There was no way of knowing whether she'd be able to continue running the gallery from wherever they were going next.

Retreating further away from Paris with the Goldsteins' collection and the priceless paintings from the Louvre made perfect sense on paper, but Charlotte had been torn with frustration. Protecting Sandrine sat easily with her. But running away from the place *she'd* vowed to protect was not something that was in her blood. If the worst happened, and the Nazis were to requisition the chateau, there was no doubt there'd not be a single thing left in Élise and Olivier's home. What was worse was that Charlotte would have to leave many of Anita's personal items behind. Anita was gone, and the reality was, the Nazis would steal everything she'd owned and loved in her childhood home. This tore Charlotte's heart.

Of course, the Louvre were taking care of the most important pieces in the Goldsteins' wonderful collection. Élise and Olivier had packed as many precious smaller items into their trunks as they could manage before their hasty retreat to America. They were only grateful for the sponsorship of Papa back in 1938, knowing how difficult it was going to be for Jews to escape Europe in the coming months as the storms of persecution and war gathered and blew over the continent. Yet, there was still so much of the Goldsteins left in the chateau.

Charlotte placed her head in her hands. If Sandrine felt she had failed Celine, Charlotte felt as if she were useless. That was the truth.

Sandrine's court shoes clicked against the polished parquet floor, and she came to stand next to the desk. "Brace yourself."

Charlotte looked up.

Sandrine glanced out the window, her eyes darting with a new sense of fear. "We have just had a call from the curators remaining at the Louvre. Bombs have fallen over Paris this afternoon. Over two hundred people are missing, and they are feared dead."

Charlotte stood up. She moved to the window, unable to do anything but nod at Sandrine. She stared out at the beautiful gardens outside. From downstairs, the sound of someone shouting in French rang up the otherwise silent grand old staircase.

"Armand and Lucie say it is as the administrators feared. Warplanes are roaring across Paris's skies. If Hitler's air force has launched an attack over Paris, we need to move the national collection far away from the capital immediately."

Just as Sandrine spoke, a truck pulled up outside the chateau.

"It is starting," Charlotte said, her voice shaking. "They are here to move us out of Chateau d'Anez." She turned wildly to Sandrine. "We shall have no time to decide what to take, what to leave. Sandrine..."

Sandrine was across the room in an instant.

For one precious moment, Charlotte allowed herself to bury her face in Sandrine's soft shoulder. She allowed the older woman to comfort her. Just for one second.

"We must be stoic," Charlotte whispered.

"We will get through this," Sandrine said. "We are together."

Charlotte pulled back, bracing herself and standing tall. "There is no time to lose."

She indicated that Sandrine go ahead of her out the doorway, and taking a deep breath, she followed the older woman out the door.

At the top of the staircase, Charlotte paused and raised her hand to her mouth. The entrance hall swarmed with guards, truck drivers, Lucie and Armand, all talking rapidly, shouting. It was as if, already, the spirit of Olivier and Élise and all the wonderful times they'd had in this home had flown with the wind, and nothing was going to bring them back again.

Charlotte ran to Anita's bedroom, threw open the door, and rushed inside to grab a small painting, unframed, that she'd found while waiting out the long months of Hitler's phony war. Carefully, she collected the little work from one of the drawers still full of Anita's summer clothes that Élise had not had the heart to pack up before she left for America.

For one, moment, an indulgent moment that Charlotte knew she might not have again for some time, she held the small painting of Anita, her mother, Chloé, her father, Laurent, and another man whom she had never seen before close to her heart. They were sitting on the lawn outside Chateau d'Anez, and in the background, the old house smiled down upon them as if nothing would ever change.

12

SOUTHWEST FRANCE, SUMMER 1940

Charlotte

The convoy of trucks sat in the curved gravel driveway of Chateau d'Anez. In the absence of covered vehicles, the curators, guards, and Charlotte had worked all night to secure crates to the open backs of the trucks, using leather straps that they all knew would be at risk of breaking due to the friction they would encounter on the road.

Charlotte stood at the entrance to the dear chateau, the key that Élise and Olivier had entrusted her with grasped in her hand, a lump in her throat as the sound of engines whirring to life rent the air. "Goodbye," she whispered, wiping a stray tear.

Charlotte closed her eyes a moment. Clothes, personal items, photographs, bottles of perfume, all the entrapments of the Goldsteins' normal life, and heartbreakingly, the personal belongings of Anita, who would never have the chance to come home again, had been hastily packed away in the orangery and in the basements of the old home by the teams of people who had arrived yesterday. The furniture was under dust covers; the Louvre staff had packed all the food in the pantries. Armand had burned years' worth of financial records, and any documentation that suggested the Goldsteins might be Jews. A black cloud had soared over Chateau d'Anez while Armand stoked the final flames. Then they'd drifted away with the wind, allowing a stunningly beautiful summer's afternoon to unfold.

Charlotte, her fingers fumbling, turned the lock in the great front door one last time, the click so filled with finality that she fought the urge to buckle over and collapse. Then, taking a step backward, she allowed herself one last, heartbreaking look up at the home that had meant the world to her since she was young. The home of the family who, due to no fault of their own, had been forced away from everything they held dear.

Steeling herself, Charlotte made her way down the front steps toward Olivier's car. The three items that Charlotte had vowed she would never let out of her sight sat under Sandrine's feet in the passenger seat. Pissarro's portrait of Élise as a little girl, Sandro Luciano's stunning modernist rendition of Anita, and the small painting of Charlotte and Martha's parents with Anita and the unknown gentleman that Charlotte had found buried in Anita's drawer.

Charlotte climbed into Olivier's old car, and when Sandrine reached across and placed her soft hand atop hers, Charlotte could not stem the churning in her stomach, nor the leaden feeling in her heart.

Keeping her head resolutely forward, she drove out of the long driveway that led into Chateau d'Anez, knowing that the final driver in the convoy would have the awful task of closing the gates behind them for one last time.

When they finally crossed the boundaries of the chateau, Charlotte leaned out the window of the driver's seat, trying to get a glimpse of the poignant procession that clogged the road out of the Loire Valley. In front of them, the road was jammed with lorries, stacked with the detritus of people's suddenly lost lives: mattresses, furniture, barking dogs, pots, and pans. Horses and carts were loaded with children, sitting atop trunks filled only with the things they could manage to salvage. There were even several cows. Men wove their way on foot through the refugees or tried to ride bicycles wobbling along with suitcases stacked on their carriers, and exhausted mothers walked steadily down the road, arms around their children. It was as if all of France, Belgium and the Netherlands were traveling in one direction. South.

"*Mon Dieu,*" Sandrine moaned.

Armand had briefed Charlotte on the instructions from Monsieur Jaujard himself, who was still in Paris, by all accounts sending final artworks, books from libraries and other treasures out of the capital. Armand had been told the tireless director of the Musées Nationaux was remaining polite, tolerant and calm. Without Monsieur Jaujard at the helm, Armand had said, without his meticulous planning toward evading Hitler's seeming insatiable appetite for stealing art, who knew where the treasures of France might be heading.

Charlotte could take an educated guess.

But Armand had also warned her. While the Nazis denounced modern art and were extremely particular that they wanted the greatest masterpieces of Europe to grace the galleries and homes of Germany's elite, not to mention Hitler's private collection itself, they would steal modern art, nevertheless. And they would destroy it. Burn it, Armand said. Burn it as an example to their people of what not to show in the galleries of the Third Reich, let alone your country house.

Charlotte knew she would have to sleep with the three paintings she would not let go of by her bed. She knew she may have to guard them with her life.

She covered her mouth in horror as they passed the corpse of a horse, lying on the side of the road. They could only crawl forward, the heat of the day searing onto the shining black paintwork of Olivier's car, the abandoned cars a stark warning that they could not take safety for granted at all.

As the sun rose high in the sky and noon approached, German planes, the low-range dive bombers, keened and wailed in the distance like screaming birds, and the air was rent with the unmistakable, pitiless clatter of machinegun fire raining on the refugees who were unlucky enough to be in their sights.

Three days later, after crawling like an ant in Olivier's car through the mass of refugees, after a night spent trying to sleep on the floor of an equestrian center of a chateau that had been turned into a shelter for thousands heading south, after a vehicle loaded with artworks including many pieces from Olivier and Élise's collection had fallen into a ditch and had to be hauled back onto the road by two powerful trucks, and after the vehicle behind Charlotte caught on her bumper, the terrain changed, there was only the occasional drone of an enemy plane overhead, and the convoy had an easier journey south.

Charlotte fell into an exhausted sleep on the third night of their journey on the floor, surrounded by a row of already occupied cots in a requisitioned classroom of an elementary school. And the following morning, she stood with Lucie, Armand, and Sandrine outside the school, when a guard in one of the other convoys from the Louvre informed them that the bridges of the Loire Valley had been blown up by the government in a bid to slow the Nazis' inevitable progress through France.

The guard spoke to the exhausted, dirty group of curators and guards, his shoulders slumped in agony. "Bombs have fallen on the Loire Valley, and German troops are already camped on the ground at Courtalain."

Charlotte turned away, her mouth working. She took in a shuddering breath. And she reminded herself, everything was different. All the rules had changed. In fact, all the rules had been blown to pieces, replaced by the day-to-day horror that came with the threat of living under the Nazi regime.

"It is difficult to conceive that we were storing some of our pieces at Courtalain just until just a few days ago. Jacques Jaujard had the foresight to ask us to move. It has all been worth it," the guard said.

There was a silence. People's hands strayed across their grubby, tired faces.

"What we don't know, is whether, down here, we will be able to keep the treasures, and ourselves, safe from the Nazis," Armand said.

Charlotte moved toward Olivier's car, holding open the door for Sandrine. They would find out how safe they were soon enough.

Just before midnight, Charlotte pulled into the driveway of an old abbey in a lonely, remote spot in southwestern France, where the Louvre had decided many of its treasures would remain safe and well hidden from the Nazis. Finally, she brought Olivier's trustworthy car to a halt. They'd traveled through a bank of dark woods to get here, and now, the moon shone down on a serene lake in front of an ancient church with a castellated building attached to it.

Charlotte's gaze tore around the serene, timeless scene. They were to sit the war out, here? The thought was impossible Not doing anything to help would be inconceivable while France fell. She leaned her head on the steering wheel.

Lucie's red-gold head appeared at the car window. Her hair was piled loosely up, and her face was streaked with dirt. "Charlotte," she said, glancing through the car window toward Sandrine. "Thank goodness you rescued Sandrine from Paris."

Charlotte reached a weary hand across to rest atop that of her mother and Anita's quiet, loyal friend.

But Lucie cleared her throat. She stared down at the ground a moment, as if troubled as to what to say next. "There is no easy way to tell you," she said finally, her voice low. "While we were tossing and turning in the schoolroom for French children, Nazi tanks rolled into Paris. Armand tells me that their flags are flying over the Rue de Rivoli from the Louvre to the Place de la Concorde."

Charlotte wrapped her arms around her body. She tightened her grip on Sandrine's arm. "*No*," she said.

Next to her, Sandrine stiffened. Charlotte heard her sharp intake of breath.

"Prime Minister Reynaud has resigned," Lucie went on, her voice shaking, but her chin lifted, her green eyes holding Charlotte's, never faltering for a moment. "Monsieur Reynaud apparently wanted to defend Paris, but he was outnumbered by those politicians who favored an armistice. An armistice with Hitler."

Charlotte curled her lip. There had been talk of disputes in the government. She'd been furious at the thought that simply handing Paris to the Nazis could even be a consideration. She swallowed, but her throat stuck. All those refugees fleeing Paris, all those families from France, Belgium and the Netherlands who were seeking solace, protection for the children, their elderly... And the government of France had signed an armistice with the Nazis?

"Paris has been declared an open city," Lucie went on.

What of the Jewish people who believed they'd be protected by their own government? Jews like Berthe Weill who would no longer be allowed to operate her wonderful gallery in Montmartre. All those Jewish gallery owners who had inspired Anita, to whom she, Charlotte, had waved to most mornings on her way to the markets? What of them?

"Henri-Phillipe Pétain has stepped up from being deputy prime minister to prime minister," Lucie said. "Our Secretary of

National Defense, General Charles de Gaulle, is apparently appalled."

"Well, that is something," Sandrine murmured.

Charlotte clicked her tongue.

"Charles de Gaulle was in London when Reynaud resigned. He has just returned but is apparently now on his way back to London. Furious," Lucie said.

Charlotte closed her eyes. So. That was it. France had capitulated to the Nazis without a fight. "Inconceivable," she murmured.

When she opened her eyes, it was only to see the groups of shocked, silent curators and guards standing with their hats in their hands, heads bowed as if in mourning for France, along with the truck drivers who had traveled for days to remove some of the most important pieces of the nation's heritage away from the very people who were now marching through the ceded capital.

"But what is the reasoning behind this?" Charlotte whispered. "Surely, Charles de Gaulle will not abandon France."

"Of course, he won't."

Charlotte turned her head to see Armand standing beside Lucie, his arm around her shoulders. A frown line ran straight down between his blue eyes. "I am impressed that you know who de Gaulle is," he said to Charlotte.

She opened the door of her car, climbed out, and eyed Armand. "Why?" she said, sending him a challenging grin. For at the thought of someone coming to fight, even one person, Charlotte felt the stirrings of something familiar, something that had drained from her as Lucie had told them the tragic news. And that was spirit. She must never, ever give into despair.

"Not many people are familiar with the brigadier," Armand said, his blue eyes softening. "Although, while I am impressed you know of him, I am not surprised."

Charlotte held Armand's gaze a moment.

"I am certain we have not heard the last of Charles de Gaulle," he said, his voice low. "But, Charlotte," he added, "we must wait."

Charlotte's eyes, blazing, stayed locked with Armand's, while Lucie moved around the car to open Sandrine's door.

And then, a voice curled out, defeated, into the dark night. "Pétain has ordered the French to stop fighting. It is over. We have lost the war."

Charlotte turned toward the old abbey. She curled her lip in disdain.

13

NEW YORK, SUMMER 1940

Martha

Everything was prepared, but the more Martha investigated it, the more it became clear that the chances of successfully bringing Élise's friend Gisela Weber to the United States seemed as slim as one of the pieces of white paper on the coffee table in Papa's sitting room.

Martha stood by the window, her hair still dressed from her day at work, her navy dress simple and professional, her feet encased in high-heeled pumps. The information she'd gathered for today's meeting with a representative from the American Friends Service Committee sat on the antique table between the sofas. She could not bear Élise's distress if she was not able to convince the committee to help.

Martha shook her head and frowned at the difficulty of the task ahead. When she'd found out that hundreds of thousands of hopeful Jewish emigrants were lining up outside United States consulates all over Europe, desperately seeking one of the existing immigration quota visas, and that in 1939, there'd been over three hundred thousand applications for twenty-seven thousand visas, she'd not been able to bear to warn Élise.

Martha folded her arms. The fact was, most visa applicants were unsuccessful, even though Gisela Weber was more than qualified to meet the requirements for researchers and academics. She'd worked for far longer than the requisite two years and had enjoyed an impressive career at the university in Vienna, until she, along with thousands of other Jewish civil servants, had been ousted from her position at the time of the Anschluss.

Like so many other victims of the Nazi government, Gisela had been reluctant to leave her home, even though Nazi rule came with sweeping reforms that discriminated against Jewish people. Gisela had tried and failed to find work. Any work. Since leaving her beloved Austria and all her assets behind, she'd had no permanent home and no savings, relying on the kindness of friends in Lyon, France. Ultimately she had been unable to obtain a long-term visa to stay there. The fact was, nations in Western Europe and the Americas feared an influx of refugees, but if Gisela remained in France, she'd be instantly deported to Germany.

In the hallway, the sound of Élise greeting the representative from the American Friends Service Committee filtered into the room.

Martha braced herself when the door inched open, only to come face to face with Papa. She walked toward him, leaning forward to kiss him on the cheek. "You are joining us, Papa? Oh, I would appreciate having you here." That was the truth. She'd tried and failed to include Papa in the research she'd done to help Gisela. He'd remained quiet, aloof.

Now, Martha rested her hand on his arm.

But his brows drew close, and he shuffled about on his feet. "Is this really a good idea?" he said.

Martha glanced toward the door, while the sounds of Élise's charming voice greeting the representative grew closer.

Martha widened her eyes. "I can't see why ever not, Papa." Her heart sank to her shoes.

He shook his head. "Élise and Olivier are like family to us. But inviting a stranger, a woman we don't know, to come and live in our home?" He shook his head and looked out toward the windows, as if seeking an answer amongst the treetops of Central Park.

Martha stilled. "I assumed we'd both want to help."

Papa's eyes grazed with hers.

Martha started at the hurt in them. "Papa?"

He shot a glance toward the door. "You and I have lived here so peacefully for years. Darling." He lowered his head, his mouth worked, and he grimaced at the floor. "Why change what is working? As much as I am fond of Élise, she is taking over somewhat. And this is my home."

Martha moved closer to him. She picked up his hands and held them. And she took in a breath. "It was not Élise who arranged this, it was me."

His head flipped up, and he shook it. "*You?*"

Martha's brow furrowed, and she spoke in a steady, low-pitched tone. "The two of us, we have hidden away from the world long enough. Don't you see?"

He shook his head, his mouth working, but no words coming out.

Martha looked into his eyes. "Dearest, Papa, hiding away will not stop the world from turning, but it is stopping us from moving forward. We must reach out. Europe is at war... Charlotte is there, doing something. I cannot be useless. Don't you see?"

He cleared his throat, and pulled his hands away from her, rubbing them up and down his trouser legs.

"In doing this, I've found something."

He stared at her, incredulous. "What?" he murmured.

Martha's voice almost broke. "A purpose. Something that will make a difference, just as Charlotte is making a difference in France."

He searched her face for a long moment, and then, throwing his head back and sighing, he took in a shuddering breath.

"Stay for the meeting, Papa," she whispered. "Let me show you, for once, what I can do."

She entreated him with her eyes, and right then, Élise swept into the room, her glasses balanced on her nose, her smile kindly, but the worry in her dark eyes more than obvious to Martha.

"Martha, and Laurence, I'd love you to meet Elizabeth Ellwood from the American Friends Service Committee."

Martha came forward to shake Elizabeth Ellwood's outstretched hand. She sighed with relief at the way the woman looked with approval at Martha's simple dress, like Elizabeth's own. She'd found out that members of the Religious Society of Friends did not approve of fancy clothes, so had deliberately set out not to offend them by wearing one of Vianne's gorgeous creations. Martha indicated that Elizabeth, who looked to be in her fifties, and whose thick gray hair rested on her shoulders, should sit down.

Martha poured coffee, offered biscuits around, and waited for Elizabeth to talk.

"I'd like to give you a little background. And please, call me Elizabeth. As a Friend, we do not stand on ceremony."

Martha shot a glance toward Papa. He was sitting back in his seat, his expression unreadable. Martha tried to still her shaking hands.

"The American Friends Service Committee was created in 1917," Elizabeth said. "It was established to take care of the humanitarian need during the Great War. We provided meals for around one million children per day after that war was done, and we were partly funded by the American Jewish Joint Distribution Committee."

Élise looked down, a sad smile playing on her lips. Martha reached out and covered her friend's hand with her own.

Elizabeth went on, her voice soft and lilting. "After the anti-Jewish Kristallnacht pogroms in 1938, we started a refugee division, to assist families and individuals in need of support," she said. "We began helping people flee Nazi Europe for the United States."

Martha hardly dared speak. To hear those words from someone was enough to give her hope, after what she'd researched in the library so far.

Elizabeth continued. "I'm afraid we field hundreds of requests every month from people seeking to flee Nazism. We help those who are struggling to obtain a visa, and we help fund passage to the United States where we can. But in the case of non-quota visas for academics, your friend would need to have a position lined up in the United States and two years' experience in her field of expertise."

Martha reached for her documents, all meticulously stacked in the correct order. "I have here the letters of rejection that Gisela Weber has received from Bryn Mawr, Vassar, Wellesley and Radcliffe Colleges." She shook her head. "I've spoken to representatives at all of these institutions and more, explained that someone with knowledge in applied mathematics would be most useful during a war."

Papa leaned forward; his hands cupped between his knees.

Martha, taking this as encouragement, continued. "I also pointed out to them that the government were placing higher consideration on applicants for visas who could contribute to important research at this time."

"And their response?" Elizabeth asked.

"Women's colleges are not carrying out research, only teaching."

Elizabeth sighed. "Exactly."

Martha folded her hands in her lap. "The traditionally male institutions, like Harvard, do carry out research but are not willing to employ women. And Jewish women?" Martha shook her head. "It seems that anti-Semitism is a problem in some of our academic institutions, as Élise feared."

Elizabeth nodded. "Gisela will not be above suspicion. She is Viennese. And they will also argue that she would be taking a job from an American."

Martha frowned. "I have variously been told that despite her leading credentials, she is too old, too female, and too Jewish to secure employment. I have to say that in all my efforts, I have learned that, sadly, the government are not interested in saving lives."

Papa coughed and shook his head. "Unbelievable," he murmured.

Martha sent him a smile.

"The Society of Friends is committed to helping people on both sides of the war, and men and women equally, so you did well to come to us," Elizabeth said. "The fact that Gisela is Viennese does not preclude her from our help."

Martha smiled at her. "But, you see, the Immigration Act, last updated in 1924, only allows for non-quota visas for *male* academics, and their wives. It seems we have no recognition of women scholars at all."

Papa, who had been quiet until this moment, leaned forward. "Tell me," he said, "how many women academics has the United States allowed in as refugees in total since the Nazis gained control?"

"Two," Elizabeth said. "Two single, academic women."

There was a silence.

Élise stood up. She moved to the window and rested her head on the glass. "That is ridiculous," she said. "I had no idea it would be so hard."

Martha hated the sight of Élise's rigid back. "We need a sponsor, someone or an organization, who could help us," she said. "This woman, who was a leading researcher and teacher in Vienna for many years, has so much to contribute. What's more, she is in dire straits. If the Nazis do get as far as Lyon, she will be deported as a Jew and as a citizen of Austria holding an Austrian passport. She cannot find refuge anywhere in Western Europe. She will be sent home, and her home is... gone." Martha shook her head.

"I think her only option would be to find a sponsor," Elizabeth said. "And a powerful one at that."

Right then, Papa cleared his throat.

Slowly, Martha turned toward him. Élise turned around from her position by the window, and Elizabeth crossed her legs and sat back in her seat.

"There is," he said, "some support amongst women in parliament for change."

Martha frowned. She opened her mouth, but out of the corner of her eye, she saw Élise lift her hand and shake her head.

"Congresswoman Edith Nourse Rogers sponsored a bill that proposed to allow German Jewish children to enter the United States outside the official immigration rules, but it never reached a vote."

Martha slumped back in her seat. Darling Papa. "I think—"

But Papa continued. "First Lady Eleanor Roosevelt is supportive of liberalizing immigration laws."

Elizabeth raised a brow. "Yes, that is true," she said.

Papa stood up. He went to stand by the fireplace, his feet planted firmly on the ground. "I read her column in the papers. She is trying to work behind the scenes to effect change."

Élise came back and sat down. She crossed her legs at the ankles, and folded her hands neatly in her lap, her eyes intent on Papa.

"What if someone were to write to our First Lady, alert her to the fact that it is almost impossible for independent, professional Jewish women to come to the United States, that they have a huge amount to contribute, and that if we don't take them in, their lives are at risk?" he said.

Élise covered her mouth with her hand and her gaze swiveled to Elizabeth.

"But the First Lady, while she has support from some women in parliament, most particularly Congresswoman Nourse, who tried and failed to secure a bill to bring out Jewish children to America, is up against some formidable challenges." Papa leaned on the mantelpiece. He smiled at Elizabeth.

Martha stared at all her papers and sat back in her chair. She sent Papa a grin. How proud she was of him. How she had not expected this.

"You see," he said, flicking Martha a tiny wink, "Eleanor Roosevelt is advocating particularly for artists and intellectuals who will be targeted by the Nazis."

Martha gasped. "Would you write to her?" she asked Elizabeth.

Elizabeth opened her mouth, but Papa continued.

"I was thinking you could write to Eleanor Roosevelt, Martha," he said.

Martha stood up. She moved across the room, suddenly needing to move. She was so grateful to Papa for thinking of this. She swung around to face them all.

"What a marvelous idea," Elizabeth breathed. "If we can get her support, then, with the Friends on board, we could make quite a formidable team, but, Martha, I have to acknowledge, if you are successful, it will be you who has done all the hard work."

Martha turned to Papa, and he raised a brow. And she saw a light in his eyes that she had not seen since she was a little girl.

. . .

That evening, it was late by the time Martha finally entered her bedroom. She'd drafted her letter to the First Lady, would check it through tomorrow and then send it off in her lunchtime break. Her heart was still full of gratitude that Papa had lent her his support.

She reached up and turned on her bedroom light. She frowned. A letter sat on her dressing table, on a small white plate that Papa had said once belonged to her mother.

Martha came forward to pick it up. It was postmarked Scotland, but the writing was not Clyde's. She fell back down on her bed and, her hands fumbling, she tore the envelope open with her bare fingers. Her eyes flew to the bottom of the letter.

Kirsty Fraser. Clyde's sister.

Martha's heart stilled.

Edinburgh, Scotland
June 1940

Dear Martha,

I hope you don't mind me writing direct to you. My brother, Clyde, gave me your address. I know that on receiving this letter from me, not Clyde, you will quite rightly feel a sense of alarm, so I shall not waste my words.

I am afraid I am not writing with good news. Clyde asked me to write to you if, for any reason, he could not, and most unfortunately, that situation has eventuated, so, here I am.

Martha drew her hand to her mouth. She sank down onto the chair by the window. A chill passed through her, despite the humidity outside, and she gathered her wrap, placing it around her shoulders.

As you know, Clyde's battalion, the 51st Highland Division were preparing for an early entry to the war. His division was part of the British Expeditionary Force serving to defend France before the German invasion. In April, they were sent to the Maginot Line.

Martha grimaced. France's great defense, the Maginot Line, had proved useless. Charlotte had written at length about it. Feverish with worry, she read on.

In May, the Germans began their offensive on Western Europe. It has been reported that the Allies had no expectation that the Germans would simply bypass the Maginot Line. Clyde's division was cut off from the rest of the British Expeditionary Force, and the French military decided to place them on the banks of the River Somme.

Martha couldn't help it; she stood up, fear lacing through her belly. She turned on the standard lamp by the window, her hand pressed into the back of her chair.

They were, by all accounts, ready for a German onslaught, and they launched an attack on the Germans at Abbeville, but suffered heavy casualties, and were forced to retreat.

"Oh, please tell me he is home, safe and secure in Edinburgh," Martha whispered.

She read on, her hand shaking, her eyes trying to read faster than she could hope to process.

But it was clear to their general that they did not have the firepower or the manpower to withstand the Germans.

In early June, the French commander refused General Fortune permission to retreat to Le Havre with due speed.

Bile rose in Martha's throat. How complicated this war was! Gisela not being able to come to America, France's own military leaders not allowing a Scottish battalion to retreat when there was no hope of success in their mission! But what of Clyde?

Forcing herself to read the entire letter, she continued with this deathly missive.

Clyde's battalion had to keep pace with the French division, and they could only march eighteen kilometers in the cover of darkness.

You will, no doubt, have heard my brother's proud beliefs that you are not a soldier if you are not a Gordon Highlander! Tears prick my eyes while I write this, but I can only imagine his battalion's frustration at not being able to march at a fast enough pace to render them safe. Their pace was too slow, and this enabled General Erwin Rommel's 5th Panzer Division, along with three other German divisions, to outflank our brave Highlanders and cut off their escape route to Le Havre.

Nevertheless, General Fortune tried to find an alternative escape route around St. Valéry, but this port is set between high cliffs, and it was not an easy port from which to evacuate. It was impossible, when the Germans broke through onto the cliffs on June 11, and while the Royal Navy had assembled over two hundred small ships to evacuate the Scottish and French forces, the Germans shelled the ships, and they could not get close enough to the port to save our men.

Martha read on, gripping the sides of the letter, and fighting the urge to squeeze her eyes shut.

And, under the safety of darkness, we are told there was also a cruel fog. Around two thousand British and French troops were evacuated from the beach at Veules-les-Roses, a small seaside town to the east of St. Valéry, however they were not from the Highland Infantry Regiments, who were still defending the St. Valéry town and coastline.

The following morning, the French forces in the area surrendered. They were exhausted, had no food, ammunition, or water, so had no choice. They were outnumbered, and outgunned, Martha, and were surrounded with no means of escape.

I am devastated to tell you that Clyde is in captivity. We are all hoping and praying that he will be freed soon, and that his suffering is not unbearable, that his courage gets him through this hour of strife.

Martha, as soon as we hear anything more, I shall write to you. I know how much you mean to him, and please rest assured that I shall keep you fully informed.

In the meantime, God Bless,

Yours truly,

Kirsty Fraser

14

Charlotte

Shadows lengthened across the deep green lawns of the abbey cloisters, and the last of the summer sun glinted on the flower beds that edged the quiet space. Charlotte sat down on one of the long stone benches that looked out over the courtyard garden. Beyond the stone walls of the cloister, refugees from Paris were camping in the abbey grounds in makeshift tents.

Charlotte grimaced. Last night, she'd asked the kitchens if she could go and help dole out food to the refugees, and she'd worked at a long trestle table set up for this purpose with some of the abbey's staff. But guilt haunted her at the fact that the team from the Louvre had been afforded sleeping quarters inside the cloisters. At night, Charlotte went to sleep in a room that had been renovated by the abbey's private owner. He'd offered sumptuous bedrooms with canopied four-poster beds and feather pillows to the curators from the Louvre, whilst the refugees were forced to sleep outside in tents.

This morning, Charlotte had seen them lining up for food from the vast abbey kitchens and she was only too aware that

most of the people here had lost their homes and their livelihoods. They had no assets and no means of survival, other than
reliance on charitable aid. Children, dirty, hungry, clutching
teddy bears and looking as bewildered as everyone felt, stood
with their eyes wide in disbelief. What was the future for the
children of France, whose little faces peered back at Charlotte
when she looked down at them from the crystal-clean window
of her bedroom here?

Charlotte frowned at the fountain, water splashing away
happily as if all of this was inconsequential.

France's government had signed an armistice with the
Nazis, and, two days later, with Italy. While Sandrine had
accepted the situation with a resignation borne of already
having lived through another war, Charlotte was raging inside.

Since Hitler had come to power in 1933, the world had
been reading of nonsensical Nazi policies. The French government, like every other democracy, had taken great pains to
demonstrate how different things were here in France. But now,
France had gone down without a fight. It seemed impossible to
imagine that things in this country were to follow Germany,
where Jews, innocents like Anita, Élise and Olivier, were being
forced to wear identifying armbands. There was deeply
worrying talk of ghettos being established, while everyone knew
that trying to emigrate from Germany, Poland, Czechoslovakia,
Austria, or Belgium was an impossible bureaucratic mess.

Last night, Charlotte had talked deep into the evening with
Armand and Lucie about the awful news that France had been
divided into two zones, one governed by the German Nazi
Party, and one controlled by the capitulating prime minister,
Pétain, based in the spa town of Vichy. Then, this morning,
they'd heard that Hitler had ordered his Nazi invaders to take
into custody all Jewish-owned valuable art and antiquities in
France.

While this was what they had expected, given Hitler's

actions in Poland, marching in, and looting Jewish families'
collections with no notice, Armand, blue eyes blazing, had
growled that the Nazis were poised to steal the entire artistic
collection of France. It seemed Hitler's appetite for looting the
old art heritage of Europe for himself was as insatiable as his
cruelty toward Jews.

Now, here Charlotte was, stuck in the so-called "free zone"
of the Vichy government. Might she as well be in New York?

Charlotte curled her lip and sat back on the bench,
stretching her legs out in front of her. Her frustration was
complex, because the whole point of this exercise was to protect
Élise and Olivier's Jewish art collection. However, what she had
not thought through was that in safeguarding their beloved art,
she was fleeing from danger and not able to stay and help those
in need. This did not sit well with her.

This morning, she'd stopped short of confessing her feelings
to Armand, Lucie, and Sandrine, when Armand had
announced that he'd sent word to Monsieur Jaujard. The
humidity in the air surrounding the abbey could pose a serious
threat to the paintings of the Louvre. Monsieur Jaujard, who
was still in Paris, was trying to negotiate in his endlessly digni-
fied way with the Nazis and their increasing demands. Charlotte had listened intently. Was Armand thinking of moving on
from the abbey? If so, where?

Yesterday, Armand had walked around the outside of the
abbey, frowning and taking photographs, and when the owners
had told him the pond out front was the remainder of a swamp
that the monks had drained centuries earlier, in a belief that the
vapors coming from it in the summer could make the inhabi-
tants of the abbey ill, Armand had visibly paled.

Charlotte had worked with Lucie and Armand, inspecting
the paintings that were stored in the chapel for any signs of
mold. She'd taken Luciano's portrait of Anita and the Pissarro of

Élise out of their crates and studied them carefully for moisture damage or any unpleasant damp smells. The small painting of Anita, Chloé, her father, and the man of whose identity Charlotte had no idea, was by her bed.

As soon as possible, Armand would be organizing readings of moisture in the air.

Charlotte was more than aware that without heating in the winter in the chapel, the works of art they'd come so far to protect would be at significant risk of damage when the cold weather set in.

When two young men wandered from the gardens into the cloisters, Charlotte stood, ready to leave, but her visitors sat on a bench nearby and proceeded to chat in hushed tones. Their whispers spilled into the quiet cloisters. The nature of their words was impossible to understand against the constant tinkle of the water in the fountain.

Charlotte couldn't help it, she let out a groan, only to earn a quick glance from one of the two men. His clear, almond-shaped brown eyes locked with hers.

Charlotte frowned at the men, both with their immaculate haircuts, their healthy, glowing tanned skin and their freshly pressed checked shirts. She thought of the poor souls in the grounds and turned away.

"You are unhappy here?" the young man's voice cut into the quiet air.

"Happiness is not something one associates with Nazi rule," Charlotte said. She stopped on her way to the door that led inside.

A flicker of something passed across the young man's features. "American," he mused, "not everyone would agree with your stance." He answered her in English, with only the hint of a French accent.

Charlotte barked out a laugh. "You are a supporter of this

ridiculous situation? At simply handing the northern half of France to the Nazis, while we sit down here safely in Pétain's 'French zone' and do nothing whatsoever to fight?"

The second young man looked down at the bench, his eyes widening and his neatly brushed fair hair catching in the sun. His mouth twisted into a thinly veiled smile.

Charlotte shuddered.

"Some think Hitler is a prophet, ordained for greatness, whose empire will rule us for a thousand years," the young man said.

Charlotte felt a bitter taste forming in her mouth. The man looked to be about her age. He was clearly well off and educated, given his command of the English language and his neatly dressed, suave appearance.

"Hitler is as likely to be a prophet as he is to be an artist," Charlotte scoffed.

The young man raised a brow.

Charlotte averted her gaze, pressing her hands against her stomach. She was starting to feel ill. "This is the man who was twice refused admission by the Vienna Academy of Fine Arts, and who at the same time considers the works of Cezanne, Gauguin, and Van Gogh to be degenerate trash. And yet, he insists he will become one of the great artists of our age?" Charlotte jerked around so she was not facing these boys. Whatever these men's sympathies, she was not going to be intimidated by them.

"You are with the contingency from the Louvre," the young man's voice came from behind her.

Charlotte closed her eyes. How on earth did he know the Louvre were hiding national treasures here? She would never reveal it to a soul. But then, she rubbed her hand across her face at her evasiveness. This was what Hitler had done. He had turned them all into suspicious folk, scared to air their views and worried about whom they might be talking to. She cringed at this mess.

"You speak very freely," the young man said. "You want to be careful; you know. You don't know who I might be."

Charlotte wheeled back around to face him. "It was not I who raised highly sensitive information about the national art collection of France." She sent him a cold glance. "Information that I shall never confirm or deny."

The young man raised a brow. "France has its fair share of Nazi sympathizers," he murmured. "Look at our government."

Charlotte stilled.

He leaned forward in his seat, cupping his hands between his knees. "There will be those who want to curry favor with the Vichy leaders in order to get ahead, and," he said, shaking his head, "with the Nazis. War profiteering is nothing new."

Charlotte let out a derisive laugh. "I have not met one Nazi sympathizer yet." She placed her hands on her hips. "And I am saddened that you have such little faith in your fellow countrymen. I believe most French citizens will not accept this situation."

The young man stood up. He came to stand next to her, and Charlotte took a step back. But, after a few moments, he held out a hand. "Louis Chevalier," he said. He glanced around the cloisters again. "I hate the Nazis as much as you do. But I wanted to find out your stance before we spoke openly of them."

Charlotte's chest tightened. She darted a gaze around the cloisters. Chevalier was the name of the family who owned the abbey.

"You are the family's son," she murmured.

Louis raised a brow. "I didn't want to give my game away until I trusted you."

Charlotte sent him a pained stare. His accent sounded British. Likely, he'd been educated in England.

"And this," Louis said, his brown eyes with their lighter flecks holding her gaze, "is my very good friend, Henri Durand."

Charlotte acknowledged the fair-haired man named Henri, who raised a hand toward her. He remained seated on his stone bench, staring contemplatively at the fountain.

"You have a name?" Louis asked.

Charlotte crossed her arms across her chest. "As you say, it's too dangerous for me to give that away."

His face relaxed into a grin, a dimple appearing on each cheek. "I didn't mean to upset you," he murmured. "I really am only a humble student trying to come to terms with this dreadful situation myself."

"Well, I cannot come to terms with it," Charlotte said, her voice thick. "I never will."

Louis's gaze was intent. His friend, Henri, wandered off to the other side of the cloisters, where an older gentleman had appeared.

"I am frustrated at my own sense of powerlessness too," Louis murmured. He glanced at the older man whose arm was around Henri. "Here we are," Louis went on, "young, healthy, wanting to make a difference."

Charlotte's chuckle was wry. "Your family are hosting refugees. You are contributing through them."

But Louis shook his head. "I am simply a student at the Sorbonne, who hoped that when I saw you sitting here in my favorite spot at the abbey I was not talking with one of those deplorables who are going to simper up to the new governments of France."

Charlotte kicked at a stray pebble on the otherwise immaculate stone floor. "Well," she said, "as you see, I prefer honesty to deception, and I prefer to speak plainly and state my views."

Louis's brow clouded. He flicked a glance across the cloisters toward the middle-aged gentleman and Henri.

Charlotte glanced up at him.

He leaned a little closer. "The Louvre contingency are traveling to Montauban to hide this part of the collection in the museum there. And..." His brows drew together, and he shoved his hands in his pockets. "If you'd like to contribute—"

"We are moving to Montauban?" Charlotte whispered, her eyes searching his face.

Montauban was an old market town. In the middle of nowhere.

She clenched her fists tight by her sides, determined not to show any more of her feelings so openly as she'd done before. Reluctantly, she had to admit that Louis was right. She must be more careful. While she was certain that the rebellious, strong spirit of France would remain intact, there would be those who sympathized with the Nazis, and who were willing to trade information for favors. There was no doubt about this.

In a swift movement, Louis reached out and took her hand.

She took in a sharp breath.

"I shall be at the marketplace in the center of Montauban at 10 a.m. sharp on Saturday morning. It will be crowded. Meet me there," he said.

Charlotte opened and closed her mouth, but her heart raced. Surely, he was not simply interested in her. That would be dull. It had to be something more. "But—" she protested.

Louis, in a sudden gesture, squeezed her hand and let it go. "Please. Meet me there. I want to talk to you." He took in a ragged breath. "I sensed your frustration earlier. It was obvious to me. And, if you think there is nothing you can do about the deplorable situation in France, well then, let me assure you that you would be wrong," he added.

And with that, Louis turned on his heels and moved across the cloisters, where the older gentleman embraced Louis and led him back inside.

Charlotte stood on the spot, unable to tear her gaze away from the door that had just closed. She should, of course, not accept his invitation. Martha, she was certain, would warn her against it. Under normal circumstances, she would agree. But these were not normal circumstances.

And she was not Martha. She was Charlotte. And if she were to move forward without this awful sense of guilt that was plaguing her in the face of the innocent refugees that surrounded her as she slept in her comfortable bed in the lovely old abbey, she knew what she must do.

Charlotte sat at the polished dining table in the original monks' dining room after dinner. Her shoes sank into the magnificent Turkish carpets underfoot and her eyes were on Armand, but her thoughts wheeled constantly around Louis's beguiling request.

"Hitler knows that he cannot simply steal the national collection of France, as the international outcry would be too big, even for a man who has no qualms in breaking the existing conventions," Armand said.

Charlotte frowned at her empty plate. In a moment, someone would come and collect it from her, take it away and deal with it. Louis had clearly grown up with undeniable wealth. But his family were not disinterested, privileged folk who had no care for those who were suffering under the specter of Nazi rule. Louis's family could have sequestered themselves away here and sat the situation out, but there had been something burning in Louis's eyes that Charlotte recognized. Deep down, she knew he held the same passion for justice that flared within herself.

She concentrated on Armand.

He gazed at the notes he had spread in front of him. "Hitler is playing another game now. He's ordering that the French national collections and all Jewish collections be returned to Paris so they can be 'safeguarded' by the Nazis."

Lucie tensed. "Does this mean the Nazis are following us?"

Armand sent her a sympathetic smile. "It is worse than that, Lucie," he murmured. "Hitler's ambassador to France launched a raid on the homes and galleries of prominent Jewish art collectors this morning."

Charlotte pushed back her chair and stood up. "Galleries?" she said. She leaned heavily against the back of the chair, her fingers pressing into the soft wood. She gasped. She'd not been able to pack all of Anita's personal things. She'd left her clothes hanging in the wardrobes and several paintings up in the attics. Charlotte squeezed her eyes shut, her head shaking from side to side. "*No*," she murmured. It was the final nail in the coffin of the woman who'd been everything to her. Imagining her gallery desecrated was unbearable. She'd failed Anita. She'd not done her job.

"I'm sorry, Charlotte," Armand's voice filtered through the room. "I know what you must be feeling."

Charlotte swallowed, bile sticking in her throat. She felt Sandrine come to stand nearby, felt her mother's friend's arm resting on her shoulder.

Charlotte forced herself to focus on Armand, but the room was swimming, and she could not free herself from the images of Anita's gallery, trashed.

"Under Hitler's orders," Armand continued, "the Nazis have hauled a huge collection of paintings, sculptures and other objects belonging to Jews into the German Embassy on the rue de Lille."

"*Armand*," Charlotte said, barking out the word. "Please. Do we know which Jewish collections were targeted?"

Armand glanced away a moment, sending the room an empty stare. "The raids are still being carried out. I don't know anything more, I'm sorry."

Charlotte's forehead began to perspire.

"The Nazis are pulling every excuse in the book to try to get their hands on the collections from the Louvre, claiming that seventy-five of our most important works were stolen from Germany by Napoleon." Armand sent Lucie an incredulous look, and she rested her hand atop his. "The list of accusations and justifications for this plan to steal everything is endless."

Charlotte clasped Sandrine's hand for a moment, then moved toward the vast windows that overlooked the gardens outside. She closed her eyes, images of Anita's warm dining room stripped, torn, damaged, the walls slashed, her personal items, clothes, ornaments, bed, bathroom, laid bare of all dignity burning in Charlotte's mind. Was dignity nothing to these people?

Charlotte hugged her arms around herself. Martha, then, had done something truly heroic in taking Élise and Olivier to New York. She pressed her hands against the windowsill. Armand's voice receded into the background, as her heart broke for Paris. And then, she stopped, for there, standing in front of the trees down in the garden, stood Louis, and in that moment, Charlotte's eyes locked with his.

He raised his hand for a split second and Charlotte stood, stock-still, until, as imperceptibly as she could, she raised her hand in return and sent Louis a small nod. Charlotte was certain his expression changed, that he'd smiled at her in return. She watched as he turned and disappeared into the trees. Right then, she did not give into her overwhelming desire to collapse with grief for Anita. Instead, Charlotte stood tall and a new, fluttery feeling started in her chest. And if someone were to ask her what it was, she'd tell them this. She'd tell them it was determination.

The confusion, the frustration, and the overwhelming sense of disbelief that she'd fought since they'd run away from Chateau d'Anez lifted like a clearing fog. Not knowing whether

Anita's home in Paris had been destroyed was impossible to bear. But even though she was powerless to do anything about that, one thing was clear. This was a war that had to be won. If the French government would not defend France, then the people of this country would have to step in and do so themselves, and Charlotte would be there amongst them.

15

THE FRENCH RIVIERA, SPRING 1919

Chloé

Chloé made her way down the narrow, pebbled lane from Roquebrune-Cap-Martin to the white-painted house, coming to a stop halfway down the narrow track. Laurence wrapped his arms around her waist, and they glimpsed the shimmering blue Mediterranean Sea through the trees. The sound of chatter, the clink of glasses and the soft laughter of their host, the wealthy designer Eileen Gray, came from one of the terraces that graced every level of the white villa on the Riviera.

From her vantage point, Chloé could see the backs of their heads, Eileen's, her dark hair cut short, along with Anita's friend Sumner Green, his languid form stretched out as if he belonged here. His American accent sounded as at home on the French Riviera as it would in a Manhattan gallery.

Chloé started at the sight of Anita as she straggled up from the steps that led down to the rocky outcrop below. Anita paused, her bathing towel over her shoulder and her tanned skin glistening in the sun. Her all-in-one bathing garment, with its short sleeves and vest-style top atop long leggings, was sleek and wet. Anita flinched at the sight of Eileen and Sumner sitting together but lifted her chin at the sound of their laughter, her dark eyes flashing toward Chloé.

Chloé didn't miss the way Laurence's grip around her waist tightened a little, just enough.

"Eileen wants another mural on the lower terrace by the swimming pool," Anita said. She turned back to face the sea. "She's asked Sumner to paint it for her. It looks like we'll be staying here longer than I thought." She frowned down at the white foam that pooled against the rocks. The sea beyond was clear aqua and a flock of seagulls rose up into the perfect blue sky.

Chloé eased herself out of Laurence's arms and turned to him. His gold-flecked eyes caught with hers, and she nodded at him. "Tell her," Chloé whispered. "Tell Anita what we discussed."

Laurence cleared his throat. "Anita. Chloé and I have come up with an idea that might alleviate some of the feeling that you are... trailing around with Sumner. Why don't you offer Eileen representation at your gallery?" His voice softened, lingering in the warm air.

Chloé waited.

In Paris, where the Americans of the war generation were filling the hotels and boulevards, the wealthier expatriates settling into the Ritz Hotel and partying with Parisian society, Sumner was going to be in demand by the fashionable set. He'd not only been painting portraits, and Eileen Gray was not the only wealthy person who was commissioning murals for her Rivera home.

"Eileen Gray? Representation?" Anita stilled. She turned her dark gaze toward Laurence and left it there. "What a devil you are, Laurence," she murmured.

Next to Chloé, Laurence raised an eyebrow. "Eileen said that the French were being slow to embrace things modern,

Anita," he said. "You heard her talking of her creative ideas. She's wanting to launch her lacquered furniture, so what if you were to host an exhibition in Rue Laffitte?" He lowered his voice, sending a glance toward the terrace, where the sounds of Sumner's soft laughter and Eileen's accompanying murmurs rent the air. A champagne cork popped.

Anita folded her arms, the dark circles that had bloomed beneath her eyes worrying Chloé. Anita had spoken honestly. She'd told Chloé that she was in love with Sumner, and so, what was there to do about this? Yet Chloé had listened, while Anita raged because it seemed effortless for Sumner to find work, while she was struggling to compete with the male dealers in the cut-throat world that showcased modern art. She'd been hoodwinked and undercut by other gallerists just when she thought she had an exciting artist on her books. Anita needed a lucky break.

Chloé squeezed Laurence's hand. Right now, if someone had asked her how much she adored her husband, she would have told them that her love for him was limitless. Laurence was the sort of man who never cooped a woman up. He'd encouraged her and supported her when she wished to work for Adrienne Monnier in her bookstore, and he'd been on the front row of every literary event she'd organized so far.

"I saw the way you were admiring her lacquer work, her weaving. Why not take the initiative?" he said.

Anita frowned.

"Why should you waste your time here?" Laurence asked. "I see no reason for it."

Chloé hardly dared to breathe.

And then, slowly, Anita raised her face. She reached out and cupped his cheek in her hand. "You are a dear man," she said, her voice quivering. "And right now, to me, you are a brilliant, ingenious friend."

Chloé grinned. When Laurence turned around, she blew

him a kiss. He had the grace to redden with pleasure and look down at the ground.

That afternoon, Chloé looked up from her wooden sunlounger on the main deck of the motor yacht that belonged to one of Eileen's friends. Laurence and Sumner stood at the ship's wheel, and Anita was seated with Eileen in the shaded dining area. Chloé was engaged in trying not to eavesdrop, while fighting to stem a curiosity that was driving her wild.

Laurence came to stand near her. "How is the lip-reading coming along?" he said.

Chloé eyed Anita, who was deep in conversation with their talented host. "I don't know," she murmured, "but I worry that if Anita doesn't pull this off, the rest of our week will be marred by her disappointment."

Laurence sat down on the sunlounger next to Chloé's. He stretched out his long legs and placed a hand in hers. "I'll make sure you won't have a bad time of it."

Chloé grinned. "Oh?" she said, turning to him.

He smiled back at her, closing his eyes against the blissful summer sun.

Chloé sat back a moment. How she'd missed the South of France, living in the cold northern parts of France. Paris was, in its own way, wonderful, but she was a girl who appreciated the Provençal light. Adrienne had given her a month off to come down here, and next, they'd be going to the magical Chateau D'Anez in the Loire Valley.

She propped herself up on her elbow.

Anita was standing up and shaking Eileen's hand, and as Eileen stood up to go into the cabin of the yacht, Anita turned toward Chloé, and Chloé could see it, her friend's face was beautifully flushed.

In one quick, surefire movement, Anita grinned at Chloé.

And Chloé clapped her hands, her heart leaping for her friend. Anita would enjoy what Chloé had now. Love, and a purpose for her life. Because, as Chloé's maman always said, if you have those two things, no matter what that purpose is, then that is the most important thing in life. And after what they'd been through, it was exactly what Chloé wanted for her dearest friend.

16

Charlotte

Charlotte sat on her bed in the hilltop town of Montauban. Her head rested against the white-painted wall in the new digs they'd been assigned by the Louvre. Outside, the sun beat hard on the pink-bricked buildings. It had faded them to the color of a peach.

The blue shutters in the old town were closed as the citizens of Montauban tried to take their afternoon naps. But Charlotte was certain that in every house in every town and city of France, someone had a wireless on. Because the news that was filtering in from Paris was breathtakingly intense.

Charlotte's muscles ached and her body yearned to rest after moving the artworks a little further southwest from the abbey to Montauban where they were to be stored. But her heart was on fire with anger because she could not stop listening to the constant stream of devastating news that was circulating around France.

Charlotte swiveled her gaze toward the small wireless that sat on the table between her and Sandrine's beds, where one of the most elaborately staged dramas since the war had begun was being described word by horrible word. Charlotte blinked in disbelief.

"It is inconceivable," Sandrine whispered from her own bed. She crossed herself, shaking her head and then drawing a hand over her blond hair. Streaks of perspiration lined Sandrine's forehead, and the skin surrounding her gray eyes was traced with tiny new lines.

"This must be one of the most dramatic surrenders in history." Charlotte slipped her legs over one side of the bed and moved to the shuttered window. She was in need of some, albeit stifling, air.

Throwing open the shutters, she leaned against the windowsill and looked down at the cobbled streets of the old town below as the wireless announcer spoke in hideously dispassionate tones. "*Adolf Hitler has insisted that the French armistice with Germany was to be signed in the very same railroad car, and on the very same spot in the forest of Compiègne, where the Germans surrendered at the end of World War One. Twenty-two years have passed since this countryside bore witness to another major world event.*"

Charlotte furled her fists into two balls as the news rolled on.

"*Nearly all Western Europe has now fallen at the feet of the mighty German Blitzkrieg. Next, Hitler has his eyes on Great Britain. And at this point, there seems little likelihood he will be deterred. With governments toppling and leader after leader handing power to the Third Reich, Germany's domination of Europe is gaining momentum at a speed more rapid than anyone had predicted.*"

"Everyone knows that Pétain is a puppet leader," Charlotte said, still gazing down at the timeless scene outside. "Everyone knows that all the power of his Vichy government flows from Berlin."

Sandrine made a sympathetic noise from her bed. "Goodness help us," she whispered, the shudder in her voice sounding as if she spoke for all the women of France.

Charlotte turned back into the room and turned the wireless off. "I am going out, for a walk," she said to Sandrine. "Will you be all right?"

Sandrine nodded. "Of course," she said. "Go and walk it off. Buy a cool drink..." She sent Charlotte a faint smile.

Charlotte placed her hat on her head and smiled right back at Sandrine as best she could. There was not a chance that she could lie down and rest this afternoon.

Charlotte strode toward the crowded market stalls in Montauban's Place Nationale the following morning. The charming square with its pink-bricked buildings and double arches rang with vendor's cries. Fresh red tomatoes, deep green leeks and fat zucchini filled the wooden boxes that lined the square. Charlotte allowed herself a wistful smile as she passed a stall filled with sunflowers. Her father used to talk of their mother's love of sunflowers, and of the warmth that those in the South of France enjoyed in the summer months.

Charlotte came to a halt under one of the arches that led to a side street. She'd done a full circuit of the market and Louis was nowhere to be seen. She shuddered at the way she'd so brazenly expressed her opinions to him now. In a matter of days, everything had changed, rendering the France she was standing in today unrecognizable compared to the country they'd known even a few weeks ago.

Sandrine had warned her to be discreet on the way here. The idea of living in a country that was divided in two, not only geographically but with people who were split and divided in their hearts, was leaving so many with no choice but to remain silent on the topic of the terrifying war that was taking place over their heads. Armand had said that many people were adopting the stance of waiting to see what living in a divided country would be like. Sandrine had warned that some citizens would be even hoping to benefit under the new governments.

This morning, Sandrine had added that she thought some of the older people of France might be too scared to risk falling out with the Nazis or the Vichy government, because, she said, those with families, children, businesses, and the responsibilities of caring for older parents could not afford to risk their welfare and loved one's lives by standing up to the Nazis, or the Vichy government. Based on the stories coming out of Germany, standing up to the Nazis was not an option if one wanted to survive.

Charlotte's heart began to race when there was a tap on her shoulder, but she did not turn around immediately to see who had followed her here. She sensed there was more to this meeting with Louis than she understood just yet. Charlotte moved a little further away from Place Nationale, toward cobbled Rue Princesse when she felt the slip of a piece of paper in the pocket of her skirt. The tall, narrow buildings loomed either side of her, and many of the apartments above the shops and the market stalls sat with their blue shutters closed against the hot sun.

Another wider square spread in front of her at the end of the street. In the distance, Charlotte glimpsed a young woman dressed in green. She was rushing away down another narrow lane.

Charlotte kept moving, keen, for some reason, not to be loitering. She curled her fingers around the paper that was lodged in her pocket and drew it up, reading the address printed upon it. There was a pencil-drawn map, and it was signed by Louis. Charlotte, a sense of grim determination forming in her belly, along with a flutter of excitement that perhaps, somehow, she could do something to help, tore the paper to shreds, scattering a little of it in one trash can on one side of the square, and placing the rest of it in another.

Her heart beat wildly and she crossed the square, following Louis's directions.

Her insides quailed when she walked down Rue Armand Cambon. This street was quieter, the pavement plain, not cobbled, and the windows in the buildings were protected with iron rails. The sun wasn't shining in this street, and the only footsteps that echoed on the otherwise silent pavement were her own.

Charlotte drew in a breath and her hands shook as she came to the address that had been scrawled on the paper. She stepped inside when the door was opened, only to come face to face with the girl in the green dress whom she'd seen disappearing from the marketplace.

"Hurry," the girl whispered in English, her light brown hair pulled back from her face and gathered in a clasp at her neck. The girl's blue eyes took in Charlotte's appearance, and a frown line ran straight between her brows.

Charlotte chewed on her lip. This young woman looked Parisian and sophisticated. Charlotte couldn't have felt more out of her depth if she tried. She had no idea what she was truly getting involved in, but it seemed certain that it would mean taking a stand. The young woman drew the heavy double doors closed behind them. Charlotte followed her companion up a flight of narrow stairs to a small landing, where the girl knocked several times on a closed door.

Charlotte stood with her heart pounding in her mouth.

The door opened to a small room with bare, dusty floorboards. It was simply furnished, with a single bed, a wooden desk and a chair. A suitcase was thrown open on the floor with the contents of a young man's wardrobe spilling out of it. Charlotte raised a brow, the tension inside her dissipating for the first time since she'd left her bedroom. The sight of that suitcase and all the clothes spilling out of it made her feel like a girl of twenty-one for the first time in an age.

Louis came through a door from the back of the apartment. He stopped and his face broke into that sudden smile. Those dimples appeared on his cheeks. His blue shirt was rolled up to his elbows and a sheen of perspiration on his forehead.

"*Bonjour*," he said, rubbing his hand across his jaw and taking a quick glance out the window at the empty street outside. He rested a hand against the desk and tilted his tall body to one side. "I am glad you came to meet us. Henri?" he called, sending Charlotte a smile.

She hovered just inside the room. When Henri entered from a kitchen beyond, she breathed a sigh of relief. Louis's intensity, she had to admit it, could come on a little too strong.

"*Bonjour*," Henri said, pulling up a wooden chair, turning it around backwards and sitting down on it, his forearms resting across its top.

The girl who'd led Charlotte here slid down a wall and settled herself on the floor. Henri pulled a cigarette packet out of his pocket, rolled a cigarette, lit it, and handed it down to the girl. Charlotte took in the fact that the girl's dress was well cut and of quality linen, and the matching green leather T-bar shoes she wore were elegant and new.

The cigarette smoke filtered through the air and Charlotte sighed at the smell she associated with Paris, with the crowded cafés and the narrow streets of Montmartre and Montparnasse. She closed her eyes a moment and remembered those streets filled with shops and galleries that she'd left behind, the shopkeepers who used to greet her in the mornings, as they pulled the blinds up to start a new day.

"Of course, I came," she said to Louis, her American accent sounding strange amongst these sophisticated young French people. "I said I would meet you and I'm here."

Louis's eyes glanced at hers for a moment, and for a split second, he showed that dimple again.

"You have met Henri," Louis said. "And this," he said, indicating toward the girl, "is Madeleine."

Charlotte moved across the room to take the girl's outstretched hand.

"That is not her real name," Louis added, his sudden change of tone cutting into the room.

Charlotte's hand stilled.

"It is safer that you do not know," Louis went on.

Charlotte swallowed and nodded. How quickly they must all adapt to this strange new state of affairs. Back at home, France was viewed as a playground, with Paris being the capital of fun. Now, none of them knew what the coming months would bring.

"Madeleine," Louis said, "this is Gabrielle."

Charlotte's eyes widened, but Louis glanced at her and came to sit on the single bed. He stretched his long legs out in front of him and accepted a cigarette from Henri. He lit up, and offered it to Charlotte.

She shook her head. Again, the feeling of being utterly unsophisticated swept over her, but the last thing she wanted to do was choke on a cigarette.

She chose a spot against the wall and slid down it, just as her companions had done.

"What do you think of the latest developments?" Louis asked, his brown eyes intent on Charlotte.

She went to open her mouth, then shot a glance toward the blue-eyed girl he'd called Madeleine, and her insides tightened. "I... reserve judgment." She almost whispered the words.

"You can speak freely here," he said. "We are all of the same opinion. Mainly," he added, grinning at Henri.

Henri swiped at him.

Charlotte folded her hands in her lap. It was all she could

do to stop herself from swiveling her gaze from one to another of these attractive people. "I am appalled," she said, softly. "It is still inconceivable to me."

Madeleine leaned back, stretching her legs out in front of her and crossing them at the ankles. "Louis tells us that you are working with the Louvre," she said. Her voice was husky and her accent was heavy, even though her sentence was formed perfectly in English.

"To call it work is a stretch," Charlotte said. "I feel surplus to requirements. I have nothing to do down here."

The others were quiet. Madeleine's blue gaze remained fixed on her.

Charlotte frowned. They were asking for her discretion. They would need to show more themselves. "You can trust me," she said. She kept her voice low and glanced from Louis, to Henri, and last, to Madeleine. "I will not repeat what is said in this room." She meant it.

Henri rested his hands behind his head. "I think Pétain will come around at the end of the summer. I'm certain this agreement with the Nazis is only a short-term arrangement."

Louis let out a loud sigh and Madeleine shook her head.

Henri curled his lip. "I'm certain the old fighter will change his mind. Everyone's forgotten that Pétain was the architect of Verdun in the last 'war to end all wars.' Why would he want to sustain an agreement with the Nazis?"

Madeleine spoke in low, confident tones. "Verdun was a folly. A battle to move the lines a few thousand yards in each direction." She scoffed. "You are talking about trusting the architect whose 'glorious battle' killed nearly seven hundred thousand French and German men!"

Charlotte's brows drew closer.

Louis blew a perfect smoke ring. "The Pétain government has already yielded on the first point of contention with the occupying Nazi'. Pétain is sending all the refugees who've come here from Germany back to the Third Reich the moment Hitler demands their return." He eyed Henri. "You can wait until the end of the summer to see if he changes his policies, I'm not willing to take that chance." Louis leaned forward and lowered his voice. His dark eyes landed on Charlotte and stayed there. "You are wondering why we asked you here."

Charlotte nodded. She pressed her hands into the wooden floor, certain that she'd made the right decision to come, but deadly uncertain why they'd chosen her.

"Henri," Louis said, "is the editor of a political student newspaper at the Sorbonne. Madeleine and I write articles for his paper."

"Only tell her what she needs to know, Louis," Madeleine cautioned.

Charlotte opened her mouth. "Forgive me," she said. "I know your name, Louis, and yours, Henri, but Madeleine and I are to remain a mystery to each other?" It made no sense.

Henri looked at her through the smoky haze, his eyes narrowing. "Women will be undertaking the missions that we want to discuss with you."

Madeleine shrugged. "They will be called up," she said. "It is the women of France who will resist. I am certain of it. And if will be the young women."

Charlotte nodded hesitantly. Sandrine had said as much. More mature adults who had children and elderly parents would not want to risk the government's wrath. So, she was the perfect target for anyone wanting to recruit people to help their cause.

Louis lowered his voice. "You must understand the risks and accept that you will only know what is necessary for you to operate with us."

Charlotte stayed quiet; her eyes trained on Louis.

"The Gestapo are infamous for their methods of questioning," he murmured. "I am getting ahead of myself. What I want to ask you is whether you would be willing to courier our articles from the unoccupied zone to Paris? Would you be willing to carry anti-Nazi literature into the occupied zone?"

Charlotte's hands froze in front of her. "Propaganda?"

Louis glanced at Henri and Madeleine, and his face broke into a grin.

"We don't like to think so," he said. "We prefer to consider ourselves the authors of well thought out, intelligent opinion articles."

"An underground newspaper," Charlotte murmured.

The others stayed quiet.

"The Nazis have tapped the airwaves," Madeleine murmured, her voice crystal clear despite her soft tone. "The only way we can try to rally young people is on the printed page with deliveries by foot. And we need couriers who will not attract suspicion from the Nazis."

Henri's expression was serious. "You would be responsible for not only transporting articles to Paris, but once we have the newspaper up and running, we would need to rely on you to bring the completed newspapers back down to Montauban for distribution in the unoccupied zone."

"You would have to watch out for French police, German police, and worse, the Gestapo," Louis said.

Charlotte lifted her chin.

"The Nazis are regularly raiding the Metro lines in Paris," Madeleine added. "This is one of the most dangerous parts of our entire student network. What we are asking you to do is extremely risky. Do you understand that?"

"Of course." Charlotte curled her lip. "That, I do understand." She shuddered. She had failed to save Anita's gallery. Chateau d'Anez was a sitting duck, waiting for the Nazis to attack it. Yes, she'd managed to save the Goldstein family's artworks so far. But she was darned if she would sit by and do nothing while France's citizens suffered under the brutality of a regime that had nothing to do with them.

Louis leaned forward. "At the hint of a raid or an inspection, you would need to be prepared to get off at the station when the police forces get on and run through the stations underground to complete your mission."

"Yes," Charlotte said. Her heart swelled with anticipation.

Louis looked at her intently. "There are curfews in the occupied zone and if you get found out after dark, you will be caught, questioned, and will be at risk of deportation to Germany. We want you to fully understand what this means, Charlotte. Like I said, this is the most dangerous job of our entire mission. But it is essential, and using couriers is the only way to spread news, rather than the propaganda the Nazis are spouting at every turn."

Charlotte cupped her hands in front of her. She stared at the floor, her pulse beating fast, her senses alert. He was right. The images of the citizens of Germany following Hitler blindly at his rallies were terrifying, but they were working. People needed to be informed about the truth behind Hitler and the Nazis' facade.

"You will have false identity papers," Madeleine added.

"You have a distribution network, I presume," Charlotte said. "A printing press, typists, paper?"

"Try not to ask questions that are unrelated to your safety," Louis warned. "Remember. The touchstone of this operation is that the less you know, the better. You are the one most at risk, so we won't tell you anything you don't need to know. You will not at any time be aware of the location of the printers," he said. "You would simply have to go and pick up the newspapers from an anonymous apartment in Paris and bring them back here. If the network sends more than one courier at a time, we will ask you to travel on separate trains so you don't both get caught, and unwittingly expose the entire ring."

Charlotte swallowed, the reality of the danger of this sinking in.

"You'd best dye your hair blond," Henri murmured.

"Blond?" Charlotte threw a glance to Madeleine, but the other girl simply nodded.

"You will tell your colleagues that you are trying to impress a boyfriend? No?"

Charlotte rolled her eyes. She might fool Armand and Lucie, but Sandrine knew her better than that. She'd have to come up with something more convincing than a boyfriend.

"I think you should wear white bobby socks," Henri added. He talked lightly, as if he were discussing a cricket match. "The German soldiers are mostly country boys. They are impressed by French schoolgirls and sophisticated Parisian women in equal measure. You would fall under the first category," he said, shrugging. "Sorry, Gabrielle," he added, when Louis grinned.

Charlotte raked a hand through her tousled hair and raised her makeup-free eyebrows. "Would you like me to carry a satchel and wear plaits in my hair as well?"

Henri waved his cigarette in the air and sent her a grin.

"You must be discreet. You will not at any time know any names of the others in the network." Louis's brow darkened. "I would anticipate that in a few months, they will all be women. My main aim is to keep you safe and inconspicuous. I want you to blend in, use charm to get yourself out of any awkward situations, and above all, keep your eyes open and be prepared to slip away at the hint of danger."

Madeleine stubbed out her cigarette in her ashtray. "Welcome to *le defi de France.*"

"Defiance?" Charlotte said. "It is my middle name."

17

NEW YORK, SUMMER 1940

Martha

Martha swore she had read the same page of her novel six times, and yet, not one sentence held any meaning for her. The stack of books by her bed was at risk of toppling over, and yet, she still borrowed novels from the library, picking them like flowers as if, somehow, she'd wake up from the nightmare that raged over Europe and she'd be able to go back to being who she used to be, a woman who found solace in stories. But she'd not been able to read one book in full since Clyde had been interred in a prison of war camp.

Worry had become her closest friend. If she was not split in two thinking of Clyde, imagining what the dear man might be enduring, she was finding herself distracted with anxiety for Charlotte. Night after night, Martha found it impossible to fall asleep. She'd lie awake until the early hours of the morning, her mind refusing to calm down.

For while everyone in the household tried to assure each other that Charlotte was afforded more protection than most people in France because she was working under the auspices of the Louvre, Martha knew better. The very safety everyone talked about was anathema to her sister. Protection was not something Charlotte would ever seek.

Martha lay back on her bed, throwing her arms behind her head and staring at the ceiling.

"Martha."

She started at the sound of Élise's voice in the doorway, and turned to see her dear friend standing there. Élise's expression was a blend of kindness and worry.

Martha stood up from her bed. She'd become more than grateful that Élise and Olivier remained in their home.

"Don't tell me," She moved to kiss Élise on the cheek. "Eleanor Roosevelt has agreed to everything we asked?" Martha attempted to smile at Élise, but the truth was, she had to force her features into shape. She saw the way Élise's eyes drifted to Martha's hands, which she was knotting and twisting in front of her dress.

Élise glanced toward the open bedroom door and moved across to close it with a soft thud. "Oh, you have no idea at my frustration that things are moving so slowly when it comes to Gisela," she said. Élise's brow furrowed. "I am only relieved that she has managed to secure a passage to Lisbon. She was fortunate to be able to get out of France and enter neutral Portugal. But now?" She threw her hands in the air.

Martha sighed. Élise had expressed her very real concern for Gisela these past nights at the dinner table. She'd been trying to communicate with her Viennese friend by telegram and had urged her to leave France. But Élise was pale with worry because the Portuguese government had limited the passage of Jews and other refugees. The papers reported that tens of thousands of Jewish refugees were trying to pass through Portugal en route to the United States.

"At least she is in the right place to embark for America, should a miracle happen and one of those universities decide to accept a brilliant woman," Martha said. She held Élise's cold hands and rubbed them. "And we know there are relief organizations in Portugal, so that is positive." She searched Élise's face.

Élise trailed a hand over her forehead. "Darling, there is something else. Another letter came today while you were at work." She swiveled her head toward the closed bedroom door and lowered her voice. "I did not mention it to your papa. But this time," Élise went on, her brow crinkling, "it was not from Scotland, but France."

Martha gasped. *Clyde.* She tore her hands away from Élise's and strode across the room to stand by the window. Outside, darkness was falling, and the trees formed strange and murky shapes. Martha struggled to gather herself, but her entire body shook. She turned around to face Élise. "Please, I must read it, now."

Élise reached into her pocket. She held out the envelope.

Hardly knowing what she was doing, not caring, for once, that another member of this household was witness to the awful, searing worry she felt for Clyde, Martha tore at the top of the envelope, her fingers fumbling. It was all she could do not to rent the precious letter in two, her fingers were slipping so much.

Martha pulled the letter out, and feverishly began scanning the words, but the letter blurred in front of her eyes. The writing was Clyde's.

Knowing the letter would have passed through German and Allied censors, Martha raced to find meaning behind his words.

Dearest Martha,

I know that Kirsty has been keeping you up to speed, and I only hope she has not been worrying you.

Martha slumped back toward the windowsill. He, in a prisoner of war camp, was worried about her state of mind!

> *I am allowed to write two letters home due to my good
> behavior.*
>
> *Dearest Martha, the thought of you and, dare I confess it,
> that dress, is keeping me going these days. And I have to say,
> the other thing that nourishes me [REDACTED] is taking care
> of the health and spirits of my fellow captives. This is allowing
> me to get to know so many of the fellows in this place that is
> [REDACTED]. It gives me a purpose, and that is what keeps
> us going in these circumstances we find ourselves in.*
>
> *Darling Martha [REDACTED] They stare at the mud
> below their feet, and I wonder what they are thinking. How
> could they possibly render this situation acceptable?*
>
> *[REDACTED] in this camp, so, most of the days, we study.
> Our senior officers, some of them intellectuals, are teaching the
> men in subjects they will find useful when we are let out:
> economics, business, and agriculture. We have a tiny engi-
> neering school. As you can imagine, my darling girl, I am
> teaching courses in medicine and first aid. Those of us with
> university educations banded together and decided this was
> the best use of our time.*
>
> *[REDACTED] as to how you fare in these places. All I
> can say is that you did incredibly well to bring [REDACTED]
> to the United States. You must be proud of that. You have most
> likely saved their lives and rescued them from [REDACTED].*

Martha shuddered. She glanced at Élise, who was looking
intently at a painting on Martha's wall. Martha turned back to
Clyde's words.

> *The Red Cross have provided us with shovels because they are
> afraid we will not be protected from air raids. We have*

[REDACTED] *with them. Some of our men have* [REDACTED].

Of course, I am not allowed to tell you where we are. But do take heart, we have built a small theater for those amongst us who are thespians, and we have begun staging plays with men dressed as women in costumes made by those who are able to sew.

Martha stopped reading. She swiped at a tear that fell down her cheek, a sad laugh bursting from her lips. Bless him.

She shook her head, her hand over her mouth, and read on.

We have a vegetable garden, although the food all [REDACT-ED]. We expect a good harvest, nevertheless, and have made plans to alter our plantings slightly next season to take advantage of the sun. As you can imagine, we have plenty of time to make plans.

"Oh, you imagine being there next season?" Martha whispered. She shook her head.

We have a good range of chaps here—mathematicians, geologists, architects and more. We are a camp full of expertise.

Darling Martha, please take care of yourself. I know you will be worrying about me. But please don't. I have simply decided to keep working here, in whatever capacity that I can help. There are fellows who are far worse off than I am, so I want you to sleep peacefully about me. And, until we meet again, sweetest of thoughts to you.

I miss you, and cannot wait until I can hold you in my arms,

Your Clyde

Martha placed the precious letter down. Her fingers pressed gently into the pages that, incredibly, had been held by Clyde in her beloved France.

"Martha?" Élise's voice seared into her thoughts.

Martha turned to face the elderly woman, who sat patiently in her chair.

"Is there something you want to tell me, darling?" Élise said, her head tilted to one side, her expression warm. "Because you know," she rested her hand on her heart, "that you can tell me anything, and it will not go any further, although, I think we both know that your papa might be ready to learn that his daughter has fallen in love."

Martha lifted her head, her eyes grazing Élise's face.

"You see," Élise said, her brow wrinkling, "I regret not always being there for my own daughter."

Martha frowned. "But Anita was so fortunate to have you. You were an incredible mother. Please—"

Élise shook her head. "I suspect, as only a mother can, that there were things Anita did not talk to me of, things that she held separate from me, and that I regret."

Élise stood up. She moved slowly, her hands reaching for the dressing table and the bedhead as she walked across the room to Martha.

"I wish I'd had the chance to help her, because while we all think of Anita as having been devoted to her career, there is not one person that I know who has never loved in their lifetime. I regret not being there for Anita when I know it happened to her."

Martha frowned. She had always wondered about Anita, who had always been so resolutely independent when she and Charlotte were growing up. There was never any mention of men, no admirers, no guests to the apartment on Rue Laffitte or Chateau d'Anez when they would spend entire summers there.

"Martha," Élise said. "Talk to me. Let me listen. And I promise, I will never judge you."

Martha looked at the elderly woman.

"It is not me I worry for," Martha said. "It is Papa."

Élise sat down on Martha's bed, and slowly, Martha handed Clyde's precious letter to her.

18

CHATEAU D'ANEZ, FRANCE, SUMMER 1919

Chloé

"Chloé, pull over. Please." Anita's voice rang above the engine of the little red Citroën that Olivier had lent them to drive to Chateau d'Anez for the remainder of their summer vacation. "I cannot, in all conscience, go on."

Chloé frowned and pulled onto the grassy verge just inside the entrance to the chateau. Anita had been quiet throughout the entire drive from Paris, but Chloé had taken this to be silent contemplation.

Anita stared straight ahead in the passenger seat, her hands clasped into a pair of tight balls.

Chloé turned to her. "You are unwell?" Selfishly, Chloé was so looking forward to this vacation in Chateau d'Anez, and the remainder of her precious month off was something she could not wait to begin.

Even in profile, it was impossible not to notice that Anita's face was pale and her expression was pinched against the vivid orange silk scarf she wore to protect her hair from the breeze.

Ahead of them, overarching trees lined the tantalizing

driveway that led directly to the old chateau, and wildflowers bloomed in the surrounding fields. Chloé sighed. The chateaux of northern France were something she'd only read about in history books and dreamed of seeing one day. And now here she was, on the way to Chateau d'Anez.

Anita pulled her scarf away and tossed it into the back seat. She leaned forward and rested her head in her hands.

"*Ma chérie?*" Chloé rubbed Anita's back.

"Nothing could have prepared me for the feelings I am experiencing now. Nothing." Anita ground out the words.

"Talk to me," Chloé said, her brow wrinkling. She balked at mentioning Anita's relationship with Sumner.

"Sometimes, the things you worry about never come to fruition, but then life hits you, like this." Anita lifted her head. She pushed her fist into her belly. "It is completely unexpected. You know?"

Chloé nodded. "I think so," she whispered. There was so much of Anita that she did know and love. But there was a side to her friend that was complex and brooding, and sometimes, Chloé worried that she didn't always have the capacity to get through to her.

Anita closed her eyes. When she spoke, her voice was low, and she recited her words almost mechanically. "Sumner and I are married."

Chloé's mouth fell open. She gasped and sat back in her seat.

Anita sent a quick glance her way, only to turn back and stare relentlessly straight ahead. "His family are Catholic," she said. "His parents would probably pull out a shotgun and shoot me in the head."

Chloé spoke in a halting, shaky voice. "You are not serious."

"Me. A Jewish girl," Anita said, her voice laced with a darkness that bit at the stunning summer's afternoon.

Chloé fumbled for words. She had to acknowledge that it

was all very well for her. There had been only joyous telegrams sent from New York when Laurence had informed his elderly parents, who were also Catholics, that he was engaged to Chloé.

Anita drew further back in her seat. "Sumner says his parents would disown him if they knew he'd married a European Jew behind their backs. I am not naïve enough to imagine that what we talk about in the cafés of Montparnasse is anything more than a fantasy," she said, grimacing.

"Surely his parents will love you, no matter what your religion. Because he loves you," Chloé said.

Anita threw back her head and laughed.

Chloé took in a deep breath. She fought the feelings of hurt and anger that threatened to swell within her. She'd thought she'd be Anita's bridesmaid and wanted, even now, though it was too late, to witness her marriage. And what about Élise and Olivier? Anita's parents?

Still digesting Anita's sudden, unexpected news and trying to come to terms with the thought of independent Anita married, Chloé waited for her friend to go on.

"Driving home to Chateau d'Anez and going to see Papa and Maman with this lie consuming me ..." Anita shook her head and her cheeks reddened. "What was, in the face of Sumner's family, an act of solidarity toward our beliefs, to the beliefs we have talked about and the new world we want to build after the war, with no one caring about race, or religion, the things that tear us apart..." Anita glowered at the driveway ahead. "Now, it feels like deception, Chloé. It feels like I have done this terrible thing. I feel that in making a secret vow with Sumner, I have broken an unspoken vow that does truly bind us together, that of family, and of doing the right thing by others."

Chloé took in a shaking breath. She shuddered. "I understand what you mean," she whispered. "I value these new ideas, of course I do, but I still love the idea of family as well."

Anita continued; her fingers pressed into her seat. "But

now, tell me this, Chloé. How can I move forward with Sumner when he thinks nothing of marrying me and not telling his parents?"

Chloé's head whipped around to her friend. "*What?* He has not even talked to them of you? Oh, Anita..." Chloé bit back her anger. She stared out the window at the peaceful countryside. A flock of sheep trotted in formation across the nearby field.

"How can I lie to my darling maman and papa and hide such a momentous thing from them in turn?"

Chloé gripped the steering wheel of Olivier's car. She stared hard at the bracelet Laurence had given her when they married. She never took the delicate little gold filigree chain off. Anita had no such token and no such emblem to recognize her marriage. Chloé hated Anita feeling so unsupported that she'd not even talked to her closest friends. Until now.

"My mother and father are extremely tied up with their artistic patronages and their society world, that is true," Anita murmured. "While we seem like the perfect family to so many, you know, we are not," she said, her eyes misting over. She swiped a hand across her face. "I thought in marrying Sumner, in falling for a real, struggling artist, that I was striking out on my own. Sometimes, I feel that the world of commercial success that my parents inhabit can seem fabricated, you know."

Chloé's mouth worked. She pressed her own hand atop her friend's. "I understand your intentions, and where you were coming from, Anita," she said.

"My parents are glamorous, elegant and rich," Anita went on. "But, you see, all their perfection, their success, forged during the Belle Époque, is something I cannot relate to because I am a child of the war. It has not been the experience of our generation to have all this success handed to us. We did not grow up in a safe world," she whispered, her eyes huge, turning to Chloé. "How could my parents begin to understand what it was to lose half the people of your own generation to war?"

Chloé reached out and leaned her hand on the dashboard. Anita had told her how Olivier had worked hard, owning clothing factories, which he had started from scratch as a young man, and in which he had manufactured uniforms during the war, only rendering him even wealthier than he was before it began. She hated to say it, but Anita had seen her own parents profiting from war, while it killed the boys their own age in the muddy, rotten trenches of northern France.

Chloé sighed. "No matter how hard it seems to talk to Élise and Olivier, no matter how difficult it might be to upset them, secrets and family do not marry well," Chloé said. She turned to Anita. "I honestly think you should tell them. Despite differing circumstances, and generations, some truths hold strong."

Anita barked out another laugh, tears falling down her cheeks now. She shook her head, her words coming out watery. "I envy you your country childhood," she said. "Simplicity is underrated in this world, darling Chloé. Perhaps I could take you to talk to Sumner's parents as well?"

Chloé chose her words with care. "Tell Sumner that you are not one to lie to your maman and papa. Set a boundary with him." She frowned. Anita was so strong in many ways, and yet when it came to falling in love, her heart was as vulnerable as any other person's.

Anita lowered her voice. "I *cannot* tell my family when he cannot tell his. And yet, I won't live with myself and hurt my parents. It is impossible. There is no way out." She turned to Chloé. Her expression was haunted.

Chloé's heart went out to her. She reached forward and pulled Anita into a hug.

"Papa and Maman would not understand his stance at all," Anita mumbled into Chloé's shoulder. "They will be furious that he thought I was not good enough because I am a Jewish girl. It is all they have worked for all their lives—to be, good enough. Collecting art, making money. Don't you see? To have their daughter rejected by a New York family would mean they failed. It would shatter them!"

Chloé rubbed her hand over her belly. Oh, how she hoped the child she would bear was going to grow into a more tolerant and understanding world. How she prayed that the next generation would not have to struggle with questions such as these!

"Perhaps it is not which generation you are born into, nor how old you are that matters. Perhaps it is the way in which you allow people to prove themselves before you show judgment that makes you truly open-hearted," Chloé said.

Anita lifted her head. Her dark eyes caught with Chloé's and held.

"Your parents might have worked hard, but there is nothing to be ashamed of in that. Élise and Olivier are tolerant. It is Sumner's parents who are in the wrong here." And Sumner, for not telling them, Chloé wanted to shout. She thumped her hand on her knee instead.

"Your child," Anita whispered, "will grow up with a pair of loving parents and with two sets of grandparents who will support them. In my case, status and money make things far more complicated than they need to be."

"I hate that you cannot be a part of his family," Chloé whispered. "That is brutal. Unfair. And they are in America, the modern world! Surely, our old-world prejudices do not have to carry on there?"

A breeze ruffled the grassy fields beyond the single line of trees, and the poppies that lined the verge tilted in the wind.

"There is more. I am pregnant," Anita said.

Chloé drew her hand to her mouth. "Both of us? At the same time?" she whispered. She reached out to pull Anita into a hug, but her friend held up a hand.

"I am carrying my parents' grandchild. I cannot bear to raise this baby without my loving parents by my side." She pressed her hand against her heart. "Without my family, this child will have half the life it deserves, and I have to consider my baby now, not just myself."

A sudden coldness hit Chloé at her core. "But a baby will change everything as far as Sumner's family is concerned?"

Anita's eyes slowly, inevitably locked with Chloé's, and in Anita's dull, haunted expression, Chloé had all the answer she sought.

Chloé woke in the middle of the night at the soft tap on her bedroom door. She reached for her dressing gown, and carefully, so as not to wake Laurence, tiptoed across the room. She opened the bedroom door, only to come face to face with Anita in the hallway, her eyes huge in the darkness, her silk nightgown wrapped around her body. She reached out to clutch Chloé's arm.

Chloé stepped toward her friend and embraced Anita's stiff, tense body. But Anita's frame was as thin as a little bird's.

"I must end it. I have decided to end my relationship with Sumner." Anita pulled back and her eyes cast about wildly. "Don't you see?"

Chloé shuddered. "But your child is Sumner's baby too," she hissed, her eyes casting about wildly in the dark. Laurence was sleeping peacefully on his back, as he always did. When Chloé glanced back at him, the father of her child, she felt the gentle stirrings of her baby moving inside her, and she reached out instinctively and rested her hand in that place where she sensed the deepest love she'd ever known. A searing, moving, protective love that was different from what she felt for Laurence or for her family. This was a love that she couldn't bear to hide from the man she adored.

She closed her eyes, allowing the slight flutters and sensations to move until they settled in her heart, where, she knew, her feelings for this baby would always remain.

Chloé gathered herself. "There has to be another way. Surely?"

Anita folded her arms, her eyes falsely bright. "I do not see that I have a choice."

Chloé stared. "But you love each other." It was simple, but the only thing she could find to say.

Anita gripped Chloé's hand. "He *must* not know about the baby."

Chloé opened her mouth. "Anita..." Her voice was a low warning.

But Anita held up a hand. She led Chloé to sit on a narrow seat underneath one of the tall windows that lined the hall.

Chloé slid down next to her friend.

Anita took both her hands and clasped them in her own. "If his family will not accept me, and he assures me they will not..." She shook her head when Chloé opened her mouth in protest. "...Then I shall give the baby away for adoption."

"Oh, no, darling Anita." Chloé shook her head, a lump forming in her throat. "We must raise them together. Love them together. It is what we fought for. This is why we looked after all those wounded boys in the war. So, we could come out of this. So, there could be a next generation!" Chloé pleaded with Anita, she wrung her hands up and down.

But Anita's gaze flickered toward the room where her parents both slept. "As soon as I set foot in Chateau d'Anez, and I laid eyes on Maman and Papa, I knew. I knew that I could not, in all good faith, tell them that I had married a man whose family would disown me and who would never welcome my child into their home."

Chloé grasped her friend's hands.

"That is no life for a baby. This child will be better off with a loving family who know none of this shameful mess. I *never* want my child to think that they were not welcomed by half of their family. It would be unsupportable. A terrible start in life."

Chloé's heart raced. Her eyes searched Anita's face. They'd been thrust into war before they were twenty. And now, with nothing to guide them except years in a bloody white tent, they were thrown out of the firepit of war into adulthood, having missed the years during which they should have grown up in peaceful circumstances. And there was no one to talk about it. They were two girls, dealing with an age-old problem that neither of them understood.

"Before you say anything," Anita continued, as if she did have the answers, as if by blustering through, she'd make this work, "were I to raise my child alone in Paris..." Anita buried her head in her hands. "It would be unfair on them," she muttered. "They would be shunned. I would be shunned. We talk of a different world, but the fact is, we inhabit this one."

Chloé stared at her friend.

Anita lifted her eyes to lock with Chloé's. The long plait that she'd tied her hair into for the night swung over one shoulder, and her dark eyes glinted in the night. "I will go to Switzerland for seven months," she said. "But I shall pretend that I am going on a tour of Europe to inspect galleries to learn more about running one myself. Because it is difficult, and I am struggling."

"No."

Anita lifted her chin. "But when I have given birth, and I have..." She swallowed. "Known what it is to give up a child, I won't care about those male gallerists. They will know *nothing* of what I have endured. And I shall run my gallery to perfection. On my own. No more men for me." She folded her arms, her lips closed tight in determination.

Chloé slumped back in her seat. "What of Sumner? He will have no say, no choice?"

"Tomorrow, we shall enjoy one last picnic with Sumner,"

Anita said. Her eyes were downcast. "And then, I shall tell him that it's over. That I can't go on. I can't be with the man who has led me to giving up my baby."

Chloé wrapped her arms around her body.

Anita turned to face her in the dark. Chloé threw her arms around her. In the darkness, she turned away from Anita's shoulder, her head down, her mouth working. And as she wiped the tears away, all she saw were shattered dreams. Dreams of her baby and Anita's baby together that would never come to fruition; of the four of them—she, Laurence, Sumner, and Anita—raising their children in peacetime because they'd fought for four years for the right to come home and create beautiful families of their own.

Chloé watched as Anita disentangled herself from their embrace and disappeared into her bedroom. Chloé moved across to the window, staring out at the moonlight that pooled in the garden, shifting and moving in secret ways.

Chloé lay with her eyes wide open the following morning. She had not been back to sleep. Now, she stared at the decorative patterns on the ceiling above her bed. Dawn pearled over the gardens of Chateau d'Anez, and outside the window, the sounds of a gardener raking the gravel lent a rhythmic, comforting sound to the otherwise silent house.

Chloé reached a hand out to touch Laurence's shoulder to stir him awake.

"Laurie?"

He stirred.

And as his eyes opened, softening at the sight of her by his side, he reached out and stroked a tendril of hair from her cheek.

"There is something important we need to talk about," she whispered, and she settled herself in the crook of his arm.

And then, quietly, she began to tell him her plan.

That afternoon, Chloé lay stretched out on a picnic rug under the linden trees that lined the great lawn surrounding Chateau d'Anez. Sumner had his easel up on the lawn with the glorious old chateau behind him. His brow furrowed in concentration. He was painting a picture of their picnic together, although he didn't know it was their last one.

Chloé rolled over onto her side, propping herself on one elbow as Sumner pulled the small canvas from his easel and brought it over to show them his finished work.

"You work quickly," Chloé breathed, her eyes searching his face, battling for the answer that had eluded her all day. Was Anita doing the right thing not telling him of their child?

Ever since Sumner had arrived this morning, Anita had been white, strained and silent. Sumner had been buoyant, exhilarated and charming. He'd charmed Élise and Olivier, and Chloé was torn for them all.

Not once had either he or Anita mentioned marriage.

Chloé stood up and peered over Sumner's shoulder at the painting of their picnic. He'd painted himself into it. A lump formed in her throat. "How marvelous," she said. He was talented. He'd go far.

She and Laurence would never see him again.

Anita caught Chloé's eye and indicated her head toward the chateau. For one long moment, Chloé held her friend's gaze, longing for her to change her mind, longing for Anita to talk to Sumner and to try to work out a way forward for what Chloé knew could be a wonderful little family if Anita were to try.

But Anita folded her arms, and, although she sat on the rug as pale as a newly washed sheet, her expression was resolute. Chloé recognized the look in Anita's eyes. It was impermeable.

It was final. She'd seen it when young men they'd cared for had died.

Chloé knew she had no choice but to let Anita break her own heart.

"Darling," she said, her fingers curling around Laurence's hand. "I'm dying to swim in the lake..." She stopped, almost saying goodbye to Sumner.

Laurence stood up. "You are welcome to join us," he said, smiling at the other couple.

But Anita lowered her gaze, and Chloé tugged on Laurence's arm. She drew him away from the picnic rug, and when she shot a glance back toward Anita and Sumner, who had gently lowered himself down to sit by her passionate friend's side, she took in a sharp breath at the sight of Anita, because she was staring at the painting of the four of them at their last picnic, and tears were running freely down her pale cheeks.

Sumner, bless him, reached out and wiped them away.

That evening, Chloé stood by the lake with Anita. She looked out at the shimmering blue-purple vista that spread before them in the dimming light. Darkness would fall over the countryside soon and the air still seemed redolent with the sounds of Sumner's car departing down the long driveway of Chateau d'Anez for good.

"It is done," Anita said. Her voice shook, but she turned to Chloé, her eyes bright with unshed tears in the twilight that hung over the lake at the edge of the gardens. "Sumner is gone for good. I shall never see him again. I shall book a trip to Switzerland tomorrow, and then, I won't ever see my baby again either." She buried her head in her shaking hands.

"Laurence and I will raise your child," Chloé said, her

words bursting out as if of their own accord. "Let us take care of your precious baby alongside ours."

And then, as darkness gathered over their heads, neither of them spoke.

When the moon threw a flicker of pearled light across the water of the beautiful lake at Chateau d'Anez, Anita turned to Chloé and Chloé felt her friend's hand atop her own. They were more like sisters than friends. They were, Chloé knew it, family.

Chloé stood firm, staring at the dash of moonlight on the water, and in the quiet summer's night, she knew she could do this, and she squeezed Anita's hand.

19

NEW YORK, SUMMER 1941

Martha

Two short blasts from the foghorn of SS *Quanza* blazed through the air above the Hudson River, cutting into the oppressive New York summer's heat. Martha stared up from where she stood amongst the cheering mass on the pier. Beside her, Elizabeth Ellwood's eyes lit up in satisfaction at the sight of the great Portuguese passenger-cargo ship that was finally, *finally* bringing Gisela Weber to the United States from Lisbon, where she'd been waiting out her visa approval in a refugee camp for months.

"This is the very best part of our work. She is here!" Elizabeth, the representative from the American Friends Service Committee waved at the great ship.

On an impulse, Martha tucked her hand into Elizabeth's arm.

The boat carrying over three hundred passengers, most of them refugees from Nazi-occupied Europe, bumped against the pier and came to a stop. Her engines rumbled before finally cutting out. There was a silence for a moment, as if the crowds gathered on the pier all took in one collective breath.

Martha's throat constricted. Here was a boat that had traversed through mine-infested waters traveling from the very continent that held Clyde and Charlotte in its dramatic, awful, heartbreaking thrall.

As news filtered in from France, Martha was reading, with a growing sickening feeling, reports of unimaginable developments in Paris, of daily Nazi military parades at the Tomb of the Unknown Soldier below the Arc de Triomphe, of swastikas flying brazenly from the buildings on the grand boulevards, of German signs swaying over the shops and theaters. She'd placed the newspaper aside in disbelief when she'd read that the Nazis had even brought the clocks forward an hour, shortening Paris's beautiful mornings, and hastening the arrival of the long, dark nights.

"They are such a bore!" Élise had sneered when she'd read how the Nazis had begun a curfew in the occupied zone.

This morning, Olivier had shaken his head sadly at the images of posters that were pasted all over Paris's Metro stations, resplendent with pictures of happy workers in Germany, while the Vichy- and German-based French governments tried to attract French recruits to man the factories in the Third Reich. "They shall never succeed," he'd murmured. "To die in battle for your country is noble, but to die while building ammunition that would destroy the Allies in a German factory would be ignoble, a travesty. The people of my country will *not* stand for this."

Martha loosened her arm from Elizabeth's. She was chatting with another worker from one of the welfare organizations who were here to meet refugees. "We heard back from the First Lady herself," Elizabeth told her colleague, her face lighting up in a beneficent smile. "But" she went on, sadly, turning to the woman, "it was not all good news for this refugee."

Martha curled her arms around her body, her fingers on her left hand lacing into one of her pockets. Elizabeth spoke a truth that was hard and unfair. Gisela had taught in Austrian universities for over twenty years, she held a Doctorate in Applied Mathematics and her groundbreaking research had been widely published internationally in prestigious academic journals, and yet, she was only granted a visa to the United States as a "*domestic servant.*"

When Hitler had sent his troops into the Soviet Union, and it seemed there was no sign of the relentless hostilities slowing down, Gisela had decided to end her battle for appropriate employment and had accepted these humiliating terms. She'd decided to come to the United States and to work as a maid.

Élise had been horrified when the news of this condition to Gisela's visa had first arrived, and the kitchen in the apartment on Fifth Avenue had resounded with great crashings and clatterings of pots and pans. "It is because she is a woman and a Jew," she had muttered. "Well," she had sniffed, when she had finally completed a beautifully braided challah, crispy and golden on the outside and fluffy on the inside, "I hope the United States realizes what a wonderful mind it has missed out on. A domestic servant…" She'd glared at the floor.

"*There is nothing for it,*" Gisela had written. "*Dearest Martha, Elizabeth and Élise, you are my champions, and I shall accept these terms graciously. Thank you for all you have done to save my life. My situation bears no comparison to the circumstances in which my fellow Jews find themselves in Hitler's occupied zones and in Germany.*"

Martha waited while Elizabeth swapped stories with her fellow aid worker. There were stories filtering out of the continent of Nazi commanders identifying and killing Jews in the Soviet Union and there seemed little doubt that this could start to happen in the other territories under Nazi rule. At the end of June, Élise had made her slow, devastated way out for a long walk in the park, when they heard on the wireless that Nazi squads were carrying out mass shootings against people deemed "hostile to German rule" in Eastern Europe. So, they were murdering them.

Papa had talked quietly, out of Élise and Olivier's earshot, of his worry over the decreasing list of countries who were willing to welcome Jewish and other refugees. He was pale with fear that the Allies were fighting in Syria and Lebanon *against* the government of Vichy France, and Charlotte was living in Vichy France.

This morning, he'd lowered his head and murmured that if America ever entered the war, Charlotte would be stranded living under the Vichy and German government, who would be enemies of the United States.

When Gisela finally emerged from the customs building, Martha brought a hand to cover her mouth. For here she was, standing face to face with a woman whose sparkling brown eyes and flushed, excited cheeks showed not a whit of the anxiety that Martha had feared she'd witness. After all, Gisela had spent days on a crowded, desperate journey across the Atlantic, and she'd traveled from a Portuguese refugee camp.

Martha stood and stared at the willowy woman whose dark curls tumbled down her back, and then, letting out an involuntary cry, and overwhelmed with the fact this woman must have seen more sadness, repression, injustice, and travesty than any person should witness in their entire lives, Martha held out her arms, and enfolded Gisela into her warm, perspiring embrace.

Half an hour later, they made their way up the hallway toward the closed Fifth Avenue apartment door. A lump formed in Martha's throat at the way Elizabeth and Gisela chatted. Both the women's relief was tangible. They came to the door, and for a moment, they paused. Martha placed Gisela's dusty old suitcase on the carpeted floor.

"This is paradise," Gisela said. Tears pooled in her liquid brown eyes.

Martha smiled, nervous, suddenly.

She fumbled about in her handbag for her key. But then, the door was thrown open, and there was Élise, wearing a white kitchen apron, and a dob of flour on her nose. Élise held her arms out, and they were shaking, as she lurched forward to clutch the woman she'd loved like her own second child into her arms.

Martha wrapped her arms around her body, her insides tingling with relief, and when she caught Elizabeth's eye, she was certain Elizabeth sent her a wink.

But, right then, Martha frowned, for she heard voices coming from inside the living room. Not just Papa's voice but the unmistakable sound of children.

"Come in!" Élise cried. "Dearest Martha and Elizabeth. How can I ever thank you enough?" Élise blew them a kiss, took Gisela by the arm, and led her down the hallway.

Martha trundled behind, slipping their guest's suitcase into Charlotte's bedroom, only allowing herself to stand in there for one moment with her eyes closed, until the sounds from down the hallway forced her to leave that dear reverie alone.

Martha frowned. Élise had clearly invited guests. Would Papa mind?

She chewed on her lip and hastily patted at her messy curls before she made her way down the hallway. But then, she came to a stop at the double doors that led to the living room, her eyes opening wide at the sight that beheld her. Not in all the years she'd lived here had Papa once entertained guests. Yet now, Élise, Elizabeth and Gisela were right in front of her, and in front of them, the room was filled to the brim. Martha almost fell backwards, for the fact was, she recognized many of the people in her home.

Here were families from the library whose children Élise read to every week. She had been talking to the children for months of the wonderful teacher that Martha and Elizabeth had been trying to bring to New York. She'd told the children, their little faces lifted toward her, their eyes wide, how the First Lady had stepped in when it seemed all was lost and even before passage was guaranteed, Élise had optimistically promised to bring Gisela into the library when she arrived in New York. Right now, Martha was more than thankful for Élise's hope in the face of almost impossible odds.

And now, here Gisela was.

Martha stayed in the doorway. One of the little girls who came each week to hear Élise read walked up to Gisela Weber, looked up at the brilliant academic, and in solemn tones said, "Welcome to The United States." She reached out and gave the dusty, delighted Gisela a kiss on her cheek.

Gisela leaned down to embrace the child, and the room erupted in cheers.

But Martha felt a hand on her shoulder.

She turned. "Papa?" she said, placing a hand on his arm. "I didn't know about this. Are you sure it's all right?" Despite all the cheers and celebrations, and the scent of Élise's wonderful, delicious food, Martha frowned into her father's eyes.

And then, she looked down. For Papa, like Élise, was dressed in a white cooking apron.

Martha threw her hands in the air. "*What is this?*"

He sighed, his eyes grazing over the happy, guest-filled room, the summer sun beaming in from outside, and the tree-tops of Central Park green, verdant and rich with *life* right outside the glass. "This is new, it is different," he murmured, his eyes searching Martha's face. "But I've come to realize, finally, that just because this is not the old life that I lost, it does not mean it is not worth living." A shadow passed across his features. "You don't think she'd mind, darling?"

"Maman?" Martha let out a huge breath. "Oh, Papa, from what you and Anita have told me, I think she'd be looking down upon you, thrilled."

A smile spread across darling Papa's face, and Martha leaned into him, wiping her eyes, and reveling in the peace that seemed to resonate from him right now.

It was a different life, he was right, and a different sort of inner peace and acceptance, discovered, strangely, in the midst of another war.

Martha accepted a glass of champagne from Olivier, who had on his cream, freshly pressed linen suit. His gray hair was combed neatly.

Martha raised her glass. "To friends and family," Martha murmured, and Papa clinked his glass with hers.

That night, Martha turned her bed down and climbed in just after midnight. When there was a soft knock at her door, she raised herself up on one elbow.

"Come in," she said, knowing it would be Élise.

Ever since she'd confided her feelings about Clyde to the older woman, and had shared Kirsty's letter with her, Élise had kept silent about her relationship with him when it came to Papa, and now, Élise entered, holding an envelope to her side.

Martha shot out of bed, the exhausted relief she felt for Gisela quickly shaking itself off. Now, she was fully awake again, and her senses heightened. Even before Élise had handed the envelope across to her, Martha scoured the writing on the front of it, trying to decipher whether it was from Kirsty, or from Clyde. Was it from London, where Clyde's sisters were nursing under terrifying conditions, or from somewhere deep in the heart of France, a place that Martha swore, if she could, she'd go to and rescue Clyde with her own bare hands?

"It is from Edinburgh," Élise whispered. She settled down in the chair.

"Thank you, Élise," Martha said, her quiet words hanging in the dimly lit room. In the light of the small lamp, Martha slid down on to the bed, and, reaching for the letter opener she kept on the table by her bed, she slit open the envelope, her fingers reaching in for the handwritten page.

And then, her heart stilled as a photograph slipped out. She drew her hand up to her face. There he was—Clyde. The photograph was not of his full body, and clearly it had been taken in the heat. Even through the blurry focus of some forbidden camera's lens, Martha gasped at the wrinkles that had formed around his sunken eyes, at the way his collarbones stuck out from the top of his collarless, dusty shirt. She let out a small moan, because unmistakably, he was smiling at her. Unmistakably, he was looking brave. And unmistakably, despite the fact he was a prisoner of war, he was still her adored Clyde.

"But how, where?" She turned to Élise, reaching across the small space between her bed and the chair, and handing the image to her friend.

"Oh," Élise said, a frown gathering on her forehead. "He is handsome, and..." Her fingers traced, for a moment, across his face. "And happy to see you, darling, and he looks starving."

Martha grimaced. She took in a ragged breath and a dark thought clouded the happiness she felt at seeing his photograph. *Had someone sent this because the unthinkable had taken place?*

Dear goodness, let him still be alive today.

Her hands shook and she turned to the accompanying letter.

Edinburgh, Scotland,
June 1941

Dear Martha,

I expect you will be surprised to receive this, and no doubt, you have opened this letter and seen the photograph of Clyde. Looking, I know, exhausted and hungry. It has been over a year since his battalion was captured, and I am told this photograph of him was taken by a fellow prisoner who smuggled the camera into the camp and keeps it hidden in a hollowed-out dictionary from the camp library. The film was nailed into the heels of an escaped prisoner's shoes.

But I am getting ahead of myself. Martha, you will have many questions, and I shall seek to answer them here. I only wish we could have this conversation in person, and, I will say this, I wish that you and I could worry together for our beloved son and sweetheart.

Martha averted her gaze from the letter. Clyde had told his mother of his feelings for her, then. She knew he'd talked of her to his sister Kirsty, but... Martha's stomach churned. She'd said nothing to Papa, and now, she felt terrible about this.

Stamping down the treachery she felt at her own betrayal, at her own secret, she scoured the letter again.

Martha, dear, first I have to say that I am only glad that my son cares for you. Please, know that when this dreadful war is over, you are more than welcome to visit in our home. We love filling the house with guests, and, you see, the one thing that gets me off to sleep at night, for worrying about my son, is the fact that after this is all over, we shall all enjoy a wee celebration—no a big one!

Martha swallowed. She glanced up at Élise, as if searching for understanding, but it was late, and after a long day cooking and entertaining, Élise's head had fallen to her chest and her eyes were closed. The soft sound of her steady breathing lingered in the room.

Last week, I had a visit from a Lt Jean-Paul Vernier. He, too, looked exhausted, starving and hollow-eyed. It turned out that he had successfully escaped from the prison camp where Clyde still remains. Jean-Paul told me that the camp was surrounded by two lines of barbed wire, and that floodlights illuminated the former military barracks at night. He said that Germans patrolled the periphery night and day with guns slung over their shoulders, but nevertheless, the prisoners had tried digging tunnels for months but that the distance from the huts to the barbed wire was too far, and they were caught, and the tunnels covered up. He emphasized, that the German officers knew very well they were there. Jean-Paul told me that he had heard tales of far worse situations in some circumstances in Germany, and that it all seemed to depend on your nationality as to how you survived in these camps.

Clyde may have told you in his letters that the Germans had allowed their prisoners to build a theater, which they deco-rated with greenery to obscure it from obvious view of the guards. This theater was between the fences and the barracks, so, using the shovels that they'd been provided by the Red Cross, the prisoners began digging a new tunnel, from their theater to the border of the camp, which was a much closer distance than they had attempted before.

Jean-Paul told me how his band of escapees had to wait for hours in the tunnel. He said it was suffocating, as it was nearly three hundred feet underground. They were malnourished, and yet, they'd dug far enough to emerge just several feet on the other side of the barbed-wire fence.

They waited and found their chance. One weekend, the Germans canceled their roll call, and over two nights, two large groups went out. Jean-Paul tells me there was so little room in the tunnel that they had to curl up into balls. He said some men fainted.

They waited almost ten hours to get out. And they all expected to see a German firing squad waiting at the other end of the tunnel.

Martha's heart raced. What of Clyde?

But once they emerged, they ran the short distance to the tree cover that was close by. And then, they all moved in different directions, under the cover of night.

By not traveling together with his fellow escapees, Jean-Paul says he managed to survive. However, he knows that several escapees were captured and returned to the camp. He only knows of one other prisoner who made it out of the occupied zones of France to safety.

"Oh, please tell me who!" Martha murmured.
She scoured the page with her eyes.

Jean-Paul told me he was a trained nurse. He is going to seek work here in Edinburgh, treating wounded military. My husband is helping him to secure a position in one of our hospitals. He was able to get into the country, as his mother was Scottish, but he was raised by his father's family in France.

Jean-Paul spoke highly of Clyde.

Martha had to bite on her fingers to stop herself from crying out loud.

He'd worked with Clyde, assisting as his nurse, treating the many starving, ill patients whom Clyde, he says, continues to treat. Jean-Paul explained that Clyde chose not to escape, because he could not, in all conscience, as a doctor, leave the hundreds of sickly younger men, with whom, it seems likely, he will be housed with for the remainder of the war.

Jean-Paul told me that Clyde was one of the steadiest, most respected prisoners in the camp. That, in the face of the food being awful, he had been instrumental in establishing the vegetable garden, which I am especially proud of, as I love to garden, and he spends his days in a makeshift clinic now, taking care of those in the camp who are ill and in need of medical attention—both on the German and the Allied sides.

He wanted you to have this photograph, and Jean-Paul says, Clyde sends you his love.

Stay brave, my dear.

Yours truly,

Elsie Fraser

Martha lay back on her pillows, tears streaming freely down her face, and she held the photograph of her proud, brave Scotsman close to her heart.

20

Charlotte

The train rolled through the French countryside on its way to Paris, passing by medieval towns with half-timbered buildings, old manor houses that had been family homes for centuries, and chateaux sitting in glorious parks. They'd wound their way through forests and past castles that had once been the hunting grounds of kings. But while France's beauty unfolded outside the window, Charlotte's eyes and ears were on the alert for officers in one of three types of uniform: French police, German police, or worst of all, Gestapo.

Louis and Madeleine had warned her that the citizens of a divided France were living under a government that was united in its loyalty to one thing: German rule. In the past months, France's homes had been witness to countless conversations and debates because people were having to choose whether to put their heads down and succumb to the Nazi regime or fight in secret.

Armand had made his position clear to the employees of the Louvre. He would opt not to make a fuss, as his main priority was the safety of the works they were entrusted to guard. What was more, he'd hinted that their collection had been joined in the Musée Ingres in Montauban by some of the Louvre's most treasured masterpieces. While this was highly confidential, Sandrine had murmured that she thought the Mona Lisa might be there. This had lent a heightened sense of purpose to Armand and Lucie's work, and Charlotte was more than aware that if she were to get caught taking any untoward risks, she'd put not only herself but Armand, Lucie and Sandrine under the Nazi spotlight.

So, each day that she was required, Charlotte had been helping in the daily tasks of caring for the collection that was stored at the Musée Ingres, where the paintings were arranged so they could be accessed easily and inspected regularly for any damage. Armand and Lucie were already worried about fuel shortages that would affect the temperatures in the cold of winter during the coming months. At night, Charlotte brought back the three paintings that meant the world to her and slept with them by the side of her bed in the lodgings she shared with Sandrine.

And yet, as Charlotte made her daily way through the marketplace of Montauban to the Musée Ingres, she'd become alarmed by hearing some townspeople saying they preferred Fascist rule to the notion of living under a Communist government. The fear of a repressive Soviet-style Communist government with their slave labor camps was very real in France.

But still, in the face of Anita's death, of the loss of Chateau d'Anez and Élise and Olivier's forced evacuation from France, in the face of the terrible stories that were beginning to leak out of Germany, summarized in a broadcast by Winston Churchill, when he announced that whole districts were being exterminated in the face of the Nazis' advance, that there had been scores of executions of innocents in cold blood, and that famine and disease would only follow in the wake of Hitler's tanks, it been simple to make the decision to work with Louis, Henri, and Madeleine. Winston Churchill had finished his speech this summer with the dire warning that the world was in the presence of a ghastly crime without a name. It was clear to Charlotte what path she must take.

She had couriered articles, messages, and letters to their compatriots in Paris, enduring freezing journeys during the bitter winter of 1940, and becoming an expert at evading the questions at the German border controls. In the face of the horror that marred their daily lives, Charlotte was proud to be part of a sure underground rebellion spreading not only through intellectuals who were ideologically opposed to Hitler, but also amongst the everyday citizens of France.

Every time Charlotte came by train to Paris, she sensed the swelling dissent unfurling in the air, in the black market that was growing by the day, an underground system where the shopkeepers of Paris were trading their luxury wares and famous gourmet foods that they did not wish to sell to the Germans for produce from local farmers in the villages outside Paris.

When the Germans had set the exchange rate so high that the franc was worth twenty times less than the Deutschmark, this had only led French shopkeepers and dealers to detest the fact that their French-made goods were all being shipped to the Reich, because even the lowliest German soldiers on leave could afford to shop extravagantly in Paris, while the spending abilities of the French were being stifled by the country's government.

Yet now Charlotte's growing sense of purpose and pride in the people of France was laced with a troubling unease. The words in Martha's latest letter to her were etched in her mind and she knew every word off by heart.

We are glued to the wireless, the newspapers, and I worry that Papa's hair will turn white with fear for you. We hear tales that the Germans are attempting to conscript French male workers to Germany, that they may extend this to women... dearest, if you were to be sent to Germany...

"But I am not French," Charlotte had murmured.

I read this morning that some Parisians are turning in support of the Nazi rule, denouncing their fellow citizens as Jews, communists, Freemasons, black marketeers and... resistants. There will be eyes watching your back everywhere, Charlotte. And I know you. Please. Don't take any risks.

We heard that the American Embassy in Paris closed this month. Without this Charge d'Affaires in place, we are hearing that almost all Americans have left.

Why then, must you remain? Please, Charlotte. Come home.

You should escape France on foot to Lisbon. Let me know when, not if, you will do this, and we will secure you a passage home. I entreat you.

You are no longer protected by an embassy. If America and Germany go to war, you will be subject to internment. Charlotte, you will be an enemy of the Nazi regime.

Charlotte sat up as the train rumbled through Paris's outer suburbs. She had stepped off trains at the sight of the police arriving on board to inspect people's identity cards. She'd run through the underground Metro stations of Paris to avoid being caught out at curfew, her fingers frostbitten, her toes bloated and red with chilblains during the winter months. And she'd mastered the art of flirting under her eyelashes with the German soldiers at the checkpoints that separated the two halves of France.

Charlotte's hand rested protectively around the old leather satchel that looked like a schoolbag belonging to a young French girl. She had it secured carefully over one shoulder and resting close by her hip. To appear less suspicious, she had dyed her hair blond, as her friends had asked her to do, and the white bobby socks she wore were those of a Parisian schoolgirl. If a

Nazi officer came aboard the train, Madeleine had instructed Charlotte to pull out an exercise book and make it look as if she were completing her homework. Charlotte was not sure how that would help, but she followed Louis, Henri, and Madeleine's instructions to a T.

Today was momentous, and she must stay focused on the task at hand. Martha's missives, while understandable, had to be placed at the back of her mind. For today, Charlotte was collecting the very first editions of *La Defense* and taking them back south to the unoccupied zone in her satchel. After months of preparation, with a network of students that traversed France, Charlotte knew that today, she must take extra care and not be caught with a hot edition of an underground newspaper on her person. Was she to be caught carrying copies of the very first edition of *La Defense* to take back south, she would be detained, questioned, imprisoned, and tortured, before being deported to a prison in the Reich, where many Resistance workers were sentenced to death, or simply shot in the heart.

But there was almost a primeval pull as she'd alight from the train and walk the streets of the once famous old Left Bank, because these were the streets where she knew her parents had danced all night in the 1920s, and where now, Paris sat in a particular shade of darkness that was specific to this Nazi war. Charlotte was resisting, to bring the Paris of twenty years ago that her father grieved for every day of his life back to the sense of freedom and joy that it deserved.

The train drew to a halt, and Charlotte prepared herself for the scenes that never failed to break her heart, the sound of the Nazi jackboots ringing across the boulevards as the soldiers marched down them every day, the sinister sight of German officers riding around the city in cars, while Parisians, not allowed to enjoy this privilege, had to get around by bus, the Metro, or pushbikes. Last time Charlotte had been here, she'd seen French citizens riding around the streets on horseback.

As Charlotte came up out of the Metro station, she held her satchel close. It was summer in Paris, but the sky was gray, leaden and heavy with unshed rain, and instead of strolling in sundresses and sipping cool drinks, her insides lurched at the small groups of citizens who were lined up, wiping their hands across their sweaty brows and hoping to be able to use their ration coupons outside the few shops that were scheduled to be open today.

With bread, fat and flour rationed, and only adults allowed a small amount of meat per week, most of the food that was being produced in France was being sent directly to Germany. The daily allowance for Parisians had been reduced to half that was needed to keep a healthy adult alive.

Everyone was talking about the prospect of severe food shortages across France, while all the spoils of Paris were at the disposal of the Nazi soldiers—cafés, restaurants, museums, and shops. The top Nazis were living a life of luxury in the glamorous hotels of the Right Bank and they were using Paris as their playground.

Soon, it was said, the Parisians would starve.

And this was why Charlotte could not, in all honesty, abandon her beloved France. This was why she had to put Martha's letter to the back of her mind. As much as she loved her sister and her father, this was why she could not walk to Lisbon and then board a boat for New York.

Charlotte moved steadily through the intersection of Rue de Rennes and Boulevard du Montparnasse, the beautiful buildings of Haussmann's Paris looking down at the large square in the sultry afternoon. On the far side, she carefully avoided grimacing at the sight of a demonstration of Hitler Youth, where French schoolchildren were being marshaled by Nazi soldiers, a small crowd gathering around to watch the spectacle.

As the Parisian schoolchildren marched around under a

swastika that flew from one of the buildings on the corner of the boulevard, looking too bright, too garish in this loaded, gray afternoon, Charlotte reminded herself of the words of Charles de Gaulle, that hope must not disappear. Defeat, he said, was not a final thing.

But as she walked across the square, her eyes averted from the sickening parade, she passed by Parisians walking with their own faces cast downward. Her heart contracted at the way their shoulders slumped, as they dealt with the daily burden of not knowing how they were going to survive the coming months when the weather grew colder again, when the severe rationing of coal to heat their homes would leave most of them to freeze. Deaths due to the freezing temperatures would be another unseen tragedy of this war.

Charlotte sighed at the sight of a young couple around her age. The fact that even though it was summer, they could not leave their homes from nine o'clock in the evening until five o'clock in the morning meant another generation were losing the one chance they had to be young.

And everywhere around, them, the streets now had German names. The clocks on the town halls struck German time, one hour less of precious daylight than she had in the unoccupied zone.

If all this theater and spectacle and veiled threats were supposed to put her off, she halted for only one second, before bracing her shoulders and marching forward. Charles de Gaulle was right. The flames of the French Resistance must never be extinguished.

Half an hour later, Charlotte stepped out of the shuttered building where she'd collected her newspapers onto the Rue Boissonade, the fresh, first editions tucked into her satchel. The very atmosphere felt laden, and Charlotte paused one moment, staring up at the sky, the sounds of the Hitler Youth parade nearby and the shouts of the German commanders still ringing through the strangely quiet street. She stood there, thoughtful, while people's wirelesses, tuned to the only German stations that people were allowed to listen to, filtered out into the air.

Charlotte took a few steps forward, her heart hammering in her chest, and a frown gathering on her forehead. Martha's well-intended words of caution, bless them, had achieved the opposite effect.

There was something she had to do.

She clutched at her loaded satchel, holding it close to her hip. The longer she spent in Paris, the more risk she was taking of being stopped. She should get on the train right now. It was imperative that she be safely out of the occupied zone by nightfall due to the curfew.

But with her dyed blond hair peeping out from under her hat, and her long legs striking along on the sidewalk, she made her way to Boulevard du Montparnasse, entered the Metro station at Port Royal and slipped through the crowds onto a train. Charlotte stood clutching her belongings until she arrived at the Opera station.

Charlotte made her way up the wide Boulevard des Italiens, averting her eyes from the shops whose frontages were desecrated with bright signs advertising the offices of *Todt*, the organization that ran slave labor camps in Germany. Her head held high, fighting not to give in to the anger that boiled inside her, not to spit on the treacherous signs, Charlotte pressed ahead, ignoring the stiff, correct, German officers who walked by her on the street eyeing her with interest. She walked at a steady pace until she reached the turnoff to Rue Laffitte. Nazi soldiers were not the only ones who understood that putting one foot in front of the other could make a powerful noise.

But when Charlotte stood in the beloved street she'd had to escape on that fateful night a year ago, she almost buckled at the familiar sight of Sacré-Cœur, the beautiful white cathedral looking down on her. Here was the magical church, where, what like seemed an age ago, she and Anita had gone to sit at sunset, enjoying the glorious pink and orange arcs over Paris, the city spreading out below.

Sobs threatening to engulf her body, Charlotte curled her fingers over the key to Galerie A. Goldstein in the pocket of her green summer dress. She walked to the front door, her forehead slick with sweat.

Slowly, she turned the key in the lock and stepped inside.

And when she did so, Charlotte barely held back her scream. The only reminder of Anita's gallery were the empty hooks on the walls. The furniture she'd left in place, so it would be there at her return was all gone. Everything.

Charlotte stood in the middle of the empty, silent room, her shoulders shaking with rage, a solitary figure, while shafts of soft light filtered through the closed shutters and left a pearly, strange mood in the air.

She shuddered. She would go upstairs next.

Until she froze.

There was the slightest shift on the floor upstairs. Charlotte's heart began to quicken. The fact was, she knew every sound, every subtle noise that this building made. What she'd heard were footsteps in the apartment.

Nausea rose in Charlotte's stomach, sending bile up through her throat.

How dare they?

While she knew that the Nazis had looted every Jewish-owned gallery and collection they could, while she knew that this was not something she should be surprised at, what she could not cope with was their having stolen from or ransacked Anita's home.

It was not fear or defensiveness that kicked in, but a great determination that swelled within her. This was her home. Anita's gallery. Charlotte set her jaw.

Shifting silently, she moved across the floor. She placed her hand on the banister, her foot sliding up onto the first stair. Her hands curled around the dagger that was sewn into her satchel.

Charlotte swung her gaze around the landing at the top of the narrow flight of stairs. Everything was deadly still.

Too still.

There was someone here.

The paintings that she'd had to leave behind still sat against the floor in the hallway.

Charlotte frowned. She eased her dagger out of place, her fingers laced around the handle. She started to inch her way along the edge of the wall, her back to it, just as Louis had instructed so that no one could attack her from behind. If they did, she swore she'd defend herself.

Swaying, Charlotte blinked hard, her heart beating a tattoo against her breastbone, a metallic taste growing in her mouth. With every fiber of her being thumping, and her eyes seeing black, red, anything but the quiet hallway in front of her, Charlotte made her slow way toward her old room. Because with the instincts borne of living in this house, she knew whoever was here was in the room where she'd slept.

And then, in one lightning move, she pushed the door fully open, and stepped inside, her eyes scanning the room. Until, suddenly, she heard footsteps rushing from behind her, and something white, a pillowcase she thought, was placed over her head.

Charlotte stumbled backward. Half falling into her assailant, she froze, her hands grasping her satchel.

The fragrance was unmistakable.

Jasmine and rose.

Jean Patou's Joy.

21

PARIS, FALL 1923

Chloé

Chloé stood in the long walk that ran through the Tuileries Garden from the Louvre. The trees that lined the path were trimmed to perfection, the leaves golden and green underneath the glorious fall sky. Her two small girls ran toward her along the neatly raked gravel path, their feet encased in their black boots, crackling the leaves underfoot, and their cherry-red coats swinging. Their eyes danced as they raced to meet their maman. Behind them, Laurence came, the leather bag in which he carried his latest translations swinging against his hip.

Chloé crouched down to greet her little ones; her arms spread wide. Martha, whose red-brown curls bounced against her collar came running up to her first, and the bewitching, dark-eyed Charlotte, with her glossy black hair tumbling down her back, followed on with outstretched arms.

"Maman!" Charlotte held up a picture she had painted today. "Don't you like the colors? Red, blue, and orange. It is especially for you!"

"That is beautiful, *chérie*," Chloé said, leaning down and

admiring the paint that Charlotte had splashed all over the paper.

Chloé gathered both the girls into her arms, and held them close, the fragrance of their freshly washed hair soft in the misty afternoon.

"It is quite perfect, a lovely picture," she said to Charlotte. "You are both perfect," she told them. Chloé stood up, holding one small, gloved hand in each of her own. "Now, we shall go to a patisserie to meet Anita, and enjoy our afternoon tea." She leaned toward Laurence as he came close, kissing her on the cheek.

"Your day was good?" he asked, keeping pace beside Chloé and the two girls.

"But of course," Chloé said. Every day was wonderful. They'd slipped into a perfect rhythm, she, Laurence, and their daughters. Chloé worked two days a week at Adrienne Monnier's bookshop, assisting with organizing the weekly readings which drew famous authors from all over France, and helping in the library part of the store, where young people could come in and borrow books, those who, perhaps, could not afford to buy from the store. The rest of her time was spent with her beloved family. The connection she had felt with Charlotte had been instant, and having been given Anita's baby, she'd felt as if Charlotte were her own too.

They strolled, their family, along the widening path, passing by the green wooden benches that lined the manicured lawns. People sat there, enjoying the last of the day's glorious sun.

Charlotte and Martha chatted away about chocolate eclairs.

As they came to the edge of the gardens, with their smart green-railed fences, Chloé came to a standstill.

"Why!" she said, stepping out onto Rue de Rivoli. Her relationship with Anita had only deepened and strengthened in the past years. Since Chloé and Laurence had decided to raise Charlotte, the sense that Anita was part of their family grew even stronger than before. The girls were developing their own little personalities and Chloé and Anita's eyes would meet with amusement when Charlotte expressed the strong sense of determination that Anita had always shown. Chloé's girls had not one but two mothers who loved them, and like Charlotte and Martha, it was as if Chloé and Anita were now truly sisters too.

Opposite her, Anita was already sitting at a table in the brasserie under the arches that lined the buildings along the grand boulevard, waving at her.

Chloé moved straight toward her, the girls' arms falling away by her side.

"*Chloé!*"

Laurence was yelling.

She turned at the sound of his voice. Whatever was the matter?

But then, she turned and saw it. A shadow, a great, lumbering, noisy shadow was bearing upon her, its horn blaring, wheels screeching.

A truck.

There were other shouts.

For one split second, Chloé swung around, the sight of Laurence standing on the side of the otherwise quiet road, holding the hands of her little girls, and she tried to move back toward them, but there was a horrible screech, a wrench of brakes through the perfect afternoon air, and Chloé screamed.

The world turned black.

22

Charlotte

The pillowcase was lifted from Charlotte's head and her hand flew to her chest. She stiffened and prepared to turn around and run. Her fingers instinctively reached for the knife inside her bag. But then she stopped. The woman standing opposite her in Anita's apartment was blond, just like she was. Her hair was clipped short to rest in soft waves on her shoulders, just like Charlotte's.

Charlotte's chest rose and fell of its own accord. The life force within her kicked into motion and while all she wanted to do was get out of here, she had to compel herself not to reach out and throw herself into the woman's arms. It was all she could do to stop herself from shouting the name that battled to burst from her lips.

But while the woman stood, implacable, it was her eyes that did it. Charlotte stared deep into those liquid, deep brown eyes and she saw the truth within them. She saw the same truth of purpose that was within herself.

"Anita."

The single, solitary, betraying, truthful word hung between them in the heavy apartment air.

Charlotte swayed. The oppressive heat that lingered needed to burst into a thunderstorm. It needed to break the loaded stillness that hung in this very room.

The woman did not flinch and she did not move.

Charlotte did not flinch, she did not move in turn and yet uncertainty stabbed her. Had some German woman come to replace Anita in a terrible twist of fate?

The woman clasped her hands in front of her body. This was the only hint that her emotions might escape her impeccable composure.

Charlotte's eyes raked the woman's face and in that moment Charlotte realized that it wasn't death that had ripped Anita away from her. It was war.

Charlotte let out a cry, and she threw herself forward.

She'd know Anita anywhere. She'd know her if she were in a room full of one million people. Because there was some pull between them that nothing and no one could break. It was the strength and yearning toward courage that was so much a part of both her and Anita's makeup. This unseen connection had drawn Charlotte to Anita throughout her whole life.

Charlotte buried her head in her friend's shoulder. Tears prickled her eyes and her heart beat louder, harder and stronger than it ever would for any other soul on this earth.

"*Why?*" Charlotte murmured into her darling friend's shoulder.

Anita held Charlotte at arm's length. "Because I am good at deception," Anita murmured. She pressed her pale pink lips together and looked down at the floor. "Sometimes burying the truth is the only way to get through." She raised her head to meet Charlotte's astounded gaze. "And I knew that it was how I must survive this war. Many Jews have escaped, and goodness knows thousands have been rounded up, but some of us decided to disguise ourselves and sit this thing through, right under the very noses of the Nazi regime."

Charlotte stood in silence. Her mouth dropped open and she stumbled backwards. She grabbed onto the strap of the leather bag she wore, and the weight of it pressed into her shoulder and sent shooting pains through her arm. But nothing came out of her mouth when she opened it to speak.

Anita lifted her head. Charlotte stared at her.

"If I were caught, you would be caught. By association." Anita held Charlotte's troubled, beating gaze. "This was the only way to keep you safe. It was the only way I could remain in the same country as you."

Charlotte paced around the room and came to a stop near the window. She gripped the leather strap of her bag. She stared down through the slits in the shutters to the glimpses of the street below. It was quiet and mercifully free of the sound of Nazi motorbikes or boots. A thunderstorm needed to break, but despite the laden air, it seemed the sky still could not rain.

"Come and sit with me." Anita's voice came from across the empty room. "Please."

Charlotte's mouth worked and her heart was on fire. Her legs wanted to buckle beneath her body. But she walked out of her old bedroom and followed Anita down the familiar hallway and into the kitchen.

It was impossible not to notice the changes that Anita had cleverly imposed upon herself. She'd disguised herself beautifully. Anita's walk was different, and she did not sway her hips anymore. A white fabric belt circled her too-slim waist and the pale pink dress she wore was nothing like anything in the former wardrobe that had belonged to the Anita Charlotte knew. Anita's pink dress with its tight belt spoke volumes. It was as if she were holding herself in.

"Please," Anita said. She slid into a chair.

Charlotte's voice cracked. "You sound different. You have

adopted a new accent." She sat down and placed her satchel down on the table in front of her.

Anita tapped her fingers on the table. She lifted her eyes. Her expression was opaque. "You cannot be associated with me, and I had to transform myself for both our sakes." She curled her lip in an almost smile. "It's been that way longer than you know."

A flicker of anger curled through Charlotte's system. "I am not a child," she murmured. "You don't have to protect me, nor do you need to look after me. If you had told me the truth, you would have spared us all so much pain. We thought you were dead." She lifted her own chin, her eyes clashing with Anita's now. "You are not under any obligation to protect me. But I believe you have an obligation to tell me the truth."

She bit her lip. She'd said too much, but the truth wanted to hurtle out of her. Every day they were living in a terrifying world where you could not speak from your heart. And here was Anita. Here was the one woman with whom Charlotte had always been able to be truly open, and she had hidden a great secret from her. She hadn't trusted her with the truth. This hurt, but Charlotte knew she could not dwell on it now.

Anita looked off to the side and she closed her liquid brown eyes. When she spoke, her voice was low, and when she strung words together, the strange new accent she'd adopted was even more pronounced.

Charlotte stared, while Anita spoke in measured, clipped tones, as clipped as the blond hair that framed her face, as neat as the pearly teeth that showed when she smiled. Not Anita's teeth, not with the endearing, unusual gap between the two front ones. She'd had those fixed as well.

"You must not tell a soul you have seen me here today. You must promise me not to put Sandrine at risk. You cannot even tell my parents I am alive. They will try to get me out, and I will not leave you here alone in France. I cannot." Anita bit out the last words.

Charlotte slumped back in her seat, raking a hand through her own blond hair. "Does anyone else know?"

Anita pressed her lips together. "Of course not."

"No one else has recognized you?" Charlotte whispered. The word formed on her lip... *yet*, but she did not dare utter it for either of their sakes.

"They have not," Anita said. She sounded reasonable and her voice was calm. "Unfortunately, or fortunately, deception comes more easily to me than it does to some."

Charlotte gripped the table in front of her. Papa had always said Anita was complex, and that no one truly knew her, but Charlotte had thought when Anita took her under her wing here in Paris, that she was different somehow. She thought she had access to the real woman behind the confident, brave facade. And yet now, she did not know.

A hard knot formed in her stomach and nagged at her. There was something else. She understood what Anita's accent was. It was German.

Surely, Anita was not working for the Reich?

Charlotte pushed aside this preposterous idea. She remained quiet, but her thoughts and feelings were in turmoil. She gripped her satchel and allowed Anita to talk on.

Anita lifted her head. "The accent is deliberate." Her eyes searched Charlotte's face. "The only thing I will tell you is that I am here in a state of defiance. A state of defiance that runs so deep, the Germans will never understand."

Charlotte barked out a laugh. Relief poured through her system and she pushed her snaking doubts about Anita's loyalty aside. She may not ever fully understand the woman sitting opposite her, but she was certain that Anita would never collaborate with the Nazis, and she also believed her when she said she was being protective.

"Oh, believe me I understand defiance. When the Nazis are concerned, it is the only thing to do." Charlotte growled the words. "I understand the feeling far more than you think I do."

She sensed Anita shifting and heard her sharp intake of breath. Charlotte noticed the way Anita pressed her hands into the table. Her back was rigid and ramrod straight.

Tears stung Charlotte's eyes. Anger wanted to rip through her, but she held it at bay. She could not halt the grief that battled to explode. "Your parents are beside themselves. Martha and Papa are devastated—"

"You never should have left your father to come to live with me. I shouldn't have allowed it. Now, you are at terrible risk. It is all my fault." Anita clasped her hands tight on the tabletop. "Everything. I am sorry."

"That is not fair." Charlotte ground out the word. "I stayed here to carry on your work!"

Anita's shoulders shook, this time, with a deep laughter, and then she reached up, passing her hand across her face. "*Mon Dieu*," she murmured, raising her eyes to the ceiling. "What a mess."

"I wanted to save everything for you. And, Anita, more than that, I wanted to be like you. I wanted to do something to protest."

"I am a coward." Anita threw her hands in the air. "I hide behind a facade, while you, dearest Charlotte, you open yourself endlessly to the world! No, we are very different. Opposites. You must not do what I do. You must go back to America and never come here again."

Charlotte scoured Anita's face, but it remained impassive and resolute. "I will make the choices that are true to my beliefs," she whispered. "And the person I most believe in is you. Even," she added, her breath shuddering, "after this."

Charlotte held Anita's gaze. She did not waver for one moment.

Anita pulled her hand up to cover her mouth. The sob she let out racked the entire, heavy, cloud-laden, stifling, room.

Charlotte stood up. She moved back to the window. Her stomach curled with determination. And then, the rain that had threatened to pour all afternoon beat down on Rue Laffitte. It bounced and ricocheted off the pavement. It sent steam up toward the relentless gray sky.

Charlotte closed her eyes. There was little time left to make the train before curfew. Were she to be caught in the occupied zones after nine o'clock, Louis, Henri and Madeleine would be betrayed. If she did not arrive back in Montauban tonight, Sandrine would be pale with anxiety for her.

Charlotte swung around to face Anita. "I understand what it is to protect those you love, but I wish you'd..." her voice drifted off. She hadn't told Sandrine that she was working for Louis. She had told her friend that she was spending the day with friends she'd met at the abbey; she did not want to risk Sandrine's safety by breathing a word of what she was doing. She could not bear to place the quiet, steady woman in danger because of any association with her.

Charlotte hated the complicated web she and Anita both woven around themselves. But then, perhaps they had more in common than she understood. Suddenly, Charlotte realized that they'd both made decisions that were selfless, not the other way around.

"If you can trust anyone completely, that person has to be me," Charlotte said.

Anita squeezed her eyes shut. Covering her face with her hands, she sat for one moment. When she spoke, her voice was small. "My artists," she murmured, her head shaking. "They are like my children. I *must* protect them. I *cannot* let them down." She looked up. "I came back to get them all out of Paris, Charlotte. One by one. They are the very epitome of what the Nazis detest." Her voice quavered. "I promised to nurture them. And they are the only children I've ever truly known."

Charlotte swallowed. Anita had said this before. Her artists were like her children. She had welcomed them into her life as if they were family. Of course she would not let them down.

"I have to get them all out of France," Anita murmured. Her eyes swiveled nervously toward the kitchen door. "My degenerates and my misfits. We are all misfits, aren't we, now?"

"Trying to force people to fit in with a ridiculously narrow version of acceptability has always been a human flaw. What can I do to help?" Charlotte whispered, her heart racing. She came back to the table and took a seat again.

Anita leaned forward. "I have two artists who are lame."

Charlotte nodded. Of course. André Picout and Leo Dupont.

"The Nazis will take them and murder them for that alone." Anita raked a shaking hand through her short blond hair, sending it up in tufts. "And right now, Sandro Luciano is sitting in the salon," she said, her eyes moving furtively again.

Charlotte sat up in her seat, her head shaking. "*Sandro?*" she whispered. "You have him hiding here?" She'd been guarding his portrait of Anita, and all the while, Anita was guarding him.

"Sandro is on the Nazis' list. The articles he has published in art magazines about Nazi disdain for modern art has captured the attention of the Germans."

Charlotte's eyes swiveled to the satchel full of underground newspapers that sat on Anita's table. She grimaced and turned her focus back to Anita.

"Sandro ran away from Rome for Paris when he was called up to join the military by Mussolini's government." Anita's words were barely audible. "I need to get him out of Paris, into Spain, and onto the United Kingdom." Her eyes combed Charlotte's face. "Charlotte. You must have come to Paris for a reason. Tell me. Can you help us?"

"You must not take him south yourself, Anita. It is too dangerous. He shall come with me tonight." Her voice was steely. "I know where to get help. Do you have papers for him? A false identity?"

"Just. I have been waiting endlessly for them." She raised her hand to her lips, chewing on her fingers. "But I cannot let you take him, darling. The risk of your getting caught with him. That is the very reason I was trying to keep away from you!"

Charlotte reached for her bag. "Get him. We shall go now." She stood up. "I shall be up here every fortnight. We will work together, as we have always done. But there must be no more secrets."

Anita frowned.

Charlotte held up her hand. "I have taken care of your art collection. Now, it's time to take care of the artists who painted them." She pressed a hand against her heart. "Remember, I worked with them for over a year while you were gone."

Anita paled.

"Their life and their work cannot be shut down by this monster who is ruling France."

Anita sagged down in her seat, her carefully made-up face falling for one, long moment. "Charlotte, I'm sorry..." she whispered. Her voice broke, and she covered her mouth with her hand, a sob racking her body. "I'm sorry I didn't tell you..."

Charlotte pushed her chair back and stood tall. She wrapped the leather strap around her shoulder and kept her eyes focused out the window on the now dripping rain.

"You have given me everything. Strength and determina-tion..." She let out a laugh. "The courage to do what it takes to survive on my own terms. And to help others."

Anita raised her face and her eyes caught with Charlotte's.

"I only wish I deserved your forgiveness. I am sorry I have caused you such sadness."

Charlotte shook her head. "Dearest Anita. You are alive and that is all that matters. Forgive me. It was the shock." Anita had sought to survive under an impossible regime. That was the end of it. Some people escaped, others stayed right where they were and fought. "Take me to Sandro. We need to depart in the coming half-hour," Charlotte said.

That night, Charlotte walked through Montparnasse station, just in time to beat the curfew. Her ears and eyes were on the alert, and her arm was tucked through Sandro Luciano's. Voices echoed through the vast space, just like they always did on a busy day. Next to her, Sandro's entire upper body was shaking. He seemed frailer and thinner now. It had taken all Anita could do to persuade him that Charlotte was more than capable of accompanying him out of the occupied zone to the *zone libre*.

Charlotte tightened her grip on the artist's arm as they passed by posters filled with the propaganda that Pétain was trying to feed to the French people: a new order was commencing, while the French national motto—*Liberty, Equality, Fraternity*—was crossed out for the slogan favored by the new government: *Fatherland, Family, Work*. Charlotte forced herself not to cringe.

She felt Sandro flinch beside her. Anita had said that he'd published articles before the Nazi takeover denouncing the measures that were being set in place in his home country of Italy, where democratic freedom was being replaced by paternalistic, top-down government.

Pétain's face was plastered everywhere on the official newsstands in the station, condemning what he called the indecency and depravity of the previous regime.

"*Jazz and, short skirts to be replaced by traditional values and family life,*" one headline screamed. Hitler's unmistakable features stared out from a foggy photo on the front page.

Charlotte guided Sandro toward the ticketing station. She fought to retain her own composure when a group of young German men on leave pushed by them. They were jostling to get ahead of the queue. Their eyes sparkled, no doubt in anticipation of a holiday in Paris with all the stops pulled out.

Sandro muttered something in Italian under his breath, and Charlotte squeezed his arm. She would be lucky to get him to Montauban in one piece, let alone with his mouth shut.

But shut it would have to stay. Charlotte was banking on Louis allowing her to accompany Sandro to his father's abbey. She was certain that Louis would know someone who could accompany Sandro across the border to Spain. From there, he'd have to make his way to Portugal.

She blinked at the small sign on the ticketing office desk: *Turning in those who resist the government is a civil duty for the citizens of France.*

What had the world come to?

Charlotte spoke in clear English with her strong American accent. But out of the corner of her eye, she glimpsed a group of German police loitering about on the platform from which she and Sandro had to depart for Toulouse.

Toulouse, then they'd switch to Montauban. She knew the route off by heart.

The young police officers stood with their uniforms neatly pressed. Double rows of brass buttons gleamed on their breasts and peaked caps sat perched atop their short back and side haircuts. Their black boots, and belts were formidable, polished and cruel.

Charlotte paid for their tickets, and led Sandro toward the waiting train.

"We shall board on the closest carriage," she murmured, keeping her voice as calm as she could. "Simply follow me."

But there was no choice but to wait in a short queue to get on the train. And as they stood amongst the quiet, murmuring Parisians who were sending fearful glances toward the German police, Charlotte noticed one of the officers scanning their line. His eyes landed right on her.

Charlotte looked down at her shoes. Her heart shuddered, but she must behave as if she were a polite schoolgirl. The steamy air curled from her lips, and she kept her breathing steady, but a heat flared in her stomach, and she had to take short breaths.

The officer approached them and Charlotte closed her eyes a moment, and then, taking a deep breath, she lifted her gaze. She was eye to eye with a man her age. His blue eyes were hard, but they narrowed and flickered with an interest that no woman could misinterpret.

Sandro took in a shaking breath.

"*Kennkarte?*" the officer said, asking for the identification card that would either make or break everything.

People behind them moved forward and passed them to board the train. Charlotte recognized the relief on their faces. They were grateful not to have been stopped. They were not feigning any interest in the young blond girl and her dark-haired companion who had been chosen for interrogation, because it could so easily have been them. Everyone was too frightened to make waves. The campaign of anti-Semitism and anti-undesirables had begun immediately after Pétain had signed the armistice with Hitler last year and had quickly turned into a full-scale assault.

It was of paramount importance that Charlotte get Sandro onto this train. But hiding him in Vichy France for any length of time would not do any good. Louis had railed just last week that the flood of orders that were coming from Vichy were not prompted by orders from Berlin.

Charlotte willed her hands not to shake as she reached into

her pocket where she'd slipped her *Kennkarte*. If she opened that leather satchel, she'd expose her newspapers and be interned for questioning immediately. She bit her teeth down on her lip, releasing a fresh trickle of blood into her mouth as her thoughts spiraled to the heated articles that Louis, Madeleine, and their friends had written burning against her side in her bag.

Charlotte handed the identification card to the officer.

The officer turned it over, slowly.

The train's whistle blew.

Charlotte's heart thumped in deep, fast, strong rhythms.

"*Amerikanisch*," he sneered. His eyes raked down her body slowly, before returning to her face. His lips curled into a lazy smile, and he kept hold of her precious identity card. Because he could. Then, he indicated his head toward Sandro, while Charlotte stood transfixed, knowing Louis would be furious with her for risking this—he'd *told* her to run if she saw German officers, and yet, in her determination to save Sandro, she had thought better of this. Now look at them! Was it over before it had begun? Had she betrayed Louis' entire circle, and would their first newspaper never hit the ground?

Sandro reached in his pocket and fumbled painfully. He pulled out a clean handkerchief and his wallet.

The officer barked a command.

Charlotte tightened her grip on Sandro's arm. She willed him to stay calm and find his false papers. She prayed that he would not collapse onto the ground.

But then the terrified Italian artist dropped his card on the ground. Quick as a whip, Charlotte leaned down and picked it up from the cement floor. She handed it to the police officer and murmured an apology.

The officer held the card between his forefinger and thumb as if it were a dirty sock. His nostrils flared with contempt. Slowly, his gaze rose to the terrified Sandro.

"You look like a Jew."

Charlotte's chest heaved, and her insides roiled, but she spoke in the rudimentary German that she'd learned at school. "If he were a Jew, he would *never* be traveling with me," she said, putting as much contempt into her voice as she could. "It would be a disgrace. You dishonor me in suggesting such a thing." She quailed at her awful words, but right now, she knew that this was what Anita would do under the same circumstances, if it meant saving a dear friend's life.

The German's eyes flew to Charlotte, and for one, horrible moment that she knew would haunt her for the rest of her days, his treacherous, cruel eyes latched with hers. Hatred for all he represented laced itself around her like a corset.

Steeling herself, she sent him a conspiratorial smile.

The guard blew his whistle.

The officer stood there unmoving. Finally, when the conductor shouted for everyone to board, he threw back his head and laughed.

"*Heil Hitler!*" he shouted.

"*Heil Hitler,*" Charlotte whispered. Her legs wanted to buckle underneath her, and she gripped Sandro's arm like a vice, but she fluttered her eyelashes, and she tilted her head to one side. It was another thing Louis had told her to do.

The German man was young, handsome, and clearly easily flattered. He bit his lip, unable to stop his grin.

They are all just country boys. Louis' words rang through Charlotte's mind.

Finally, the German officer waved them on. "American, Italian? You are my friends. Go."

And Charlotte murmured, as they got on the train, "I wanted to spit in his face."

When they found a seat, Charlotte slumped down into it. Next to her, Sandro was silent and pale. He rubbed his sweaty hands together and leaned down, his head between his hands.

The train rolled forward, and Charlotte leaned into him. "Please," she said. "Relax. You will be fine."

The only indication that he'd heard her was in the rigidity of his body.

Charlotte sat back. It was ironic. A few years ago, young people were escaping the outcome of the Spanish Civil War to come to France. And now, they were having to escape persecution in the country they'd hoped to call home.

It would be the least she could do to help take Anita's beloved artists to safety. She'd come to respect the fact that they were creative souls who saw and expressed beauty on their canvases, where, sometimes, there was none to be found in the real world.

The train quickened its pace and rolled out of Paris.

Charlotte laid a soft hand over Sandro's shaking arm.

The following morning, Charlotte opened her eyes at the gentle shake on her shoulder. She leaned up on one elbow in bed and came face to face with a worried-looking Sandrine.

"Sandrine?" she whispered.

Late last night, she'd managed to guide Sandro from the nearest train station to the abbey using a hand-drawn map from Louis. He'd assured her in the middle of the night that his family would help find someone to lead Sandro across the border to Spain. She'd arrived back at her lodgings exhausted, but relieved and fallen into bed.

"I was awake when you came in," Sandrine said, her voice lowering. "I know you are not just going to see your new friends from the abbey. Please, Charlotte. I feel a responsibility to keep you safe."

Charlotte frowned. She was suddenly awake, but she could not put Sandrine in any danger by revealing her whereabouts in the last day. At the same time, she yearned to share with one of her oldest friends the fact that Anita was alive.

"If you cannot trust me, who can you trust?" A hurt expression crossed Sandrine's features.

Charlotte slumped back in her bed. If Sandrine knew anything of the journeys she'd taken to Paris or of the fervent trip to the abbey yesterday, guiding Sandro from the safety of Louis' apartment across the red-russet landscape, with only low shrubs to hide themselves, Sandrine would not have slept at all.

Charlotte closed her eyes. This was the very reason Anita had kept her activities secret from Charlotte. Where did the circles of truth and deception end in war?

She would never forgive herself if anything happened to Sandrine. Sandrine was enjoying working with Armand and Lucie as it gave her some connection with the antiques business she'd lost. Armand had said he valued Sandrine's quiet assistance looking after the treasures from the Louvre. The role was perfect for her.

But there was a growing resistance to the Nazis in the area surrounding Montauban, and that meant there could be an increase in suspicion against this in the region as well. The local bishop had spoken openly in opposition to the Nazi ideologies that the Vichy government had embraced without question. Monsignor Pierre-Marie Theas, the Bishop of Montauban, had given a speech condemning the Vichy government for following in the steps of a regime worked in cruel and inhuman ways.

Sandrine's eyes darted to the door.

Charlotte pressed her lips together in silence, but her heart broke at the sight of Sandrine's pale, worried features, at the way she looked so hurt.

"I was a friend of the Goldsteins too," Sandrine whispered. "I have a personal stake in this as well." She pressed her hand to her heart. "Don't think that I am less sickened than you are. Charlotte, don't think for a moment that I don't care."

Charlotte's brows drew together. She stood up and pulled her wrap around herself. "Sandrine, I wouldn't have been able to run Anita's gallery without your support, your guidance. When Anita left, I..."

"*Left?*"

Charlotte closed her eyes. She swallowed, but her throat was thick. "I am tired," she said. "I meant, when Anita *died*."

Sandrine folded her arms. "I detest the fact that that, as a Jew, Anita could not be on the public streets of Paris except at certain times of the day. She would have to ride in the back carriage of the trains on the Metro in the city she so loved. The only solace I can begin to find in her departure..." Sandrine frowned at Charlotte, "is the fact that she is at peace and away from that nightmare." She paused. "But, Charlotte, if you are hiding something, you cannot hide it from me. Please."

Charlotte swallowed. Lying to Sandrine went against every fiber of her being. And somewhere deep inside her, a voice cried out that Sandrine had guessed.

But revealing that Anita was alive and in disguise? Charlotte grimaced.

"While we are all aware of the Nazi atrocities being carried out across the border, I don't think any of us ever thought they could be happening here in France," Sandrine continued.

Charlotte stayed quiet. She'd promised not to tell a soul, not Élise and Olivier, not Martha, not Papa. But Sandrine was here with her. How would she feel if Sandrine were to find out Anita was alive when Charlotte had not told her so?

Sandrine's voice broke. "Darling, if you are carrying on in the brave manner that I know Anita would have done, if you are doing something truly to resist this terrible, unthinkable situation that our government has put us all into, then, I want to help. Please. What are we humans if we cannot help each other?"

Charlotte covered her mouth with her hand. She swallowed

back the tears that wanted to spill down her cheeks. Was she underestimating Sandrine's quiet determination? Sandrine had lived through a war before.

She'd assumed Anita had taken her own life because it was all too much, and she'd also assumed that Sandrine wanted to lead a quiet life, but maybe she was wrong.

Sandrine's mouth worked. She struggled to get out the words. "Armand told me that when Marshal Pétain came to Montauban, he gave a speech in the Place Nationale before a wildly cheering crowd. I can't stand by and do nothing, particularly if you are putting yourself at risk. And, without you telling me a thing, I suspect my worries are confirmed."

Charlotte looked down at the floor.

"I cannot be a part of a France that is disloyal to the values of freedom and democracy that we fought for in the last war," Sandrine went on. "You must know how this is killing me. I don't agree with sitting and waiting, but I understand why Armand and Lucie are doing so. How could I live with myself if I did nothing to help my fellow countrymen and those who are being persecuted for no reason?"

Charlotte knew Anita's truth. Did Sandrine deserve to know hers?

Sandrine was pale. "Yesterday, I passed the Poult building in town. Montauban housed some sixty foreign-born Jews as prisoners there last year. While the bishop speaks against the Nazis, the local government does not. I *shuddered* as I walked past the old factory." She lowered her voice. "I am terrified to think where those poor souls who were incarcerated there are now. And I will not stand by while you risk your life, because I am certain that is what you are doing. Let me risk myself too."

Charlotte took in a shaking breath.

"I worry that things are going to become even more shameful in France," Sandrine said, her voice steady and sure. "I worry that we will see our French-born Jews sent to

Germany. How can I go on if I am not doing a thing? I see far more risk to my state of mind in sitting here with a guilty conscience than doing something to help, Charlotte."

Charlotte walked across the room. The specter of roundups in Paris sickened her. The specter of Anita being found out was unbearable. But she did understand what Sandrine was saying. It made perfect sense because it was getting to the point that all people in occupied France had to make a choice: collaborate, resist or wait.

Charlotte stood solitary by the window. Louis had said it when she first met him. The Resistance was going to become a network of women—women just like her and Sandrine. Sandrine was middle-aged but she only had herself to put at risk. If Charlotte did not allow her to help her network, she might go work with another cell of Resistance run by strangers.

"If you do not tell me," Sandrine said, "I shall join the Resistance anyway."

Charlotte stilled. Sandrine had read her mind. After a long moment, she turned to face her. "Prepare yourself," she said.

Half an hour later, Sandrine's face was strained. "My old friend is brave, but she dances too close to the fire." She walked the few steps across the room to the wooden dressing table that did for them both.

Charlotte stared at Sandrine's face reflected in the mirror. Her eyes latched with those of her mother's friend. Sandrine's gray eyes might be quiet, but they held a determination that was undeniably strong.

Sandrine opened the single drawer to the dresser, where she and Charlotte each kept the most rudimentary of things. And then, Sandrine held up a key.

"We must convince Anita to live in my apartment." Sandrine's brow furrowed. "My apartment was once the home of my late husband's family, of tall, blond Parisians. The Germans will *never* consider going to search it because it is completely inconspicuous."

Charlotte held out her hand, and Sandrine placed the key in it, folding her fingers over Charlotte's palm. She, Anita, and Sandrine would wage their own private war, just as Anita and Sandrine had done in the last war with Charlotte's mother, Chloé.

The following day, Charlotte made her way through the quiet streets of Montauban to Louis' apartment in the narrow lane off the square. He and Henri remained, to all intents and purposes, simply students. Madeleine was a quiet girl from Paris who lived by herself. No one suspected that the three of them were integral to *La Defense*.

Charlotte took care to look as if she had not a worry in the world. The fact was, she was not only about to deliver the very first editions of the newspapers they held so dear, she was about to inform the trio that she'd found another courier to travel between Paris and Montauban. She was about to lend Sandrine's support to their network, and the only solace she felt was that at least she could keep an eye on Sandrine herself.

Charlotte knew the network was extensive and she knew that she was only one of many women transporting underground newspapers around France. There was a major cell in Lyon, and there was one in the French government's headquarters in Vichy. Surely, her friends would welcome Sandrine to their group with open arms.

But Charlotte fisted her hand into a ball as she came to a stop outside Louis' building.

The first edition in her satchel had come with a proclamation stating the aims of *La Defense*: to galvanize people into action, to share a common feeling of expression of the young and to provide a common study into the hearts and minds of the youth of France. The front page proudly announced the establishment of a movement of national freedom, and articles discussing the last month's political activities in France. Charlotte only hoped Louis, Henri and Madeleine would accept the help of a middle-aged woman when it came to *La Defense*. The majority of their network was made up of young people in their twenties, not middle-aged folk as yet.

Charlotte pressed the bell. Louis came down to greet her and she started at the dark expression on his face. Once they were inside his apartment with the door closed, she handed him her leather bag bulging full of the very first editions of the newspaper he held so dear.

He picked up the printed pages in a reverie. His eyes raked over the paper and when he lifted his face to Charlotte, she swallowed at the sight of tears pooling in his eyes.

"There are not words," he whispered.

Madeleine came into the room and pulled Charlotte into a hug. "We cannot do this without couriers, and you are some of the bravest people in our cell," she said to Charlotte. "I am proud of you. Thank you."

But right then, Louis reached for a document that sat on the table where he wrote his articles for *La Defense* and handed it to Charlotte. He walked across to the window and pressed his forehead against the glass.

Charlotte glanced at the paper in her hand. "*No*," she murmured. She bowed her head. She had minimized her contact with Louis since she'd met him. Were they seen together, they could risk the very thing they were fighting for— freedom. But on some occasions, she'd sensed him looking at her. She'd thought the expression in his eyes was tender, and sometimes, when he spoke to her, there was a softness to his voice that he did not show toward Henri or Madeleine.

It had been there the first time they met, but caught up in

the war and their united purpose, anything romantic had seemed soft. But now, it was too late for any such notion.

He'd been called up. She might never see him again.

Charlotte placed the paper back down on the desk and spread it out gently with her fingers. Slowly, she lifted her gaze until her eyes locked with his. "Louis..."

Louis rubbed a hand over his chin. His eyes were dark with fire. "Madeleine will be your contact," he said. "I will miss—"

She turned away and folded her arms. The words she wanted to say locked in her throat.

"If things had been different," he began, speaking gently. "In another time, Charlotte..."

Charlotte shook her head, her mouth widening into a forced grin. Tears stung the backs of her eyelids, and she shuddered and bent her face to focus on the letter from the French military. "But times are not different," she murmured.

"No."

She was achingly aware of him standing there, and she'd miss his presence in this space where they'd worked together. Who knew when she'd see him again. But she forced herself to focus on the documentation in front of her instead. She must focus on reality. Fantasies had no part in war.

"I have another courier for *La Defense*," she said. But her heart ached for Louis. He was being forced to fight for a government whose actions he detested. Instead of resisting them, he was going to have to kill on their behalf. "We can trust my contact. She is a family friend whom I've known all my life."

"There won't be a 'we' any more," he said, his voice lingering in the room.

She let out an involuntary sob. If only she could go to war for him, she would!

"Charlotte."

Charlotte lifted her head and her eyes locked with his. In one fast, mad impulse, he was across the room. He held her face in his gentle hands and then he leaned down, his eyes raking over hers.

Charlotte reached up, her hand cupped his face. "I shall always remember you," she murmured. "Thank you for allowing me to be a part of this. I am honored. And I shall not let you down, Louis. I promise. You can count on me."

A smile spread across his features, and he reached out to tuck a stray strand of hair away from her face. "Dearest Charlotte, once this is over, I will find you. I swear it."

In one tiny, yet momentous movement, she nodded, and he leaned down, his lips touching hers in a fiery kiss.

23

NEW YORK, FALL 1942

Martha

It had been nineteen years since Chloé's death. Martha sat on a wooden bench in Central Park. Papa was by her side and, opposite the lake, the trees were a multicolored glory spilling down to the water, where their reflections sat like perfect mirrors. A couple rowed along the glass-like surface of the lake. Every year on this fall day, Martha would come and sit here with Papa, and they'd remember Chloé. A sharp breeze drew up, and golden leaves fluttered down from the trees.

"She was lovely," Papa said.

"I know." Martha turned to him. She scanned the dear, familiar lines on his face. Her mother had never been able to witness these expression marks, because she had not had the privilege of growing old next to him. "You know," Martha said, swallowing hard. "The last memory of my mother is one I have clung to, in case, goodness knows, it was to go away."

She closed her eyes. That stunning fall day in Paris still vivid in her mind as it could be. It was the scents of the

Tuileries Gardens and the memory of her mother holding out her arms to her and Charlotte that had stayed with Martha. She still remembered the sound of her and Charlotte's little shoes on the gravel beneath their park.

"You couldn't walk on the grass." Martha smiled and wiped a stray tear from her cheek. "I remember being so cross about the rules." She sighed, and Papa chuckled softly next to her.

"They say we remember things we associate with feelings," Papa said. "I shall never feel anything as keenly as I did that day, Martha." He sighed heavily. "Chloé got me through the last war," he murmured. "But the battle I fought for years after she died was the hardest one I've fought all my life. I will never get over it. How someone can be here one day and gone the next. It is one of the cruelest forms of loss."

Martha turned back to face the lake and the glorious, changing trees. "I think we all know that time is so precious now," she ventured. "If you want to move forward, then I think you must." She turned, her eyes with their golden flecks catching with his, as he turned his head to meet her gaze. "I don't want you to suffer anymore." She lowered her voice. "And I know that mother wouldn't want you to either."

He stared out at the water, his blue eyes focused yet far away.

"Gisela is lovely..." she said. It seemed more important than ever to tell Papa that she'd noticed how Gisela looked at him. Now, the United States was at war...

Martha was certain that he'd have Charlotte's blessing too. She'd written and told Charlotte how Gisela was giving Papa a new lease of life. Charlotte had written back, delighted that he was enjoying Gisela's stories of her life in Vienna. She was pleased that he liked to sit with her while she told him of her passion for teaching mathematics and for developing opportunities for girls. Martha had told Charlotte that she'd noticed Papa's brow darkening when he said goodbye to Gisela after breakfast, when he went to his study, and she had to go to clean the houses of wealthy Manhattanites. He railed to Martha over the fact that this educated, brilliant woman could not translate her passion for girls' education into anything concrete in the United States. It was clear. When it came to Gisela, Papa was beginning to care.

"Gisela is brave, kind, and also a role model for me." Martha lowered her voice. Dare she voice it? "If Maman had lived, I know she would have been a role model. But, Papa, I feel lucky to have another inspirational woman in the house. It is almost," she went on, taking a deep breath, "as if with Gisela here, and you, and Élise and Olivier, that I have parents and grandparents all under one roof."

There. She'd said it.

Papa sat back against the bench, spreading his arms along it.

Martha's feelings were in a turmoil. She stood up. "It has been nineteen years, Papa."

He looked up at her, his tawny eyes bright. "We are only friends."

Martha threw back her head a moment and contained her tears. And then, drawing breath, she leveled with Papa. "If you had one day left to live your life, right now, this moment, everything considered, what would you regret not doing?"

Papa leaned forward in his seat, his hands dangling between his knees. "Martha..."

Papa raised his head. He stood up, a solitary, dear man. "We should go home."

"I think I shall stay in the park a little longer," Martha said. "You go though," she whispered. "Go and talk to her. Please."

The expression on his face was unfathomable. He pulled her into a hug and she leaned into his sweater. "Thank you," he said.

"You have my blessing if you want it, you know that," she

murmured. "You know how important it is to me to see you happy and at peace."

He pulled back, and she stood and watched him disappear from view.

Martha shoved her hands into her pockets, and her fingers curled around the latest letter from Clyde. She asked herself one brutal, honest question. Did she want Papa to be with Gisela, so that she, in turn, could be with Clyde?

She hated the fact that she could not bear to be honest with him.

And she hated the fact that the longer she left this, the stronger her feelings for Clyde were turning out to be.

But, most of all, she hated having secrets from Papa.

Martha leaned over a table in the New York Public Library. She was sorting through the hundreds of books that had been donated for the Victory Book Campaign that had been organized to send books to the army camps, both here in the United States and overseas, to the navy as a way to lift morale. Martha ran an expert eye over the current selection. As usual, the books that folks had dropped in to donate were largely fiction. She started sorting these into stacks. The staff had been instructed that some of the books were not to be deemed suitable for the armed forces and were to be sent to women and children in industrial areas, and Martha began placing some of these aside.

The Victory Book Campaign had been a wonderful success so far, and every now and then, the library hosted jazz concerts and events on the front steps to increase awareness amongst the citizens of New York.

But, again, the unsettled feelings that she'd fought to overcome yesterday in the park threatened to overwhelm her. Here she was, safely in her job, while Élise, Olivier and Gisela had all lost their homes, their livelihoods and every aspect of the life they'd known. It had all been stripped bare.

And then, as she sorted through a pile of books, she stopped. Martha frowned at the familiar cover that she held in her hands. Virginia Woolf's *The Years*. It had been the book she was reading when Clyde had approached her aboard the ship to France.

Suddenly, a feeling of complete unease seeping through her, Martha placed the book down and moved away from it. She couldn't help but shake the feeling that something was wrong. And she couldn't help but hate the thought that she was here, doing nothing toward the war, and useless. As usual, hiding away in the sanctuary she'd sought.

"Oh, please," she murmured. "Clyde, Charlotte. Be safe."

Martha stared at the quiet shelves and the rows of books that had provided her with a retreat from the world since she was a little girl. Right now, her old haven felt like a fortress. Keeping her in, not keeping her safe at all.

The next morning, Martha was folding laundry with Gisela. The only way to deal with the uncertainty that was snaking through her insides was to keep busy, she knew that. She folded a blouse of Élise's and put it into the ironing pile. She sighed with thanks at the sight of a fresh bunch of flowers that Élise had popped into the laundry room.

"Élise would make a welcoming home wherever she lived," Gisela said, her voice kindly. "It is one of the things I have always adored about her. The ability to make a home anywhere."

Martha stopped. "She was a second mother to you, as Anita was to me," she said quietly.

Gisela nodded. "Anita had Élise's ability to make people

welcome in her home, but she is of my generation, and we had slightly less traditional ideas. Anita was independent."

Martha stood still.

"There is, of course, nothing wrong with being happy on your own terms," Gisela went on, her eyes far away. "Goodness knew, in Vienna, it was the way I operated."

"Do you miss it dreadfully?" Martha asked. There was something fascinating about this attractive, wildly intelligent, yet down-to-earth woman. And yet, these days, it was a sensitive topic to ask people about what they did before the war. People whose lives had been upturned.

But American lives were being upturned now. Since the bombing of Pearl Harbor, most families had sent at least one son, father, brother, uncle, or cousin to the battle zones in the Pacific and Europe. And while Martha had not known families who had experienced loss in the first months since that momentous day in December last year, she was beginning to know girls who had lost brothers or sweethearts, and the reality of the situation was starting to hit home across the country.

Gisela sighed and a faraway look clouded her dark eyes. "I miss the old Vienna every day," she said, finally, in answer to Martha's question. She shook her head. "I also think that doing something practical is not a bad thing for academics." She lowered her voice. "Sometimes, when I am cleaning houses, I imagine my male counterparts at the university in Vienna scrubbing bathtubs, and dusting lamps, and I have a chuckle. Manual labor puts an uneasy mind at rest sometimes," she added.

Martha took in a shaky breath. If only such a thing would work for her. Last night, she had come so close to broaching the topic of Clyde with Papa that she'd hovered outside his study for a long moment, only to hear Olivier talking to him. So, she'd turned away. She'd written a long letter to Charlotte instead because she was yearning to know if her sister was safe. Yearning to know if the strange feeling that had over-taken her in the library had been an omen or simply her own fears borne out of the anxiety that everyone felt because of the war.

"I am thinking of writing more books on mathematical instruction for girls," Gisela said. "I have been talking with your father about approaching publishers in the United States." She shook her head. "There is no law saying that I cannot write a book, thank goodness. And maybe I can reach more people by writing than by teaching anyway."

Martha took one of her cotton summer dresses from the wicker basket and placed it alongside Élise's blouse. "How wonderful," she said, meaning it. She still felt embarrassed that she and Elizabeth had failed to secure an academic visa for Gisela.

"I wonder, do you want to follow in the path of indepen-dence, Martha?" Gisela asked quietly. "What are your dreams, dear?"

Martha hesitated. "Papa ensured that Charlotte and I had a wonderful education, and I will never waste it. But..."

There was a silence.

"But?" Gisela prompted.

Martha placed one of Papa's shirts down. Her eyes traced over the familiar patterns on it. She swallowed, knowing how it would look on him. Could she bear not to see him every day? How could she stand it? They had never been separated their whole lives. And yet, if she did not start to talk of her strong feelings for Clyde to anyone beyond Élise, she would only exac-erbate her own distress. "I have fallen in love with a man who is not American, Gisela," she said.

Gisela's head tilted to one side. "Oh, Martha," she murmured, "You are worried about your papa."

Martha nodded and tears sprang to the sides of her eyes at the quickness of Gisela's response. "Papa and I have always been together," she explained. "I cannot bear to leave him. And so, you see, it is hopeless."

"But sometimes, if our destiny is far away from home," Gisela whispered, "we must go find it. Believe me," she whispered. "I know how that feels."

Martha turned away, her heart breaking.

Why, why must things not remain the same? And why must decisions be one of the hardest things in life?

Charlotte

Charlotte walked through the Place des Vosges, one of the oldest squares in Paris, in a city occupied by one of the world's newest and deadliest regimes. She'd deliberately chosen to walk through the beautiful square on her way from the station, her bag bulging with the latest edition of *La Defense*.

She moved toward Sandrine's apartment in the Marais district where Anita had agreed to live in order to conceal her identity more completely from the Nazis than were she to remain in Rue Laffitte. But the task that loomed ahead was going to be one million times more difficult than anything Charlotte had attempted in the last months, during which time she'd helped Anita rescue six artists from Paris, accompanying them south to Montauban. Sandrine had assisted her, traveling in a separate train in case anything went wrong. Charlotte had then taken them to safety at the abbey, where Louis' father helped them to a network of safe houses on the way to Spain. If this was resistance, it was simple, and she, Sandrine and Anita had worked together not only as part of a larger home-grown network, but most importantly, as a small, tight-knit team.

But now, everything was about to erupt. Charlotte and Sandrine had to convince Anita to leave Paris now.

There must be no delay and Charlotte knew they had to act immediately. Armand, worried, had informed everyone that they would have to move the artistic collections out of Montauban in the coming week, because the United States and the United Kingdom were preparing to invade North Africa, and the colonial power in the region was France.

There was worried talk that the Nazi government would, in retaliation, take over the government of France in its entirety, and that meant that Montauban and its surrounds would be overrun by German police.

Armand and the team from the Louvre wanted to try to find a more isolated place for the protection of France's artistic legacy, but he feared they may not have time to move at all. Desperately, he was casting about for somewhere to go. He was trying to negotiate with the Vichy government and to explain to them that, in Montauban, they may be at risk of Allied air strikes and there would be no protection for the treasures in their care.

But Charlotte couldn't sleep at night for thinking about Anita.

Last winter, the freezing weather, accompanied with the never-ending search for food, had left Anita thin and cold. She'd suffered a terrible case of influenza and Sandrine's apartment, like those of most Parisians, had been glacial. The idea of Anita in this solitary flat, spending another winter alone, hungry and freezing in Paris was impossible. Electricity was limited, and Anita had given up any rations she had for coal for a little gas for an hour at noon, but this winter, even that would not be possible, as she'd combined rations with a neighbor so that one of them could cook one meal each day.

Last time Charlotte was here, Anita had realized she had no cooking fat left. The contraband market was thriving, but coffee, eggs, chickens, and wine were all ten times their pre-war prices and things were only going to worsen with the war in Northern Africa.

And yet, still, Anita insisted on dyeing her hair blond and remaining under a false identity, right under the noses of the German government.

But a Jewish woman in Paris? It was a time bomb waiting to explode. And now that she'd rescued the foreign-born artists for whom she cared so deeply, it was time for Anita to save herself.

If there was one thing Charlotte wanted to do in this war, it was not to lose Anita. Not again, not ever again.

Charlotte fought the instinct to disappear into the shadows that overcame her every time she was in Paris. Instead, she walked openly through Place des Vosges that was overlooked by the old aristocratic mansions with shadowed arcades running beneath. In a rare break of sunshine in this cold day, a few others walked through the formal gardens, admiring the buildings' red-brick facades.

Charlotte made her way out of the square. She folded her arms around her body to stave off the quick wind that flew through the streets of the Marais and stopped at the road crossing, checking assiduously to the right, and left, always, always. These days, everything seemed to haunt her, Chloé's sudden death nineteen years ago, the living death that pervaded the Parisian streets and the fear that people would never again feel the joy they'd known before this war began.

What was also worrying was that Louis was based in Casablanca, where the Germans were carrying out air strikes against the Allied forces in a show of support for the Vichy government. It was a potboiler of a situation, because the Germans remained in control of the French troops. Charlotte's heart went out to her brave, loyal friend. The kiss they'd shared had been brief and passionate. But she still hated the fact that this passionate Frenchman would have to fight alongside the Germans and the Vichy government, the two things he abhorred.

Charlotte was tossing and turning at night, because her other deepest worry was that the Vichy government had not only been arresting and deporting foreign Jews and separating families from their children, but the roundup of July at Vel d'Hiv had shaken her to her core. Thirteen thousand Jews had been arrested in Paris and transported to a labor camp in Germany.

Today, Charlotte knew she must convince Anita to come south. She had to persuade Anita to make use of the network of safe houses that Charlotte had built up with Louis' family. There was only so long a Jewish person could hide in disguise under the Nazis, and if they were going to take over France in its entirety, then the places for hiding would be countable by the fingers on one hand.

If the Nazis discovered Anita's real identity, there was absolutely no doubt she would simply vanish without a trace. And if Charlotte was living under German rule, as an American, she would have to check in regularly under her real name with her new governing rulers. Moving around with false identities and getting through checkpoints was going to move from dangerous to outright impossible if the Nazis ruled all of France.

Charlotte hurried through the streets of the Marais. She turned down the narrow Rue de Sevigny where Sandrine's apartment sat. The afternoon was wearing on, and Charlotte knew that once night fell, it would be the worst time of all in occupied Paris. The city would be almost deserted, a deathly silence hanging over the streets.

The only thing that ever broke the darkness of Paris at night was the tramp of nailed Nazi boots. Charlotte, like everyone else in this city, lived in fear of the sound of *la botte allemande*.

Yes, the thing she had most come to dread was the sound of synchronized feet, and the shouts that accompanied them. *Ein, zwei, drei. Halt!*

Charlotte came to halt outside Anita's home in Sandrine's former building in Rue de Sevigny. Automatically, she glanced around to check the pretty street was clear.

The clouds thickened overhead, and the weak sun disappeared in the closing afternoon. The sudden pepper of a machine gun in the distance rent the Parisian air.

Charlotte froze when, at the corner a couple of houses up, a powerful car rushed by.

She checked her wristwatch. Sandrine, who had traveled on a separate train as she always did for safety purposes, should, by Charlotte's reckoning, already be here.

Charlotte reached for the duplicate key she held to Sandrine's building, and stepped inside, knowing that this would be one of the hardest conversations she'd ever have. She made her way up the staircase to the apartment that had once been the family home of Sandrine's husband, Jacques Mercier. Here, Charlotte's family friend, Vianne Mercier, had grown up during the Great War, dreaming of creating beautiful garments for women to wear once her struggles were done. And she'd made it.

Charlotte paused a moment outside the apartment door. Vianne was an inspiration. Charlotte closed her eyes. One day, she, Charlotte, would hang Anita's sign outside the gallery in Rue Laffitte again.

She turned the key in the lock.

Now, she faced the biggest challenge so far.

Saving Anita.

This was the one thing at which she could not fail.

Charlotte stepped into the apartment. The cold hit her as soon as she entered the front hallway. Damp patches bloomed on the walls and the minerals from the bricks leached through the old wallpaper. Freezing air curled white from Charlotte's lips.

"Anita? Sandrine?" she called softly. Charlotte gathered her coat around herself and made her way down the long passage that led through the apartment. There was no sign of Sandrine, and the apartment was deadly quiet.

In the last months, Anita had become too cautious to open her front door to anyone, and so Sandrine had given Charlotte a key to her home. Charlotte wanted to ensure that Anita was not frightened by her arrival, so she continuously called her name.

Anita was strong, she'd seemed invincible to Charlotte at times, but cold and hunger and the constant news of Jews being rushed away by the Gestapo to Germany to never be seen again would pray on the mind of the bravest soul. Anita had worked so hard to remain in Paris and to live under the Nazis with false papers, a disguise and a new name. Hiding and taking on another identity had been brave, and Anita's decision to help her adored artists to safety had been heroic. But now, with the war taking a heavy toll on Anita's health, it was Charlotte's turn to handle the reins that Anita had always held so strong for her.

The silence that greeted Charlotte's calls only served to prove the urgent need to remove Anita from the worsening situation in Paris. Poking her nose into the dining room, Charlotte winced at the way it was covered in dust sheets. The air was misty and cold and the shutters were drawn closed, enveloping this strange, empty apartment in darkness. This was no way to live.

When, finally, she moved down the long passageway, Charlotte stopped outside the bedroom that Anita was sleeping in. She'd only inhabited three rooms during her time here—the kitchen, the bathroom, and her bedroom—and now a sliver of light cracked underneath the closed bedroom door.

Charlotte pushed open the door, only to stop, bringing her hand to cover her mouth. For there sat Anita, on the little velvet stool that Sandrine had told them once belonged to Vianne, in the room where the famous designer had grown up as a little girl.

In the reflection of the mirror, Anita's dark eyes caught with Charlotte's, and held for one, long moment. For one long moment, neither of them moved.

The older woman turned, her mouth working, the dark circles that loomed around her eyes seeming even more pronounced. Their purplish-blue shade was stark against the unaccustomed paleness of her skin. The simple dress she wore hung like a sheet on her body that was once so voluptuous and curvy. Anita's eyes that used to dance with joy held a dead expression that made Charlotte want to curl up on the bed and cry. How could anyone be expected to stay healthy when they were only allowed to eat enough for a small child?

Charlotte moved toward Anita, toward the woman who had given her every opportunity she'd known. Placing her bag, filled with the newspapers that riled against the Nazis, on Vianne's old bed, Charlotte came to kneel in front of her friend.

"Hello there," she whispered.

Anita reached out. Her thin hands were bloodless and she clutched Charlotte's fingers like a pair of bird's claws. "My apartment in Rue Laffitte was ransacked by the Nazis last night," she murmured, her eyes swiveling around the room. As if the perpetrators were here.

Charlotte's heartbeat started to race. She opened her mouth, but no words came out. Instead, she simply stared at Anita in disbelief.

"A neighbor sent word to me." Anita widened her eyes, and in the semi darkness of the late afternoon, they appeared overly bright.

Too bright.

Two vivid spots appeared on Anita's cheeks.

Her hands started shaking violently in Charlotte's. "You

see, two of my neighbors, whom I thought I should be able to trust, recognized me recently. No matter how much I denied it, they had worked out who I was," she whispered, her head shaking from side to side now. "One of them sent her son here this morning to tell me that the Gestapo were looking for a blond woman who was a Jew in disguise. They searched everything in my apartment, destroying, looting, stealing. They held my neighbor at gunpoint and threatened to torture her if she withheld the truth."

Charlotte set her jaw.

"They know I am alive."

"Anita, we shall pack your bags." Her heart raced and fear spiked her insides. They couldn't hang around any longer. If Charlotte had known how urgent it was to get Anita out of here, now it was imperative.

"My neighbor broke down and could not inform them I was dead. It is only a matter of time. They will come for me. It is over." Anita grabbed Charlotte's arm. "Darling, *you* must go. Leave me. I will not risk your life for mine." Anita ground out the last words, and something in her voice made Charlotte reel backwards.

She stared at the older woman, and she almost fell back physically at the determination in her eyes. But then, something equally as strong and determined reared up within herself, a strength, and a power that she knew had always been a part of her.

"Never," Charlotte whispered. "I have made the journey south a hundred times. I will get you to safety. You must come with me. There is no time to delay." She turned her head toward the door.

Sandrine should arrive any moment.

Anita swept her hand across her forehead, as if in some vague effort to remove the sweat that was building there despite the cold, in spite of the freezing air in this apartment. "I can't put you at risk for me. I have already put you through too much." Anita raised her head, her eyes grazing Charlotte's. "You have no idea how much. Darling..."

Charlotte stood up. She cast her eyes about the room. "Now. We must go. We must not be conspicuous, and we cannot take anything." She held her breath at the way Anita had been living. She'd been a woman reduced to the most rudimentary of basics. A change of clothes, only enough food to feed a sparrow, a freezing bed, no fuel, little milk, and hardly any meat... no more of this. Charlotte was determined. "Now. Come with me." From the mess of clothes on the bed, she found a warm coat and a hat.

"Go, Charlotte, I will not put you at any risk for me," Anita whispered, as if like a refrain from some old song. A song they both knew only too well.

Charlotte held Anita at arm's length. Lifting her chin, she forced her shaking breath to calm. "We stick together," she said, her voice firm.

"It is more than I deserve," Anita said, her eyes raking Charlotte's face.

And just then, Charlotte froze. There was a disturbance in the street outside the apartment. The unmistakable sound of a car pulling up. A shout. In German.

Charlotte reached up, her hand covering her own mouth as she fought to stop herself from screaming out loud. She bit her hand, her stomach reeling.

Anita frowned. She stood still for a split second, clearly taking in the terrifying sounds out in the street. Then, as if in complicit agreement that Charlotte was right, Anita reached for the coat, her hat and a handbag. Anita nodded at Charlotte and indicated that she follow her. In that split second, it seemed that Anita had taken control again.

They moved, Charlotte's chin trembling and her head shaking as she followed Anita, now, in the lead, down the passageway. For once, she had no destination in mind, other than to get out of this cold, terrifying building, of this place that had been torn from Sandrine. How Anita had stood living here for months was beyond her. Being here for a few minutes had felt unbearable. Charlotte ached for the poor citizens of Paris, and her anger flared for the top-ranking Nazis living in the city's most exclusive hotels.

And then it happened. An ear-splitting crack rent the air outside in the street.

A woman's scream.

Shouting.

Nazi voices barking instructions.

Charlotte froze. And then, in one horrifying leap, she wove her way through the dining room, around the shrouded table and to the window, where she slipped the closed shutters open a fraction.

Only to recoil in horror. Gasping for air, her skin clammy, Charlotte clutched her chest.

For there, sprawled out on the street for everyone to see in Paris, was Sandrine's body.

The Gestapo had found their blond woman outside Sandrine's apartment.

But they'd found the wrong one.

"What is it?" Anita murmured, moving up behind Charlotte, and in that one, quick, terrifying, fatal second, Charlotte, almost retching all over the floor, averted her gaze from the window and took Anita's arm.

"*Nothing.*" She ground out the words.

Charlotte's heart split in two. But she steeled herself not to look back at the blood-spattered, dear dead body of the woman she'd shared a room with these past months, of the woman who had kindly guided her through the machinations of running a business on her own, the woman whose quiet, determined generosity and friendship had made her an invaluable friend to the young Chloé and Anita during the last war. Sandrine's apartment had afforded Anita safety these last months and had probably saved her life too.

There was more than one type of hero during a war, and Sandrine was a quiet achiever.

Charlotte swallowed back the tears that threatened to engulf her chest as she took Anita away from the scene.

"I presume there is a back way out?" she asked. She glanced to her left and her right as they left the Merciers' apartment, hypervigilant for what they might find.

"Come down to the ground floor. There is an exit to the rear laneway."

Charlotte's heartbeat thrashed in her ears. Her lungs and her chest wanted to explode. She would never forget the image of Sandrine's body laid out on that street. She would never forget her, and her mother's long-trusted friend, but now she had to focus, more than she ever had in her life, in saving the last of their friendship group.

Fingers of pink and orange light spread slowly across the sky in a magnificent dawn, too beautiful for the morning after Sandrine had died. Charlotte stared up at the patterns of brilliant light that pearled between the treetops in the thicket she'd come to know only too well because it afforded precious shelter between the terracotta bricked town of Montauban and the abbey that Louis' family owned.

There were few places that provided cover on this route, and Charlotte had become deft at knowing them all. Sometimes, she'd slipped into gardens of abandoned or empty homes. She'd hidden away in the hedges that lined the narrow roads, but this thicket followed a narrow walkway that ran for part of the route toward the abbey.

Charlotte leaned back against a tree. Next to her, Anita

slept. She was curled up on the damp grass and her face was streaked with dirt. Anita's too thin body shivered involuntarily every now and then, and her eyes fluttered like the tentative wings of a fledgling.

Charlotte had not been able to speak of the sight that had haunted her ever since they left Paris, Sandrine's body spread out on Rue Laffitte, a Nazi officer standing over her. She was poleaxed and too stunned to be able to iterate the heartbreak that wanted to flow, that wanted to shout at the stars for the terrible loss of an innocent friend who'd been murdered outside the front steps to her rightful home. Murdered by impostors. She would not tell Anita for fear of what it would do to her.

Charlotte had drawn on some primal life force, some well of strength she had no idea she possessed, in order to leave darling Sandrine's body where it lay. She'd fought every instinct that burned inside her, shouting that she needed to turn around, to go and defend her friend's body, to hold it and give her the burial she deserved.

What if she'd gone down to the street to find Sandrine still breathing? What then?

Instead, she'd clutched onto Anita's weak, spindly arm, that felt, shockingly, like that of a child's, propelling them both to the Montparnasse station and hiding in the shadows of the cobbled laneways whenever she heard a sound that sent her senses to full alert.

It was lucky that they had not encountered any Nazis on their way out of Paris, because if Charlotte had come face to face with one, she did not know whether she could trust herself to behave. Like a pair of shadows, Charlotte and Anita had wound their way through the dismal streets of Paris. They had bought a train ticket and headed to Montauban via Toulouse.

It had been when she was sitting on the train with her hat in her hands and her blond hair bright under the strip lights for any passenger to see that Charlotte's heart had sunk even further into despair over the complete disaster that had unfolded on her watch, and she realized her own error.

She'd left her bag containing Madeleine's newspapers in Sandrine's apartment.

Right on the bed Anita had been sleeping in. There for anyone to find.

Charlotte had glared out the window at the darkness that enveloped the train, while Anita had slept beside her.

Now, Charlotte squeezed her eyes shut. "I am sorry, dearest, Sandrine," she whispered to the trees. "I shall miss you so very much."

Charlotte swallowed. She gently leaned forward to stir Anita awake.

"Anita," she whispered. "We must depart again. Dearest, it is not too much further until you shall be safe."

Anita stirred. Her brown eyes opened, and her gaze landed on Charlotte's face.

"Thank you," she whispered, her lips forming a brave smile, despite the fact her cheeks were as pale as new fall of winter's snow.

Charlotte fought back the urge to burst into tears when they arrived at the abbey. She limped into the cloisters and eased Anita down onto one of the stone benches that lined the lawns.

Assuring her dear friend that she'd be safe there, Charlotte moved away to find help. But as she did so, Anita gripped her arm with surprising strength. Despite the exhaustion that had overcome her after months of malnutrition, Anita's eyes held a determined look.

"Come with me, Charlotte," Anita whispered, her voice rasping, her lips dry and cracked. "You must get out of France too... you are in as much danger as I."

Charlotte's brows drew close. She glanced across the timeless cloisters with their fall display of pansies, whose little faces peered straight up to the noon sun. This was the very place she'd met Louis all that time ago. It was the place where she'd first felt the stirrings that she might be able to do something to help.

"Don't be silly," she whispered. Charlotte ran her hand through her hair. "Darling Anita, we shall meet again, at the end of this ghastly war."

But Anita's mouth worked, and she shook her head. Her eyes searched Charlotte's face. "You cannot stay in France. It is not safe for you." Anita seemed to struggle with something, her mouth worked, but she simply shook her head and pressed her lips tightly closed.

Charlotte took Anita's hand, covering it with her own.

She'd turn around and go back to Montauban as quickly as she could. Despite the exhaustion that threatened to split her head in two, despite the hunger that gnawed at her stomach, the only thing that was going to keep Charlotte moving forward, after the tragedy of losing Sandrine and after the ache of having to say goodbye to Anita, was her job. And that was to work with Armand and Lucie, and to help safeguard the treasures of France, and those that belonged to the Goldsteins, who, through no fault of their own, had lost everything else.

"*Go back to town and quickly. The Germans have invaded the Free Zone of France.*" Louis' father's words, whispered to her as she held Anita in a long hug for one last time, pounded in Charlotte's ears as she rushed through the streets of Montauban later that day. She'd torn herself away from Anita's entreaties that she run away and leave France. But as the chilly afternoon closed into evening, and twilight spread a dull blanket over the old town, Charlotte came to a slow, dreaded halt.

The streets were silent.

The old town was too quiet.

And she knew this stillness; it was a silence that every citizen of Paris and every person who lived in a territory occupied by the Nazis would never forget as long as they lived. It was in the dark, pervading fear that lingered when people fled into their homes and were too scared to come out.

The sound of a lone motorcycle beat through the empty streets. Charlotte slipped into the small park opposite the Musée Ingres, shadowing herself under a solitary tree.

"Dear goodness," Charlotte whispered. "Help us all now."

Her eyes followed the motorcyclist as he buzzed past. She'd know that uniform anywhere.

Charlotte whipped out from the park. She scanned the great iron gates that led into the Musée Ingres' courtyard. They were closed. The gates were chained. If Armand and Lucie had still been there, light would have shone from the windows of the basement where the collections of the Louvre and the Goldsteins was being kept.

Charlotte turned, and keeping her head down, she took the laneways and the quietest, cobbled streets through the town to the Place Nationale. But as she crossed the empty, eerie square, its pink-bricked buildings framed by arches only reminded her of those in the old Place des Vosges in Paris, where she'd been two days ago, right before Sandrine was killed. And now, here she was, the only woman standing solitary in this old square.

Arches and old buildings were places people came to admire in peacetime. In war, such beauty only served to highlight the things they'd lost.

Charlotte struggled to stem the emotion that wanted to engulf her over Sandrine. If she could collapse right now, buckle down and cry, she would. But there was one thing she must do before she went back to the safety of her landlady's house.

Madeleine.

Charlotte must go and check on her friend. She must warn Madeleine that in the scurry of a Nazi attack, she'd left the latest editions of *La Defense* sitting on Anita's bed in Paris. While she reasoned that there was no link to Madeleine in that bag containing the latest editions, Charlotte couldn't be too careful. Madeleine was not the girl's real name, and there was no way that anyone could connect her with Charlotte. She'd used a different name to travel up to Paris and back, a hundred times. Trying to soothe herself with this thought, repeating it over and over in her head, Charlotte picked up her pace.

But all the while, another thought curled in her mind. If the Nazis were already aware of the underground paper, they'd go for Louis' apartment the moment they arrived in Montauban.

And they had arrived in Montauban that afternoon.

Charlotte started to run. As she hurried out of the square, a refrain beat through her head with the relentless ear-pounding beat of German boots on solid ground. The Nazis were ruthless. The Nazis were detailed. The Nazis would leave no stone unturned. The Nazis would systematically destroy any person whom they thought undermined their regime.

And, despite her best efforts, they'd discovered Anita was alive.

Charlotte raced across the square and moved toward Rue Armand Cambon. But the eerie feeling that had overcome her since the first time she'd walked down this narrow street swelled a thousand times.

She stood at the narrow road's entrance, unable to move, her entire body shaking violently.

Charlotte gripped onto the nearest door, her fingers laced with sweat as she stood, frozen, immobile, her chest heaving at the sight of the men out front of Louis' home, out front of the apartment where Madeleine was living and working and writing her articles for *La Defense*.

Until now, she'd been safe.

Charlotte turned rigid at the sight of those uniforms, the telltale dark green, the shoulder pads and collars that were brown, the caps that were peaked and polished, and the expression on their faces that was uniform.

Unrelenting. Jaws set. Downturned mouths.

The Gestapo.

They'd come for Madeleine.

Charlotte's feet wanted to melt into the pavement. But she slipped into the doorway of a building whose windows were lined with bars. In the silence that she knew would only last a few seconds before doors were beaten down, and Madeleine lay in a pool of blood on the pavement exactly as Sandrine had done, Charlotte was hit with a sudden coldness. It ran like quickfire to her core.

She had two choices. Turn and run away, run to the safety of Armand and Lucie, and be protected by the auspices of the Louvre, or she could step out into this street and give herself up.

Only she could save Madeleine.

As the slow rumblings of a German army truck rent the silent air, and an open-backed vehicle appeared, replete with German police in back, it all became icy clear. They would take Madeleine away. If Charlotte left now, Madeleine's family would never see her again. She would become one of the thousands of victims of the Nazis' insidious Night and Fog decree, where people in occupied territories who were engaged in activities intended to undermine Nazi rule simply disappeared for good.

It was happening all over France.

N.N. That was what the Germans put next to the names of their political opponents. One day here, next day, gone, leaving their families in agony, waiting for news of their loved ones that would never come.

Her belly fluttering, and dizziness threatening to overwhelm her, her heartbeat racing a thousand-fold, Charlotte

knew she could not live with herself if she allowed Madeleine
to be caught. She had already lost Sandrine. She could not bear
to lose another friend. In one split second, Charlotte stepped
out into the middle of the street.

She opened her mouth and shouted at the top of her lungs.
"Casse-toi! Plouc!" Get lost! Country hicks!

And then, she stood there, legs akimbo, arms on her hips, as
the wretched men in their polished, pristine uniforms turned
and, like a pack of wolves, pounded down the street toward her.
And out of the corner of her eye, from where she stood, Charlotte almost collapsed with relief as a hand came out and the
shutters of Louis' apartment were drawn closed.

There was a back exit to Louis' building. He'd told them to
use it a thousand times if they were in danger. And so. Just as
she'd escaped from Paris, just as she and Anita had run, now, it
was Madeleine's chance to go free.

Charlotte turned on her heels, only to come to a hopeless
stop. They were coming from every direction, their relentless,
rhythmic jackboots pounding against the old cobblestones.

And their shouts rang in her ears.

Shouts of boys her age.

She threw back her head. *In normal times, would they be
dancing together?*

Charlotte stiffened as they grabbed her upper arms,
wrenching them behind her until she reeled with pain. She
stumbled, her arms pinned to her sides as she was dragged down
the street where she, Louis, Henri and Madeleine had dreamed
they could make a difference.

Charlotte did not flinch as she glimpsed Madeleine's horrified face at the window. She only wished she had the courage to
spit in the face of the officer as he hauled her into the back of
the truck.

And as they drove her at gunpoint through the streets of

Montauban, Charlotte forced herself not to be physically ill at the proximity of the very men they'd all tried to fight against.

And yet her gaze did not falter when the few citizens of Montauban who were out stared at her, their faces creased in sympathy.

Because, her head held high, she vowed right then that no matter what they did to her, she would never, ever tell the Nazis a thing.

25

NEW YORK, FALL 1942

Martha

Martha was sitting in the window seat in her bedroom. She gazed down at the trees in Central Park, their branches skeletal and sitting in ghostly, haunted shapes. On the wide lawns below, she glimpsed children in mittens and warm woolen hats throwing the last of the fallen golden leaves up in the air, only to watch in wonder as they drifted back down to rest in the rich earth below. The clouds were gathering over Central Park like a misted blanket that would envelop the city in the coming months, layering New Yorkers with winter's quiet cold. At least here in the United States they had coal.

They had electricity and warmth.

Their food might be rationed, but they were not starving.

Their driving and gas might be curtailed, but they had public transport.

Their boys might be fighting in the Pacific and in Europe, but the citizens of this country were not living under a dictatorial regime. Martha could only imagine what life was like for her beloved sister.

Martha's brow furrowed at the knock on the front door. She gathered her cashmere wrap, and, throwing this around her shoulders, pattered down the hallway.

She'd come to her room for a bit of quiet. Papa and Olivier had been talking all day about the fact that the Germans had taken over France in its entirety. The sound of them grinding over and over this topic was not helping the rushing nausea that flittered through Martha's belly at the implications of this for Charlotte. There was no escaping the news. And having loved ones involved only caused it to sear to the depths of Martha's soul.

There was no more Vichy France. There was only Nazi France. Martha tried to console herself with the reminder that the Vichy government had never provided a real buffer between the unoccupied zone where Charlotte lived and the north of the country. Now that the Allies had invaded Northern Africa, the Germans had retaliated by simply marching south and taking over all of France.

Martha opened the door. In front of her, there stood a boy. He was holding a telegram from France. Martha gathered her shawl around her shoulders. A sudden wave of cold air shook her to her core and she took in a sharp breath. An involuntary gasp flew from her lips, and she took a step backwards, almost falling into the hall table and knocking it over, but the boy did not flinch. His job was to deliver missives. He would have had a long day.

Martha shuddered. She reached out. Her fingers curled around the white envelope and thanked him.

The envelope was from Montauban.

Martha shut the door behind her. She leaned against it a moment and closed her eyes. These things could go either way. The line between good news and bad news was as slim as the envelope in Martha's hand, and every family in the world was hovering somewhere between the two. Whenever Martha saw people taking plates of food to other apartments in the building, she knew this meant things had gone the wrong way. Bad news. She'd cross herself, bow her head and move on. Condolences and despair were the accompaniments to war and they'd linger like a hangover for nobody knew how long.

Martha knew. She'd lived with Papa's grief throughout her childhood and into her adult years. Was there more grief to be added?

Her fingers fumbled as she tugged open the small envelope. She allowed herself a moment to close her eyes. Here she was. Not knowing. But was not knowing better than the total devastation of bad news?

Finally, she held her breath and read the white slip of paper. And she sank back against the door, sliding down it, her knees buckling and her face dropping into her hands. The telegram floated to the floor and sat like a discarded handkerchief that nobody wanted to claim.

She cupped her hand over her mouth and fought the urge to run outside, and, in true Charlotte fashion, tell the telegram boy that this message was not, indeed, intended for this home, that he'd got it all wrong. That everyone in this family were safe. Surely they were safe? Charlotte was brave. She was not a victim. It couldn't be true!

The sound of Papa and Olivier's voices rose from the study. They were arguing a fine point and now there was no point.

Martha reached for the envelope, bit back a loud sob and stood up. Somehow, she knew not how, she managed to stumble to Papa's study. Soon she was there and the door was open and there they all were.

Gisela was sitting on the cherry-red sofa by the window, the light cast by the standard lamp falling on her dark brown curls. Papa was kneeling at the fireplace, about to start a fire on this cold night toward the end of fall. Olivier was at the drinks cabinet holding the decanter of sherry. It was a still life. It was a picture that Martha knew would remain imprinted on her mind for years to come.

It was the point between knowing and not knowing. Panicking, she felt an irresistible impulse to turn around and run away.

But here came the rustle of Élise's footsteps and the gentle touch of the elderly woman's hand on her shoulder.

"Was that the front door, dear?" Élise asked.

It was a simple enough question.

Papa turned around and stilled.

Martha stood stock-still, her breaths coming in fast little hitches. She was struggling to breathe, let alone talk.

Then they were all looking at her. Somehow, Élise had propelled her into the room, and Olivier had come up behind her, and Papa had lowered his glasses and Gisela, bless her, was standing over Martha's shoulder, one arm protectively resting there.

Charlotte didn't have any such protection. Charlotte was not surrounded by loving family. She was at the mercy of the cold killing fields of war.

Martha raised her hand to cover her mouth. Bile threatened to choke her throat and her stomach heaved.

"Martha!" Papa moved toward her.

But then, as quickly as it had come, the feeling passed, and a wave of quiet calm spread throughout her body. Martha stood still. Would she ever see her sister again? Did disappeared mean dead, imprisoned, escaped, or murdered at the hands of an enemy who knew no boundaries when it came to inflicting suffering upon their fellow human beings?

"Charlotte is missing," Martha whispered. She'd gone with the night and the fog.

She lost the grip she'd had on the telegram, and it fluttered down to land atop the rich Turkish rug.

"Charlotte is gone," she said, her eyes misting with tears. "And it seems that Sandrine is dead. She was shot outside

Vianne's childhood apartment in Paris. Oh, I cannot bear it, Papa..."

Martha sank down onto her knees, and silently, she buried her head in her hands. Dry sobs racked her body, but her tears would not come out. Any relief that crying would bring was held deep inside her. Her tears were stuck somewhere that the Nazis neither knew nor cared about. All Martha felt was a dreadful silence slipping over her. It was the same veil she'd seen on people's faces in the train. The Great War had caused an entire generation to be lost. Would this war, with its insidious, calculating cruelty that was utterly incomprehensible, leave her generation unable to speak?

Papa had picked up the telegram. He blanched and sank down into the nearest chair. Martha raised her eyes to meet his, and it was as if all the lights had gone out of him at once. It was as if all the hope of a new way forward that Martha had watched unfolding in him since Gisela had arrived had slipped away into nothing. He did not have to say a word and Martha knew that he'd retreated into that cold dark place he'd inhabited after Chloé died.

Martha buried her face in her hands. She would retreat too. It had been a mistake to try to engage with life. In that moment, she knew she would never, ever trust this false world again.

26

FRESNES PRISON, PARIS, WINTER 1943

Charlotte

Charlotte sat with her knees hugged to her chest in the formidable gray prison outside of Paris where she'd been confined to a solitary cell. Deliberately, she kept her eyes and nose faced toward the barred window in an attempt to avoid the stench of the filthy gray blanket that was spread on the hard cot beneath her jutting-out bones. This freezing room had become her beginning, her middle and her end. There was no chance of her stepping outside these walls unless she were to betray two of the people she loved most in the world.

Charlotte reached up to pull helplessly at the short tufts of dark hair that were all that remained of her locks. When her roots had grown out, exposing her black-as-night hair that matched her dark eyes, her captors had scoffed at her. Lips curled, they'd called her a Jew.

They'd cut what remained of her blond locks off. They'd stopped short of shaving her head because they wanted to see the tiny tufts of black hair that proved she was not Aryan. She was not one of them. She was not worthy of being anywhere except in a prison cell because she had betrayed the Nazi regime.

"I'll give you a choice," the officer in the newly acquired prison in Montauban had told her. His cold blue eyes were set so close together that Papa would have said he looked like a criminal, which is what he effectively was, or worse, a monster.

Charlotte had stared at him openly, having been transported through Montauban on the open back of a truck. She'd not responded to him. Silence was the only weapon she had left.

"Either tell us everything you know about Louis Chevalier and Anita Goldstein or go to prison until you do. It's up to you how this plays out," he'd told her.

She'd folded her arms and shaken her head. She had resisted the temptation to spit in his face. Instead, a wry smile had passed across her features. She'd braced herself for torture, but she'd been thrown into a solitary prison cell instead. Charlotte had hidden in a corner, her knees curled up to her chest like a little girl's. The walls were dripping wet. The floor was icy cold. Her teeth had chattered uncontrollably, but she'd closed her eyes and reminded herself that she was one of thousands. She would never betray the people she cared about.

Since then, Charlotte had learned how it felt to be treated as if she were nothing.

When they hauled her into a stark white room for interrogation, there was a single white lightbulb hanging from the cracked ceiling. Paint was chipped on the walls, and the constant drip of a leaky tap only served to remind her not to say a thing. No matter how much she wanted to rail at them, no matter how much she wanted to scream that they were murderers, she would not budge.

But what pierced her soul was not knowing whether Madeleine, too, was behind these grim walls. She had no idea whether her brave friend had escaped the ruthless determination of the Nazis in their relentless search to eke out the Resistance members in Montauban.

Charlotte stared at the barred window. She'd made up a game where she tried to capture the odd flicker of sunshine. But it was winter. She could tell by the unending, gray winter sky. It would be winter in New York, in Paris, Montauban and North Africa where Louis was based.

Sometimes, she spent entire days thinking about the people that she loved and the people whom she'd loved and lost, such as Sandrine. She focused on the memories that helped her keep her faith. She'd while away hours dreaming of the linden trees at Chateau d'Anez, of trips to the markets with Élise, and of the joy she felt when she laid eyes on a painting that a new artist had brought into proudly share with her in Rue Laffitte.

In this gray, dark, cold place, she dreamed of color. She dreamed of fields full of poppies in Normandy and flower carts filled with pastel-colored roses in old Paris. She thought of Papa's warm study with its bookshelf-lined walls, and she remembered the feel of his soft sweaters when he hugged her tight. She remembered Martha and the childhood bedroom they'd shared, twin beds covered in blue and white counterpanes on each side of the room. How they'd wake each other in the mornings by asking "Are you up?"

Had she taken it all for granted?

She'd smile to herself. No, she had not. Because if she'd learned one thing in this cell, it was that she'd never take the good times for granted again.

Even though her entire body shook with cold all day and all night and even though her stomach was so empty from hunger that it had stopped growling all together, and even though her body only ached to shut down, her spirit would not die.

Even though her ribs stuck out above her concave belly, and her hips were like needlepoints, even though when she lay on her side, her bones stuck into the bed and her body was covered with bedsores, her arms and legs pairs of twigs so thin she feared they might break in two, there were three things that kept her going—truth, love and hope.

Charlotte tended to these things within her as if they were tiny flames. And soon, she came to understand what the most important thing was in life. It was hope. Because if she lost hope, she had nothing left. This world might be tough and unrelenting, but somewhere, in the haze of each passing, freezing, lonely day, she'd come to realize that sometimes all we could do was create our own inner happiness.

When the guards had dragged her out from this dreaded room and asked her the same questions repeatedly, *Anita Goldstein? Louis Chevalier?* When they had sneered that Anita was dead, and Louis had been killed in action on the front, she'd opened her mouth to speak for the only time in months. She'd told them that if Anita and Louis were both dead, why were they of interest? Knowing that they were alive somewhere was also keeping her strong. Louis would be strong. Anita would be strong.

Lies were the Nazis' weakness; truth was her strength.

She closed her eyes and imagined how Madeleine's story had played out. She liked to think that Madeleine had time to flee that day, that she had hidden in the woods or lain in the hedgerows until she'd come to the abbey, hugging Louis' father and eating warm bread. Perhaps she had been given some warm milk, before being escorted across the Pyrenees to Spain. There, Anita would be sitting in the sun, and they'd both be safe, she thought.

When the tap-tap-tap of a Morse code message was relayed on the open pipes from prison cell to prison cell, Charlotte eased her aching body off the cot.

Someone had come back from interrogation. Charlotte swallowed, her throat tasting of rust. Her teeth were filthy and she'd become used to her own grime.

We will win in the end. Do not tell them anything. I survived it and so can you.

She repeated the messages down the line.

Her fingers frigid from the contact with the glacial pipes, Charlotte managed to shuffle across to stand near the window, the freezing-cold air settling its thick fog on the grimy pane. And she leaned her forehead against the unhospitable bars. How many others were incarcerated across Europe in this despicable war?

When her door was thrown open, and a cold, blue-eyed prison officer stood there, his arms folded and a baton in his hand, Charlotte lifted her chin in defiance. He came forward and grabbed her. He shoved what was left of her stumbling, emaciated frame down the hallway, until she fell to the ground outside a closed door in the dark hallways of the prison.

They hauled her in.

The door closed.

Rough hands stripped her body of the shredded rags she wore.

She stared at the freezing-cold bath. Ice cubes bobbed on the surface like apples on Halloween.

Halloween, home. Papa, Martha, Anita, Élise, Olivier, Louis.

Love. Truth.

Hope.

Charlotte closed her eyes.

Held her breath.

Let them do their worst. Nothing would make her tell.

The sky was blue when they came to move her again. She'd decided it was spring but had no way to know. She stiffened when they dragged her by the armpits down the rattling, echoing hallway. The rows of locked doors were only broken by the sigh of guards standing firm. Charlotte glanced at their upright bodies. The brass buttons on their uniforms gleamed under the bright lights.

Her captors shoved her to a stop inside a formidable metal door. Bolts drew across it and she had no idea what was on the other side. She had not been here before.

But they'd warned her last time.

The door heaved open and she was staring at a grim court-yard. But the sky soared above her and, for one glorious moment, she threw her head back and let her pale face draw in something of the sun.

The officers barked orders around her.

There was a cattle truck parked across the courtyard.

It was happening. They were putting her on a train.

A few moments later, she stumbled across the courtyard while a woman with a German Shepherd hauled her by the neck. Charlotte was in the back of the truck in no time and she was gasping for air after the effort of crossing the outside space. Her eyes would not adjust to the brightness of the sun and all she could see was a searing yellow, so she leaned her head against the back of the truck until her eyes flickered in recogni-tion when she gazed over and saw the chipped, bloody lips of a batch of fellow prisoners. She recognized their bloodless cheeks.

But there was something else there too. Her eyes caught with those of another woman around her age, and in them, Charlotte saw truth. Silently, she nodded, and the woman nodded back. Then everything went dark for a while, and Char-lotte could not remember anything until the truck came to a stop.

When they hauled her off onto the platform of a railway station, in some quiet, dismal station where they could carry out their atrocities and no one would know, Charlotte took in the next cattle truck in front of her. This time, it was on rails. This particular journey would be a one-way trip out of Paris. She'd heard rumors of where she'd end up. Charlotte stood there, her arms clasped around her tiny waist. She heard the silence of three hundred prisoners speaking louder than any screams or shouts.

A guard grabbed her arm. It was a woman again with another slathering dog.

Charlotte ripped her arms away from the woman. And, her head held high, she climbed into that one-way train on her own.

Through her half-closed eyes, she estimated that three hundred souls were crammed into the cattle truck. It was standing room only on this one-way journey. Around her, the stench of human suffering caused some to drop to the ground and others to faint. Charlotte knew there would be deaths on this journey.

There was one putrid bucket in the corner for a bathroom.

All of them were starving.

The relentless officers closed the doors with a clang.

It was dark inside now, and Charlotte knew that the best way to deal with this was to close her eyes. So she rested them in the blackness and she waited for the sounds of the train's engine to unfold. Was it the beginning or the end? She hardly knew anymore, but she knew that these poor souls who shared her carriage had no idea, no control, no choice and as little chance of survival as doomed animals being sent to the abattoir.

What to make things better then? What could she draw out of herself to try to give these people hope?

And then, as if out of nothing, her heart suddenly swelled with the most beautiful violin strains in the world, and in a clear, pure voice, she began to sing Mozart's most moving song. *Lacrimosa, Dies Illa, Qua, Resurget Ex Favilla—Mournful, That Day, when from the Ashes Shall Rise...*

As the music poured out of her, for what better language was there than music to transcend a war, Charlotte felt the unmistakable touch of a hand on her shoulder, and a human arm around her birdlike body. The arm was thin, and the arm was frail, but here was a person. Here was something beautiful in the face of some of the worst evil the world could bring.

And as the tears rolled down her cheeks, she fought to focus on Martha's delicious laugh, and Élise's wonderful cooking, and Olivier's kindness, and the fact Papa was always there, and Anita who had been everything to her and Louis who had captured her heart as they worked together like two sides of a coin, and Sandrine, dear Sandrine whom she hoped had gone to a better place, a place where things were kinder.

Charlotte heard someone whisper next to her.

"*Requiem.*"

EPILOGUE
CHATEAU D'ANEZ, WINTER 1946

Martha

The trees that lined the great lawn around Chateau d'Anez sat unnaturally still. Their bare branches were devoid of any new spring life and the air was crisp and cold. Martha stood on the front driveway with her hands hanging limp by her sides. When would the grief caused by war ever end? France was filled with a beautiful stillness that was impossible to bear.

She'd searched for answers, but there were none. She'd searched for peace, but couldn't find it. She'd searched to feel the connection she'd once felt with Charlotte, and knew she'd never experience it again. People were irreplaceable, and that was the greatest price of war.

Martha turned around, her heart breaking at the sight of Élise and Olivier making their slow way down the front stairs of their old chateau. Their arms were interlinked, and they took each step with great care. Anita walked behind them and her expression was consumed with the same sadness that Martha was finding impossible to bear. She'd survived the remainder of the war in London, working in a hospital for wounded British soldiers. She, Élise and Olivier had broken down with relief when they'd heard of her survival and now Anita was back working in her gallery in Rue Laffitte, slowly rebuilding her life and the careers of those artists she'd saved during the war. Out of all of them, Sandro Luciano was starting to rise to prominence, and had vowed that he'd always allow Anita to represent him. She had helped save his life.

Along with Charlotte.

Clyde stood tall next to Martha, and his hand curled with hers. She leaned her head on his shoulder. Her Scotsman. Like so many young couples who'd fallen in love during war, the time they'd spent together had been sweet and brief before they'd been forced to part for years. The time they'd spent apart had been lengthy and marred by worry on Martha's part. But the fact was, Clyde had survived the entire war in a prison camp and his fellow prison inmates had told Martha how he'd endeavored as a doctor to not only alleviate the sufferings of his fellow prisoners but also to aid in the suffering of his German captors.

Clyde often said that if he hadn't been captured, he probably would have been killed in the D-Day landings. In Edinburgh, he'd introduced her to his family and shown her the funny little mementos he'd brought back from the prison camp, which he said he never wanted to visit again. He'd shared with her the menus he'd written in good cheer for Christmas dinner each year, while all they'd had were potatoes and turnips to eat. He'd said that at Easter time, he'd been pleased to hear stories of a French farmer nearby giving a cigarette to a passing German officer because it was Easter, and the Frenchman thought the chap deserved a cigarette too.

Clyde had learned German during those years interned in close quarters, and he'd told Martha that he'd stuck to his principles of behaving humanely toward everyone no matter what their race. All of this had helped her fall more deeply in love with him than she ever could have imagined. His courage and good spirits in the face of an experience no person should ever have to endure was remarkable.

Even Papa had come to respect and admire Clyde when he had been to visit them in New York. Papa had forged a connection with the Scotsman when he'd described his experiences helping those on both sides of the battle, and Papa had said this was the embodiment of what he and his friends had yearned for after the last war.

The old chateau sat empty in the middle of a desecrated France, not one piece of the family's furniture, not one of their items of clothing, not one light fitting remained. Chateau d'Anez had been silent when they'd arrived. Flotsam fluttered across the floors and was a sad reminder of the desolation the Nazis had wreaked.

Martha stilled at the low rumble of a truck's engine approaching the chateau. Tires crunched on gravel and broke into the hushed air. When the truck pulled up, its brakes screeching, Élise gave out a cry.

Martha closed her eyes a moment, then moved toward it. "You must be Lucie," she said softly to the red-headed woman who was behind the wheel.

Lucie held Martha's hand. "There are not words," Lucie said. "Dear Martha. I feel as if I have known you and your family for years."

Martha stared at the ground. The gravel was all neatly raked again. She grimaced and managed to maintain control. Just.

Lucie's husband, Armand, appeared around the front of the vehicle and Lucie introduced her blue-eyed husband to the Goldsteins. Armand's eyes were filled with understanding when he shook Élise's hand.

"You are ready?" he asked the elderly couple.

Olivier reached out and stroked Élise's cheek. "Darling?" he whispered.

Something fluttered in Martha's stomach. She turned away a moment, gathering herself.

But Élise nodded. "Yes, I am."

Armand led them around to the back of the truck, and with Lucie's help, he hauled the great door open.

Martha placed her arms around her stomach and stared at what was inside. Neatly stacked boxes of paintings lay upright against the walls, while taller, square wooden crates clearly held statues, Olivier's beloved statues.

And while they stood there, heads bowed, Élise brought her hand to cover her mouth. "It is all there. She saved it all," she cried.

"I know," Armand said, simply.

Lucie moved closer to Élise. "Madame Goldstein, you will forgive me, but there is something else." The curator moved to the front of the truck, and taking three packages out, carefully wrapped in brown paper that she'd clearly had resting at her feet, she laid them down against a wheel. "Charlotte slept with these," Lucie said. "She guarded them with her life. In here is a small painting that she did not think was valuable in monetary terms, but that seemed particularly important to her. She rescued it from your bedroom, Anita, on the eve when we left the chateau." Lucie lowered her voice, her words catching in the cold air. "You know, Armand and I spent this war protecting the grand heritage of France, but in the end, it seemed, it was the personal mementos that meant the most to Charlotte."

Anita let out a moan. Her legs went from underneath her, and she buckled down onto the driveway. Clyde rushed over to her and knelt by her side.

Martha went to crouch down next to him. Élise, Olivier and Lucie and Armand's shadows hovered over them.

Then, finally, Anita opened her eyes.

The silent air, pregnant with the ache of war, was filled with a soft, gentle breeze that floated through the gardens outside the old chateau.

EPILOGUE

Martha

Martha stood high on a hillside in the mountains of Alsace, a cold sweat pricked her skin. One clammy hand rested in Anita's, the other in Clyde's. Gasping for air, she forced herself to stare at the beautiful, devastating landscape in front of her eyes. Before them spread the only concentration camp that had existed in France. It was freezing here, so high in the hills, and a chilly wind whipped around the place where repression and punishment, execution and unimaginable work conditions had been too much for their darling Charlotte. It was here that she had drawn her final, weary breath.

Behind them stood two young people, a dark-haired, dark-eyed young man called Louis and a young woman who had introduced herself as Catherine, but whom Charlotte had known by her code name, *Madeleine.*

There was a red-granite quarry in the distance, where more than fifty-thousand prisoners had been forced to labor, and in front of them there was a double barbed-wire fence, watchtowers and a gatehouse that guarded rows of barracks on steep, terraced grounds.

Anita swayed violently.

Martha squeezed her friend's gloved hand tight.

Atop the main gate in front of them, was a sign that read *Konzentrationslager Natzweiler-Struthof.* Running down the side of the camp, there was a long sloping path that led to the prison, and the crematorium.

"They called it the *Ravine de la Mort,*" Catherine whispered behind them. "The little death valley, because of where it led."

Martha bowed her head.

Louis had told them the camp's former commandant, Josef Kramer, had been executed by hanging late last year. He'd been sentenced to death by a British tribunal.

Martha closed her eyes. Retributions were of little comfort to her. She'd seen photographs of inmates dressed in striped frocks featuring the red triangle with an 'F,' denouncing them as French political prisoners.

Right then, a rustling sound drew Martha from her thoughts. She started as Anita drew a small painting from her bag with her free hand.

Martha peered at it. Her heart constricting at the sight of Anita, her parents, and a fourth, handsome young man. They were sitting on the lawns at Chateau d'Anez, and it was summertime. The linden trees were verdant green.

"Anita?" Martha said, her gloved finger pointing at the strange man.

Clyde leaned in next to her, and Martha strengthened her grip on his hand.

"She died to save her mother and her grandparents, you see," Anita whispered, and then tears fell freely down her cheeks.

Martha lifted her head. Her gaze clashed with Anita's.

And for one, horrible moment, Martha was unable to find any words.

But Anita, her cheeks wet, her dark hair blowing in the wind only stood there, shaking her head.

And then, after an age, Martha's heartbeat slowed. She looked down at the painting and her eyes scoured the image of the man who lounged on the picnic rug.

Martha took in a ragged breath. Had she always known? Charlotte had never settled down with her and Papa. Had her battle been to find out who she truly was? Yet, to Martha, Charlotte would always be her beloved sister, because she was certain that was the way her mother, Chloé wanted it to be.

Martha looked at the rough grass. It was beaten flat by the families who came here daily to see their loved ones' final resting place. She sensed Anita glancing down at the little painting that was the size of a postcard. It was a letter from the past that had been written without words.

Anita moved to a nearby rock, an outcrop sitting high above the camp, and she placed the little painting there.

"Goodbye, my darling," Anita said.

Martha stared, fiercely, at the small painting. She fought to swallow down her tears. But a lump formed in her throat. For the painting told the story of a family that had never had a chance to know what they could have become.

Martha lifted her head to come face to face with the silent, beautiful mountains.

"Are you all right?" Clyde whispered, next to her.

She turned to meet his warm eyes. And after a long while, she nodded. "Yes," she said.

Her battle had started when her own mother died. It had been a struggle that, as Martha looked out over the distant hills, she knew, had to stop. She had lost her mother, but now she understood that Charlotte had never known who her mother was.

Martha would never be as courageous as Charlotte, nor would she ever try to fill her shoes, but now, standing here, she knew one thing, and that was that her life was a gift. She must no longer only exist; she must start to *live*. She had to stop being afraid. This was the last gift of many that Charlotte had given her and she must take it with both hands.

Clyde drew her close, and she leaned her head on his shoulder. "I'm coming to Scotland," she whispered. "I shall write to Papa and Gisela." Papa and Gisela. They were going to build a new life as a couple out of the ashes of war. Papa had been devastated by Charlotte's death, and only now did Martha understand what a true father he'd been to her.

She smiled through her tears at the way Clyde rested his head atop hers.

"Charlotte did not live for nothing..." Martha continued, her voice resonating through the landscape. She, Charlotte and Papa had been a family, and Anita and Madeleine would not be alive if it were not for her courage. Charlotte had known no limits when it came to protecting those she loved. Martha would never forget any of it, her past, nor this beautiful, sad day. She would take all of it into the future, and Charlotte would always remain in her heart.

Martha gazed into the far distance, where nature soared before her in all its beauty, well beyond the weakness and horrors of any war. And just then, the little painting caught on the cold wind, and it carried it, high above the line of trees, whirling it away into the distance.

A moment later, a lone bird sang, an exquisite song that echoed all through the old hills of France.

A LETTER FROM ELLA CAREY

Dear reader,

I want to say a huge thank you for choosing to read *The Lost Sister of Fifth Avenue*. If you did enjoy it and want to keep up to date with all my latest releases, just sign up at the following link. Your email address will never be shared, and you can unsubscribe at any time.

www.bookouture.com/ella-carey

This was such a moving book to write. I'm so emotionally involved in it that I'm sure you'll understand how devastating the research was, and how heartbreaking the sight of that concentration camp in France was for me.

I hope you loved *The Lost Sister of Fifth Avenue* and, if you did, I would be very grateful if you could write a review. I'd love to hear what you think, and it makes such a difference, helping new readers to discover one of my books for the first time.

I love hearing from my readers—you can get in touch on my Facebook page, through Twitter, Goodreads or my website.

Thanks,

Ella x

HEAR MORE FROM ELLA

www.ellacarey.com

 facebook.com/ellacareyauthor
twitter.com/Ella_Carey

ACKNOWLEDGMENTS

My deepest thanks to my editor Laura Deacon for your wonderful guidance with the direction of this novel and my career. I appreciate you enormously and am incredibly grateful for your support. Hugest of thanks to my publicist Sarah Harvey for your amazing work in promoting my books. Thanks also to Kim Nash and Noelle Holton. My thanks and appreciation to my brilliant copyeditor Jade Craddock for your detailed and meticulous work on so many of my books including this one, proofreader Anne O'Brien for the same, editorial manager Alexandra Holmes and Mandy Kullar. Thanks to Alba Proko and Iulia Teodorescu for bringing my books to life in audio format. Huge thanks to Laurence Bouvard for doing such a lovely job in narrating the book for the audio edition. My sincere thanks to cover designer Sarah Whittaker for the beautiful cover. I adore it and think it is stunning.

Huge thanks to my agent, Giles Milburn, for your amazing support and for your management of my writing career. Thanks also to Emma Dawson at the Madeleine Milburn Literary Agency. My sincere thanks to Liane-Louise Smith and to Valentina Paulmichl at the Madeleine Milburn Literary Agency for selling my books into so many foreign territories.

I would like to acknowledge the brilliant Bookouture authors. Your support and friendship is invaluable, and I am honored to be a part of the Bookouture family.

Deepest thanks to my children, Ben and Sophie, for your

ongoing wonderful support of my writing, and to Geoff for his support and belief in my work.

Thanks to my readers, some of whom have been with me since *Paris Time Capsule* was first published back in 2014, and my thanks and hugest of welcomes to my new readers—it has been lovely to chat with some of you so far.

My thanks and special appreciation to the bloggers and reviewers who read and review my books. I appreciate your time and effort enormously.

Finally, my sincere thanks to my former editor, Maisie Lawrence, for your incredible support and editorial direction when I moved to Bookouture. This book is for you.

You all mean the world to me. Thank you.

Made in United States
North Haven, CT
05 July 2022

20955269R00193